Servant of the Kingdom

Servant of the Kingdom

A Message of Hope

The Servant Series: Book One

DARCI D. WALSH

RESOURCE *Publications* · Eugene, Oregon

SERVANT OF THE KINGDOM
A Message of Hope

The Servant Series: Book One

Resource Publications
An Imprint of Wipf and Stock Publishers
199 W. 8th Ave., Suite 3
Eugene, OR 97401

www.wipfandstock.com

PAPERBACK ISBN: 978-1-6667-6430-7
HARDCOVER ISBN: 978-1-6667-6431-4
EBOOK ISBN: 978-1-6667-6432-1

04/26/23

Cover Art by: Lyndsay Krebs

With all sincerity, this book is dedicated to *you!* In all the hours spent writing and rewriting and editing, I would think about you. Yes, *you!* You each have a unique story of your own. Every day you are living it! I wonder what *your* story will tell? I am excited to hear about it! I hope that reading Anya's story will be an encouragement to you as you live out your mission for the King! Blessings!

Contents

Editor's Note

Dear Reader,

You are beginning a fascinating journey. The book you are holding tells part of Anya's story. It is one of mystery, challenge, missed steps, forgiveness, and discovery. Hers is our story too, for we also need the King's Message.

I was privileged to work on the manuscript, so I was one of the first people to read it. I found the story compelling and the message life changing. It was refreshing to my soul and nourishing to my spirit. Your journey now begins, and the adventure awaits.

In service to the King,

Rev. Samuel P. O'Donnell, MATS, MSL

A Note from the Author

Greetings Dear Reader,
When in the late nights my sleepyhead did nod;
as over keyboard clicks my weary fingers trod,
to write the visions placed within my skull,
lest time or mere distractions erased to null.
Setting off on my pilgrimage, I took flight,
to transform years of notes and scribbles
into meaningful insight.
This story is but mine, penned upon my heart,
of how, within God's plan, I am a precious part.
Tho I, temporal as mist that clings
to dew-drizzled hills till morning springs,
then is gone again without a lingering trace,
so is my humble presence in this place.
And yet, upon God's vast eternal scope,
This tale of a mere servant girl holds hope;
perhaps to only I, this simple pilgrim be,
but, I pray, this hope I have, I share with thee.
Earnestly yours,
Darci D. Walsh

Acknowledgements

I CANNOT BEGIN TO express my gratitude to all the amazing people I have the pleasure of walking life's paths with! First, my children who have cheered mom on and been a constant source of light and energy in my life. You are each a joy and a blessing to me! To my husband, my best friend and a stabilizing voice in my life, Morgan, your belief in me has kept me going when it seemed I had so far yet to go. Our journey has just begun but look how far the Lord has brought us and how faithful He has been!

Pastor Sam and Kim O'donnell, thank you for affirming that this was a project worth doing and for your many hours of reading and editing to bring this book together! Your wisdom and knowledge of the Word has fostered valuable conversations that have grown my faith and understanding. Not to mention, the lessons you have taught me on grammar and the literary graces!

My sister-in-love, Loretta Villanueva, thank you for your support and help in so many things, but also in the proof-reading and preparation of this book!

None of this would have been possible without the support and encouragement of my family and friends, old and new. You mean more to me than I can possibly tell. My heartfelt thank you to each of you!

Prologue

My name is Anya. I am a servant of the Kingdom. I've lived in the palace of the Most High King ever since I could remember. Actually, the earliest memory I could recall was having a wash rag in my hand, washing the floors in the palace kitchen with an old bucket filled with warm soapy water by my side.

This story begins in my fourteenth year, and though I had many unanswered questions of how I came to be in the house of my King, I could not imagine being happier anywhere else than here, amid the warmth of the kitchen's large brick ovens and the inviting smell of the bread baking in the morning.

Marita is the head of the household; she oversees all the daily operations of the staff. I've never had a mother or a father that I could remember, but over the years, it was Marita who taught me my duties in the palace. Now, if you met her, you would know that she comes across as very stern, with her quick, decisive speech and the rigid, poised way that she carries her stocky frame. But under it all there is kindness and gentleness; she has been like a mother to me, and I've always felt like her main duty has been looking after me.

She tries her best to help me be a servant worthy of the Kingdom; humble in service and doing all things with excellence. She would tell me that in anything I do, I should do it as if the King is right there watching me and that I should aspire that He would be pleased with His servant.

Marita's high standards, though difficult to live up to, do keep the household running smoothly. Over the years she has never let me get away with doing anything without excellence and care. Nothing! Not even making my bed could be done without taking the time to do it right! I'd protest in jest that the King would never see it if my sheets were not perfectly tucked, or my pillow was not fluffed! I cannot count the number of times that I've gotten that look that says, without saying a word, "Do it again. And this time, do it correctly." What she *would* say was, "How you do anything, is how you do everything." Or "If you're careless small, you'll be careless big." Her little sayings were always with me, and still are today.

My main duties in the palace had grown over the years, from just washing the kitchen floor to now arising before the sun to get the fires started for the ovens, helping to prepare food, and washing the dishes, but one of my favorite duties was to sweep and mop the long, brightly lit hall that leads past our kitchen door and continues to the throne room of the King.

I was never allowed to wander far from the kitchen. This hallway was like a sanctuary for me. It was very simple compared to other magnificent parts of the palace, but it was the only place where, for a few moments, I was left alone. Well, I'm never fully alone. Pari is always with me. That shaggy white dog has been my constant companion and my best friend.

The morning when it all began, I had finished my duties in the kitchen, and had stepped into my 'sanctuary' with my bucket and a mop in my hand and Pari by my side. I could feel the warmth of the sunbathed stone floor through the simple canvas shoes that I wore.

I let out a contented sigh at the quiet, familiar hall. Pari found a warm beam of sunlight next to the kitchen door. Turning around several times before he settled himself into his usual place; he let out a loud open-mouthed yawn and dropped his head onto his paws. I set about my tasks joyfully, humming the song of the King. I may have lingered a bit longer embracing the peace and sunlight if I had known this would be the last morning for a long while that we would be soaking in this warm glow. The mop became my metronome keeping time for the song that always played in my heart. I had never dared to sing boldly in the daily assembly before the throne. However, there in the serene hallway, when I was alone, I could not contain it.

I have a good reason to sing. I knew very little of my past, so any crumb that I did learn was savored like a feast, a feast that did not happen often. One morning, years ago, while we were hurriedly getting ready to begin our day, I had asked Marita about a scar that I had across my shoulders. I had always had it but was wondering how it was I had gotten it.

I must have asked her at just the right time. She was distracted securing my hair into two neat braids. She started to say, "When the King rescued you and brought you into the Kingdom . . ." realizing she had just said too much; she quickly finished the statement, "you had been injured."

I looked at her, hopeful that she would continue to tell me more of who I was and where I had come from. Sadly, looking into my desperate eyes, Marita sighed and placed her hands on my cheeks. "I'm sorry, my child. That is all that I can tell you. Now run along and finish dressing for the day."

She was very careful after that, and I knew better than to ask more questions. But that day I had learned that it was the King who had rescued me and brought me to be a citizen of His Kingdom. He welcomed me into His own palace. That one glimpse into my past has fed my heart ever since and watered the seeds of my love and gratitude for my King.

There in my sanctuary, with eyes closed, the song of the King would burst forth, bouncing off the low arched ceiling and down the quiet halls. That day something new happened. My song came from a deeper place within me and as the sound reverberated back at me, another voice, deep and strong, joined in and sang over me. Melody and harmony mingled together; and my heart stirred. Beauty and wonder, awe and joy filled my soul. A wave of energy flowed through me. It radiated from the bottoms of my feet to crown of my head. I could not stop the song and didn't want to. Never had I more willingly, and so completely surrendered myself into His song until that glorious moment in time. Abandoned in the last resonating note, the mop slipped from my hand and landed with a sharp slap on the stone tiled floor.

Snapped back into my senses by the noise, I jumped and opened my eyes to see my King standing at the end of the hall. It had been the voice of the King that had been singing over me and with me! I quickly took a knee before him. When I dared look up, my King smiled at me, his servant, and looking into His kind eyes, this servant smiled back at him, then He continued on His way.

I will forever cherish that moment, but I did not know that the encounter with my King would be the start of a grand journey.

1

The Pearl & the Call

EACH MORNING THE ENTIRE palace gathered in the throne room for our daily assembly, where we would kneel before our King, receive his blessing for the day and sing His song. Everyone had their place in the assembly. Mine was on the right-hand side of the throne room, right in front of Marita. The smooth white wall was adorned with an inlaid diamond-shaped stone made of blue marbled lapis, centered under one of the tall windows that lined the room. That marker was where Marita had shown me how to kneel before my King. There were several times over the years, while our heads were bowed, I dared to peek and look at Him. Each time I did, I was shocked to find that the kind eyes of our Lord seemed like they were always upon me.

The very next morning, when the assembly was adjourned, I stood and looked to the throne. The King turned to me and smiled. The court herald approached Marita as we were about to leave. "The King requests a moment." Pursing her lips together thoughtfully, she nodded solemnly then looked to me, "Wait here."

This was something new. I stood in my place and watched her approach the throne. The King smiled warmly as Marita drew close. His Majesty took her hands and held them gently. They talked to one another as if they were old friends who were just catching up.

They both turned their heads to look in my direction. By the look on Marita's face and her furrowed eyebrows, I could tell she was thinking very deeply about whatever it was the King was saying. Finally, she looked up to our King and taking a deep breath, she nodded her head decidedly. Again, they both looked toward me, and Marita beckoned me over with a small wave of her hand. It was obvious they must have been talking about me.

I stumbled forward, quite ungracefully. I was afraid of what they were going to say and my legs had turned to jelly. My mind began to race. "Maybe I'm in trouble for singing too loud in the halls. Maybe I *did* forget to make my bed!"

I cautiously walked toward the throne. I had never been invited to approach the King before. My heart was pounding in my chest! Pari trotted happily along behind me, I could hear his claws making a soft clicking noise as we crossed the gleaming stone floor.

His presence made me feel more secure. However, when I arrived beside Marita, Pari did the most preposterous thing I'd ever seen him do. He leaped right up onto the platform, placed his large paws on the arm of the throne, and licked the King's face from chin to forehead. He then sat down! I took a deep breath and held it. I looked at Marita expecting her to reprimand Pari for approaching the King so boldly. She did not, and much to my surprise, the King sat down and placed his hand on the dog's shaggy head scratching him lovingly behind his ears.

Curiously, I watched them greet one another "Hello my old Friend." Affectionately, Peri leaned his head in and nuzzled the King's hand. I almost did not recognize my hairy companion. His dingy white coat seemed to transform to gleam pure white.

Old friends? How was that even possible? Pari had *always* been in the kitchen with me! Hadn't he?

The King turned his full attention to me. He leaned forward resting his elbows on his knees and smiled. "Hello, Anya." He greeted me gently. His sincerity drew me in; any apprehension or worry I had melted away.

Forgetting all formalities, I blurted, in awe, "You know my name?"

He and Marita chuckled merrily; Marita put her hand on my shoulder and explained, "Our Lord gave you your name," "Wow! Really?" I asked breathlessly. This nugget of insight to my past was like a precious jewel to me. I could not believe it! Not only had He rescued me, but I had been named by the King too!?

"Yes, Anya." The King responded, nodding his head. Looking back, one would think that I would have asked all the other questions running through my head. I stood silent at the wonder of it; no further explanation was given.

The King continued, "Anya, beyond our Kingdom, and the seven realms, there is a land shadowed by a great darkness. The inhabitants of this land are people whom I love. The darkness is pressing in all around them. Many are hurting and confused. They are fighting each other, greedy, and have lost hope. These people are searching and in great need. I can give them the weapons they need to overcome the darkness. I already won the battle for them, but many have closed their eyes and forgotten that they need only look to Me. I have a precious gift for them, a message to encourage them, give them hope and remind them to seek the answers I have. Someone must travel to them and deliver it."

The King continued, "It will be a long journey, across the sea and beyond the evening sun. The one who brings the gift will have to find someone in that land who is meant to use the gift to its potential. They will turn the tide and influence the people to seek my Kingdom's provision and to press back and take hold of what has been lost. I have chosen you, Anya, to bring them this gift and with it, a reminder of my message of hope."

The King drew out a leather bag, unfastened a large brass buckle, and folded back the flap revealing a soft glowing light. Putting his hand deep within the bag, He pulled out a crystalline sphere. It fit perfectly into his hand and gave off the gentle white light. He held it out toward me. Mesmerized, I took a step forward to peer at the swirling white mist that it held within. The sphere's surface had an iridescent shine, like a bubble. Yet, the white wisps inside gave it the appearance of a giant pearl. "Anya, as a faithful servant of the Kingdom, you are called to deliver this gift to the one to whom it is destined. Will you receive the call?"

Maybe I was caught up in the moment or in shock that the King would use a simple kitchen girl for such an important delivery. Without hesitation or question, I responded, "Yes, my Lord. Your servant accepts the call!" A feeling of destiny and excitement captured this moment in my memory. I could almost feel the shift happen, as if, by my acceptance of the call, my life had taken on a new meaning. A new path had opened for me.

The world was suddenly bigger than my corner of the palace. I had no idea of what life was like beyond these walls or what I had just agreed to do. The pearl the King laid gently into my hands would be the agent of great change, for the lives of those to whom I was to be sent, and for my life as well.

I held the pearl gently, I could feel the cool, hard surface brush my fingers, like a ball of solid glass. However, it was nearly weightless and so delicate that I felt compelled to put my other hand over it so the ball could not float away.

The thought of doing something important for the Kingdom became real and immediate when the King proclaimed, "Preparations will be made, and you will leave in the morning. I am proud of you, Anya. I know that you will serve the Kingdom well," Placing his hand gently upon my shoulder, He added, "And return safely to us."

The King returned the pearl to the bag and draped it securely over my head and one shoulder. It lay comfortably across my body, with the pouch resting on my hip. It all happened so fast I didn't really have time to be afraid of the journey ahead. I tried to soak in as much of what the King said as possible. "Anya, you will have seven days in the other land to deliver the gift to its destination. You will not be alone; Pari will be with you." Pari gave a proud, "Hrmpf". I had never been a day without him, so I was relieved that he would be going with me.

Questions spilled into my head all at once. I quickly sifted through them to ask the one that seemed of most importance, "How will I know who I am to deliver the gift to?"

"Anya, the one who you seek with have four qualities: the ability to influence a generation, they will be a leader among men, they will inspire others to take action, but most importantly, they will be willing to receive the call, just as you have."

"They will *see* the gift you bring, and their desire will be to spread this message of hope. It will shine a light to their land and give glory to My Kingdom, for they too are citizens because of their faith." So it was; in one morning, my entire world as I knew it was expanded, and changed forever!

2

Equipped

I DID NOT RETURN to my duties that day. While everyone in the palace continued their regular routine, Marita and I prepared. A short walk from the palace gates, was a small village, which until that day I had only seen over the palace wall from the kitchen patio. I never visited there myself. When we entered the market, I marveled at the bright colors and pleasant smells as we passed. There were piles of fresh fruits and vegetables, tables filled with fresh bread and pastries. We walked past baskets filled with pungent spices and racks lined with bunches of fragrant flowers. The merchants greeted Marita with a nod or wave, occasionally someone would call out a greeting.

When we were about to leave the big square where the produce booths were set up we passed a large cart filled with shining red apples. The man standing there smiled warmly as he noticed me gazing at the apples. "Good day," he said with a nod and small bow to Marita. "An apple from the King's orchard for you." With a charming flourish, he extended a hand to each of us, handing Marita and me a large, gleaming, apple. "Thank you!" I said receiving the juicy treat with both hands. "You are very welcome, little one. The King provides for all in His Kingdom." "Good day, George." Marita bid him farewell as we continued to a side street lined by little shops with various signs hanging over the doors.

The windows of the shops were filled with displays of shoes, stacks of books, glass bottles and fixtures, foods, tools of all sizes and colors, fine fabrics, garments, and many other useful wares. By evening, we headed back toward the palace gates with low leather boots, new leggings, a green embroidered tunic with a hood, undershirt, stockings, and undergarments.

That night after I had bathed, I sat in my nightgown at Marita's feet while she braided my wet hair into my two usual golden braids. This time she secured my hair into a ring around the back of my head. The next morning, we would rise before the sun to meet the ship at the harbor.

A mist still hovered above the fields as we made our way down the winding road that led from the palace to the sea. The sun had not fully made its appearance above the horizon behind us. The light of the approaching dawn illuminated our way as we rumbled down the path in an open carriage drawn by two proud black and brown horses.

In the chill of the morning, I was thankful that our small carriage made it a cozy ride. Marita had draped her thick blue cape over both our shoulders and Pari lay across our feet keeping them warm.

Suddenly the thought of leaving Marita's side sent a wave of panic over me. I knew that once we reached the bay at the bottom of this next hill, I would have to leave that safe, warm place beside her. Pari and I would be on our own. "Marita?" I said softly.

She looked down on me and raised her eyebrows inquisitively, "Yes, child?"

"I'm afraid!"

She smiled and took my hand in hers, "Yes, Anya, every journey begins with a fear of the unknown ahead. Fear can stop you if you let it, but when you do the thing you fear, you'll find strength and courage on the other side. Fear itself is the coward if you face it."

"I've always felt safe here, Marita." I admitted. "Out there, I don't know what lies ahead."

The sunlight slowly worked its way over the hill behind us, chasing the mist away and illuminating the tops of large masts below us. The sails were gathered up as the ships were at rest in the port, and they gleamed like brilliant white puffs of cloud hanging from the masts.

"Do you see that beautiful ship tied up at the dock?" I looked down our path at the ship, now fully illuminated and gleaming in the sun. I nodded. Marita continued, "We do not know what perils the trip ahead may bring; the storms the ship may face, the lands it may find. This ship, here in harbor, is safe but staying in the harbor is not what this ship was created for." She lifted her gaze to the expanse of horizon beyond the busy docks and ships. "It must journey beyond the harbor to complete the purpose for which it was made. To stay where it is safe and familiar for the rest of your life, will keep you from the adventure for which you were created."

I thought about that for a moment. I felt the gentle weight of the pearl, securely held in the messenger bag on my lap. Marita put her arm around me, holding me close for a moment. I could feel this was not easy for her either.

Marita set her jaw resolutely, scanning the scene before us, "We serve the Most High King and it is our duty to serve Him joyfully and courageously. Whatever and wherever He directs our hands and feet, we go." The emotion in her voice betrayed her usual sage-like demeanor. "Take courage little one, the King has called you for this moment." I leaned into her and placed my head on her shoulder; we rode in silence.

As we rounded the last bend and rumbled over the last rise, we could now see the men at the docks working busily to ready the ship for departure. "I've never left the Kingdom before." I pondered out loud.

Giving my hand a squeeze, Marita softly explained, "Anya, the Kingdom is not a place to be left. You are a citizen of the Kingdom; it is in you wherever you are."

We arrived at the bottom of the hill. Before us stood the tall masts of the ships bobbing at the docks. Some were being loaded and others unloaded. Some vessels were preparing for a journey and others had arrived through the night.

Marita took my face in her hands, not quite ready to let me go. "Our Lord has gone before you and prepared your way."

"The King has been to this land before?"

"Oh yes!" She assured me and placed a kiss on my forehead. She hung my messenger bag across my shoulders and courageously took a step back.

Looking up at the ship I saw its name painted in gold letters. "Shema" I whispered the name. This was the vessel that would take me where my King was sending me. I took a deep breath and a few moments later I watched the land slip away and Marita waving goodbye from the end of the dock.

"Anya!" She called, hurriedly, giving me one last instruction, "Remember, to enter His gates with thanksgiving and His courts with praise." I waved back, not exactly sure the meaning of her words, but I received them and tucked them away. I knew Marita has never been careless with her words. Perhaps they would make sense at just the right moment ahead, I thought. How right I was.

3

Sailing to the Other Side of the Sun

I STOOD BY THE rail for a long time. The shimmering white palace, the only home I had ever known, grew smaller and smaller on the distant hills. I looked away from the safety of the harbor, and I noticed something surprising. Now that I had taken the first steps of my journey, the fear I felt a short while before was replaced with a tenacious spirit and excitement for what lay ahead. As usual, Marita's words were true.

I climbed up on a crate I found lying along the railing. Pari and I sat facing the water. We passed by the Filigree Islands. I had seen their intricate pattern swirling away from the land on a map of the Kingdom. Now, the archipelago I had seen upon dusty parchment was real before my eyes!

There were seals basking on the rocks, soaking in the morning sun. I could hear their lazy bark mixed with the birds squawking as they swooped among the islands searching for food. When we passed by the last rocky outcroppings, several of the seals flopped off the rocks and slid into the crystal-clear water. I smiled at the way they transformed from an ambling mass to an agile arrow moving quickly under the water. I leaned over the edge to watch them play in the water below.

The shallow waters soon sloped away, and I could no longer see the fish darting here and there or the seals chasing them for a meal. We were now in the deep open sea; surrounded by nothing but water and the sun as it traveled its arc over us toward the horizon to which we sailed. The wind pressed us forward, its gusty breath filling the billowing sails making them ripple and quake.

Sailors bustled here and there amidst the heavy crates of cargo that were stacked on the deck and, I am sure, filled the hull below. They were filled with precious goods and fine things from the Kingdom. The crew members busily moved the cargo and scurried about the deck checking lines and adjusting the sails. Occasionally, one would start a sailor's song and the others would join in. It was a delightful addition to the excitement of the day. Pari and I tried to stay out of their way, however, with my new-found sense of adventure and independence, we spent the day exploring the ship. As the sailors passed us one of them would pause to ruffle Pari's fur or smile at me with a quick wink or a nod. They all seemed delighted to have us aboard. Eventually, we made our way to the bow at the front of the Shema.

I was mesmerized by our ship breaking through the gentle waves as we sailed toward the setting sun. A pod of dolphins joined us in our journey and playfully raced alongside us, leaping out of the water then sliding gracefully back below the surface. My grand day on the sea was ending. My legs grew tired, and my eyes stung from the salty air and the brightness of the sun.

When the sun kissed the horizon, its brilliance reflected off the surface of the water then slowly began to sink into the water. The moon and the sun shared the horizon for a moment as they made their slow exchange of places in the sky. Pari and I found a little nook in some coiled-up ropes to sit and rest. I pulled my leather-bound journal from my bag along with the writing stick that Marita had given me and began to write about the first day of my journey.

With tentative steps I did depart
From the safety of my home and comfort.
Your Kingdom, now far across the sea,
Travels in my heart with me.
When your call I do pursue,
My flame of courage is made new.
Entrusted with this gift, unique,
Its destination I will seek.
As the setting sun bends to kiss the sea,
My lips give praise, my King to thee.

As the light of the day faded and night fell upon our ship the air and wind took on a wet chill that caused me to shiver. A kind sailor appeared and wrapped a gray tattered blanket around my shoulders.

I smiled up at him gratefully, "Thank you." He smiled, still silent, nodded and was gone again. Wrapped in the surprising warmth of the threadbare blanket my eyelids soon began to droop, I leaned back against the bow of the ship and sleep overtook me.

Pari was nuzzling my cheek with his cold, wet nose, as the first rays of morning light now shone upon my face. When I opened my eyes, I felt like I had only blinked, it was as though we had pierced the setting sun and a moment later had come out the other side. I blinked my eyes to fully wake from my slumber, Pari whined softly and nudged my arm urging me to stand up. Could it be that our journey across the sea was complete? I stood and turned around; there stretched out before me was our destination. Pari and I had arrived at the other side of the risen sun.

4

Sunrise in a New World

I WAS AWESTRUCK AT the panorama all around me. A domed palace, encircled by flags, had two high towers standing proudly on the huge stone pier. Nearby there was a towering wheel stretching up into the sky high above the buildings. At the ends of the white spokes hung large blue baskets. Beyond them, more palaces and courtyards extended back towards the mainland. But that was just the beginning.

On the mainland, in place of hills or fields, were hundreds of enormous towers that reached to the heavens! Some were made with stone, and others looked like they were made of glass. The colors of the morning sky reflected off them.

Though the sun was shining brightly on the morning horizon, everything it was shining on seemed dull and faded. I thought this was strange and tried blinking my eyes to clear the haze. The muted colors remained. It was like looking at a reflection on dusty glass, still beautiful but not quite as brilliant as the real thing. It lacked the vibrant colors I was used to in the Kingdom. Even so, I stood in awe at the immensity of the city before me. My eyes tried to take it all in. There was so much to see!

Pari nudged my hand with a grumble and a huff, "Alright, let us begin.", I obliged. We started to walk toward the gangplank that had already been let down to the stone pier. The blanket that the sailor had given me the night before was still draped over my arm and when I saw him standing near the ramp, I thanked him and held the blanket out to him. He put his hand on my shoulder to stop me. He took the blanket from my hands and folded it carefully. Then raising his eyebrows, he held it out to me offering it as a gift. It folded up surprisingly small. I was actually very grateful for that tattered old blanket, and I tucked it into my messenger bag.

My silent sailor friend then nimbly hoisted himself over the rail, landing on the platform. He held out his hand to help me down the gangplank onto the pier. Before he boarded the ship, he pulled out a folded paper from his back pocket and handed it to me. Looking down at the paper, it appeared to be a map of this new land. A map! That was just what I would need!

Overwhelmed with gratitude I hugged the map to my chest and bowed politely, "Thank you for your kindness. Do you know where I am to begin?" As he backed onto the ramp, he swept his hand across the land before me and with a smile and a wink, he pulled the gangplank back onto the ship and gave a whistle. Two other sailors pulled the ropes from the moorings and still others prepared the sails as the large ship began to pull away from the pier.

With magnificent swiftness the good ship "Shema" departed across the sea into the rising sun. She was soon only a speck on the horizon before disappearing from our sight. Pari and I watched her go.

Taking a deep breath, I lowered to one knee, bowing my head as if the throne of my King was before me. "May I bring you honor, my King." I whispered. A breeze off the sea swirled around me playfully and the warm morning sun caressed my cheeks. A soothing feeling tingled through me, comforting me. Smiling, I opened my eyes and stood. My feet felt nimble and my mind at peace.

Nearby, we found a bench that looked out over the shimmering waters. We sat to study our map. It was unlike any map I had ever seen in the palace library. It had charts and graphs with lists and numbers. A labeled grid with colored lines stretched out from near the pier. From what I could figure I was at the end of the pier that led up to the main city.

"CTA Bus & Rail Map" I read out loud. I looked at Pari, he tilted his head thoughtfully, then whimpered softly. "I do not know what that means, either." I shrugged, "But the King has sent us here on a mission so somehow He will show us what to do next."

Reaching into my bag I pulled out the sphere and held it gently in my hand. Though still light, it seemed to have a new weightiness I was responsible for supporting. "We will find where this gift belongs. Perhaps something in this palace will give us the direction we need." Pari barked in agreement.

We spent the morning exploring the pier and the palaces and gardens that it held inside and out. One building housed a beautiful botanical wonderland, with fountains that played above my head, shooting a jet of water from one fountain to the next. I walked among the raised flowerbeds and under the tree fronds that reached up to the glass ceiling.

It was early, and at first, I was alone wandering the pier. However, it was not long before some strangely dressed people began to enter the garden. I studied them, excited and nervous to meet the people of this land. At home in the Kingdom, I had not made many introductions and knew very few people. I was not even sure how to start.

Some children raced playfully from one fountain to the next trying to catch the beads of water before they splashed into the next pool. The children's joyful laughter echoed through the air and mixed with the gurgling and splashing sounds of the water. What a fascinating and beautiful place this garden was!

A group of children entered the garden through the door at the far end. I had never seen anyone else my age before and I watched them in wonder as they laughed and talked with each other. A man was ushering them all into a gathering area. He had dark skin and was dressed in short pants with a strange cap on his head. The whole group wore the same bright green shirts with matching designs.

"Mr. Johnson's students, circle up!" His deep voice echoed through the garden. It was clear that he must be their instructor. This seemed like an exciting way to learn.

Back in the Kingdom when our duties for the day were complete, Marita instructed me in my lessons. Most days we did our bookwork at our small table in the corner of the kitchen. Somedays, as a special treat, Marita would bring me to the palace library filled with rows and rows of towering shelves stocked with books on any subject I could imagine, and millions more I had never even dreamed of. As impressive as the library was, we had never traveled outside of the palace walls.

Mr. Johnson addressed the children, "Class, this is our first stop. We have a big day ahead of us. We've got about 20 minutes here in the 'Navy Pier Botanical Garden'. Mrs. Carlson, your science teacher, insisted I have you check out the tropical plants and trees in the garden and see how they are different from the flora that are native to Illinois."

Some of the students had already begun to lose interest and started to wander away or chat, so he raised his voice, "Meet up right here in," he glanced at his wrist and a large black bracelet that he wore, "18 minutes. We will be loading up on the river cruise boat at 10:45 to ride downtown to meet the King of Chicago." The words, 'King of Chicago' were music to my ears! Could it be that this land had a king? Surely, *he* would be the person who could use this gift!

I was amazed at how these children were educated! Not only were they visiting tropical gardens, riding down rivers, but they were meeting kings! These must be princes and princesses to receive such an education!

I knelt next to Pari, "Do you think they could get me an audience with the king of this Chicago land?" Pari wagged his tail and licked my cheek with his rough, wet tongue. Wiping my cheek dry, I smiled "Ok! Stay here, I will come right back." Pari sat down contentedly next to one of the benches that lined the path. He kept his eyes protectively on me as I slowly approached the teacher. "Mr. Johnson?" I said cautiously.

"Yes?" He turned around expecting to see one of his green clad students, and got a puzzled expression when he saw me instead, "Oh, hello?" "Mr. Johnson," I began again, "My name is Anya. Do you think that I could join your students for your audience with the king of Chicago today?"

"Oh, Annie? Oh my gosh! You're the new kid that is supposed to start tomorrow, right?" Clearly flabbergasted, he continued without letting me correct him or answer his question. "I can't believe they didn't tell me that you would be coming today! Did you just get *dropped off* here?" Truthfully, I answered him, "Yes, I did."

"Oh geeze!" He flagged over the other two adults nearby who were also wearing green shirts. Once they got close enough Mr. Johnson said to them, "So this is Annie, her family just moved to Aurora from North Dakota. We weren't expecting her until tomorrow, but it turns out she just got dropped off here!"

Both the man and the young woman raised their eyebrows, looking shocked. "Annie, this is Mr. Reed, his daughter, Sophie, is in our group, so he is helping to chaperone this day trip into the city." A middle-aged man with a kind smile and thick glasses nodded at me, "Hello Annie." Mr. Johnson continued, "And this is Ms. Moore, she is new to the school this year too. She's our new art and graphic design teacher. And I teach Social Studies and Economics classes."

The bouncy lady with her red hair pulled back and tied up with a green ribbon that matched the shirts, stuck out her hand to me, "Hi Annie, welcome to Riverview Middle School. Not every day is quite as exciting as a trip to the big city, so we're lucky you could come today!"

Ms. Moore's eyes lit up, "Hey Mr. Johnson, I happened to grab that extra t-shirt that was for my sister, who was signed up to be a chaperone." Turning to me and leaning in, she smiled big and lowered her voice like she was letting me in on an exciting secret, "Her son Carter, my nephew, is one of your classmates, but she couldn't come because she ended up having her baby a few weeks early."

Straightening up, she continued, "Needless to say, the t-shirt is a kind of huge, but you could wear it and match the rest of the group if you want to!"

Mr. Johnson added, "That also left us with an extra ticket to the river cruise and an extra lunch, so I guess it all works out. Welcome to the class, Annie."

5

Going to See "the king"

I COULD NOT BELIEVE how fortunate I was! I had only been there a few hours and now I was about to deliver the pearl into the hands of the king of this land, or so I thought.

There were still a few minutes before we were supposed to "circle up" and leave for the river boat. It would take us to see the "king of Chicago." I pulled the new green shirt over my head; it hung down to my knees. I ran back excitedly to where Pari was still patiently waiting.

There were several kids wearing green shirts, talking to him and petting him behind the ears. Pari wagged his tail lapping up the attention. He faithfully had kept his eyes on me. He let out a happy bark when he saw me approach, causing the children to jump, then erupt into a fit of giggling.

"Pari, I see that you have made some new friends." I was so excited to talk with some children my age, but suddenly I became a bit nervous about what to say. Turning to them, I could feel my face start to flush, "Greetings, my name is Anya." I said rather quietly, "and this is Pari."

One of the girls, with her black hair braided into many tiny braids that were pulled together at the back of her head, jumped up, noticing me wearing the class shirt. "Hi Anya, I'm Sana! Are you a part of our class now?" She spoke excitedly.

"I am for today." I vaguely admitted. I did feel a bit guilty that I did not correct Mr. Johnson. He really thought I was someone else. I was sure it would be quite a shock when the real Annie arrived the next day as planned. I put it from my mind; Pari and I would soon be meeting with the king and things were moving along quite nicely. I was so pleased that we were on our way to completing our mission on the very first day!

The boy and girl who were kneeling next to Pari piped up in unison, "Will Pari be coming with us?"

Giggling, Sana explained, "That's Tommy and Teri. They're twins," she added, smiling, and rolling her eyes, "and they do that all the time!"

"We do not!" they both exclaimed. Then looking at each other burst out laughing again. Sana and I laughed too as we plopped down on the bench next to Pari, Tommy and Teri.

Once the laughter died down, I replied, "To answer your question, Pari is with me wherever I go."

Sana's eyebrows lowered in thought, "Oh, so he's like a service dog?"

I did not know what that meant, but *I* was a servant of the Kingdom, so it sounded about right that Pari was a *service* dog. I nodded in agreement, and Sana, Tommy and Teri exchanged looks and said, "Cooool!" I think that meant it was a good thing.

Just then Mr. Johnson blew a short whistle blast from the meeting place, and we jumped up and hurried over to where the group was gathering. Pari trotted along with me and when we got to the circle, he sat at attention next to me. Looking up from his clipboard, Mr. Johnson's eyes narrowed when he saw Pari. "Now what is this!?" he said, sounding rather exasperated.

Tommy chimed in and answered him, "That's Pari, it's Anya's service dog!"

Rubbing his forehead, Mr. Johnson muttered, "A service dog! Of course, Annie has a service dog!" Shaking his head and looking back down at his clipboard he said, "Seriously, nobody tells me anything!"

After that, Mr. Johnson split the class into three groups and handed tickets to Ms. Moore and Mr. Reed. Our group followed Ms. Moore to the other side of the pier where several, two story boats were moored. We walked over a ramp onto one of the boats.

"Let's head up to the top!" Ms. Moore said, cheerfully leading the way. Only our class and a few others were on board, so there were plenty of open seats for Pari to sit up next to me and look out over the water. He leaned over the railing with his tongue hanging out, happily letting the wind of the sea ruffle his fur. Something below us began to rumble and move the boat away from the pier. Sana sat beside me, and Teri and Tommy sat next to Ms. Moore right in front of us. Turning in her seat so she could see her part of the class, Ms. Moore counted to make sure all of us were present.

Satisfied that we were all where we should be, she reached back and patted Pari's head. "We're lucky that these boats are still running this late in the season! It's usually too cold by now to take the river tour downtown.

Luckily, we've had such a mild autumn that they extended the season into this week! Today is the last day before they officially close for the winter!"

The wind off the open water was the only hint of winter approaching and held an icy chill as we rounded the end of the pier and turned in toward the city. Turning to look at me, Ms. Moore asked, "So has it been nice in North Dakota, too?"

Just then a man, with a messy mass of copper curls on his head and thick black rimmed glasses, stood up in the front of the boat. He was wearing a blue coat and green suspenders that held up his tan pants, pushing his glasses up his nose, he began to talk into a wand he held in his hand.

His voice echoed from all around us as he welcomed us in a sing-song cadence to the Chicago River Architecture Tour. I was thankful for the interruption since I did not know how to answer Ms. Moore's question. I had no idea what or where this land of North Dakota was!

When we got closer, I could see that the river flowed right into the heart of the city. The man at the front began talking about the design and significance of each of the colossal buildings that we passed by. I tried my best to pay attention, but soon I was lost in my own discovery of this strange new world of massive structures and grand bridges.

When we entered the city the first thing I noticed was the constant noise! It was so different from the quiet world I was used to; I kind of liked it. It was like an oddly tuned orchestra where each player played music of their own. I also noticed that there were people everywhere! It seemed like most of them were just rushing around, pressing to get to some unknown location with their heads looking down at their hands. I was surprised; they didn't even look up at the wonder around them.

In front of us was a bridge that was made of giant rust-colored beams of metal that zig-zaged up and down as it spanned the river. Across it moved many strange carriages. I was amazed; none of them had a horse or oxen, or anything pulling them.

The closer we got to the bridge I started to hear a rattling and screeching noise. Then a large metal creature burst from a tunnel and shot across the top of the bridge. It looked like a giant metallic snake. I jumped in surprise and clung to Pari! I could tell by the smooth way that it moved that it was not really a living creature, but a long string of enormous containers connected together that zoomed over the bridge above the carriages. They all seemed to be pulled along by some invisible force.

It was so amazing and busy, not at all like the quiet and peace of the palace. I turned my head in every direction, trying to see it all as the warm sun shone down on us and gleamed off the beautiful buildings and the river.

The grandeur of this land made my head spin! What an amazing kingdom the king of Chicago had! It was loud and overwhelming, and I loved it!

Sana had been watching me and smiled, "Never been to Chicago before, huh?" I smiled sheepishly back at her and shook my head.

My attention was brought back to the man who was standing. In a more animated voice he said, "Mr. Johnson's class, I understand you all will have the pleasure of touring Talon Tower. Congratulations on winning the," he paused to look down at a notecard in his hand, "Talon Industries Community Connections Video Contest 'Making a Difference in Illinois' Communities." The class cheered at the recognition.

At that moment we rounded a bend in the river, and he swept his hand dramatically toward the magnificent building that came into view. He resumed his speech, "Talon Tower was built 14 years ago by shipping mogul Stephen Talon. His family has had a major influence in the Chicago shipping industry for the last 150 years. Under Steve's stewardship, what started as a small shipping enterprise here in the Great Lakes is now a worldwide leader in shipping and logistics. Mr. Talon is often referred to as the "King of Chicago " for the contributions that the Talon family has made to the development, culture, arts, and infrastructure of the city. Up until recently, Talon Tower was the highest building in Chicago offering breathtaking 360-degree views of the city and Lake Michigan from the offices at the apex of the building. These are the personal offices of Mr. Stephen Talon himself."

Mesmerized, I stared up at the gleaming palace of the king of Chicago. Surely someone like him would have the power and influence to use my King's gift!

Soon our boat was docked at a small landing within the heart of the city. We stayed in our group with Ms. Moore and climbed a set of stairs that led to the street above. Along the side of the street there was a smooth, paved walkway bustling with herds of people moving in a steady stream back and forth. Ms. Moore tentatively led us into the crowd and urged us, "Stay together! This way!" Mr. Johnson's and Mr. Reed's groups were in front of us. They waited just inside the huge gold-gilded doors of Talon Tower. The dark stone floors and walls gleamed; elaborate gold fixtures hung from the high ceiling. As opulent as it was, compared to the beauty of the palace in the Kingdom, this luxurious estate seemed dark and cold.

We waited near the door while Mr. Johnson approached a woman behind a marble counter at the far end of the large expanse. The woman picked up an object and held it to her ear, saying something into the mouthpiece. Several minutes later two huge men appeared from a long hallway and joined Mr. Johnson. He stuck out his hand toward them in greeting; they stared blankly at him then stiffly shook the teacher's hand. Mr. Johnson motioned toward the class. The men nodded and walked with Mr. Johnson over to us.

With his chest puffed out, he addressed us, his voice sounding deeper than before, "Class, these are Mr. Talon's personal bodyguards; they will be escorting us up the Talon offices." Soon we were following the two giant men across the echoey chamber.

Leaning over to Mr. Reed, I heard a new excitement in Mr. Johnson's voice, "You know, no matter what anyone else thinks, I'm a huge fan of Stephen Talon. The guy is larger than life! I mean he's ruthless in business, brilliant in negotiations, not to mention filthy rich. I've studied him for years. Back in college I even dreamed that I'd end up having some big important job working for Talon Industries in this very building.", he said, looking around at the lavish surroundings.

A high-pitched sound made him turn to look at a group of boys that had fallen behind. A boy with platinum blonde spiky hair was using his shoes to make obnoxious squeaking sounds on the smooth tile floor that echoed through the chamber. Once he had done it, the other boys with him had to try it too. Snapping his fingers at them Mr. Johnson gave them an exasperated look that made them grin mischievously back at him and tiptoe, stifling laughter the rest of the way across the room.

Rolling his eyes, the excitement had faded slightly from his voice, "Guess life did not work out that way, huh? But man, I've always dreamed of seeing the view from those offices!"

Chuckling uncomfortably, Mr. Reed responded, "Living the dream today then?"

Slapping Mr. Reed on the back, Mr. Johnson laughed and agreed, "Yeah, I guess you're right. That's probably why I got so excited when I heard about this video challenge from Talon Industries. But really, the kids caught the vision and got on board coming up with ideas to make an impact and improve our community. It was so great when they won the challenge and got that grant from Talon Industries for the community improvement proposal, and they did one heck of a job raising support and transforming that abandoned lot next to the library into an outdoor reading garden. Then to be invited to Talon Tower to meet this king of Chicago in person, what a trip! Who knew it would be this group of crazy middle-schoolers that would get me to the top of this tower!"

By that time, we had walked past the marble counter and were waiting outside several sets of golden doors. The smile had returned to Mr. Johnson's face, and he fondly ruffled the hair of the blonde boy with the squeaky shoes.

"Sorry coach!" he said sheepishly. Mr. Johnson joked, "No worries, Kyle, I'll just have you do some extra laps at basketball practice tomorrow to work those squeaks right out of those sneakers." The boys with him laughed and punched Kyle on the arm and playfully he pushed them away. "I don't know what *you're* laughing at boys, he'll have you jokers to keep him company." Mr. Johnson finished with a sly grin.

In the hallway there were three sets of doors to our right and three to our left. At the end of the hall was another set of gold doors that were set apart with two large sconces on either side. It was these doors that we headed to. The special set of doors parted to reveal a tiny room with mirrored walls.

One of the guards turned to Mr. Johnson and said, "This is the private elevator to the Talon offices at the top of the tower. We will take you up in three groups." Mr. Johnson's group piled into the room with one of the guards and the doors closed behind them. The rest of us waited in the hallway.

Above the doors some numbers lit up. I began to wonder what they could possibly be doing in that tiny room. Several minutes passed and then the doors slid open again. I gasped. They were all gone! Mr. Johnson and all the children had vanished! Only the guard that had gone in with them was left behind.

I backed away from the strange room in horror, but no one else seemed bothered by their disappearance. When the guard motioned to Mr. Reed, without fear he led his whole group right through the golden door frame!

Turning to Sana, I whispered, "Where have they gone?"

"Um, I think the offices we are going to are on the 100th floor. These other elevators," she motioned over her shoulder, "do not go that high. I think they stop at the 99th floor, so the *only* direct access to Mr. Talon's personal offices is by this one private elevator. Cool huh?"

As we waited, some other doors in the hallway opened. People went into the tiny rooms, then the doors would close behind them. When the doors reopened those people were gone and new people came out. One thing was for certain, things moved very quickly in this land, it was nearly impossible to keep up.

Finally, it was our turn to go into the room. The sound of my thumping heart filled my ears and a chill slithered up my spine. I clutched the messenger bag to my side; I could feel the pearl it contained. Completing my task for the King was more important than my fear. We were about to have an audience with the king of Chicago, and, as far as I could tell, braving this ill-boding room was the only way to get there. I gulped as Pari and I followed the others through the golden doors.

6

Palace in the Sky

THE INTERIOR WALLS OF the elevator were made of black panels that were polished like mirrors. Everyone turned around to face the doors as they slowly closed. I noticed right away that there were no other exits. Where had the others gone? Suddenly, I felt the entire room jerk and began to move! My stomach dropped to my feet as I clung to the gold railings along the wall. This palace was terrifying but exhilarating! Ms. Moore and the other children seemed to enjoy the excitement of the ride as well. Pari let out a huge yawn; he did not seem impressed.

After a few moments we slowed to a stop. When the doors opened, we had somehow been transported to a lavish reception chamber. The dark elegance of the first floor paled in comparison to the radiant personal chambers of the king of Chicago. The floor and walls were made of white stone that gleamed in the sunlight streaming in through the windows. It was bright and spacious.

Across from us was a large, curved table where a woman with a pleasant smile greeted us. "Well, hello there! Welcome! The rest of the class is right around the corner." Her dark eyes twinkled. Turning to the men who were with us, she added, "Olivia is waiting for them outside Conference Room A."

We met up with the class and together we followed the guards down the large hallway. Tall white vases lining the path were topped with large vibrant green leaves, giving the only splash of color to the crisp white surroundings.

A slim woman with short dark hair stood at the end of the hall, apparently waiting for us. She was wringing her hands a bit nervously. Dressed neatly in a smart navy skirt and coat, she wore a striped scarf tied in a bow around her neck that was draped to one side. "Well, if it isn't Mr. Johnson's class! Welcome and congratulations on winning the Talon Industries video challenge! My name is Olivia and I'm the PR director for Talon Industries." Taking a deep breath, she smiled and added, "Mr. Talon is very excited to meet you, however, he is presently finishing up a very important meeting with our overseas partners, so he has asked me to," She paused slightly, "to give you a tour of our offices."

Mr. Johnson nodded enthusiastically, not noticing that she seemed to have made that up on the spot, "Okay, sounds great!" Ms. Moore and Mr. Reed exchanged a befuddled look then shrugged. Olivia proceeded to march us up and down the halls showing us places like the employee lounge, the marketing offices, operations department, research and development and accounting offices, and explained at length what each of them did for Talon Industries.

Finally, Olivia filed us into a big room with the huge glass table that was surrounded by white leather chairs. "Please wait here, I will go and see if Mr. Talon is ready." She smiled and turned to leave, then noticed Pari standing with me near the door. With a startled gasp she put a hand to her chest, "Ohhh my," she stuttered nervously, "is, is that a dog?"

Ms. Moore, who was standing next to me piped up, "Oh, this is Annie, she is new to our class, and this is her service dog, Pari.", she explained, "He really has been such a gentleman; sometimes I forget he's even with us.", she added reassuringly.

Olivia bit her lip, thinking, "He does seem very nice, but you see, Mr. Talon is very allergic to dogs." Looking at me she said, "Annie, do you think it would be alright with Pari if he waited with our receptionist, Mrs. Kelly, for just a few minutes while Mr. Talon visits with the class?"

Pari nodded with a huff; standing up he started toward the door in response to her question. I smiled up at Olivia's shocked expression and answered, "Yes, I guess he's alright with that." I turned to follow him out into the hall.

As we approached the large desk and the gold doors again, Olivia called down the hall in a slightly panicked tone. "Mrs. Kelly?"

The plump, dark-skinned woman with a cheerful face who had greeted us when we arrived, appeared from around the corner, "Yes, Ms. Olivia?" In hushed tones, Olivia gave a quick explanation, Mrs. Kelly assured her, "Well of course, I'd be happy to look after him."

Motioning to me, she smiled with that same friendly twinkle in her eye, "Come with me, Honey, we'll get him all settled in, then you can go join your class, ok?"

With a sigh of relief Olivia put her hands up and mouthed, "Thank you!" She turned and with a deep breath, headed back down the hall to a large set of double doors.

Mrs. Kelly and I went back to her desk. I liked Mrs. Kelly right away and so did Pari; she had a genuine kindness about her. Once she had plopped herself down in the big white chair behind the marbled desk, she held out her hands palms facing up toward Pari, inviting him to come closer, which he did immediately. He sniffed her hands and sat down contentedly beside her chair. Scratching him under the chin, Mrs. Kelly crooned, "We're gonna be just fine, aren't we, you handsome boy?"

I hurried back to the rest of the class. I could not risk missing an audience with the king of Chicago! I felt sad that Pari would not be with me at such an important moment, but I felt assured that he had a friend in Mrs. Kelly. There was something about her countenance that reminded me of home.

What had Olivia meant when she said that Mr. Talon was *allergic* to Pari, I pondered. From how Olivia reacted, the king of Chicago would not have been happy to know that Pari was there. How strange, I thought, no one in the Kingdom had ever had a problem with Pari. In fact, anyone who belonged to my King's land welcomed him as a friend.

I was almost back to the room that Olivia had called the conference room, when I saw her standing outside of the two doors that I assumed belonged to the king of Chicago's private quarters. One door was open and I could hear someone talking with Olivia.

"I understand what you are trying to do here, Olivia. But this was not *my* idea, it was *yours*. You go entertain them and wipe their noses. I *do not* have time to babysit a bunch of children wandering through my office. I am trying to run a *billion-dollar* enterprise and I don't really care if people think I am a self-centered, greedy, egotistical jerk."

"Mr. Talon, you know it is very important that our state and communities see Talon Industries as having their best interests at heart." Olivia slid inside of the door, but through the partially open door I could still make out their conversation. I didn't mean to eavesdrop. I also did not stop myself from listening.

"Olivia, if that is not already evident from the millions of dollars' worth of community investments the Talon family has shelled out over the last 50 years, then I don't think taking some pictures with a bunch of brats is what is going to suddenly change people's opinion of me."

"Look, Stephen," Olivia leveled with the king, "You agreed to let me do the challenge and award a grant. And these kids worked really hard putting together a proposal, earning that grant money and they really improved their community. I know this was not your idea, but it would be a shame to let this opportunity go to waste. At least just come and say hello to them."

Finally, the king gave in, "Fine, five minutes, Olivia, that's it! Five minutes, three pictures and *you're getting me out of there*. I've got a lunch meeting with Ivan in 20 minutes. What do I need to know?"

"Well, these kids are middle schoolers from out in Aurara,"

"Oh, don't tell me they're from some magnet school." Mr. Talon interrupted with a groan.

"Yes, they are." Olivia responded shortly, then continued, "Mr. Johnson, and his Social Studies class are the ones who started with the grant proposal, but then they got all the other school programs on board too, the Art Club, the STEM group, the Reading Club, and the school Newspaper."

Olivia's excitement was building as she told the story. "They really got enthusiastic about making their community better. With our help they were able to purchase an abandoned lot that was next to their public library and transform it into a reading garden using all sorts of recycled materials."

"That's enough Olivia." Mr. Talon cut her off. "Mr. Johnson, Middle schoolers, Aurora, Reading Garden. Right?"

I could hear Olivia sigh, "Right. Thank you." As the door started to open, I quickly stepped inside the conference room.

Mr. Johnson was standing by the floor to ceiling windows overlooking the tops of the other towers and the sea of Lake Michigan. "Now that's what I'm talkin' about! Imagine sitting here looking out at this every day!" he exclaimed to a few of the students that were standing next to him. I had to agree; the view was truly astounding!

Olivia reentered the room with Mr. Talon and began with introductions. Mr. Johnson spun around and seeing Mr. Talon, started to navigate around the table, past his students to make his way to where they were now standing.

"Mr. Talon, this is Mr. Johnson and his class who won our Talon Industries Community Connections video contest."

Mr. Talon's voice was now relaxed and friendly as he said, "Oh yes, welcome, Mr. Johnson, well done." He held out his hand in Mr. Johnson's direction.

Excitedly, Mr. Johnson nearly tripped over every chair before he made it to grasp the king's hand enthusiastically. "Well thank you Mr. Talon, but really it was these kids who put it all together. I just provided some guidance and a little direction."

Turning toward the children, Mr. Talon lauded them, "That's what I hear. Way to go," He began boldly, but faltered having forgotten what Olivia had told him, "doing that thing you did for your community."

The children beamed proudly.

The king continued, regaining his poise, "On behalf of myself and Talon Industries we would like to thank you for partnering with us to make our state a great place to live and work. We are so pleased to be a part of your idea, and help it come to life. Your ideas today as middle schoolers will change the world we live in 15 years from now, so keep creating and innovating. One day, maybe Talon Industries could use your talents to reach the furthest corners of our world!"

I was so perplexed at what to make of this king of Chicago. One minute I was convinced he could not be the one I was seeking. He did not really seem to care about anything but his own productivity. The next minute, I was inspired by his encouraging words and desire to make a positive impact in the world. The most confusing part was that it felt like he sincerely meant both.

I thought back to my King's words, "Anya the one who you seek with have four qualities." I mentally listed them as the king of Chicago circled the room shaking everyone's hands.

The ability to influence? Mr. Talon certainly had the ability to influence. Mr. Johnson's reaction to him was evidence of that! The king said it himself that he was a leader of a "billion-dollar corporation" (whatever that meant). So that made him a leader among men. Could he inspire others to take action? From what I had heard from his speech to the class, he could be not only encouraging, but empowering! He could definitely inspire others. That left the last quality; willingness to receive the call. There was only one way to find out if he was who I was sent to find. I looked for the opportunity and stirred up my courage to address him.

Raising his eyebrows toward Olivia, he volunteered pointedly, "I imagine that Olivia here would love a few pictures of all of us for the company newsletter, webpage, social media and all that jazz; if you wouldn't mind, that is." Jovially he threw an arm around the star-struck Mr. Johnson.

"Yeah! Yeah, that would be great!" Mr. Johnson stammered.

The class, teachers and Mr. Reed all stood together, "Here sweetheart, you stand right here next to Mr. Talon." Olivia motioned to me, then stepped back and tapped on a device she held. The king cleared his throat several times then I noticed him pull a handkerchief out of his pocket and dab his nose with it and return it to his pocket.

Mr. Johnson piped up, "Oh, here." Holding out another small, flat box to Olivia, "Would you mind getting one for me too. Maybe a few, just so we make sure we get a good one."

"Well of course, sure!" she grinned, then noticing Mr. Talon's perturbed look and his glance at the large gold clock he had on his wrist, quickly added. "Then I better get Mr. Talon on his way, he does have a very important meeting to attend."

She quickly tapped the device several times then handed it back to Mr. Johnson. The king shook Mr. Johnson's hand again and with a big smile and a wave to the class he was gone.

We heard a loud sneeze echo down the hall, then a door slam shut. Olivia jumped in, "Oh here, I almost forgot, before you go; these are some commemorative coins from Talon Industries for you as a token of our appreciation for your great work and participating in our challenge."

She handed each of us a golden medallion that had a picture of Talon Tower on one side and on the other side was a message.

"These commemorative coins were minted for our 100th anniversary back in June. Thank you so much for coming out from Aurora to visit us today! Glen and Frank will see you down to the 99th floor so you can take the other elevators down to the lobby."

With that she ushered us out into the hall where the large bodyguards were opening a door directly across the hall from the conference room and leading us down the stairs.

I hung back trying to think of a way to get to Mr. Talon to present my gift. My mind was racing, if I didn't talk to the king of Chicago now, I'd lose this chance. Panic was starting to set in as we were already on the stairs and the door closed behind us with a loud thud. Then I remembered Pari. "Ms. Moore, I have to get Pari."

Turning to the bodyguard behind us, Ms. Moore pleaded, "Oh my gosh! Annie's service dog is still up with the receptionist."

"Come with me." He growled back, using a small circle that he pulled from his belt on a stretching string, he held it to panel on the wall next to the door. It glowed green and then beeped. He opened the door for us then let it slam shut. Ms. Moore and I were back in the hallway of Talon Industries.

Just then the door to the king's private quarters opened and Olivia stepped out followed by Mr. Talon. Olivia's voice was bubbling, "Look at these pictures! They are precious! I'm going to get these posted this afternoon." Turning to Mr. Talon she added sincerely, "Thank you! See? That went great!"

Raising an eyebrow, he smirked slyly and replied, "Yeah, now you owe me."

Olivia continued down the hall to the right of Mr. Talon's quarters, and the king started down the hall toward us, I had to think fast.

"Ms. Moore. I'm not who you think I am. My name is not Annie, it's Anya. I let Mr. Johnson think I was from the land north of Dakota. But I was really sent from the Kingdom on the far side of the sunrise, by my King, to deliver a message. It may be for the king of Chicago. I'm sorry, I can explain more later, but I must do this."

Confused, Ms. Moore just looked at me with her mouth open trying to find words.

I took a step forward, blocking Mr. Talon's way. "Stephen Talon, king of Chicago" I addressed him, bowing from the waist as I had seen emissaries from the seven realms bow to my King.

He eyed me suspiciously but allowed me to continue. "My name is Anya, your majesty. I come to you from the Kingdom of the Most High, bearing a gift from my King whom I serve. I have been sent to your land to present this gift and the message it carries. May you use it to bring hope to your people. I hope you will accept this gift and this call?"

Kneeling, I reached into my bag and lifted out the pearl. It radiated light and the mist within drifted in swirling wisps, responding to the touch of my hand. I held the pearl out before me, proudly offering it to the king of Chicago.

He wrinkled his nose, "What's this? The Drama Club?", half-heartedly putting his hands out to mimic mine.

I moved to place the pearl into his hands, but before I could, he pulled them back, scoffed, and started to step around me. "Look kid, nice performance, but I've got important places to g-guahh," before he could finish his sentence, he started to fight back a sneeze.

"Gesundheit?" Ms. Moore said meekly.

The sneeze stifled, Mr. Talon shook his head, "Thanks." then noticed Ms. Moore for the first time. He turned looking up and down at her admiringly, "And you are?" he purred.

"*They* are just leaving," Mrs. Kelly interrupted, coming around the corner from behind her desk. "I believe *you* have a lunch appointment to get to Mr. Talon?"

"Yes, of course." Mr. Talon cleared his throat and turned to head to the elevator. As he got closer to Mrs. Kelly's desk, he began sneezing uncontrollably.

Recovering, Mr. Talon barked over his shoulder as he jabbed a button on the wall, "Mrs. Kelly, call maintenance and tell them to come clean the vents! Something is wrong with the air in here!" Pulling his handkerchief from his pocket he dabbed his runny nose and watery eyes. The golden doors opened, the king stepped into the mysterious room and was taken away.

Once he was safely out of hearing, Mrs. Kelly chuckled and shook her head. Staring down at the pearl, I murmured, "It was like he couldn't even *see* the gift."

Looking at me, Ms. Moore questioned, "What gift Annie?" catching herself she corrected, "I mean, Anya?" I held out the pearl up for them to see.

Mrs. Kelly gasped, "Oh my word!" and drew close to me, to look at the pearl. "What is it?" she whispered awestruck.

"It's a message, a reminder of hope from my King. I was sent to bring this gift to someone who could use it. I had hoped the king of Chicago would be willing to receive the call and carry the gift of hope to the people . . ."

". . . But he couldn't see it." Mrs. Kelly finished for me.

Lowering herself to kneel beside me, Mrs. Kelly put her hand on my shoulder. She mused, "Honey, it's beautiful!" The light of the pearl shone upon her face, drawing her in. Then as though she saw something familiar from deep in the mist, Mrs. Kelly looked at me curiously, "I don't know exactly where you came from, but I think I know the King you serve."

With a sigh I confided in Mrs. Kelly. "I don't think the king of Chicago is who I'm looking for"

"Mr. Talon? No, that man shut his mind and heart off to the miraculous years ago. To him there is no calling higher than his own ambitions. To serve a king besides himself and his own success, he'd consider an inconvenience and waste of productive working time." She smiled at me, "Keep searching for who you're looking for. Your gift is precious. I've got a feeling its gonna change people's lives if they let it!"

Ms. Moore had been standing back watching us, "We better catch up to the rest of our group."

"Oh yes, I'm sure you're here for Pari then." Mrs. Kelly slowly stood then offered a hand to me.

"Yes! Thank you for taking care of him!", I smiled. Taking her hand, we made our way around the desk to where Pari had patiently been waiting out of sight.

She ruffled his shaggy fur, "Well it was my pleasure! He's pretty special, Anya!" Lowering her voice she confessed, "This may sound a bit strange, but it feels like we've been friends my whole life."

I assured her, "That does not sound strange at all, everyone in the King-dom feels that way with Pari, even the King himself calls him 'Old Friend'!"

Seeing us off, Mrs. Kelly bid us farewell, "Bless you, Miss Anya. May you find who you're looking for. And goodbye Pari, my 'Old friend'!"

Pari and I rejoined the bewildered Ms. Moore in the hallway. With the pearl safely tucked back into the messenger bag, we left the palace of the king of Chicago. We walked in silence back to where the other students were waiting to reboard the boat.

For the first time, I noticed a slight weight to the orb pulling down on the bag. It was beginning to make an indent where the strap had been resting across my neck. I shifted the messenger bag around to the other side to relieve the pressure.

I was disappointed that Mr. Talon had not been the one to accept the call, but I would not be discouraged. I was sure of the conviction that I would find them soon, whoever it was. The bounce quickly returned to my step.

7

Up in the Air

"THERE YOU ARE!" TERI rushed over, followed by Sana and Tommy. "Where were you?" Tommy chimed in.

"Ms. Moore and I went back to get Pari. I also had a very short audience with the king," My voice trailed off; I was unsure how to continue.

Raising his eyebrows, Tommy questioned, "The king?"

Sana laughed, "You mean Stephen Talon? He's called the 'King of Chicago' but he's not *really* a king, Anya. They just call him that because he's got a lot of money and influence."

Tommy jumped in again, "Yeah, he just throws some money around and usually he gets his way."

Teri leaned in, "Yeah, but that doesn't always work." She glanced up at one of the other towers that loomed over us. "He threw a big fit when World Tech announced they were building a tower higher than his! But in the end, even *he* couldn't stop it from happening."

Crossing his arms, Tommy leaned back against one of the posts and looked up at the buildings, "But that's the game, right? You build the tallest building in town, and someone's bound to come along and try to build one bigger than yours."

Sana and Teri both nodded in agreement as we gazed up at the palace of the *so-called* king of Chicago.

Our boat arrived; we boarded it and started up the stairs to the upper level again. Ms. Moore climbed the stairs behind us. She had been especially quiet; I could tell something was bothering her.

When we were about to take our seats, she leaned over, "Hey Annie, could I chat with you for a minute?" I noticed that she was calling me 'Annie' again. I nodded and followed her to the row of seats along the back of the boat. Pari sat on the floor between us and placed his head on Ms. Moore's knees.

Absent-mindedly she smoothed his shaggy fur, biting her lip trying to collect her thoughts. With every stroke of Pari's silky brow, the deep furrow in her own began to soften.

Taking a deep breath, Ms. Moore looked at me, "How are you feeling, Annie?" she probed.

"Well," I began, "I was disappointed that Mr. Talon was not a real king or willing to receive *my* King's gift. However, it is only my first day here in this land. I must not let myself get discouraged." It was so nice to be able to be open and honest with Ms. Moore.

I continued, decidedly, "Mrs. Kelly was correct, I just need to keep searching for the one who will accept this gift. They will remind this beautiful land of the hope they have in my King!"

She was still studying me very closely, her youthful face strained again, in concern, "Ok.", she sighed very tentatively and took another deep breath. "I'm going to be honest with you, Annie. Alright?"

I nodded innocently at her. "I didn't see anything either, when you were talking with Mr. Talon." she explained.

"You couldn't see the gift I was offering him?", I asked.

Ms. Moore leaned back in her chair, "Well, I have to admit that I felt like there was something there, and I wanted to believe it. But just like Mr. Talon, I couldn't *see* anything. Just because you want something to be real, Annie, doesn't make it real." She continued tenderly, "Tomorrow when you come to school, I have someone I'd really like you to meet. Her name is Mrs. Guster, she is the school psychologist. She is very nice and she helps lots of kids with adjusting to new things."

"Oh, well that's very kind of you Ms. Moore, and I'm certain that she is very nice, but I will be continuing my journey tomorrow to find out who this gift is for. Besides, the real Annie from the North of Dakota will be arriving tomorrow."

Ms. Moore rubbed her forehead and tried again; "So, back at the U of M, in my psychology class, I learned about how sometimes when kids deal with something traumatic, like a big move, it can trigger the imagination to become more active. Does that make sense, Annie?"

I smiled at her, "Yes, change can be very difficult for children. I'm sure that Mrs. Guster will be very helpful for Annie. But my name really *is* Anya." I corrected her. "I really *am* from the Kingdom of the Most High. I have seen the Kingdom with my own eyes. I have been entrusted with a *real* gift, sent from my King to the people of this land, whom he loves dearly. It is very important that I deliver this message to the person who is waiting for it."

By this time the boat had docked back at the pier, so I stood to depart, "I thank you and Mr. Johnson so much for allowing me to accompany your class today." I left her speechless in the chair.

The class had already started filing down the stairs and then onto the pier, but Sana waited for Pari and I to catch up. As we started to descend the stairs, my stomach rumbled loudly. Marita and I had packed enough provisions for the journey across the sea, but Pari and I had eaten those when we were traveling on the 'Shama' the previous day. With all the excitement of meeting the king of Chicago I realized that I had not eaten yet. I was suddenly very hungry.

Sana, who was going down the stairs right in front of me, giggled and looking over her shoulder, commented, "I'm starving too! Our bus driver, Don, is waiting for us with our bag lunches from school." she wrinkled her nose, "Nothing fancy, just sandwiches and stuff, but we get to spend some extra time on the pier. The PTO pitched in some money and got us tickets to ride the huge Ferris wheel. So that will be cool. You can see the whole city from up there! My mom gave me money to get some popcorn too! They have the best caramel corn here! I'll share some with you if you want."

Sana chattered all the way down the stairs and ramp. Tommy and Teri were waiting at the pier and joined in talking about all the kinds of foods and delicacies that were native to this land of Chicago; something called pizza, churros, iced cream, candied nuts and hot dogs. They all got excited when Tommy mentioned the popsicles and pretzels. I didn't know what any of those things were, but they sounded delicious. I could tell I was not the only one who was hungry!

It turned out that 'bag lunch' consisted of a pliable bottle filled with water, a small amount of bread, meat and cheese stacked together, some small carrots, a tiny apple and a bag with something crunchy called 'chips'. They were greasy and extremely salty; I offered them to Sana and she was glad to have them.

I was thankful for the food but was shocked at how bland it was compared to the food of the palace kitchens. As I ate, I broke off strips of meat and tossed them to Pari who jumped to catch them. The other children laughed and cheered and soon everyone around us was also tossing bits of meat into the air for Pari as he playfully jumped and spun, seeming to defy gravity.

By the end of our meal, Pari had also had his fill. He laid down contentedly at my feet with a full belly. I slid the half full bottle of water into my bag for later. After the meal we were quite refreshed and accompanied the other children up the pier to a fantastic courtyard. It was filled with mechanical marvels that people rode upon for enjoyment.

One had chairs that were suspended on long chains. People sat in them and swung around in a wide circle making them soar high in the air. On another, the people sat on painted wooden animals that bobbed around a beautifully ornate platform. Looming before us, in the center of the courtyard, was the enormous wheel that I had noticed when we first arrived. I craned my neck to see the top and noticed that it was traveling in a slow circle carrying large baskets filled with people up, over the top and back down again, stopping every minute or so to let people in and out of the bottom baskets. Mr. Johnson was leading us to a raised platform with a long line of people standing in the wheels shadow.

Along the way a few of the children stopped to attain items from the merchants. Sana rejoined us after she had acquired the 'caramel corn' she had spoken of earlier. As we waited in the long line to board the baskets, she offered some to me. It was delicious! By the time we got closer to the front of the line, we had devoured the whole bag!

In front of us Mr. Johnson and Ms. Moore were passing out slips of paper to each of the students. When they got to us Ms. Moore presented me with a slip and offered to sit with Pari while I rode in her place. She explained that dogs were not allowed inside of the baskets, and she would be happy to take care of him for me since she was not a fan of heights. Ms. Moore also offered to hold my bag. The weight was beginning to dig into my other shoulder. I reluctantly nodded, and carefully removed the bag.

Pausing, I earnestly petitioned, "Please watch over it very closely. As you know, it contains something tremendously precious and valuable."

"Of course." She replied with a reassuring smile. I placed the bag in her hands and a look of surprise registered on her face when she felt how heavy the bag was. Ms. Moore and Pari retreated to a bench just off the platform to wait for us to return.

It was our turn to board the basket. Unencumbered by my messenger bag, my steps were light and easy. The sun was shining brightly through the windows of the basket. Without the cool breeze coming off the sea of Lake Michigan, I soon got very warm with the oversized shirt layered over my clothing. I took it off and draped it over my arm as we waited for the other baskets to be filled.

Sana, Tommy, Teri and several other students were in our basket. Mr. Johnson rode with a group in the basket in front of us and Mr. Reed rode with the last group two baskets behind us.

"Hey new girl, what's with the outfit? Is the peasant look the in thing back in your little village?", sneered one of the girls sitting in the seats across from us. The group who sat with her all snickered at her comment.

Sana jumped to my rescue and shot back, "Lay off Kimmy, you'll probably be dying to wear something just like it in six months. And her name is Anya."

Rolling her eyes, Kimmy dismissed her, "Whatever!" but in a more friendly tone added, "Cute boots though."

I looked down at the new boots that I wore and then noticed the boots she had on were very similar to mine, I grinned, "Thank you, Kimmy! I like your boots too." She grinned back and we were then friends, apparently.

With the doors securely closed, the wheel began to move. We all turned and pressed our hands and noses against the glass to look at the city as we were lifted into the sky.

"Oh my gosh!" Kimmy squealed suddenly looking over our shoulders. "I think I can see the park where Zahara will be performing tomorrow night!" The wheel stopped to let the lower baskets empty and be reloaded with people standing in line.

Kimmy motioned to Tommy, "Quick, change places with me! I want a better view!", she commanded. A confused Tommy reluctantly obeyed.

Leaning with her hands on the glass window and looking out over a large green gardenlike space beyond the pier, Kimmy said proudly, "It's gonna be at that big pavilion concert stage over in that park. My dad bought us tickets to her show tomorrow! It's going to be epic!"

"Who is Zahara?", I inquired.

"What?!" Kimmy responded incredulously.

"You really have never heard of Zahara? The actress, singer, song writer, model, activist who just finished her autobiography?", even Sana was in disbelief. I just shrugged my shoulders and shook my head.

Kimmy slowly shook her head, "What do you even do in North Dakota if you don't know Zahara!?" Kimmy continued, her words dripping with adoration, "Zahara Amaryllis is totally my hero! She is an amazingly talented artist, her music is so deep, it speaks to me. Like she totally gets me! You've *had* to have heard her song, 'Look at Me'!`` She started singing a song that didn't sound like anything I had ever heard before, but the other girls knew it and joined in singing with her.

Even Sana and Teri eventually sang along.

"Look at me now, I'm in the spotlight.

Party with my friends, shinin' like the sun.

Takin on the world, doin' my thing.

Look at me, look at me, look at me now!

I'm gonna be your shooting star,
Glowin' in the sky, speaking my mind,
listen to me, listen to me, look at me"

Tommy joined in on the last word, ridiculously throwing his head back and clutching his chest for the high notes at the end, "nooo-ooooo-ooow!"

There was a second of silence then Tommy rolled his eyes, and blankly stated, "I hate that song." We all burst out laughing, even Kimmy.

"Anyway," Kimmy got back to her point, "Zahara also stands up for causes and fights for justice. She's a major influencer! Like that time that she totally boycotted zoos and told all her fans they should too because the penguins looked so sad and had to eat gross food."

"Um, I don't think that's a very good example, Kimmy.", one of her friends spoke up.

Teri seconded, "Yeah, she had no idea what she was talking about. The zoo almost sued her for defamation. She had to make a formal apology and delete her post about it. They only dropped it when she agreed to go in and help the zookeepers with the penguins to learn about how they take care of them. I can't believe you didn't see the dozens of pictures she posted of herself in that little zoo-keeper outfit holding baby penguins."

Kimmy retorted, "Of course I did! They were *so cute*! Anyway, tomorrow night's concert is to raise awareness about homelessness. *My* tickets in the pavilion seating were $300 a piece for VIP, but people can also sit out on the greenway and watch for free! She said she wanted everyone to be able to enjoy her music, even the homeless."

"How generous." Tommy blandly mocked, rolling his eyes again, leaning back he quietly commented to the girls next to him, "What would Zahara know about being homeless, anyway?"

Kimmy huffed, "Well, for your information, Tommy, her family was almost homeless once. She talked about it in her new autobiography. Her dad's job moved them from Atlanta to San Diego and they had to move into an apartment until their house sold in Atlanta. It was horrible and she was forced to share a bedroom with her sister!"

Sana shook her head in disbelief, "That's hardly homeless, Kimmy."

"Close enough!" Kimmy said quietly then quickly turned away to look back out the window. The basket shook slightly as the big wheel started turning again, carrying us higher.

Teri looked over at the other girls who were now sitting with Tommy, "Are you guys going to the concert too?"

One girl with wispy blond hair parted neatly to one side flipped it over her shoulder and replied with a sigh, "My mom said no, that it's an hour from home and on a school night. Plus, the traffic getting out of the city after the concert would be madness, so we couldn't go."

Kimmy looked back from the window and smirked, "Yeah, my mom said that too, so I just asked my dad. It's been super easy to get whatever I want since the divorce." Her smile faded slightly, and her gaze fell to the floor for a second before she recovered her smug expression.

The wheel stopped turning again, this time we were at the very top. On one side, we could see the city laid out before us and on the other, the sea of Lake Michigan. Kimmy seemed relieved that our focus had moved back to the view out the window.

She and Tommy switched back to their seats and the girls soon started chattering about what Kimmy was going to wear to the concert. I looked out over the sea twinkling in the sunlight and Kimmy's words about Zahara played through my head, "Zahara also stands up for causes and fights for justice. She's a major influencer!"

"Maybe Zahara is the one I was sent here to find," I thought to myself.

Soon the wheel began rotating again and the basket lowered closer to the ground. Below us I could see Ms. Moore sitting on a bench, tapping on the small box in her hand.

It seemed like the people were very fond of these boxes; nearly everyone had one. My messenger bag lay beside her on the bench and Pari sat at her feet, his eyes fixed on the wheel waiting for my return. Once he saw me and knew I was watching, he stood up and took action.

Using his nose, he pushed my bag closer to Ms. Moore. I watched her try to pet him to calm him down, but he persisted, pawing at the bag gently urging her to pick it up. She pulled the bag protectively into her lap. Pari slipped his muzzle under the loose flap and flipped the bag open. She seemed to be having an internal battle within her whether to look inside or not. Finally, she decidedly looked to her left and then to her right; and cautiously peered into my messenger bag.

A moment later, she leaned back looking a bit satisfied that she had been right all along; there was nothing to see. Pari tilted his shaggy head crossly, one ear flopping up and the other down; I could almost hear that low grumble of frustration he had made at me many times. He lifted her hand with his snout and pushed it toward the bag that was still open on her lap.

She looked at him curiously then to appease him, she put her hand deep into the bag. Ms. Moore's eyes widened. Her hand made contact with something she did not expect to feel. She raised her eyes and saw me smiling down at her. The wheel began to move again.

It was almost time to say goodbye to my new friends. I felt a tinge of sadness; they were the first friends my own age that I had ever had. They would be traveling back to their homes; but I would not. Not yet. The mission still lay before me. My time with them was done and I knew this was my chance to slip away.

The students began to exit the baskets. They gathered near Mr. Johnson, preparing to depart. I grabbed Sana's arm and pulled her aside. "Thank you so much for befriending me today. You, Tommy, and Teri made me feel so welcome. I shall never forget you. It's time for me to continue my journey. A new girl will be arriving tomorrow in my place. Please give her the same reception and warmth that you have given me. She will be so blessed to have a friend like you!", I hugged Sana, and she hugged me back.

"Will we meet again?" Sana thoughtfully inquired, trying to soak in what I had told her.

I lifted my shoulders, "We shall see, but I hope so! Farewell, Sana, my friend!"

I turned away and rejoined Ms. Moore and Pari. Ms. Moore stood next to the bench, speechlessly, holding my bag with both hands. Her face was pale.

Tentatively, she held out the bag to me, "You're really *not* Annie from North Dakota, are you?"

Receiving it, I draped it over my shoulders. Having the weight of the pearl back again was a comforting feeling. I smiled and shook my head, no. I could see the realization sink in; she finally believed in something she couldn't see but could only feel.

Handing the shirt back to Ms. Moore, I said, "Please tell your sister thank you for letting me use her shirt."

Pari whined softly and raised his eyebrows at me, as if he had something to add. I know it sounds strange, but after all the time Pari and I spent with each other, I could understand him. It's like we had our own language. If he was trying to tell me something, I could just look at him, and he would give me a special message. Sometimes it was a message of encouragement or wisdom to uplift me or keep me from some trouble or danger. Sometimes the message was for someone else.

Turning back, I added, "Ms. Moore, you don't need to worry about Carter's new baby sister. Your niece is going to be just fine. That problem with her heart has already been healed."

Ms. Moore's face went slack. "How did you know about that Anya? Did Carter tell you that about his baby sister?"

"No, Ms. Moore," I smiled looking down at my shaggy companion, then back to her, "Pari did."

8

A Walk in the Park

PARI AND I WALKED in the other direction until I was sure we had faded into the crowd, then we doubled back and found our way to our bench from that morning. I tucked my bag at my feet under the bench to relieve my shoulder. Again, I had begun to feel the heaviness of the King's gift.

I sat on the bench and gathered my thoughts. I was encouraged that I had an idea of what to do next. Zahara sounded amazing, maybe she *was* the person of influence that others would listen to. After all, she fought for what was right, or at least what *she* thought was right. All I had to do was find her and talk to her. Then I would know if the gift was for her. I took out the map that my sailor friend had given me.

Thinking back to what Kimmy had said about seeing Zahara, she had mentioned something about the pavilion. I figured that must be a place nearby. I scanned the map in the direction of the park Kimmy had been pointing to and to my delight I found a gray shape labeled 'pavilion'.

"That must be it, and it doesn't look *that* far!", I glanced down at Pari, who had taken the opportunity to doze at my feet. He seemed content to remain at the bench, but my energy had been revived with new hope of proving myself on my very first day. How impressed the King would be if I completed in one day what I was given seven to do?

Raising my eyebrows at Pari I proposed, "Maybe we should go there today to see if we can find her."

Pari groaned and put his paws over his eyes.

"It's not *that* far." I pleaded, "How hard can it be to get right over there?" I held the map in front of him and pointed to the green patch on the map where the pavilion was.

Eventually I would learn to listen to Pari's gentle resistance, but my excitement drove me on. I started toward the place where the pier met the land.

Things moved faster the further we got from the pier. The carriages, like the ones I had seen earlier, buzzed over roads that were held up on giant pillars. They were stacked one road running over the top of the other. People wearing domes on their heads pedaled on two wheeled contraptions, swerving around me as I stood in the middle of their path squinting up at the roads then down at my map, discerning the best way to get to the pavilion.

This was exciting! I had never been out of the palace before and now, here I was, navigating a foreign land! Up ahead I spotted a set of stairs that seemed to lead up to the first level of the road. A sign pointing up read "Lower Lake Shore Dr."; which I was excited to see, matched the name of the road on my map. This road would lead to a bridge that would bring me closer to the park.

I looked down at Pari and encouraged, "This is going to be quite simple, really!", or so I thought. I have come to find that most things that seem simple in the beginning, prove to be more difficult and troublesome than expected. I enthusiastically headed for the stairs. Pari trailed reluctantly behind me.

"Come on!" I urged him as we got to the top. I led us to the left and was thankful to see a wide path that led alongside the road. Aside from the unsettling thunder from the constant queue of carriages that rumbled above, beside and beneath me, it was quite a pleasant walk and only occasionally did we need to dodge oncoming domed peddlers. The bridge was longer than I expected, and we walked for quite a while.

Eventually, we crossed over one long bridge then another before our path sloped down. The road met the land again, then continued along the edge of the sea of Lake Michigan. Back on the ground, the path led away from the roadway. The gray, stone scenery gave way to a strip of brown grass covered with the crunchy leaves of the bare trees, now ready for their winter slumber. There was a marina to my left and several small vessels bobbed in the water.

At the sight of them my mind wandered to the "Shema" and her arrival on those shores. It seemed almost like a dream that it was only that morning that Pari and I watched her sail into the distance. For a moment, I allowed myself to wonder how I was going to get home again. Would the Shema return for me? The King had never said how I would return. At the thought of home my heart ached ever so slightly, but I pushed that from my mind. The task in front of me was to find Zahara.

I paused at a bench overlooking the marina to check the map that I was still clutching in my hand. "We should be almost there!" I said optimistically to Pari, still a little out of breath from the pace of our brisk walk. Pari's tongue hung out of his mouth, but he did not sit. Looking at me he turned in a circle and whined softly, moving back toward where we had come from.

"We can't go back now, Pari! We are already so close!" The beginning of the park I was looking for was now visible on the other side of the busy road. I could not see any safe way to cross these channels yet. The steady streams of carriages sped relentlessly by, and the lanes were divided by stone barriers. I decided to continue along the paved path. Eventually there had to be a safer crossing.

Pari returned to where I was sitting and put his head wearily on my lap. I stroked the fur on his loving familiar face and felt a tinge of doubt about my choice to not listen to him.

I rationalized, "I'm sorry Pari, but we are almost there. I must see if we can find Zahara today. Just think of how pleased the King would be if we completed the mission the first day we were here!" Pari didn't move but let out a discouraged groan.

"How about we continue on this path and find something to eat?" I had resorted to bribery. He sat up and sighed complying with my request. Pari has always been a gentleman. Even when he is trying to save me from what lay ahead, he stays with me and protects me from my own decisions.

The sun was starting to sink behind the towering buildings to my right. Their giant ominous shadows began to creep across my path. We walked further. Up ahead a road intersected ours where the traffic was stopping. I could see people crossing to the other side. Encouraged, I quickened our pace.

We were almost at the intersection when a pleasing aroma reached us, causing us to both slow down and look around. It was the smell of grilled meat coming from a little green hut with colorful signs. It was set a little way from our path, closer to the water's edge. Tables were set around it, each with a red and yellow umbrella sticking up through the middle. Several people stood in a line at an open window in the side of the hut and others were walking away carrying paper baskets of food. Pari and I glanced at one another. We both had the same thought and veered off the path led by our stomachs toward the food hut.

A stout man dressed in workman's clothes and boots was lumbering away from the hut as we approached. He carried a kind of sausage laying atop a small loaf of bread in one hand and a large cup in the other.

I addressed him, "Excuse me sir, what is that that you have there?"

He stared at me, bewildered, as if I had just asked him if he had two noses, slowly he replied, "It's a polish and a soda?"

I nodded, "That sounds delicious! You received it from the good people of that hut?"

He raised his eyebrows and replied flatly, "Yeah"

Pari yipped happily and I interpreted, "Thank you Franklin!"

His face went blank as we left him and walked toward the hut, waving back at him for his kindness. His wide eyes stared at us for a few moments before he shook his head. Still dazed, he continued walking away.

We stood behind the queue of people waiting at the window. When they had gotten food from a loud, slim gentleman inside of the hut they moved along, either sitting at a table nearby or walking away like Franklin did. When we got to the front of the line, we stepped up to the window and peered inside. Two others were inside that tiny hut as well, one at a large cooking grill and another using a large press to squeeze the juice from the sweet-smelling fruits. The savory aroma of the grilled meat and the fresh tangy scent of lemons and oranges wafted around me. My mouth watered; I was hungrier than I thought!

"Fantastic," I whispered mesmerized.

Rather crossly, the thin man behind the window growled, "Ya gonna order or not?"

"Yes, please." I replied brightly, though I had no idea what he meant by that.

After a pause, he spat, "What do you want?"

Now I understood, remembering what Franklin had said, I confidently ordered, "May I have a Polish and a soda?"

He punched some buttons on the box in front of him. "That it?" he grouched.

"Oh, and the same for Pari as well."

The man leaned out the window and looked down at Pari, raising his eyebrows, "You want a Polish and a soda for your dog?"

"Yes please, kind sir. Thank you for providing food for us and for the people of your city!"

He leaned back and eyed us suspiciously, "Yeah, so that will be thirteen dollars."

"Pardon me sir, thirteen what?" I questioned.

Slowly and deliberately he enunciated, "Thir—teen dol—lars."

Astonished at his generous offer of thirteen of whatever that was, I assured him, "No thank you, you've been more than kind." I smiled sweetly at him.

The girl who had been running the juice device, appeared at the counter with two containers containing the bread and meat and asked cheerfully, "What kinds of soda did you want?"

The thin man put his hand out to stop her, "NO," he said sharply. Turning to Pari and I he pointed in my face, "No money, no food! So, unless you've got thirteen bucks, stop holding up the line and get out of here, kid!" he bellowed, grabbing the sausages off of the window ledge.

"Next!" he hollered at the people who had lined up behind me.

I backed away from the hut, hungry and puzzled. The next person approached the window, made their request then handed him some papers. The thin man seemed satisfied by this and gave them some food. I lingered trying to understand this strange exchange. The next person didn't even give him anything, they just used a rectangle shaped object and rubbed it against a box on the counter. This also seemed to please the thin man, and they too received food. These papers and rectangles must be very important in this land. There were none like these in the Kingdom. I knew nothing of them.

Disappointed, I put my hand on Pari's head, "Sorry Pari, I'm not sure how things work in this land yet."

Pari leaned his head against me appreciatively, I assured him, "Maybe we will find something to eat at the pavilion." This was not to be the last time I was disappointed by the ways of this land.

We walked away from the hut and the queue of hungry people, still waiting. My attention returned to finding a way to the pavilion. Nearby, Lake Shore Drive crossed in front of us again. A small group of people were already crossing; we joined in behind them.

A green sign above us read 'E. Randolph St.' Once we reached the other side, the others branched off in different directions, leaving us to continue straight on our own. I paused to glance down at the map; the green patch that we were searching for looked like it should be to our left shortly.

By then, the sun had sunk completely behind the buildings, so the chill of the evening and a wind off the sea gave the air a sudden bite. I shuddered, looking down at our map, "We should be getting close now." I reasoned as we continued along Randolph Street. To our left a garden opened up and we could see a pathway leading through the trees. Pari moved to start down this path, but I stopped him.

Looking at the map, I beckoned him, "Come on Pari, that's not the one yet. I think it will be closer this way." I pressed on and Pari trailed behind me. Soon I had led us into a dark tunnel, once again proving that ignoring Pari's promptings was unwise.

The tunnel was lit by a few orange glowing lights hanging on the huge dark beams that arched over our heads. The path narrowed as we entered the tunnel and the echo of the carriages speeding past us reverberated off the low ceiling. The air was thick and foul, and when I breathed in, it caught in my throat making me cough. I tried holding my breath as much as I could and hurried toward the next opening in the tunnel up ahead that let another road pass through. I was thankful for the rush of fresh air it brought in.

Looking further down the street of Randolph, the raised path that we walked upon completely disappeared. The carriages drove right next to the wall; I could go no further in the tunnel. I decided the best move would be to get back out into the open. Besides, I could see a shiny metal bulge above the trees that resembled the picture on my map. We were so close! Yet it seemed that we just could not get where I wanted us to go!

We found ourselves looking up at a large wall that stood between us and the park where the pavilion stood. Frustrated, I searched for an opening in the wall but found none. We passed under a silver arch that went over the road and finally found a set of stairs that led up into the park area.

Looking at the name etched into the stone wall, I found it on my map and groaned; we had completely passed the pavilion and would need to back track. It was getting harder to muster my energy and excitement. I could not make my tired feet move any faster as I dragged them up the stairs. At the top of the stairs an open garden space was finally spread out before me, I collapsed onto a wooden bench nearby. While I caught my breath, Pari sat down right in front of me and halfheartedly stared at me letting out a huff that caused the fur around his jowls to fly up.

"Don't be cross with me, Pari. I thought I knew the best way. But now we really are almost there." Loosening my boots, I rubbed my sore feet. Even with the winter approaching and the glory of the summer flowers gone till spring, the garden still offered a peaceful retreat for the people of the city. What a contrast to the smoky tunnel and the gray stone roads. Just beyond a line of trees I could see the shining roof of the pavilion across the park.

With the sun gone, the sky was growing dark. I pulled my boots back on and quickly stood up. The muscles in my legs ached; protesting my drive to keep moving.

"Let's go see what we can find. I'm sure we didn't come all this way for nothing. There must be something here that will lead us to Zahara!" The wide path was free of any other walkers and the scenery would have been pleasant had we not been moving so quickly.

Soon we saw the beginning of the silver arch that we had walked under when we were outside of the park wall. It was a walking path that lead over the busy road in the direction of the path that Pari had urged me to enter. It was clear to me that his path would have been much more efficient and safer.

Pari looked up at me knowingly, and yipped, reproving me for not trusting him to know the best way to go. I knew I was still going against his guidance, but I just thought I was on the best path, and obsessively I could not let this idea go until I knew if Zahara was here. However, it would prove that the path I was on only led to trouble. The tranquil tree-lined garden opened to a clearing revealing a monstrous frame of arches spanning a massive lawn. In the distance a bulging, silver structure held a large platform. Many workers were busy on lifts and ladders hanging strange cans that lit up, illuminating the platform with many colors of light. The temperature had dropped again, and I was still breathing heavily. My hot breath began to catch in the cold air and condensed into a light cloud.

I pressed forward. "This must be Zahara's performance space for tomorrow night." I thought to myself. As I approached the platform the grassy area gave way to that same smooth stone that covered most of the city and contained rows and rows of red chairs filling up the space in front of the platform.

Men were placing barricades between the lawn and the seats creating a clear dividing line. The place was buzzing with activity, and I was able to walk past unnoticed. There was no sign of Zahara, except for several enormous banners that were being hung across the back of the platform of a curvy woman with a sultry look in her eyes striking different poses. By the giant letters down the sides of each banner that read 'Zahara', I could safely guess that this was who I was looking for. She had dark glistening skin, and deep eyes with bold eyebrows and full, glossy red lips.

"Good to know what she looks like!" I chirped, still trying to stir up enthusiasm in Pari. I began to scan the area but saw no one who looked anything like the sultry woman on the banners. In fact, the only woman I could spot was standing on the stage holding a clipboard and directing the workers.

She had pale skin and long red hair and smart black glasses. She wore long pants with crisp lines and a tight-fitting pink sweater with a large bow that curled over her shoulder and pointy shoes with little sticks for heals. Currently she was motioning for the workers to adjust the banners to allow for a giant elephant statue to be able to pass through the middle of them.

"What in the world is that for?" I mumbled to myself. I would find out the next night, but I had no time to worry about that right now. Off to my right some movement caught my eye. A large carriage stood there with tall doors open to the container in the back. Inside were all sorts of boxes and cords that must have been for the concert.

Several young men were cautiously approaching the open doors. One of them peered around the corner of the vehicle and motioned for his companions to come closer while he continued to scan the stage area.

"Perhaps they are also looking for Zahara" I said excitedly. I motioned to Pari, just like the boy had motioned to his companions. Pari groaned at me but followed anyway. I called out loudly to the boys waving my hand in the air to get their attention.

"Greetings!" They froze, and I continued toward them, "Pardon me, could I ask you . . ."

The boy who had been watching the stage, glared at me before bolting down the path away from the park followed by the others.

I began to run after them calling, "Wait! I just wanted to ask you if you know where I can find Zahara." They kept running, not looking back at me. However, several men nearby wearing navy uniforms that had the word 'Security' printed across the back in yellow letters *did* take notice and started toward me.

Still determined to catch up with the boys, I kept running after them with Pari at my heels. The boys disappeared into some bushes, and we rushed after them. Pari leapt over the top of the shrubs, but I had to push through them with the twigs catching on my clothes with their bare hooks and branches snapping back and scraping me. I came out on the other side with a stinging scrape across my cheek and welts on my legs and arms. I could not stop and nurse my wounds now.

"Please wait!" I hollered after the boys as they launched themselves over the wall and out of the garden.

From behind me I could hear the 'Security' men shout to each other, "Over here! The hoodlums are by the wall!" When Pari and I got to the low wall I could see that the drop was about ten feet to the bottom on the other side. I recognized that it was the path I had trudged up after leaving the tunnel just a few minutes ago. Before the men found their way through the line of shrubs, I impulsively copied the boys and launched myself over the wall. The drop felt further than it looked and when I hit the ground I rolled through the bushes and dried leaves; it took me a few seconds to regain my bearings. Suddenly Pari was beside me and nudged me to get up with his cold nose.

The voices of the men were growing closer and sounded aggravated. Why were they chasing us? Were they going to try to harm us? Had the hoodlums done something wrong? What was a 'hoodlum' anyway? Mr. Johnson had called the boys in his class 'hoodlums', so perhaps it was a term of endearment. These men did not seem to be using the term very fondly though. Either way, I guessed it must be a name they called their youth. These thoughts went through my mind as I jumped up and started following the boys again.

They had jumped over a barrier and onto the roadway running down a ramp leading under the park. Over our heads there was a sign with an arrow that read, 'Parking'. My heart was pounding, and I felt a panicky fear rising up in me, like I needed to be running away, but I didn't really know why. It gave my legs a strange burst of energy and speed.

Entering the tunnel, the walls began to squeeze in closer as we reached the bottom of the ramp and several carriages blasted a loud horn at us as they buzzed within inches of us. The hot breath of them pressed us against the walls. This was the first time since arriving that I felt truly afraid. The sound of my heart pounded in my ears. Pari and I found we were running right into a kind of holding pen for carriages. Several had been abandoned here in orderly rows marked with white lines.

Catching my breath for a moment, I looked around for the hoodlums They were nowhere to be seen; I had lost them.

Discouraged, we walked away from the tunnel and after passing by many carriages and empty carriage stalls, we found some stairs leading up. We climbed the stairs and peeked around.

It had led us back up into the park, not twenty feet from where we had leaped the wall. I had gone in a circle, angered the security men and lost the hoodlums. I was not making any progress. The sun was now fully set, and the air had a very crisp chill. The breath of the security men made little clouds around their heads as they spoke into some black boxes and used sticks that shone light out of them to search through the shrubs that we had jumped through.

"Keep a look out for 6 adolescents, last seen skulking around the pavilion staging area attempting to steal some sound equipment. Five males, approximately fourteen to sixteen years of age and one girl with a big white dog."

Gasping, I quickly crouched down on the top step behind the stairwell wall hiding from them and listening to what they were saying. Hoping my own breath wouldn't give me away. Wide eyed, I looked at Pari, pleading silently for help.

His stern look said it all; those men knew the boys were thieves, and now thought I was one of them! Two of the men met each other a short distance from the stairwell where I was hiding.

"Those were some of 'Scrumps' boys. I've seen those punks before. Usually just causing trouble and picking fights. Looks like they were out to score some AV equipment out of one of Zahara's trucks. The guys checked it out and nothing was missing. We must have spotted them before they had a chance to nab anything."

Another man approached them. "I found this in the bushes. It must have torn off their clothing."

"I've never seen fabric like this," one of the other men commented, "I think it was from that girl. Haven't seen her running with them before, but she was wearing that color green."

I looked down and noticed the tear in my tunic. It must have gotten caught on one of the shrubs and ripped, leaving a small strip of it behind.

Marita would be disappointed that I had ruined my new tunic already, but I had no time to worry about my wardrobe right now. It was obvious now that Zahara was not here. The men barked into their boxes for 'reinforcements' and asked for someone to contact something called 'CPD' to increase the patrol cars in the area. I didn't know exactly what all of that meant but gathered that this was not where I wanted to stay.

Pari and I quietly crept down the stairs back to the carriage stalls. I owed Pari an apology.

Once we were a safe distance away, I turned to him, "I am so sorry for my strong headed actions today Pari. We had such good fortune with meeting Mr. Talon so quickly that I thought I could still find who we are seeking on our first day." I humbly confessed, "But my ambitions led us astray and my brilliant plan only led us on a wild goose chase for nothing. I could have gotten us into trouble and put us in danger. Please forgive me."

I looked down at the map in my hand. I had been clutching it tightly while we ran, and now it looked sad, soggy, and crumpled.

"A lot of good this map has proven." I scoffed, giving Pari a half smile. I moved to put the map back in my bag when I realized, to my horror, that I had not had my bag this whole time!

9

Abandoned

A CHILL RAN THROUGH me. It was not from the cold this time, but from the realization that I had abandoned the very reason I had come to this land in the first place.

Mentally, I retraced my steps and remembered setting the bag at my feet back at the bench on the pier.

"How careless could I be!?" I berated myself. "Pari, I left the King's gift at the pier!" In my foolish excitement I had come all that way and left my bag and the pearl behind. I felt like I was about to cry, then stopped myself. That wouldn't help me. I had to get back to that bench. Maybe there was a chance that my bag would still be where I had left it. I had to at least try; it was my whole purpose for being there!

Recalling his hesitation to leave the pier, I desperately looked to Pari, "I should have listened to you in the first place!" I had caused this problem myself, but I couldn't fix it on my own. "Please show me the fastest way back." I asked him simply.

He needed no further prompting; Pari had been waiting for me to notice my mistake and be willing to be led. Pari ran ahead of me and, to my surprise, instead of running toward the pier he ran in the other direction, back toward the entrance of the park.

I was in no position to argue with him. I had caused enough trouble by *not* listening. Leading me through the shadowy paths, we arrived at the entrance to the silver ribbon pathway.

The security men were still patrolling near the bushes on the other side of the garden and took no notice of us. We made our way quickly over the road following the path, winding like a serpent, down into the next garden.

Not slowing, Pari continued to run through the garden turning down one path, then another, zig zagging our way around the trees and bare flower beds. We emerged from the park near the bridge for Lake Shore Drive. It was the simpler path that Pari had wanted me to take before when we first saw this garden.

Under the bridge I could see the green food hut again. The small green hut was now very quiet. The que of hungry people had dispersed; the angry thin man and the others had gone away. Metal shutters blocked the windows and chains were wrapped around the chairs and tables. One lonely lamp flickered high on a pole giving an eerie yellow glow over the scene.

Pari barked, urging me to continue. Again, we burst forward, not under the bridge toward the hut, as I was expecting, but across the road and up another large ramp. A bright yellow carriage came blazing down the ramp toward us. We threw ourselves against the cold stone wall and out of the way. The carriage narrowly missed us., but sounded an angry horn blast and screeched as it swerved away.

I looked back to see the man inside shaking his fist in the air, but Pari paid it no attention and continued at full speed. I *had* asked for the fastest path, not the safest. We ran close to a low wall as the road rose higher from the ground and soon, we were running above the river.

From the high road I could see the lights of the towering wheel on the pier still slowly spinning. Hope fueled my steps that no one had found my bag and that the pearl was still safe where I had left it hours ago.

Many of the oncoming carriages zoomed past us oblivious of our presence, but an increasing number did notice us. Some responded by sounding their horn or quickly swerving away from us. The bright lights shining from the fronts of the carriages glared at us in a steady stream as they rushed at us.

I squinted my eyes and looked down. I could only focus on Pari in front of me and the wall beside me.

"Just keep moving." I kept telling myself, occasionally daring to glance up at the glowing wheel in the distance to gauge my progress, it looked only slightly closer now.

By the time we had crossed the River, my legs were burning and pangs in my chest pleaded with me to stop, but I could not.

For a time, the wheel vanished from view, blocked by large buildings and trees. I just had to believe that Pari knew where to go, even when I could no longer see my destination. I chose to trust my guide this time.

In the distance blue and red flashing lights were headed toward us accompanied by a high-pitched wailing. Pari made a sharp turn to the left around a break in the wall and led me down another ramp. The wailing sound was growing louder behind us. As we reached the bottom of the ramp, Pari turned and went under the road and suddenly stopped, so abruptly that I nearly tripped over him. He circled me and leaned against me, pressing me into the shadows, urging me to stay hidden. I slumped down against the painted wall, my legs had turned to jelly. I gasped for breath.

The lights and wailing moved over our heads and continued toward the bridge, the way we had just come. I wondered what this strange event could be. Maybe a ritual or warning of some kind. I would hear this same kind of sorrowful wailing many times in this land.

Pari let me catch my breath for quite some time before finally nudging me to my feet. I knew we must continue. My mind and heart agreed, but my body protested, and it took all my willpower to make my throbbing legs comply.

Throngs of people were streaming away from the pier. I could see the glowing wheel towering above the palaces. Being so close fueled my desperation to get back to the King's gift.

We frantically wove our way through the crowd, which thinned to a trickle as we finally approached the palaces on the pier. The wheel had stopped turning and many of the shops were dark and closed. I retraced my steps back toward the bench. When it came into view, my heart sank. Peering around the last of the dispersing crowd, I could not see the bag.

A young man was standing in the middle of the path facing the last of the departing crowd offering any who passed him a colorful card. I noticed that the ground was littered with cards that people had discarded immediately after they had received them.

When we got near to him, as if sensing my presence, he suddenly spun to face me, raising his eyebrows hopefully, he smiled. Stepping forward, he looked relieved and offered one of his cards to me. Something about the spark of light in the blue eyes of this stranger caught me off guard and caused me to pause long enough to grab the paper he held.

Pushing past him, I slowed to a walk, had I really lost my King's gift forever? He had entrusted it to me, and I had abandoned it in my zeal to prove myself! I fell to my knees and with my last thread of hope I ran my hand under the stone bench.

To my relief my hand brushed the leather straps of the messenger bag that someone had tucked safely out of sight under the bench. Quickly, I looked behind me just in time to catch the young man smiling at me before disappearing around a corner.

Who was he? Had he been *watching over* the King's gift? I could not be sure, but it did seem like he had been waiting for me to come back. Pulling the bag out of its hidden place I clutched it to my chest as tears of relief washed my cheeks.

The pier was completely abandoned. Pari and I were, again, the only ones here. It was just as it had been at the break of day when we were watching the Shema sail into the distance. What a journey we'd had already!

Still kneeling on the ground, I pushed back the flap of the messenger bag and reached inside to lift out the precious pearl. It glowed brighter as my heart throbbed with joy at the sight of it. This was my assignment to serve my King and I would never again be so careless as to abandon it to seek after my own ambitions.

Pari sat with his tongue hanging out happily keeping his watch over me. My faithful guide, my gentle companion, he (and the young stranger) had rescued me from disaster! I reached out pulling him close and my tears of gratitude wet his shaggy fur. He nuzzled me affectionately until the tears had dried and the cold wind blowing off the sea made me shiver.

I returned the pearl safely to the bag and picked up the crumpled map which had fallen from my hand. Lying next to it was the paper I had received from the young man. Picking it up I looked closer at it. A chill ran through me, but again, not from the cold.

He *had* been here waiting for me. The brightly colored paper matched the banners that had been at the pavilion, and the card held the image of Zahara on the cover of a book. The words next to the book read, "Zahara wants to meet you!" On the back of the card was a strange seal, and then some other words and numbers. I did not know how to interpret this yet, but this was the answer I had been seeking!

If I had only been patient, the answer was already on its way to me, in the form of this dark-haired, blue eyed, handsome young stranger with an invitation from Zahara herself!

I looked around. By the hundreds of invitations that littered the ground, he must have been here for hours watching for me to come back.

Pari nudged my tired arm, "You are right, Pari. We need to find someplace warm for the night." The inviting glow from the indoor garden beckoned us and we made our way inside.

Protected from the wind, the welcome wave of warmth hit me as soon as we entered. I shuddered as I shook off the cold. When the numbness left me, exhaustion, thirst, and hunger arose.

I found a place in the shadows at the corner of the garden and sat down next to one of the trees. I slumped back against it. Retrieving the bottle of water from my bag, I drank deeply from it before offering Pari the rest of the water which he lapped from the air as I poured it out for him. I returned the empty bottle to my bag, thinking we may again have need of it in this land.

Pari went to a large canister nearby that was overflowing with cups and boxes and other discarded things. Standing on his back paws he delicately grabbed a large flat box that had been left atop the cylinder-shaped receptacle. Returning to me, we opened the box that read, 'Giorgio's Pizza' to reveal two pieces of bread topped with cheese, some vegetables, and several bits of meat. I lifted out the triangle shaped food and Pari and I paused in thankfulness for a moment before we devoured our feast. Although it was still not the same as the food in the Kingdom, it was quite tasty and not a morsel remained when we were through. How kind that someone left it there for us.

Only one need remained. Now that my belly was full, my drooping eyelids hungered for rest. I pulled the tattered blanket from my bag along with my journal and writing stone. Before giving in to sleep I wrote of my day:

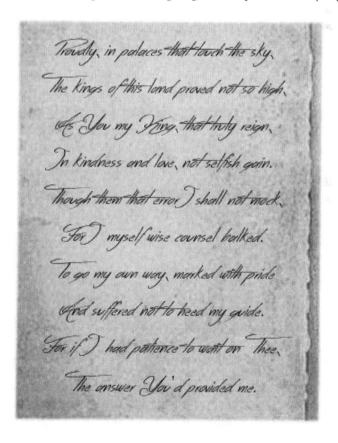

Proudly, in palaces that touch the sky,
The kings of this land proved not so high,
As You my King, that truly reign,
In kindness and love, not selfish gain.
Though them that error I shall not mock,
For I myself wise counsel balked.
To go my own way, marked with pride
And suffered not to heed my guide.
For if I had patience to wait on Thee,
The answer You'd provided me.

I tucked my book back into my pack and leaned back against Pari. Pulling the blanket up over us both, I gazed out at the twinkling lights of the giant wheel that shone through the glass ceiling until sleep overtook me.

In the morning the soft trickle of the fountains awoke me as the sun peeked over the sea of Lake Michigan. It filled the garden with golden light. I deeply breathed in the new day, and quickly gathered up my things, folding my blanket and tucking it into my bag. As I did my hand brushed the pearl.

Pausing, I gently lifted it from the bag and held it in my hand. I dropped to a knee before the throne, just as I had every morning. My braids tumbled down over my shoulders, having broken loose from where Marita had fastened them several days ago. Clutching the pearl, I was brimming with new hope. Maybe today I would find the one who I was looking for; the one who could use this gift to spread hope to this beautiful land and its dear people.

I had seen so much on my first day there, and now I had people here whom I considered friends. I thought of Sana, and Tommy and Teri, Mr. Johnson and Ms. Moore.

My heart bubbled with gratitude, and I spoke to my King as if He were right there with me, "Thank you, my King, for sending me to this strange new place. I have seen so many wondrous things and found friendship and favor with those I've met. May your servant succeed and bring you glory, my Lord."

I did not know whether the King could hear me, but there in the warmth of the tranquil garden, it seemed only fitting to address the one to whom I owed it all, even my very life. I was honored that He had entrusted this mission to me, His humble servant.

10

To Catch a Falling Star

LOWERING THE PEARL BACK into my bag I arose, refilled my bottle with water from the fountains and made my way to the nearest door with Pari close behind. "Today we have an invitation to meet Zahara! Now we just have to find out where."

Pari and I stepped out into the crisp morning air and looked toward the city. Just the same as the morning before, it was an inspiring sight, but still dull and faded somehow.

I pulled the card I had gotten from the blue-eyed stranger out of my bag and turned it over to look at the back. Somewhere in this vast land of towers and busy roads Zahara was waiting to meet me, and this card held my clue.

Again, we sat on our, now familiar, bench to think of what to do next. I looked at the back of the card again. "State Street", I read out loud, that looked familiar, but from where? Then it came to me, it was on the map! Pulling the map out of my bag, I frantically scanned for that word. Pari let out a sigh and put his big head in my lap, right on top of the map.

This time I got it, "You're right, I don't know how to find where Zahara is. We need someone to help us."

No sooner had I said that than we heard a joy-filled chuckle. Squinting into the rising sun, I could barely make out the silhouette of someone standing nearby leaning against the railing. Had I completely missed them, or had they just appeared? I never did find out which.

The person must have noticed me looking at them and cheerfully called out, "Mornin' pal!" It was a woman's voice, spunky and upbeat and it drew me in with its warm and friendly tone.

As she approached, I stood and put my hand up to shield my eyes and try and see her through the sun. I could not make out any features other than that she had short hair, a stocky build, and the shoes she wore were bright red with white laces and white soles.

"Can I help ya with something?" she inquired.

"Well, yes, actually!" I was rather shocked that she had suddenly appeared and offered her assistance at just the right moment. "We have an invitation to meet someone, but I'm not sure how to find this place." I held out the card for her to see.

"Zahara huh?" she said sounding rather impressed. I nodded, proudly. "May I see it?" the woman asked, holding out her hand. Turning the card over she studied the back for a moment, "Oh yeah! This is at the bookstore in the mall over by Millennium Park. If ya get on the 124 up here at the bus stop and take that around to Michigan Avenue, you're gonna get off at the corner of Washington. You'll find it about a block and a half down on the right. Take the first entrance to the mall, go down the hall and you'll see the bookstore on your left."

I continued to squint into the sun completely lost.

She looked down at my hand, "Well, you've got the transit map right here, kid!"

Slowing down, she very carefully gave me detailed instructions. Taking my unfolded map, she pointed me to where a grey line swooped close to the pier. Among the many numbers on it was the number 124 in a little grey circle. "You get on bus 124 right here. It will say 124 above the front window", she slowly continued. Then tracing the grey line, she explained, "Then get off the bus right here at the bus stop at the corner of East Washington Street." She pointed to a little blue square on the map next to Millennium Park and the pavilion I had been to the day before.

I could feel Pari look up at me with his head cocked to one side knowingly. He remained silent; we both knew I had learned my lesson. I followed her bejeweled hand as she continued to point the way. "Then walk down Washington till you pass under the CTA tracks and enter the first set of doors with an awning over it. This is the entrance to the mall. Inside, you'll walk straight down that hall, the bookstore is on the left, you can't miss it!"

I nodded slowly trying to take it all in and remember the details. "Here," she said, pulling something from her pocket, "you'll need this for the bus." She handed me a flat, blue rectangle. "And getting around will be a whole lot easier if *you* wear this, Pari!" From her back pocket she pulled a red vest-like object. Pari stepped over to her and allowed her to buckle it around his large chest then she ruffled Pari's fur.

I was amazed at the kindness of this stranger. I glanced down for a moment to tuck the card into my bag and looking back up, began to say, "You have been so helpful! Thank yo.", but when I did, the woman had vanished.

The sun had risen above the horizon now and there was no one else on the pier. Astonished, I pondered for a moment how help had arrived right after I'd asked for it.

"Wait," I uttered suddenly, turning to Pari, "how did she know your name?"

Pari let out a short yip, to the effect of "You'll see."

"Fine, keep your secrets." I pouted. We headed back toward the land to the place the woman had shown me on the map. Along the way checking the cylinders to see if someone else had left us food like we had found the night before, but all the cylinders had been emptied.

A man with a cart was roasting nuts, they smelled amazing on an empty stomach and as I passed, he smiled and offered me a small cup of them. "Good morning! Would you like a sample?"

Gratefully, I accepted, "Thank you!" We continued toward the spot marked on the map. I held out one of the sweet roasted nuts to Pari; he turned his nose up at them. I thought they were quite good, though I was still hungry when they were gone.

We got to the end of the pier and found a sign that said 'Bus Stop' near where the road looped around then headed back into the city. It was still early but the city had already woken up; the streets were busy, and several people were jogging or pedaling on the contraptions I had seen the day before. We waited for a while before we saw a long box-shaped carriage coming around the loop toward us.

Above the front window little yellow dots of light made the number 124. It screeched to a stop in front of us and made a loud whooshing noise as the entire carriage lowered closer to the ground.

A man inside pulled a lever that made the doors open for us. After staring up at the balding man for a moment, he impatiently barked, "Ya getting on or what?"

Timidly, I inquired, "Is this a 'bus'?"

"Nah, it's a submarine." He rolled his eyes. "What kind of a question is that? Of course, this is a bus!" He repeated himself, "Ya getting on or what?" more impatient than before.

Very tentatively I followed Pari up onto the first step of the bus. "Wait," the man said in a quieter tone, "is that a service dog?"

I looked down at Pari wearing his red vest. Sana had called him that too, so I guessed that he was. In all honesty I looked up at the man and replied, "Yes, he is."

"What's he trained to do?" he asked suspiciously. Confused, I struggled to answer, "Um, well, many things, but mostly he guides me and keeps me from running into danger."

Fumbling with some knobs and levers on the bus, he muttered, "Oh geeze, it's a seeing eye dog!"

Standing up flustered, he changed his tone, "Let me help ya, miss. I'm real sorry, I didn't realize." He nervously chuckled, "No wonder you was asking if this was the bus."

Gently, he guided Pari and I to the first seat right behind his. "Where ya headed to, kid?"

Thinking back to the woman's directions, I remembered, "Michigan and Washington?"

Sitting back down in his seat, nodding his head, "Yeah, I'll get ya there, Miss."

Reaching into my bag I pulled out the blue card and held it up, "Oh, I have this. It's for the bus?"

Nervously chucking again, he said, "Here, let me, ah, get that for ya." Looking at my reflection in a mirror above his head, he reached back and grabbed the card and waved it in front of a box next to him.

The box made a loud tweeting noise before he reached back with the card slowly, "I'm handin your card back to ya, ok?"

I studied his worried expression in the mirror, taken aback by the doting attention he was now showing to me. Pari leaned over me and took the card out of the man's hand, holding it gently in his teeth and placed it on my lap.

Still watching me in his mirror, the man pulled the lever to close the door again. The carriage lifted, and we began to pull away from the bus stop.

What an experience it was being *inside* of one of those carriages! The man used a large wheel to move the carriage back and forth, with some strange power propelling us past other smaller carriages and around corners. We went under Lake Shore Drive and rumbled into the city. The bus stopped several more times just as it had for me, and other people entered and found a seat.

Only minutes passed before the man behind the wheel looked in his mirror at me again and politely said to my surprise, "Alrighty Miss, this is your stop." I could not believe we were already at our destination! He opened the door and motioned for several people entering the bus to step aside and wait for Pari and I to pass first.

Pari led the way down the steps. Turning back toward the bus, I waved and called "Thank you, kind sir!" to the man through the line of people entering his bus. He awkwardly waved, then shook his head and called, "No problem, Miss."

The bus pulled away and just beyond where it had stood, I could see the top of the silver pavilion shining in the morning sun above the trees. I could not help but laugh at the fruitless journey I had taken us on the previous day.

"Not a word, Pari." I said flatly as he sat smugly next to me. He stood and turned to walk away from the park, and I followed. In the distance I could see a kind of bridge that ran over the road and in the middle was a large circle with the letters 'cta' across it. I remembered the woman's words and knew that just beyond that bridge I would find a door with an awning, and I would be at my destination to meet Zahara.

The lesson from this part of the journey was not lost on me. It was amazing how easy the path was when I slowed down and followed my guide and asked for help, instead of rushing off after my own ideas. Pari never again brought it up, but I never forgot.

Soon we reached the entrance to the mall. A blast of warm air hit my face as we entered the two sets of doors leading from the street into a wide hall with shops on both sides. We didn't make it far into the mall when we saw right where Zahara was going to be. Huge signs with Zahara peeking out from behind her book stood on both sides of an entryway to a shop.

I passed by a long queue of excited people, most of which were holding a copy of the same book as in the pictures. Two men in blue uniforms with black talking boxes hanging from their belts, very similar to the 'security' from the night before, stood on either side of the entrance which was blocked by a chain curtain.

"Excuse me, sirs, good day!" I began, pulling the invitation from my bag. I held it up for them to see. "Could you give me your assistance? I have this invitation to meet with a woman named Zahara today."

"Yeah, you and half the city." The guard scoffed, "Wait in line just like everybody else. The doors don't even open for another hour."

He pointed back the way I came. My eyes followed the line of others waiting to see Zahara. It wound from the door of the book shop, looped around the corner, and then snaked down into the next hall. A thin strand of red rope held on black pillars corralled them in and Perri and I walked along it until we finally found the end and stood behind a group of girls a bit older than me, who were giggling and talking excitedly as they sipped beverages from paper cups.

The line continued to grow as more and more people of all sorts joined in behind me. A woman with a tiny baby in a rolling cart, a young man with baggy pants, shaggy hair and a shirt much to long for him, a woman and man who stood very poised and collected in their crisp, pressed clothing and their impeccably clean shoes tapping the floor impatiently, an elderly woman accompanying two young girls who wore shirts with a picture of Zahara painted on them, and many more in the growing line that I could not see fully from where I stood.

One thing was certain; many people followed this Zahara and would listen to her. I was practically bouncing with anticipation that Zahara could be whom I sought, when a man carrying a large box with a white number 6 on it appeared and hoisted it to his shoulder. It had a strange 'eye' looking out of it, and he stood a little way off pointing the eye toward the line, then stopped to focus on a man who was speaking into a stick.

The man with the stick began to interact with the crowd and everyone around me got excited about this and seemed to want the man to talk to them.

He made his way toward us, and when he approached, he singled me out and came my way, "So what brings you to the mall today, young lady?" he asked in a sing-song tone then held the stick in front of my face.

Maybe he could help me find Zahara, I thought. Holding up my invitation, I boldly told him, "I received this invitation to meet Zahara. I need to speak to her about a gift I have brought! My King has sent."

He cut me off and in a loud excited voice asked, "Who's here to meet Zahara?" The crowd roared and cheered, and the man returned to talking to the box, finishing with, "This is Ted Hartly for Channel 6 News." Then he and the man with the box were gone again and the line resumed their excited chatter. I guess I was not the only one that Zahara had invited.

After what seemed like a very long time, a cheer erupted from the front of the line, and I craned my neck to see what was happening. The guards pulled back the chain curtain and the woman named Zahara stepped out from behind it waving and blowing kisses to the waiting crowd.

She really was quite stunning! Tall and slender, she wore a bright yellow suit hugging every curve and accentuating her long legs with a slight flair at the bottom. A huge fur-like mane wrapped around her neck with a tied bow on her hip. Her ebony hair was now long and straight, quite different from the short tight curls in her pictures, and streaked with the colors of honey and cinnamon. Her moves were smooth, calculated, and sensual. Her dark caramel skin glistened as if dusted with starlight. Large, dark glasses covered her eyes, but her plump red lips and sparkling white teeth drew your eye as she smiled and spoke with large, exaggerated moves to the people waiting at the front of the line.

Her presence seemed as large as the banners of her, and she paused to pose with a group while someone flashed a light at them from a small box with a long tube at the end. She had an entourage of people with her, including the woman with the dark-rimmed glasses and red hair I had seen at the pavilion.

Today the red head wore a simple black dress with tall, spiked heels and some flashy jewelry. But all eyes were on Zahara as she threw her long hair over her shoulder and the red-haired woman stood back and held out a small rectangle object which she tapped, moving to different angles as Zahara greeted the adoring crowd. The woman smiled in satisfaction and gave Zahara a nod. Zahara took the cue and retreated to a table that had been set up just inside the entrance to the shop.

One of the security men called out, "Hey Angela?" The redhead, Angela, hurried over and gave some instructions. She pointed to a small counter where a girl sat with a large flat box in front of her and stacks and stacks of Zahara's book surrounding her.

'Angela' joined Zahara at the table while the security men started shouting instructions to the crowd, she discreetly handed Zahara a white cloth. She quickly wiped her hands with it before sitting at the table, which Angela had just wiped down with another white cloth. I got the impression that Zahara did not like touching anything that could get her hands dirty.

I was so far away I could not hear what they were telling the people at the front of the line. Two huge men with large muscles emerged from inside the store. Their biceps bulged out of the short sleeves of their black shirts which made them look especially intimidating.

They positioned themselves one on either side of Zahara while the other security men stood at the beginning of the line of very excited people. At the nod of the muscle-bound men they started to let people approach the table with their book in hand.

Occasionally they would direct one of the followers to go to the girl at the counter to receive a book before going to speak with Zahara.

As I observed, a girl approached the table, squealing with excitement. For just a few moments Zahara addressed her and the girl in happy tears gushed something back. Angela held out her hand for the book the girl had brought. Opening it, she placed it in front of Zahara. Zahara scribbled something inside the cover of the book, then the security guard took it from the table and handed it back to the girl. She clutched it to her chest as the muscle-bound guard directed her to move away from the table. I did not understand their strange ritual, but it repeated itself, almost identically, with person after person as my place in the line crept closer and closer to the book shop. Eventually Pari and I made it to the front of the line.

The security man grunted, "You got yur book?" When I shook my head, he pointed me toward the girl at the counter with the stacks of books.

The girl was tapping on the surface of the panel in front of her as I approached, "That's $27.89." she chirped cheerfully before I had gotten all the way to her counter.

Confused, I asked "I beg your pardon, but I am not familiar with how this exchange works."

A little shocked, the sweet girl smiled and explained, "We accept cash or cards. With taxes the book comes to $27.89."

Pari nudged my bag with his nose. "Card?" I asked him, then exclaimed, "That's right!" I had a card that the woman had given me! Maybe this girl would like to tap it on the box thing like the people from the food hut yesterday! I was finally figuring out this strange land! I pulled my card out from my bag and proudly presented it to the girl.

She furrowed her eyebrows and looked at me with a concerned expression, "Um, this is a transit card? It only works for the bus and train." she whispered. My countenance fell and my cheeks flushed red. I guess I had *not* figured it out yet.

Sensing my hesitation and noticing the line forming behind me of others waiting for a book, she said kindly in a quiet voice, "It's ok, you don't have to be embarrassed. I wouldn't have had enough to buy an expressive book like this when I was your age either. Here, you can use this promo poster for your Zahara autograph!"

She smiled sweetly and handed me a poster, which was a large image of Zahara on thin shiny paper and returned my card. Smiling up at her, I was thankful for her quick thinking and kind heart.

"Go ahead." she said, encouraging me and nodding toward Zahara. Tucking the card back into my bag, I rejoined the line, with Pari trotting along beside me. The guard motioned to me that it was my turn.

My heart was thumping hard, and I took a deep breath as I slowly approached the table, Angela held out her hand and smiled weakly when I handed her the poster.

I bowed before Zahara then straightening up I began my address, "Graceful Zahara, I am Anya, servant of the Most High King. I have been sent from the Kingdom, bearing a gift . . . ."

Zahara looked up and interrupted with a forced smile and in a bored, sing-song tone, uttered, "Hello Anya." She paused looking at me curiously, "What's the costume for? Are you in a movie or something?"

Without waiting for me to answer she looked down and as she scribbled something into the poster she continued, "What production are you coming from?" she said, sounding slightly intrigued.

"I am from the Kingdom of the Most High King." I responded respectfully.

Turning to her companion, Angela, she bragged, "I think I was sent a script for that one. It was some original streaming production or something like that. My agent keeps trying to get me to do a cameo for old times' sake. But I've told him a million times, I'm not going back there!"

She laughed and rolled her eyes. "Here, little one, let me do you a *huge* favor." Motioning for me to come closer to the table, she dropped her voice and leaned in, "Believe it or not, I was once a nobody in the industry, just like you and only *wished* I could have had someone big like me come along and help *me* out. Look, you're *cute* right now, but in a few years your *cutie points* are going to run out, so you're going to have to find a way to stand out. Intrigue, drama, controversy, sizzle," She purred, winking at me. "That will keep their attention." She motioned to the throng of people still waiting in the line.

"Picture time!" chimed the red-head, and she held the box out toward Zahara and I. A bright light flashed in my eyes.

Zahara leaned over and told the red-head, "Post it on all platforms. Say, 'Met my biggest fan today! She is following in my footsteps to be the next rising star! #helpingoutthelittleones, #payitforward, #Kingdomof . . .'" she wrinkled her nose looking back at me, "What was the name again?"

Confused I slowly said, "Kingdom of the Most High King?"

"Kind of a redundant title, don't you think?" She laughed, shaking her long locks, she turned back to her companion, "Got that?"

Angela nodded, tapped a few more times on her box, "And sent! That was super cute! Your followers are going to eat that up!"

Her good deed done, Zahara tilted the tinted glasses down on her nose and looked over them to dismiss me, "Run along now little one, and you're welcome."

As her unhidden eyes locked with mine, her smug expression melted, and her sentence slowed to a crawl. Looking into her eyes, it was like her soul was laid bare before me, and I saw deeply rooted fear, desperation, and loneliness.

My heart was moved with pity for her desperate state. Compassionately, I leaned over the table and put my hand on hers, and quietly comforted her, "Do not be afraid Zahara, my King is sending a message of hope for your world."

My words washed over her fragile heart, and tears instantly gathered in the corners of her eyes. The man next to her quickly grabbed the poster from Zahara's frozen hand and shoved it toward me, directing me out into the hall.

"But I haven't even . . . ." I began to protest, but the man said sternly, "Move along."

I walked back toward the hall, following Pari. Turning back, I saw Zahara again hiding her eyes with the glasses and shaking her head as Angela and the man were asking her questions and looking deeply concerned over her reaction. Zahara's eyes now followed me as I backed away from the scene.

Suddenly a voice called out from behind me, "Hey pal, over here."

11

Kingdom Spirit

SHOCKED, I SPUN AROUND to see a woman sitting at a bench in the middle of the hall.

I looked down at Pari, "Was she talking to me?" I looked over my shoulder to see if there was someone else she could have been calling to.

"Yea, you!" She chuckled with a small smirk. It was like she had read my mind. The woman was relaxed, leaning back, one arm draped on the back of the bench, one foot propped up on her knee casually observing the frenzied crowd clamoring to have their moment to meet Zahara face to face.

I made my way over to where she was and noticed that this woman had a radiant lightness about her. It was something I could not quite explain fully at the time. She was dressed like the other people I had seen in this place so far, blue denim pants, long-sleeved plaid shirt and a warm, plush looking black vest. Around her neck was a chain with a single key hanging from it. On her feet she wore bright red shoes with white soles and laces.

Red shoes! "It was you who helped us on the pier this morning!", I exclaimed. With a smile and a nod, she motioned for me to sit down on the bench.

"I did not have a chance to thank you for helping us! I am very unfamiliar with the ways of this land."

Brushing it off, she waved her hand toward me, "Ah, it's no problem kid! I was happy to help." After watching the crowd for a minute, she turned to me and nonchalantly asked, "On a mission for the King, huh?"

Shocked, I quickly looked at her and gasped "How did you know?"

"You always can tell a citizen of the Kingdom, Anya. My name is Jen, I'm a warrior in the army of the King."

"And you're here on a mission too?" I asked excitedly.

"Umm-hmm." She nodded. Suddenly the radiance about her made perfect sense! "Hey Pari, come here buddy!" She greeted him. Pari trotted happily to her, and she embraced him as a friend ruffling his fur ruggedly. Everyone in the Kingdom seemed to know Pari!

We sat watching the crowd again as Pari sat at our feet, "Funny the way they do things here isn't it?" she commented, nodding her head toward Zahara and her flock of followers.

"Yes. I am here to find someone to deliver a gift to. It is from the King and I thought it *could* be for that woman Zahara. But I don't think she is who she tries to be. She's not the one." I sighed sadly.

"Come on kid, let me get ya both a hotdog." Jen invited. I didn't know what a 'hotdog' was, but my hungry belly was willing to try anything!

We walked down the hall and found a shop where Jen asked for "Three dogs, one plain, two with the works, chips, water and 2 colas." She gave the man behind the counter some paper and he handed her some back with some silver and copper coins.

"How does that work? And why do they want that paper?" I earnestly asked, wanting to understand this custom.

"They think that things *belong* to them. They like it if you give them this stuff in exchange for what they have." She explained, holding up the green papers and coins.

Raising my eyebrows I pondered, "That is so odd, in the Kingdom everything belongs to the King, and He provides everything for us that we could need."

Jen snorted, "Yeah, the funny thing is, everything here belongs to Him too and He provides for them just like He provides for us. He made it all for them! But most of them do not understand that."

The hotdogs and drinks arrived for us and we sat at a small table nearby to enjoy this new delicacy. Jen unwrapped one of the hotdogs and tossed little chunks to Pari, and pulled the top off of the cup of water, holding it for him to drink. Soon our hunger and thirst were satisfied for the moment, and the next few hours brought much joy as Jen, Pari and I walked and talked of things of the Kingdom.

I was so encouraged and refreshed by her company! Even though we had just met, it felt like we were long-time friends. We left the mall and soon found ourselves walking in the park around the large grassy lawn before the pavilion.

People were buzzing all around, some appeared to be workers preparing the grounds, and many, many other people were finding a place on the lawn and spreading out their blankets or chairs and getting settled for Zahara's performance that night. We circled around the back of the oval lawn and found a bench to sit at and watched the gathering crowd.

I sighed. Although Zahara was in desperate need of what the King's gift could bring, I knew in my heart that she was not the one who could bring it to her world. I was at the end of my ideas; I didn't know what to do next and a wave of self-doubt came over me.

"Jen," I confided. "I am only a kitchen servant in the household of the King. I am not a warrior like you. I am truly a nobody in the Kingdom. Maybe I am not qualified for something like this." I placed my hand on the bag in my lap that held the pearl. "Everything I've tried so far has failed."

Placing her hand on my shoulder, she gently corrected me, "There is *no such thing* as a nobody in the Kingdom, Anya. You don't have to *feel* qualified to serve our King; *He* has qualified you. Just be willing to listen for His voice and take action when you hear it."

Taking my hands, she closed her eyes and as if she was standing right in the throne room, she petitioned the King on my behalf, "My King, may your favor continue to fall upon your faithful servant, Anya! Give her courage and wisdom to complete the mission you have given her."

Squeezing my hands, she opened her eyes, "I must leave you now, Anya."

I enjoyed her company very much. It was so refreshing to my soul to walk with someone else from the Kingdom. I had quite hoped we would be continuing this journey together.

"Perhaps as we follow the King, our paths will cross again," she smiled. I could not find the words to respond to her, I just bit my lip and nodded.

Jen continued, "Oh, and here! I won't be needing any of this stuff anymore. Perhaps it can help you." She held out a wad of folded rectangles of green paper like she had used to exchange for the hotdogs earlier.

Still holding the silver and bronze coins in her hand, she studied them, "If you don't mind, I think I'll keep these as a trinket of my journey here, I find them fascinating." She jingled them in her hand playfully.

I unfolded the slightly crumpled papers and smoothed them out. I noticed that several of them had the number one on them, one had a number five, one had twenty and another had one hundred written across them. I had no idea what these numbers meant. I studied the pictures and symbols on them for a moment before I folded them again and placed them in my bag.

Jen reached down and affectionately held Pari's head in her hands scratching him behind the ears, "Thanks for taking good care of her, my friend." She stood and so did I and she opened her arms invitingly. I jumped forward and hugged her, tightly holding on for as long as I could.

When I let her go, she chuckled in her joy-filled way and said, "Farewell, Anya!"

She stepped back, and when she did a crowd of people passed between us. When they had gone, Jen was nowhere to be seen. I felt a great loss, but also hoped that I would someday see her again in the Kingdom.

12

One Face in the Crowd—Part One

THE SUN WAS SINKING lower in the sky and I could no longer feel it's warmth. The shadows of the buildings darkened the park again. This did not deter the people who were now arriving in droves and filling the grassy expanse.

The lamps that surrounded the space flickered and illuminated. Kimmy had mentioned that this concert was to raise awareness of homelessness. I was not familiar with this term, but assumed it meant people without a place of residence. All the people I could see seemed very well cared for, so I wondered where all the homeless people were, after all, this concert was supposedly for them.

I decided to explore the pavilion grounds. Pari seemed glad to comply. Perhaps we would see the homeless closer to the front. I continued around the oval shaped walkway that was around the perimeter, observing the people I saw.

Soon the park was overflowing. Most of the people were happy and laughing with groups of others, but a few were arguing over a space on the grass.

I curiously watched as one woman stormed over and yelled in another woman's face, "Find your own spot! We got here first!"

The other woman yelled back, "Well excuse me if you need twenty feet to hold your fat." the man with her pulled her away and with a huff they left in search of another spot. The first woman sat down triumphantly on her place marked by four large blankets, proudly guarding her turf.

I continued toward the front of the pavilion where the grass gave way to the stone slab that sloped down toward the platform. The chairs in this space were mostly empty and there were guards stationed at the entrance. As people approached, they would show the guard a badge that they had hanging around their neck that had large letters V.I.P stamped on it, and the guard would admit them access. These seats must be the 'VIP seating' that Kimmy spoke of.

Suddenly a voice from behind me said, "*What* is going on?"

I spun around. "Kimmy!" I exclaimed, joyful to see a face I recognized, even if that face was glaring at me. "I was just thinking about you!" I beamed at her.

She raised her eyebrows at me contemptuously, "Whatever!" She paused, shook her head and continued, "Anyway, so Mr. Johnson was *fa-reaking* out yesterday when he found out you didn't get on the bus back to school. Ms. Moore had to talk to him for like 20 minutes before he calmed down enough to not turn the bus around. Then this morning this other girl shows up and says *she's* Annie. She looks *nothing* like you, she's dressed like a normal person and does *not* have a dog. And the worst thing is that Sana, Tommy, Teri *and* Mr. Johnson *and* Ms. Moore tried to act like nothing is the matter with this. So, *what is going on*, Annie?" As she said 'Annie' she put two fingers from each hand in the air and curled them down. I think she knew that my name was not really Annie.

I have found that the truth is always the best option when facing an accuser. Marita would always tell me that the truth is like a lion, let it loose and it will defend itself. Besides, I was never any good at lying, so I resolved that I would tell the whole story to Kimmy. Whether she would believe me or not was up to her.

"Kimmy, my deepest apologies for causing confusion. That was not my intent." I took a deep breath, "My real name is 'Anya." I confessed. "This really is Pari." I said referring to Pari who was obediently sitting beside me, who gave a short bark of introduction. "We are not from this land, but we've been sent here to find someone. When I saw your class and Mr. Johnson yesterday, I overheard that you were on your way to see the 'king of Chicago' and I thought if there was anyone who could help me it would be the king of this land. I just had to get an audience with him. But when I went to introduce myself to Mr. Johnson, he must have misheard me and he just assumed I was Annie, so I let him.", I dropped my eyes ashamedly to the ground.

"You see, I have been sent here from the Kingdom of the Most-High to deliver a gift." I reached into my bag as my story gushed out. "A message of hope for the people of this land. My King told me that the person I was look-ing for would influence a generation, be a leader among men, and inspire others." Hesitating, I lifted the orb just out of the top of my bag. I was not sure if Kimmy would be able to see it. So far, only Mrs. Kelly had acknowledged it was there, and even though Ms. Moore had felt it, she and Mr. Talon could not see it. I continued, "But Mr. Talon was not who I was looking for."

Before I could continue, Kimmy, whose eyes were wide, put her hand up and stopped me. Pushing my hand and the orb back into my bag, she looked around cautiously, "Wait," she looked up and locked eyes with me, "you wanna get some hot cocoa?" Her voice was very real now, the shell of offense was completely gone, and had been replaced by an open vulnerability which surprised me.

"Yes, I would like that very much!" I smiled back at her appreciatively. Actually, anything 'hot' sounded very inviting since the chill of the evening had set in.

She smiled, "Hang out right here for a second, ok? I'll be right back." Kimmy jogged to the nearest of the guards and held up the badge she was wearing. Once she was admitted to the seating area, she ran down the aisle until she was near the bottom, then walked halfway down one of the rows of chairs to talk to a man who was sitting with his arm draped over the shoulders of the young woman beside him. I saw her point up at me and wave, I waved back. The man smiled and gave a wave and a nod, then handed Kimmy something and she made her way back up the aisle to where I was waiting.

As she approached, I asked, "Is that your mother and father?" The idea of a family was so fascinating to me; the thought of having a mother and father together with their children warmed my heart.

"Yeah, that's my dad," Kimmy rolled her eyes, and continued disdainfully, "and the floozy, homewrecker, secretary that he calls his fiancé." They were still watching us, and Kimmy flashed a very fake smile and waved at them. "Come on. Let's get outta here."

We walked to a nearby cart and Kimmy asked for two hot cocoas. The man handed her two steaming cups and she passed one to me, "Here you go."

"Thank you, Kimmy!" I was excited to try this hot cocoa drink! As she gave him a plastic card, I wrapped my hands around the hot cup and the steam rose and warmed my face.

"Mmmmm, it's chocolate?"

"Yeah," she laughed, "you've never had 'hot chocolate' before?"

"Mmm-mm" I shook my head lifting the cup to my lips.

"Careful," Kimmy warned, "it's called 'hot' for a reason!"

She caught me just in time, and I very gingerly sipped the liquid chocolate, "Yes, hot! But it's good!" I confirmed and we both laughed.

We continued sipping our cocoa and strolled toward the back of the yard away from the seats, Pari trotted along between us and as we walked. Kimmy explained, "So my dad works for this politician running his election campaign." She pointed to a sticker that was on her denim jacket, I leaned over to read it, 'I VOTED'.

"So you voted?" I inquired.

"No!" Kimmy laughed, "My dad thought he was being funny when he put the sticker on me, then lectured me about the importance of the political process." She groaned and rolled her eyes.

"Oh I see," I said blankly. I did not see, but I let her continue as we walked.

She took a deep breath, "This year was an election year, so my dad was gone a lot, but my mom didn't really think anything of it since he was just traveling around the state campaigning with his boss. But I guess he was doing more than just passing out campaign fliers and designing billboards."

She stared down at the sidewalk. "So, this summer he comes home for the weekend, and out of the blue he hands my mom divorce papers and tells her that he doesn't have feelings for her anymore. My mom was crushed, so she just signed it. She didn't find out until after the papers were signed that he had been having an affair with his boss's secretary, Abigail, the whole time." She clenched her teeth and an angry tear rolled down her cheek, she quickly swiped it away.

"So, mom and I moved from our house here in Chicago to Aurora where my Grandma lives. Dad said he would sell the house after the election was over and split it with my mom, but last time I *had to* go there for the weekend, 'Abby' had moved in, so I doubt he's going to follow through on that promise either. I bet he thinks he has so many 'friends' in the right places that he will get away with it. My mom had to start working at the nursing home in Aurora to pay for the dumpy little apartment we got. Don't get me wrong, my dad buys me anything I ask for because he thinks I'll stop being mad at him if he does. But it's not going to work. I still think he's the biggest jerk that ever lived!"

She let out a frustrated cry, trying to control her emotions, "It just isn't fair. He just gets to keep going like nothing's happened, and my mom has to start all over." Kimmy slowed down and turned to face me, "The craziest part about it though, is that my mom is actually much happier now than I've ever seen her. She is taking classes in the evenings to go back into nursing, and every Sunday she goes with my grandma into the city to go to church. She says that her faith has grown so much during this time and that *that's* what is getting her through. But I feel like I lost my faith completely. I used to go to church with Grandma too, read my Bible, go to youth group, and pray all the time," Kimmy sighed, "but after the divorce, I just couldn't."

We had arrived at a large open space on the other side of the grass. In the middle was a huge shiny, monstrosity shaped sort of like a bean. We stared up at our exaggerated reflections on the polished surface. I wondered what function it had for the people of this land. In our reflections I looked into Kimmy's hurting eyes. What she had said struck a chord. 'Faith' was a word I *did* understand, it was the complete trust and confidence that I had in my King.

Kimmy sighed and looked away from our reflections, "Anya, I feel like I just dumped all that on you. I'm sorry! There is no one at school who I've told any of that to. I just tried to keep up appearances, they all just think I'm the new rich kid because I dress nice. So, I guess I've been holding it in and putting on a show to keep it all together."

I turned to her and assured her, "No apology is necessary, Kimmy. I am honored that you would confide in me! But why do you say you've lost your faith?" I gently inquired.

Kimmy motioned to a bench that was nearby. We sat down and Kimmy leaned her elbows on her knees and earnestly confessed, "After all that happened, I just thought if I can't even trust my own dad, how am I supposed to trust someone I've never met or seen? So, I gave God an ultimatum. 'Show me you're real and that you care about me; give me some kind of evidence that I can see with my own eyes, or I'm done believing in a God who would let something like this happen.' And then, when you pulled that ball thing out of your bag, I saw my answer and I felt a hope that I haven't had for a long time!"

She looked up at me, her eyes brimmed with tears, "You *are* my sign, Anya! God answered me!"

Relieved, my eyes filled with tears too. I cried, "You could see it?"

She raised her eyebrows, surprised, and dabbed her eyes with her shirt sleeve, "Well yeah! Of course, I saw it!"

"Not everyone can." I explained.

"What exactly is that thing?" Kimmy whispered.

"It's a message of hope. I'm just a servant of the King, delivering it. My King has sent me to find the one who will share its message with this world."

"Right!" Kimmy chimed in, trying to recall, "Like you were saying before; someone who can influence a generation, be a leader among men, and inspire others?"

"Yes! That's it exactly!" I exclaimed, surprised that she remembered what I had said earlier.

Placing her finger thoughtfully on her lip, Kimmy decided, "This world really *needs* hope. I think I can help you!"

"Well Kimmy, you already have." I explained. "It's because of you that I even went and met with Zahara!"

Kimmy froze, "What!? You *met* Zahara?"

"Yes, but she is definitely not the one I was sent for. When I looked into her eyes, all I saw was fear and loneliness behind that shell of who she thinks people want to see."

Kimmy's eyes dropped to the ground, and she smiled weakly, "I guess Zahara and I have that in common too."

Looking up, Kimmy brightened, "But I think I have an idea of someone else who has influence and power. I can't guarantee that he's who you are looking for either, but he certainly has a way with people. It's the guy my dad works for," Kimmy glanced down and tapped at a band on her wrist, "and unless something really crazy happened in the polls, in about two hours he will officially be reelected as governor of Illinois."

Kimmy dug in a little pouch that hung on a thin strap slung across her shoulders under her jacket, like a small version of my messenger bag. "Here! This is my dad's business card. See that address, it's not that far from here, right down that street."

Kimmy pointed in the direction of the street I had walked down earlier with Jen, "About five or six blocks, I think. That's where, if everything goes like my dad expects, they will be having a big party and press conference at the hotel next to his office tomorrow morning at ten. The guy's name is Anthony Warner; but he goes by 'Tony'. He should be easy to spot; big smile, black hair slicked to the side, everyone will be shaking his hand and patting him on the back," Kimmy rolled her eyes, "plus he will be giving a big speech."

Back in the pavilion the crowd erupted with cheers as a voice rang out over them. Kimmy shrugged, "I guess I better get back." We stood up.

"I am so fortunate to have seen you again Kimmy. Thank you for your help, and the hot cocoa, but mostly for letting me get to know you, the *real* you!"

Kimmy leaned in and gave me a big hug, "No, I should be thanking you, Anya. I have hope again, and a lot to talk to my mom about." Releasing me, she smiled, and not just a fake smile on the surface, but glow from the inside, "I really do hope you find who you're looking for."

The beautiful glow washed over me, and I smiled back, "Me too!" Before she left, she pulled a box out of her bag, like the ones everyone in this land seemed to have and holding it in front of us, it captured an image of her and I standing in front of the silver bean; her smiling and me with an astonished look. She left the square, stopping to look back over her shoulder and waved before walking out of sight.

Soon it was just Pari and I and the giant bean in the empty space. The other people who had been wandering around had rushed to the pavilion for the start of the performance.

I lingered and stepped closer to the odd mirrored surface. I raised my hand to touch the reflection that stared back at me. The neat braids that Marita had fastened together had fallen loose and now hung over my shoulders with little hairs sticking out here and there looking a bit disheveled. The tear in my tunic, though small, drew my eye and had started to fray on the edges. Aware of my tattered appearance I tried to smooth the stray hairs down.

From the pavilion loud music began to play and the crowd roared again. I smiled at the funny, straggly girl in the 'bean', and she smiled back reassuringly; I had direction again. I would find this Anthony "Tony" Warner. He governed the people and already had a voice to lead them. Who better to use the King's gift for good?

Tomorrow morning seemed like a long time away, so I wandered back into the pavilion to see what these thousands of people had been drawn here for.

When I entered the performance area again, I was surprised at how loud it suddenly was! A song had just ended, and the crowd was roaring. I did not see Zahara on the stage, someone else was telling some kind of story about the song they were about to sing and then with a shout of "1,2,1,2,3,4!" an intense amount of noise emanated from the stage, I had to place my hands over my ears to drown some of it out!

Pari hung his head low as we walked in the direction of the stage, hands still over my ears, to investigate this barrage of sound, something seemed to be amplifying their strange instruments and voices.

The man on stage was crooning, "The way you move, girl, it pulls me, your legs they call me, your lips say come find me. Well, here I am!" What strange things to sing about! In the Kingdom we sing to the King alone, and those were *not* the kinds of things I would say to *Him*.

The singer and the musicians were not *bad* exactly, but to my ears it was ever-so-slightly out of tune and compared to the music of the Kingdom it was quite grating. I was near the seating area again when I felt a timid tap on my shoulder.

13

One Face in the Crowd—Part Two

I TURNED AND LOOKED behind me. It was Franklin, the man from the evening before at the food hut. He was carrying another 'Polish and a Coke'. Smiling, he yelled something above the din, but I shook my head, I could not make it out. I leaned in, taking my hands away from my ears and he tried to repeat himself, but again to no avail. He motioned for me to step out onto the walkway toward Washington street. I followed him and surprisingly, just out of the oval of the pavilion the sound was greatly reduced!

"How'd you like your polish sausage yesterday?" Franklin asked, smiling nervously.

"Oh!" I exclaimed, finally able to understand, "Well, actually I was not able to get one." I shrugged. "The man was quite frustrated with me for not understanding the process of obtaining food here."

Franklin looked devastated, "Oh. Well, I, uh . . ." Franklin stammered, then blurted decidedly, "Here, you gotta have a polish if you never had one!" He continued, assuring me, "I'm just killing time till this thing is over so I can bring all this stuff back to the airport in my truck," He motioned toward the stage, which was still visible from where we stood, but thankfully, drowned out a bit, "I already had one earlier, so I don't really *need* another one."

He held out the food sheepishly. His genuineness and meekness won me over and I gladly accepted. We sat down on the ledge of a raised flower-bed watching the festivities from outside of the bubble of the pavilion.

"Ya know, since yesterday, I was hoping I'd run into you again." Franklin admitted, looking down at the grass and pushing a few leaves around with his foot. I looked up from the package I was unwrapping.

"Really? Why is that?"

Franklin continued, "So my real name *is* Franklin, but nobody has called me that in a long time." He dared to look up at me. "How did you know?"

Smiling, I admitted, "I didn't, but Pari did." I looked down at Pari and smiled. I pulled the 'polish' in half and held part of it out for him. Pari gently took it from my hand and lay at my feet to enjoy his dinner.

"He told you that?" Franklin questioned skeptically, leaning over to stroke Pari's neck.

I shrugged, "Pari just knows things and he tells me." I looked up at Franklin and switched the topic, "So why doesn't anyone call you Franklin?"

He smiled looking down at the grass again, "Only my grandmother used to call me that, but once I started school, they all said 'Franklin' was too smart a name for a dumb kid like me." He sniffed and tried to laugh it off, "So Frankie always seemed like a better fit."

"Well, Franklin," I said rather formally, using his 'smart' name intentionally, "it is my pleasure to meet you! And thank you for this!" I lifted the polish in my hand. "My name is Anya."

Franklin noticed I hadn't started eating and urged me, "Well go ahead and try it, let me know what cha think!" I took a big bite. I must have been hungrier than I realized because the food was starting to taste better and better. "Mmmm! Vats prebby goob!" I mumbled with my mouth full. Franklin smiled. We sat and listened to the crowd cheering while I finished eating, enjoying the moment.

Finally, Franklin inquired suspiciously "You ain't from here, are ya?" With my mouth full of the juicy meat and tangy sauces, I looked up and just shook my head.

"Didn't think so. There's something different about you." He quickly added, "I mean in a good way!"

We chuckled and after I had swallowed, I inquired, "Are you an associate of Zahara then?"

"Me?" Franklin shrugged, "Na, I'm just the guy they hired to haul some of the sound equipment to and from the airport.".

"That sounds like a very important task!" I assured him before taking another bite.

"Yeah, I guess." He said unimpressed, looking up at the stage. "It pays the bills and keeps a roof over our heads." There was a note of disappointment in his voice.

"This is not what you want to be doing?" I guessed.

He shook his head, "Nope. But I've got a great wife and three kids to provide for, so it's not the time to go chasing dreams." He fumbled in his pocket and pulled out his rectangle box and tapped on it. It illuminated and after a few taps he proudly held it out for me to see an image of a plump woman standing with Franklin and three grinning children around them. In the glow from the box, I could see Franklin smiling fondly at the image.

I could tell that he was willing to do whatever it took to take good care of his family, but my interest was piqued, and I could not help but inquire, "What would you want to be doing?"

He leaned back and shook his head again, "I've got a great family and we live ok. I should just be happy with it. But there's just this gnawing feeling I have, and no matter what I do, I just can't get away from this *idea*." He paused not wanting to say it out loud, Pari was now sitting up and listening intently to Franklin.

Urging him to go on, I pried, "What's your idea?" He threw his hands up, but he seemed to come alive with energy, "That's the goofy part, it's the one thing I struggled with all growing up, and now it's the one thing I just feel like I need to do."

Franklin paused, finally plucking up the courage to say it out loud, "I want to go back to school and become a teacher." He rubbed his forehead, "I've got all these ideas rolling around in this head about how to help kids who are having a hard time learning, like I was. But who's gonna listen to someone who barely made it through high school."

"I just," He faltered, losing his conviction. "I just don't want to start something, only to fall flat on my face and fail my family." Franklin clenched his fists in frustration, going through the same battle of doubt in his mind that he seemed to have been having for a long time.

Leaning back, he confessed, "I can't get over this feeling that someone," He pointed at the sky, "is trying to tell me to *do* something!"

I looked up at the bare tree branches above our heads, wondering who he was pointing to. No one was up in the tree.

Pari stood in front of Franklin and barked excitedly. Franklin looked at him in surprise, "What's up with your dog?"

I laughed, "I guess *someone* is telling you to do something, Franklin. Pari just said that you have been given a brilliant mind and a kind heart. Follow that heart and let your mind be free from the lies of the past. You're not going to fail your family. They are going to be so proud of you!"

Taking a handkerchief out of his pocket, "He said *all* that?", he sniffed and wiped his nose and dabbed his eye. "Now you sound like my Grams!"

He looked out over the crowd then nodded his head decidedly, "I'll do it!" looking down at the box in his hand he took a deep breath and added, "Now I just gotta tell my wife."

He stood up and looked back at me, "Thank you, Anya! Thank you both!" He looked down at Pari.

"Best wishes to you, Franklin!", I responded proudly.

He stepped away from us tapping on his box and held it to his face. We could hear him as he walked away, "Hi Sweetheart! Nah, the show just started so it's gonna be pretty late. But, um, I had something I wanted to talk to you about. Do you have a minute?"

In the distance, Franklin paced down the sidewalk talking excitedly. I could not help but smile, I looked down at Pari, and ruffled his fur.

Inside the pavilion, the first performance was winding down and the crowd was frothing with excitement as I reentered the bubble of sound. The man and the other musicians on stage yelled something and then waving and pumping his fist in the air he exited the platform.

The stage went dark. Around us the city was now completely covered by the black of night. The glow in the windows of the towers provided star-like points of light while the lamps high on the poles spilled pools of illumination onto the paths and roads.

Suddenly, eerie music started to play. The dramatic effect that it created was mesmerizing as rays of colored light sliced through the air with a buzzing noise, eventually focusing to a point at the center of the platform as the suspense swelled!

Suddenly a flash of light lit up the stage and with a mighty trumpet the large elephant statue emerged with Zahara perched on the top wearing a dramatic feathered cape that draped around her. Huge circles hung from her ears and her face was painted with white dots and lines.

The sound of elephants trumpeting and drums beating rhythmically combined with the sound of the crowd was deafening! Huge flat sheets on either side of the stage showed moving images of Zahara as she regally gazed out over the crowd from her perch.

The two muscled men I had seen earlier today, accompanied her on-stage, now shirtless, wearing strange skirts of grass and furs. They lifted her from the statue when it arrived at the middle of the platform and the drums beat faster as she slowly and dramatically moved to the front of the stage while the elephant and men retreated. She struck a pose and the drums and trumpeting stopped suddenly.

Zahara vocalized and the crowd stood silently mesmerized by her. She paused dramatically, letting the silence caress the city for a moment and then suddenly tossing off the cape she launched into the song that I had heard Kimmy and the others sing the day before. "Look at me now!" The crowd erupted!

One of the men guarding the area approached me and shouted, "Move along. The general seating area is back on the grass." He shooed me toward the back of the park. I followed the curve of the oval-shaped lawn and Pari and I found an empty bench along the wall. We had nothing else to do until we would go find Anthony Warner in the morning, so Pari and I settled in to watch the rest of Zahara's performance.

She was quite the performer, I had to admit that. I noted the calculated motions she took, very precise, practiced, and smooth as she moved across the platform. Though, I'm fairly certain that Marita would not have approved of her attire, or even considered it clothing at all. It barely covered her slender body. A cool night breeze swept across the park, I shivered, not able to fathom how she could not be freezing.

At one point she stopped and gave a passionate speech about the problem and horrors of homelessness. I scanned the crowd again looking for the homeless people whom she spoke of. I saw no one I could identify as having no home, and honestly, I had no idea what a homeless person should look like anyway. I thought of the peddlers that I would sometimes see traveling with their pushcarts coming and going from the village outside of the palace walls. I would watch them from the kitchen balcony, but I had never met any of them.

The crowd hung on her every word. She was doing all the right things; smiling, moving, and pausing at just the right times, but I could feel that her heart was not settled, it was too calculated, too rehearsed. Subtle notes of self-doubt crept into her voice before the next act took over. Although no one else seemed to notice, it was all too clear to me.

Despite Zahara's larger than life persona, she needed hope just as desperately as anyone else. I pulled my messenger bag up onto my lap and held it close. My heart ached for Zahara's hidden pain. This gift could hold the answer she didn't know she was looking for. This world needed hope; she needed hope.

14

One Face in the Crowd—Part Three

EVENTUALLY THE ELABORATE PERFORMANCE ended and after the thunderous applause and cheers died away, the crowd began to disperse. Within minutes, only a few people lingered on the expanse of grass.

"Can we pet your dog?" a sweet little voice interrupted my thoughts. I looked down to see two sets of deep brown eyes looking up at me from their dark little faces, illuminated only by the lamp that hung behind us.

A little girl with puffs of kinky black curls pulled neatly into two buns on her head, repeated herself politely, "Can me and my brother pet your dog?" Her brother stood silently next to her sucking on his fingers, with his wide eyes fixed on me.

Their sweetness melted my heart, I could not keep the smile from my face, "Of course you can!"

Excitedly they gasped and turned all their attention to Pari, who loved every second of their hugs and their shrill squeals when he licked their faces.

A short distance away, a stout woman was sitting on a blanket in the grass with two other children. She noticed that two of her little ones had wandered away and called out to them sternly, "Keyana and Keagan! You get over here! Leave that nice girl and her dog alone!"

In unison, they both replied, "Yes Mama.", and returned to their mother.

To my delight, Pari trotted off after them, looking back at me as if to say, "Are you coming?" Charmed, I gladly followed him; a bit slower as the heaviness of the pearl was beginning again to wear on me.

As we approached the place where they sat, the mother shook her head and laughed apologetically, "I'm sorry about those two, they see an animal and they just go right for it!"

Pari had made it to their blanket and all four of the children were huddled around him scratching him behind the ears or stroking his fur. The older children, a boy and girl, were not too much younger than I was. The girl patted the blanket beside her urging Pari to join them, and, of course, he did. To the children's delight, he made himself right at home among them.

Their mother explained, "They've been beggin me to get em a dog pretty much since they could talk." She held out a hand to shake mine, "I'm Rita, you've met Keyana and Keagan." The two younger ones peeked over Pari's furry back and smiled up at me. "And these other two are Keziah and Kensington." Kensington nodded in my direction with a cool smile before returning to smoothing the mop of fur on Pari's shaggy head.

Keziah looked up, smiling and prompted, "What's your name?"

Finding my words I replied, "My name is Anya, and this is Pari."

The littlest one, Keagan, repeated, "Pawie" and threw his arms around Pari's neck. Rita and I chuckled at his adorable display of affection. His siblings laughed and shook their heads. Pari responded by lovingly lapping at his chunky cheeks causing a melody of squealing giggles. The sound of it was pure joy.

With a discerning tilt of her head, Rita invited, "Would you and Pari care to join us for dinner?"

"Yes please!" I responded gratefully sitting down with them, "Thank you!" Besides, Pari and the children were enjoying each other's company so much, I could not bear to divide them now.

Pulling a basket toward her as she started to unload its contents, Rita shared, "My shift at the nursing home didn't get done until late today, so we barely made it here for the concert. I figured we would make the most of it and enjoy a late celebration dinner right here at the park."

"Celebration?" I questioned, "Why do you celebrate?"

Kensington chimed in proudly, "Mom just finished her nursing degree, and passed her big test. She will be starting her new job as an *official* nurse next week."

The children looked at their mom beaming, and Keyana crawled into her mother's lap hugging her.

Rita's eyes grew moist with emotion, and she admitted, "It sure was a long road, and calls for celebration and thanksgiving." She lifted her eyes to the sky for a moment giving her daughter a squeeze and then resumed pulling small, wrapped packages from the basket next to her.

"Peanut butter and jelly sandwiches for everyone!", she exclaimed. The kids groaned as she passed the humble bundles to each of them and one to me as well.

"Hey, the food for this party may not be fancy, but the entertainment cost a fortune!" Rita jokingly boasted.

"Mom, it was a free concert!" Keziah rolled her eyes.

Rita retorted, with a sassy smile, "Maybe for you it was." Keziah shook her head; her mane of brown curls bobbing around her and returned her attention to Pari.

As I helped unwrap the sweet sticky sandwiches from their coverings for Keagan and Keyana, Rita quietly explained, "I had to switch shifts and work a double this weekend to make sure that we could even get to this concert. Keziah loves Zahara, and I just *had* to make it work. We'd never be able to afford tickets to one of Zahara's regular concerts. If there's one thing that girl wants *more* than a dog, it's to be singin'."

Rita took a bite of her meal, and I followed suit. The sweet and nutty flavors burst in my mouth. It may have been simple and humble, but it was comforting.

As we sat and savored our feast, Keziah, who had finished first, was gently stroking Pari's face and singing a little concert just for him.

"Look at you now, I've put you in the spotlight. Don't be afraid, I know you'll shine like the sun. You've come so far, you were made for this moment. Look at you, look at you, look at you now! Your gonna be my shooting star, lighting up the sky, just by being who you are, look at you, look at you, look at you, Now"

I stopped eating and just watched this little girl as she cupped Pari's big head in her hands and poured out *her* version of Zahara's song over him. The *tune* was the same, but this song was *nothing* like Zahara's anthem to herself. I liked Kaziah's version much, much better.

"That was beautiful, Keziah!", I breathed. She looked up and realized that we had stopped talking and were watching her.

Sheepishly she smiled looking down at the ground, "You were listening to me?"

Pari barked appreciatively, and I agreed, "You keep singing from your heart just like that and people will come from far and wide to listen you."

She bit her lip and nodded, letting that soak in for several moments before a huge grin lit up her face and determination shone in her young eyes.

Meanwhile, her brothers and sister secretly fed bits of their sandwiches to Pari till they were gone.

"All done!" Keagan chimed proudly holding out his now empty hands. "Chips pwease?", he begged with a big grin. Rita, who had seen everything, smiled, shook her head, and pulled a small bag of those salty, crunchy things from the basket and handed them to Keagan who gleefully took them and leaned back triumphantly onto Pari's warm belly to munch on his prize.

The park was nearly empty. I gazed across the grass that was strewn with cans and debris abandoned by the exiting crowd. I remembered the question I had at the beginning of the concert; I posed it to Rita, "If this concert was meant for the homeless people, where are they?"

She paused thoughtfully, and slowly replied folding her hands in her lap, "Two years ago you would be looking at em. A few years back we hit a really rough patch. It'd just been me and the kids for a while by then and we were living, not even, paycheck to paycheck." Rita took a breath, then continued, "I had a medical situation come up and for two months I just couldn't work. Thankfully, my job kept me on, but with no money coming in, we went backwards fast and couldn't keep our apartment. My sister let us sleep on her couch out in the suburbs, and that worked most of the time. But there are more times than I'd like to remember where I knew we didn't have the gas to get out there and back again to get me to work or the kids to school and daycare. So we'd just find a place and sleep in our car for a few nights till I got paid and we could afford to drive back to my sisters."

Stunned, I listened to her story, "Are you still homeless?"

Rita shook her head, "No! Thankfully, we got connected with a wonderful ministry that helped us get into an apartment and helped me get into school. I always wanted to be a nurse my whole life, but I never had a way to do it before. That's why this celebration for us is so special, Anya. I've got a chance now to give my kids a better life, to give them a better place to start from than I had. I am so thankful to the Lord for that."

Tears glistened in her eyes as she looked at her children. By now Keagan was laid back on Pari's soft belly, sound asleep with crumbs from his chips stuck to his plump cheeks and the half empty bag hanging loosely in his hand.

"Speaking of home, I better get these crazy kids to bed." Rita smiled fondly.

I helped Rita and the kids clean up their celebration feast and as Rita lifted a floppy Keagan to her shoulder and wrapped him in the blanket, she looked at me. She was suddenly very serious, "Anya, where are you headed tonight? Have you got a place to be?"

Thinking of my cozy spot amid the fountains in the garden, I assured her, "Yes, I do."

She eyed me suspiciously, "You sure?"

I nodded confidently, "Pari and I better get back and get some rest too. We have a big day tomorrow. Thank you, Rita, for sharing your story and your celebration with us."

Satisfied with my answer, Rita had Kaziah write some numbers on a small bit of paper and hand it to me, "The pleasure was all ours, Miss Anya. You can call me at that number if you need anything. You take care, ok?" Taking the paper, I nodded and reluctantly we parted ways.

In a dreamy haze from the pleasant and encouraging encounter with Rita and her children, I was more hopeful for this land. Maybe it was that, or the growing weight of my burden hanging over my shoulders, coupled with the weariness from the long day that put me in a less than alert state.

I didn't notice that as I left the park, Pari and I were not alone.

15

In the Shadows

PARI AND I CROSSED the street, which was now very quiet and looked up at a sign that read 'Bus Stop'. I figured that if the bus brought me here from the pier, it would be able to take me back, right?

I stood next to the sign and felt around in my bag for the card that had granted me access to the bus earlier in the day. The green papers that Jen had given me were shoved haphazardly into the bag and were now in the way, so I grabbed them out and held them crumpled in one hand as I searched in the folds of my blanket for where the card had slipped.

Finally, my hand connected with the smooth surface. I retrieved it and pushed the papers back in before I closed the flap and looked up.

Out of the shadows behind me I heard a snarling voice, "Well look what we have here?" I spun around to see a group of boys stepping into the fringe of light that surrounded me from the lamp above. "You're the girl from the park yesterday, aren't you?"

I strained my eyes to make out their faces in the shadows. This had not started in a friendly way, so I was cautious with my reply, "Yes?"

The boy who was speaking stepped a bit further into the light and in recognition I innocently exclaimed, "Oh *you're* the hoodlums!" recalling the name the security men had given them. The boys all exchanged a look. A few of the boys at the back snickered.

Taken back, the boy who seemed like the leader of the pack, gritted his teeth, and tried to continue, "You know you really messed with our plans yesterday. The people who sent us to nab that stuff out of the truck weren't very happy about that and I had to pay the price for it."

He stepped a little further toward me and the light fully illuminated his face; a face that looked much younger than his angry voice let on. Though he was several inches taller than me, he too was still a child. I gasped and chill ran through me when I saw his eye and cheek with a puffy discolored patch around it, and a split in his swollen bottom lip.

He took another aggressive step forward, cracking his knuckles, and his companions followed suit, "And now you're gonna pay for it too!"

In an instant Pari leaped between the boys and I; transformed into a furious snarling beast.

The boy threw his hands up to protect himself and stammered, "I, I wasn't gonna hurt you! Just, just give me what's in your bag and we'll leave you alone!"

I clutched my bag to my chest, it contained the pearl, my treasure, my message from the King. I backed away, shaking my head in fear and disbelief. With a low threatening growl, the usually amiable Pari, crouched in front of me, frothing at the mouth. His eyes were now ablaze, and a dazzling white light glowed from within him.

The rest of the boys had abandoned their fellow hoodlum, fleeing down the street at the sight of Pari. Trembling with fear the boy with the black eye shouted, "Call off your crazy dog, you *freak*!"

One of the boys who was already down the street hollered back, "Forget the girl! Come on Danny, let's get out of here!"

A screeching and rumbling noise approached and lamps from the front of the bus carriage shone toward us.

The boy seethed with anger, and backed away defeated, "This isn't over!" One last snarl and bark from Pari sent him running into the shadows just as the large carriage screeched to a stop behind us.

The threat now gone, Pari's gentle demeanor, and humble dingy appearance were suddenly restored, and he trotted past me toward the bus. My eyes followed him, but I stood frozen, he may have bounced right back, but I was still in shock from what had just happened. Pari looked back at me with a soft whine, urging me to move.

The doors of the bus swung open, and I numbly followed Pari up the steps of the bus carriage. He patiently nudged my hand that held the card to prompt me to hand it to the driver, who paused for a second and then took the card from my hand and held it to the box in front of her. Silently, she returned the card to me. If she was concerned by my blank expression, I did not notice. I shuffled down the aisle after Pari.

An emotional fog hovered over me as we sat several seats toward the back. The bus rumbled, bumping, and swaying for many minutes, stopping, and starting as it went along, moving further away from the pier before looping back again. I think several people got on and got off, but I stared expressionless at the back of the seat in front of me, until the bus came to a stop at the familiar loop where we had begun the day. Pari stood and started toward the front of the bus, and I followed.

Before opening the door to let us out the driver stopped us, "This is my last run of the night and there's really nothing open on the pier at this hour. Are you sure you want to get off here?" she questioned. I nodded my head slowly.

Unable to form words, I just stared at the floor. The driver finally consented, "Okay then. Suit yourselves." and opened the doors. I followed Pari down the stairs and off the carriage.

16

Out in the Cold

STANDING ON THE SIDE of the road, I listened to the bus pull away and fade into the other noises of the city. Pari and I were finally alone. The night air was even cooler here as the damp wind off the sea swept around us. The chill reawakened me and I began to shudder uncontrollably. I slowly let out my breath and it hung like a cloud in the air as the numbness melted away and hot tears began to stream down my cheeks.

"What just happened?" I sobbed, finally letting it all out in a flurry of emotions. I fell to my knees and Pari gently came close and pawed at me reassuringly. He had been sent with me as a guide, but I didn't know I would also need him as a protector. I buried my face in his soft, warm fur and he leaned in supportively as I clung to him.

Shaking all over, I trembled as questions tumbled out, "Why would that boy act like that? Why was he so angry? *I* didn't do anything to him! Why would he threaten me and try to take the King's gift from me?"

I was not familiar with the feelings I was having. I felt anger toward Danny; I felt attacked and mistreated. I began to despise him for the way he had accused and threatened me.

"*He* doesn't deserve the King's gift!" I cried through clenched teeth.

Calmly, Pari intervened. Whining softly, he gently nudged my cheek. Infuriated, I looked up into his soft brown eyes. I was surprised to find they were filled with compassion, not only for me, but also for Danny, the boy he had just defended me from. I didn't understand. How could Pari feel that way about the boy who had just threatened me and tried to steal something so precious and important?

He licked my face with his warm rough tongue. I thought of Danny's black and swollen eye. There was a wicked cruelty that infected this land. A sickness of heart and mind that caused people to disregard the dignity of one another. Someone had hurt Danny, and he was passing that infection on to anyone else in his path. Gasping back sobs, my callusing heart softened and filled with a deep sorrow and compassion for my offender. Thanks to Pari, I felt the sickness of hate leave me. "I forgive him." I finally whispered when my sobs had subsided, and I had caught my breath.

The bag that lay across my knees felt heavier than ever and the burden of the King's gift pressed down on me. It took quite a lot of effort to stand up and carry the messenger bag. The place where my bag had been rubbing across my shoulder all day was tender and raw. It felt better to cradle it in my arms with the strap gently draped around my neck than to let it hang from my aching shoulders. I hugged it in front of me as I struggled to walk toward the pier.

The wind had picked up and in addition to being quite cold I was now emotionally exhausted. My longing for the warmth and tranquility of the garden was the only thing that drove me across the pier and up a set of stairs. The park with the enormous wheel was now eerily quiet as I passed by the silent giant. It loomed overhead while I searched for the door that I had entered the night before.

Weary and cold, I finally found the door to the garden, only to discover it was locked up tight. I searched a little further to try another door, but it too was locked, as was the next and the next. My hopes of the warm garden faded, and I slumped down with my back against the wall. The card for the bus was still clutched in my hand and with much trembling I brushed back the flap of the bag to tuck it safely away. I would need it in the morning to find Anthony Warner.

Inside my pack my hand connected with cloth, and it felt invitingly warm. I began to carefully pull out the tattered blanket, having to push the green papers and card down next to the pearl so they would not be blown away by the wind. Standing up again I wrapped it around me and immediately I was draped with warmth and my eyelids threatened to close right there.

My legs could hardly hold me, and I was sure they would give out at any moment from exhaustion. I knew I could not stay there out in the open; I needed to find a safe place to rest. The wind was getting colder and had picked up significantly. Each gust swirled around my feet and snuck its way up the bottom of the blanket attempting to slide up my back and snatch the blanket away.

I clutched the blanket tightly around me and pressed on into the night, stumbling along the wall until I found a place where the wall receded and was partially covered by wooden panels. It created a small reprieve from the wind next to a door with a flickering lamp on the wall above it. I leaned into the sheltered corner slumping down on top of a crunchy pile of leaves and other debris that the wind had deposited. Pari huddled close to me and provided me with a soft warm pillow. With relief I laid my heavy head against him but just as I was about to pass into the bliss of slumber, I shook myself awake and retrieved my notebook and pen from my pack and quickly wrote what I had learned that day.

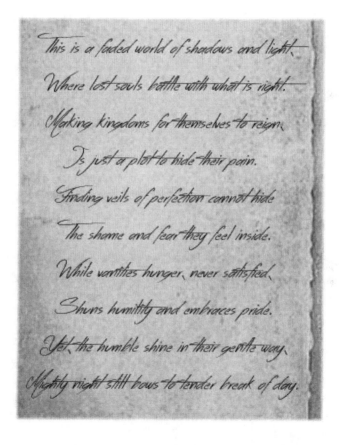

This is a faded world of shadows and light.
Where lost souls battle with what is right.
Making kingdoms for themselves to reign.
Is just a plot to hide their pain.
Finding veils of perfection cannot hide
The shame and fear they feel inside.
While vanities hunger, never satisfied,
Shuns humility and embraces pride.
Yet, the humble shine in their gentle way,
Mighty night still bows to tender break of day.

I tucked the notebook and pen away and spread the blanket over Pari and I. We created a cocoon of warmth and immediately I drifted away . . . from the cold . . . and the wind . . . and the darkness of the land.

17

Broken Dawn

I DON'T KNOW HOW long I had escaped from my senses, but at some hour in the morning something caused me to return to myself. I laid there for a moment with the fog of sleep still clinging to me, eyes closed, my mind groggy, wondering where I was and what had awoken me. Was Marita calling for me? Had I forgotten to rise and start the fires in the baking ovens? I was still bundled from head to toe under the warmth of the blanket, but beyond that shell I began to perceive a frosty chill in the air.

My hips and legs could feel cold radiating from the stone slab below them, separated only by the thin layer of paper and leaves I was laying on. Most of the rest of my body was draped over Pari's sturdy, warm frame with my head resting on his back and my hands wrapped up in the fur under his chin.

Suddenly his body tensed, with a soft warning growl. My senses quickened, and prying my eyes open, I became very aware of where I was. We both lay still under the blanket peering through the threads when the door beside me was quickly shoved open with a loud creak, just missing us.

A thin gangly figure of a man emerged. He placed a small white stick in his mouth, while propping the heavy door open with his foot. He ignited a small fire in his hands and lit the end of the stick. Holding the smoking stick in his mouth he proceeded to drag large black bags from inside the door and deposit them roughly into a large bin.

When he had finished, he reached up and groped his hand on top of the lamp above him. He grabbed a block of wood that had been stashed there and used it to prop the door open a crack. Leaning back against the wall he inhaled deeply through the stick, causing the coal at the end to glow red and then breathed out a stream of smoke that curled around him. Kicking the leaves at his feet, he looked around still casually puffing on the white stick.

The smoke of it made its way over to us and snuck under the blanket filling our nostrils with its pungent smell causing Pari to sneeze softly. The man froze wide eyed with the stick hanging loosely from his lip. Suspiciously he squinted into the shadowed corner where we lay.

Pushing himself off the wall he started to crouch down to get a closer look. Slowly and cautiously, he reached out his hand toward the blanket that hid us; we held our breath.

From behind the door a voice called out, "Hey Greg." Startled, 'Greg' fell back, sitting down hard on the ground as the door was flung open again and a stocky man emerged, looking around and then finally looking down at the man, "What the heck you doin' down there?"

With a goofy grin, Greg looked up and taking the stick out of his mouth, he used it to gesture, "Smoke break?"

Shaking his head and laughing, the man replied, "Well, smoke break is over, we've got a delivery truck to unload! Comon."

Greg jumped up, flicked the white stick onto the ground and stepped on it before he grabbed the block off the ground and tucked it back into its hiding place. Glancing once more at our corner, Greg laughed at himself and shook his head before letting the door slam shut behind him. Pari and I continued to lay still, afraid that the door may fly open again.

Minutes passed, and I began to slowly sit up. I ached all over from the odd position I had been in and the hard ground beneath me. The corners of my eyes were crusty, and my throat felt dry and sore. I tried to clear it, but that only made me cough.

The sky had started to lighten as the day approached. Making it to my feet, I shook the leaves and debris from the blanket and quickly folded it; I tucked it away in my bag. We slipped out into the brisk morning air.

The wind had died down, but the frosty chill of the night still lingered. During the night my braids had begun to unravel and even the light breeze was enough to blow the loose hair into my face. I pushed the hair back over my ears and pulled the hood of my tunic up over my head and began to leave the pier.

We passed by the place where the Shema had been docked on that bright morning only a few days prior. I had arrived with such hope, excitement, and fascination for this new place. It seemed like a long time ago, though it had only been two days.

The morning sun did not appear on the horizon at all that day; the gray sky just got less dark. Like the overcast sky above, my sunny expectations had been replaced with dull clouds of weariness.

I slumped down on a bench near the bus stop, "I thought this would be easier." I sighed, giving voice to the desperation I was starting to feel inside. At that moment a dark spark of doubt was lit in my mind. What if I failed? What would the King say if I disappointed him? Would I even be able to get back home to the Kingdom?

I looked around. It was still early, and the bus carriage was nowhere to be seen. Trying to clear my throat again, I opened my bag and retrieved the bottle of water to quench the dry scratchy feeling. But I would find no satisfaction from the water it contained. Before the cool of the water reached my lips, the odd smell reached my nose. I recoiled. This water I had gathered from the fountains in the garden was tainted and not fit for drinking. I shook my head as I poured it onto the ground, "Sorry Pari, we cannot drink that."

I sighed, putting the empty bottle back into the bag. Peering down into my bag my hand lingered over the orb. It was now gray and dull, reflecting the sky, its glow had been diminished and it seemed a bit more transparent than before. I let my fingers fall on the cool surface; at my touch a soft glow pulsed faintly from within. My mind fueled the flicker of doubt that had crept in. "Maybe the message is losing its power the longer it takes me." Guilt now ignited that doubt into a tiny flame.

Drooping forward over my knees, I hung my head, discouraged, when a cold wet nose interrupted my worries, I lifted my head to look into his soft brown eyes. He yipped encouragingly, breaking the silence. I tried to arouse my enthusiasm again, "You're right, Pari. Today . . . maybe today will be the day. Maybe Anthony Warner *is* the one the King sent us here to find." The flame of doubt still burned in my mind.

I slid off the bench and onto one knee, bowing my head. I had nearly forgotten to start my day, as we did every day in the Kingdom, kneeling before the throne of the King. Weariness, cold, affliction and discouragement had distracted me, but it would not keep me from giving Him honor. My King had given this task to me; I would see this through. What other choice did I have? This was *my* mission! The King would not have sent me here to fail! He knew the plan he had for me and had provided for me this far!

The bus carriage made a sharp screeching sound as it rounded the corner and headed toward the place where Pari and I waited. Standing up, I retrieved my card from the bag and quickly closed the flap over the top, concealing the orb within. The doors of the bus opened with a warm woosh of air and Pari and I stepped aside for several people to get off. We climbed the stairs of the bus and I shuddered as a blast of hot air melted around me.

The same man from yesterday was behind the big wheel and greeted me, "Well good morning, miss! Didn't know if I was gonna see *you* again."

I tried smiling up at his friendly greeting, and clearing my throat I replied weakly, "Good morning, sir."

He did not bother hiding the concern on his face, "Ya ok, kid?"

I held out the card, nodding, "Yes, just cold. But it is nice and warm in here." I replied, shaking off another layer of the chill. The driver handed the card back to me and Pari and I dropped into the seat behind him.

"Yeah, I'm afraid there's a big storm rolling in. Could be a regular old 'White Hurricane' if you ask me, with the air pressure dropping like it is. I can feel it in my bones.", he stated ominously, closing the door of the bus with a loud creak.

The bus began to move away from the pier. As the silhouettes of the palaces and Ferris wheel shrunk behind me, I stared out the window at the city that was just beginning to wake up for the day.

The gloriously warm air that had greeted me when I first stepped onto the bus, continued to waft around me and the tension relaxed from my cold muscles. I slumped further down in the seat. Several minutes passed. Lulled by the warmth and hypnotized by the herky-jerky, starts and stops of our carriage I was not paying attention to where we were going.

I was thinking of the warmth and comfort of my little bed in the cozy quarters that Marita and I shared next to the palace kitchens. Nestled up against the rear wall of the brick ovens, the cooling of the bricks let me know when it was time for me to get up and stoke the fires in the morning. I realized that my first thoughts upon waking that morning was of my home in the King's palace and my duties there. A wave of longing washed over me. I had not appreciated the comfort and peace it provided, until I was absent from it and at the mercy of this land.

Finally, the driver got my attention and called back, "Hey kid? I forgot to ask you, where ya getting off at?"

Startled, I fumbled to retrieve the card of paper that Kimmy had given me yesterday that listed the location where her father worked. Nearby, I would find the 'hotel' where I could find Anthony Warner later that morning. After a few moments of trying to get my watery eyes to bring the tiny print into focus, I remembered that Kimmy had directed me to go down the same street where I had gotten off the previous morning.

"Washington?", I replied, hazily, making it more of a question than a statement.

"Oh geeze, kid. I'm sorry! We passed that like five blocks ago." His round face looked disappointed, "I could let you off here, but you'd have to backtrack on foot." He paused then offered, "Or you could ride around the loop, and we'll be back at Washington in about an hour, if you've got the time."

I nodded wearily. His worried expression in the mirror softened a bit, "Why don't you just rest, and I'll let you know when we are back around, ok?" I nodded again and settled back watching the land of Chicago pass me by as I leaned my head against the cool glass of the window. My eyelids drooped and soon I was sound asleep with Pari curled up at my feet and the kind driver keeping watch over us.

A short time later I awoke to a gentle tapping noise on the partial wall that separated the driver and I. "Hey Miss? Miss? The next stop is yours, kid." The driver called and smiled kindly back at me in his mirror.

"Thank you, sir!" I replied gratefully, stretching my arms and legs, my muscles now warm and rested. I felt refreshed and the world around me seemed brighter and more hopeful than it had in my cold and tired state.

The carriage screeched to a stop and Pari and I rose to exit. The driver put out his hand to stop us before he opened the door.

"Say, kid? Right down here on Washington there is a little dinner on the left about a block down. It's called Lulu's. Why don't you stop in there and get yourself something warm to eat." Slowly and with great compassion he continued, making sure we caught every word, "Tell em' Charlie sent ya. They'll take care of you. Ok? Can you do that, kid?"

My smile had returned, and I nodded, "Yes!" Pari groaned softly, looking up at me, "Pari says, you're a good man, Charlie. Thank you!"

Blushing slightly, Charlie chuckled and opened the door, and we left the warm bus for the brisk city street. Looking back at the bus I waved at Charlie, still smiling as he pulled away.

There I stood, back at the corner where I had been the morning before, hopeful again that I was about to deliver the King's gift into the hands of someone who could use it to reignite hope into this faded world. But first, 'something warm to eat', like Charlie had said, sounded like a very good idea!

Down the street a little way I could see a lit-up sign that read "Lulu's". Excitedly Pari and I bounded toward it! We raced each other playfully, weaving around other people who, with their heads down, clutched their coats around them against the gusts of wind that surged down the street. With the hopes of a warm breakfast, Pari and I hardly noticed the wind.

However, crossing the street to get to Lulu's became quite an ordeal since I had yet to learn the meanings of the colored lights that made the carriages stop and start, or the purpose of the lines drawn on the streets. Many carriages of different shapes and sizes moved this way and that and we stood for quite some time timidly searching for a clear path across.

Finally, one of the men behind the wheel of a bright yellow carriage waved at us to cross and slowly and tentatively we did. However, by the time we had made it to the other side there were several other carriages that had stopped in the middle of the intersection, having to wait for us to cross and making a chaotic symphony of horns to announce their displeasure.

Triumphantly, we arrived at the door to 'Lulu's Bakery and Café'. Tucked in between the intimidatingly large stone structures, the tiny building with its whimsical black and white awnings and a homey appearance, seemed completely out of place. I was curious to see what the inside would look like.

Pulling on the heavy door, we heard a bell clanging overhead. Pari and I stepped inside letting the door shut firmly behind us. The air inside was laced with the smell of brewing coffee and sweet syrup. I stood in the entryway to the small dining area breathing heavily, firstly because we had just raced down the chilly street and secondly, just relishing the warm fragrant air. A thin, worn-out looking woman wearing a black apron noticed us and narrowing her eyes, she rushed over to us impatiently.

"You can't have that dog inside here. The sign is clearly posted on the door." She snapped at us pointing toward the door. Shocked, I said nothing and looked at her, puzzled, she reiterated, "If you're going to stay, your dog has to go. Tie him up outside or something."

Realizing that she had meant Pari, I looked to him unsure of what to do. Indignantly complying, Pari turned with a huff and we returned to the windy street. Pari followed along the wall and sat down, planting himself beside one of the large windows outside of the café.

Looking up at me, he tilted his head toward the door. "You want me to go in without you?" He tilted his nose up, as if to say, "Go on!" I opened my mouth to protest, but Pari barked sternly and turned from me, taking a regal and resolute position looking into the window of the café. He was determined to stand guard and wait there for me.

Stubbornly, I stood my ground for a few moments. Finally, my growling stomach won out, "Fine," I conceded crossly.

I pulled the door open again and at the jangling of the bell the irritated woman looked back toward the door and rolled her eyes. She stayed standing next to one of the tables jotting down what the people seated there were telling her, then went to the back and returned to their table with mugs and a carafe before she begrudgingly came to talk to me.

Before she got to me, I remembered Charlie's directions and blurted out, "Charlie sent me." The woman's shoulders slumped down even further as if all the air had just leaked out of her, and her face went slack. "Fine, have a seat.", she groaned, motioning toward the tables near the windows.

Gratefully I slid into the chair nearest to where Pari was still staring intently at me. The woman turned and shook her head as she went to the back and hollered to someone who was hidden from view, "Caroline, someone is here for you."

"Co-ming!", a sing-song voice chimed from somewhere behind the wall. I could hear the familiar sounds of chattering voices mixed with the clanging of pots and pans and dishes being moved about, so I assumed it must be the kitchen.

Just then, a radiant being emerged. She was brightly colored from the fiery hair spiked atop her head to her glittering shoes. The deflated woman looked especially drab next to her vibrant counterpart, to whom she was now talking in hushed tones and pointing exasperatedly at me. The bright woman raised her eyebrows and peered curiously in my direction. Nodding, 'Caroline' said something I could not hear and began to tie a black frilly apron around her waist, dismissing the drab woman to retreat behind the wall. Grabbing a shiny booklet from a bin and a glass of water she started for my table.

"Good morning!" she sang as she drew nearer to where I sat. She set the glass of water and the booklet in front of me. "My name is Caroline, and I will be serving you today." She said rather dramatically pointing to a button on her apron that had her name scrolled across it.

Honestly, I would not have seen it unless she pointed to it due to the numerous other buttons and shiny pins that covered the top of her apron. It was an odd, yet intriguing, collection of things from antique looking broaches to pins shaped like kittens or musical symbols and a white mask with a rose to funny statements like, "We provide sarcasm at no additional cost." Or "I'm here for the pie." And "Unicorns don't believe in you either."

"So, you're a friend of Charlie's?" she inquired, raising her red eyebrows over the metallic purple shadowed eyes.

I nodded meekly, drinking deeply from the cup of cool water. Clearing a tickle from my throat, I found my voice, "Yes, my name is Anya. Pari and I met him on the carriage that he drives. He told us to come here, to Lulu's."

She tilted her head and laughed. "I've never heard the city bus called that before. Who's Pari?" she questioned looking around for another person. I looked out at Pari's furry face peering into the window next to me.

Startled to see him staring in at us, she jumped and put her hand over her heart! "Oh geeze!" she exclaimed. Finding her composure, she continued, "Is he yours?"

Smiling, I looked out at Pari, feeling rather guilty, "Pari is my companion and my guide. I couldn't have made it this far without him." Looking back at Caroline I explained, "The other woman said he could not be in here." Caroline's jaw clenched and a fire lit in her eyes as she shot a disgusted look toward the kitchen area.

Very seriously, she arched her bright red eyebrows and whispered, "Wait here." Backing sneakily toward the door she craned her neck to make sure no one was coming out of the kitchen.

The other patrons had started watching her, curious and amused by her dramatic antics. Opening the door, Caroline patted her leg calling Pari to her by making a smooching noise with her lips. He trotted over to her, and she led him inside to my table and lifting the tablecloth she motioned for him to slip underneath.

Crouching down she cooed at him, "Did that cwanky lady make you wait outside? Well, we don't need to listen to grouchy old Debbie now, do we?"

Smoothing the tablecloth back down, she smirked at the other patrons nearby and winked. Several young ladies at the next table giggled and resumed their conversation; a man dressed in a crisp suit, shook his head, and went back to reading a large paper that he had held up in front of his face; and the elderly man in the corner winked back at her smiling.

"I'll give you a few minutes to look over the menu then I'll come back to take your order. Can I get you some coffee, tea, or hot cocoa?"

My eyes widened, "Yes, please! Hot cocoa! I tried one of those yesterday and it was quite lovely!"

She was pleased by my excitement, "A hot cocoa it is then, young lady!" she spun to return to the kitchen area, calling to the elderly man, "You need a refill on your coffee, Mr. Stevens?"

She was so full of life! I just enjoyed watching her as she bustled about to interact with the other people seated at the tables. She called many of them by name; they must have come to Lulu's often. Caroline's laughter and playful banter lit up the space. I liked her right away. Her energy was contagious.

By the time Caroline came back with hot cocoa topped with whipping cream and chocolate sprinkles, the room had a new buzz about it. I was surprised that one person could change the entire atmosphere in minutes. Pari liked her too, especially since every time she came past our table, she had a new treat for him. I giggled at the way she made sure the other server, who had returned by then, was not looking in her direction when she slipped a bit of sausage or bacon discreetly under the tablecloth.

It was not long before Caroline was setting a warm bowl of porridge and a plate of buttered toast in front of me, then, to my surprise, she settled into the chair across from me holding a cup of tea.

Leaning forward with her elbows propped on the table, she cradled the cup in her hands and closed her eyes, savoring the warmth of it for a second before she spoke, "I'm just starting my break. Mind if I sit with you," she peeked under the tablecloth, "and Pari too?"

I smiled, nodding with my mouth full of warm toast. My heart was light again, and Pari and I were warm and hopeful. Our hunger was satisfied and at present our company bright and pleasant.

"Soooo, are you from this area?" Caroline pried, trying to sound casual.

Between bites I managed to get out, "No, I've never been to this land before." I turned the question back to her, "And yourself? You are a citizen of this land?"

Taken aback that I was asking about her, she began, "Well, I live in Chicago now, but I grew up in a little rural farm-town." She seemed pleased at the invitation and began to tell me about her upbringing and what had brought her to, as she put it, the 'windy city'.

"So, I came here to really *become* something. I thought there would be more opportunities for me, but here I am working at Lulu's and being a volunteer with this really cool afterschool program here in downtown Chicago. You may think I'm crazy but working with those kids is the highlight of my day. Music and theater are still my passions, but now I am beginning to wonder. Maybe I'm supposed to become a teacher and go back home to bring the kids there some opportunities that I never had."

I finished my breakfast while listening intently to her story and sat back dabbing my mouth with the paper napkin, I sincerely encouraged, "You'll make a wonderful teacher, Caroline! I would be so blessed to be a student of *yours!*"

Caroline took a beat, nodding to herself, then looked up decidedly, "Thank you!"

She used this pause to slide a small booklet across the table to me, "Funny you should mention that because, at least for now, you can find me every weekday from 3 to 7 o'clock at the Learning Center. It's not too far from here and it is *a safe place* for kids to come after school and get a snack, get help with homework, or life or whatever. Anya, I want you to know that you're welcome any time, ok?" With a tender smile she waited for my response.

Sipping my warm cocoa, I nodded, "Ok."

Her invitation was delivered, so Caroline turned the question back toward me, "What brought you to Chicago?"

"Well, I came here on a ship, called the Shema."

"Shema?" Caroline whispered thoughtfully, "That means something." She pondered trying to recollect something forgotten.

Pari nudged my hand and groaned softly, "Pari said it's from the Hebrew language of your land, it means 'to hear, obey, and respond."

Reaching under the table she rubbed Pari's fur, "Did he now?" she exclaimed, raising her eyebrows, impressed.

I continued, "I am here for seven days, two of which have already passed. I have been sent to find someone."

Leaning in, Caroline looked concerned, "Who are you looking for, Anya?"

"I don't know yet." I sighed, then listed off the qualifications that the King had given me, "All I know is that it will be someone who is an influencer of a generation, a leader among men, inspiring others to take action *and* who is also willing to receive the call. I have a message to give them that will help remind your people of the hope they have already been given. So far, I have met with the wealthy, and I have met with the famous. But they are as much in need of hope as the rest of this land, sometimes even more, I fear."

Looking down at the table I thought sadly of Mr. Talon, the king of Chicago, and his misguided ambition, and Zahara with her endless hunger for attention. The weight of the orb, hidden inside the bag, pressed down on my lap. "This task has proven to be more difficult than I expected." I confessed, finally looking up.

Caroline set down her cup. Leaning back, with her hands fallen into her lap she murmured "Where have you come from, Anya?"

Before I could answer, the door opened and a group of laughing people walked in from the cold street, setting the bell above the door tinkling merrily. Caroline's fellow server, Debbie, who had been wiping down tables looked up at them and sighed.

Walking past us to seat the new arrivals, she grouched, "A little help here?"

Caroline smiled and shook her head, "I guess I had better get back to work."

The time for Anthony Warner's press conference was fast approaching. I set my cup on the table, preparing to be on my way as well. I reached into my bag and inquired, "What is the cost for the meal?"

"Oh, Anya!" Caroline assured, standing up, "If Charlie sends someone to me, I can count on it, he'll be by this afternoon to cover the tab."

Thankfully, I smiled up at her, "I had better be going then, I have been sent here with a gift that I must share."

Leaning down she laid a dainty hand on top of mine, giving it a squeeze, she spoke sincerely, "I believe that you have." She turned to go back to her work, and I stood to leave when suddenly Caroline paused and looking back at me over her shoulder, she urgently whispered, "Hurry, Anya!"

A chill ran through me. The light had left her eyes and in its place was a deep sorrow that caught me off guard. My breath caught in my throat, and the sudden added weight of the orb nearly made my knees buckle beneath me. For a moment I saw her hidden despair. Then, like nothing had happened, her playful nature returned and her boisterous banter with the patrons again concealed the brokenness, as she danced about serving them. I was shaken. If a person who looked so happy was also filled with the sadness that I saw in Caroline's pleading eyes how could one message of hope even help.

For the most part, the people of that world looked nice on the outside, but I feared that nearly everyone was broken beneath the surface. I did not know how I could help, but I had to try. It was the very reason that the King had sent me. Maybe the answer *would* be found with Anthony Warner. I had been sent here with a gift to deliver and I was now more resolved than ever that I *must* deliver it.

Laboriously, I adjusted the leather strap over my shoulder. Pari and I left the warmth of Lulu's and started toward the offices of Anthony Warner.

18

A Leader in a Haystack

THE WIND WHIPPED A fine mist through the streets. It surged between the buildings pelting my face and wetting my hair which was now completely disheveled. I pulled my hood over my head and shivered as Pari and I pressed down the street. Soon we got to the corner where the road named Washington met with a crossroad. I retrieved the slip of paper that Kimmy had called a 'business card'. One of the words on the card matched the name on the sign.

"I *guess* this is where we should go." I tried to shout to Pari, but my words were carried away by the wind. Despite the deteriorating weather conditions, the walkways were quite busy. People rushed by with their chins tucked into their coats and their heads down. I had grown used to the constant din of the carriages that filled the roads and even the sharp wailing sirens that came from the white or red box-shaped ones that periodically whizzed by with flashing lights.

I turned the corner and continued up the next street. Here the wind was much less powerful being blocked by the tall buildings. I peered up into the windows as I passed. I half expected to see Anthony Warner standing inside just waiting for me.

He was not. I checked the card again and came to the realization that other than the name of the sign, I was not sure *how* to locate the place I was looking for. I peered down the busy road as far as I could see. Feeling lost and overwhelmed, my pace slowed, and I let my eyes travel up the towering buildings that lined both sides of the street. There were so many buildings, with so many, many windows I started to wonder how I could ever find one particular person in this vast ocean of windows.

"Like finding a needle in a haystack . . ." I whispered to myself, remembering the phrase that Marita would sometimes say when trying to locate a particular serving spoon from all the others in the drawer. I never realized what she had meant until that moment. I felt discouraged when I saw how daunting and tedious the task may be.

The thought of Marita made my stomach twist into a knot. I longed for home. I had never been away from her, at least never that I could remember. I wished I could ask her what I should do next.

I stopped in the middle of the sidewalk. Pari was several paces ahead. He barked loudly, encouraging me to press on. It was then that I noticed the line of people wrapping around a building up ahead. Bundled up and shivering in the cold, they seemed to be waiting for something. "People here must get really used to waiting in lines for things." I commented to Pari, catching up with him. "Maybe one of them could tell me where to find Anthony Warner." He yipped approvingly.

We quickened our pace again and approached the man standing at the back of the line. He was wearing a warm hat, leather gloves and a long brown coat. Hanging around his neck was a black box with a large tube on it like the ones that the men had pointed at Zahara and her fans with flashes of light coming from them.

"Excuse me, Sir?" I cautiously started.

The man turned toward me with an eager, bright smile, "Yes?" he replied.

"Um, I was wondering if you could help me. I am looking for a place and I'm not sure how to locate it. Do you know this land well? Could you help me?"

Striking a proud stance, he stated in a matter-of-fact tone, "I make it my business to know this land well." Chucking softly, he relaxed and in a more casual voice introduced himself, "I'm Tim Calloway, reporter for the Tribune. And you are?"

Clearing the persistent tickle in my throat, my voice crackled, "My name is Anya."

"Well Anya, what are you looking for?" he got straight to the point.

I held up the card and explained, "I'm looking for someone named Anthony Warner. I was told I could find him nearby. Do you know of this place?"

Taking the card and studying it, Tim inquired nonchalantly, "So why is a kid like you looking for Anthony Warner, anyway?"

"I have been sent to find him and maybe deliver a message to him. It's vitally important, the fate of your land may depend on it.", I somberly replied.

This had caught Tim's full attention, "Interesting.", he murmured, then leaning in, he delved, "What's the message?"

Suddenly very protective of the King's gift, I took a step back, lowering my eyes, "I'd rather not say."

Curbing his aggressive inquiry, Tim professionally continued, "Well Anya, this appears to be the card of Anthony Warner's campaign manager. And this address is for their campaign offices just down the street here." He pointed back the direction I had come from. "But" he continued, "today is your lucky day, because just around this corner good old 'Tony' happens to be holding a press conference in about.", he pulled up his coat sleeve and glanced down at a band on his wrist, "10 minutes. And I happen to be standing in line right now hoping to catch a few statements and pictures for a piece I'm working on."

Quickly he pointed his box at the card and pressed a button causing a bright light to shoot out of it and then handed the card back to me. Blinking from the flash I took the card and he continued, a bit sheepishly, "Yeah, I know what you're thinking,"

Truthfully, I had no idea what he was talking about, but I stood silent and let him tell me what he thought I was thinking. "If I was really with the press, how come I'm here waiting *outside* of the press conference. Well, I *do* work for the Tribune," he assured me, "mostly covering special interest pieces like dog shows. But that is not what I got into journalism to do. There are just so many in my field who are reporting based on what is trending or catering to whoever is willing to scratch their back, but I think people deserve the facts. *That's* what I'm looking to report, not seeking favor from some politicians." He had become quite passionate, and something about the young reporter's dedication to uncovering the truth inspired me.

"I came down here on a hunch, *unofficially*, of course.", Tim confessed, then turned and smiled mischievously at me. "But I've got a feeling that maybe you and I have not met by accident."

At that moment the line began to move, and Tim urged excitedly, "Come on! Let's go in and see if I can introduce you to Anthony Warner."

Following the line, we rounded the corner and came to an opulent building with flags hanging over the entrance. The long line of people filed through two enormous glass doors into a large open area with dark wood, plush furniture, and thick draperies. Sparkling crystal chandeliers and striking paintings hung from the ceiling and walls. The crowd was being directed across the shiny marble floor to a massive staircase, with gilded banisters.

It appeared to lead to an open reception area at the top. The opulence reminded me of the palace as meticulous care had obviously been put into every detail. Unlike the palace, this place had a mysterious, dark feel to it.

We were half-way from the doors to the staircase when a polite man in a black and gold double breasted coat stopped me, "Excuse me miss? My apologies but our hotel policy requires me to ask you a few questions about your dog."

"Oh, about Pari? What would you like to know?" I asked innocently, looking from Pari to the man then back to Pari.

"Is 'Pari' a service animal?" the man inquired gently.

"Yes, I suppose he is." I answered, fairly confidently, since my friend Sana had called him that our first day in this land.

The man smiled and nodded, "Is he trained to help with a disability?"

"Oh no! Definitely not!" I adamantly declared.

Struck by what I had just said, the man tried to clarify, "What *is* he trained to do?"

Puzzled, I thought then answered truthfully, "Well, I don't think Pari is *trained* to do anything, he just knows how to help me." I smiled up at his worried expression.

Tim had made it up the first few stairs when he looked back and saw the man talking with me about Pari. He pushed his way through the stream of people that were flowing up the stairs and tried to jump into the conversation to help me.

Shaking the man's hand, he introduced himself pointedly, "Tim Calloway, with the Tribune. Look, this girl is not looking to cause any trouble here. This is obviously a service animal, he's well behaved, he's wearing a vest." In a quieter, more confidential tone he added, "Can't you just let him in."

Remaining polite, but firmly holding his ground the man answered very diplomatically, "And I am Geoffrey, the head bellman here for over 20 years, and with all due respect, Mr. Calloway, it is my duty to uphold the hotel's policy regarding service animals and the safety of our guests. We are well within the ADA guidelines to ask these questions."

He looked to me apologetically, then crouched down slightly, gently rubbing Pari behind his ears, "He seems like a very well-behaved dog, but we are a strictly pet-free facility. I am very sorry, but your dog can not be in here."

Trying to decide what to do, I looked to Pari, "I don't want to leave you outside again, but I'm not sure if we will get another chance like this to meet Anthony Warner."

Pari whined and pawed at my hand to reassure me. "Alright, if you're sure you'll be ok."

I looked to the young reporter, who was watching our exchange with fascination, "Mr. Calloway, you go on ahead and I will catch up."

Glancing at the people who were already moving up the staircase ahead of him, Tim agreed, "Ok, I'll head up and see what I can do to get us in, and you just come right up these stairs and to the left and I'll meet you up there, alright?" He waited for me to nod, before he turned and sprinted up the staircase after the crowd.

The bellman, Geoffrey, walked with Pari and I back to the large glass doors and held the heavy door open for us. Pointing to a small outdoor seating area a little way down from the door, Geoffrey offered, "He's welcome to wait right out here, miss."

Pari and I walked toward the benches while I complained out loud, "Why does this land seem to resist you? *I* seem to be accepted here, but I'm continually pressured to leave *you* out! Pari, I can't do this apart from you!" I dropped despondently on the bench and Pari jumped up and settled down next to me.

He yipped softly in response, and I challenged, "How can you *always* be with me if this world is always trying to tear us apart?" He leaned his soft head on my chest and raised his snout to lick my cheeks. I wrapped my arms around his furry body. Conflicted, I didn't want to leave him, but the burden of the pearl was getting so heavy, and my spirit was growing weary from carrying it. I had to deliver it, and soon!

Finally, I stood. "I must get back in to find Anthony Warner. Wait for me right here? I'll be back as soon as I can."

His reassuring bark echoed off the overhang above us as I rushed back inside. I was so thankful to have Pari with me. The world was so loud and busy; I was sure I would have been overcome by it without him.

Once back inside I took a deep breath and boldly climbed the staircase. When I reached the top, I looked around the crowded area for Tim. I didn't see him anywhere. The doors to the left had been closed and two men in dark suits stood in front of them as sentinels with their hands clasped in front of them. Cheers, followed by applause, and laughter came from behind the doors; maybe Tim had gone inside already. I approached the door tentatively. The men eyed me with suspicion, but neither of them gave any indication that they were going to move to let me though.

"Excuse me. Can I get in to see Anthony Warner, please?" I asked timidly looking up at their stony faces.

Looking down on me with a condescending tone, one of the men sneered, "This is a press conference, not a girl scout meeting. Move along."

Flatly, the other man explained, "No one gets in without a pre-issued press pass."

I reached into my bag and pulled out the card that Kimmy had given me and held it up to him. Humoring me, he took it, glanced at both sides and then shaking his head, handed it back to me.

"Sorry, invited press are the only ones permitted and a press pass is required."

"But I don't have one of those." I admitted.

"Then I guess you can't go in." the other guard busted in, obviously done with my interruption, "Move away from the door or we will have you removed.", he threatened.

Perplexed, I backed away from the door, unsure of what to do next. If only Pari was there, he could always show me which way to go.

"What would Pari tell me to do right now?" I thought to myself. And as I did, an idea began to form up. I'd have to be patient, but it just might work. I turned and started back down the stairs and when I was out of sight of the guards, I looked around to find a place to wait.

"Hey, up here!" a voice urgently whispered. I looked up and saw Tim peering over the gilded railing motioning to me. I climbed up a short set of stairs and joined him in a small lounge area that, while perfectly hidden from the guards, still gave an unobstructed view of most of the lobby and the group of eager looking people who were also not allowed inside the press conference.

Leaning back in a plush red chair, Tim gave me a halfhearted smile, "Wouldn't let you in either, huh?"

I dropped down into one of the other red chairs, and shook my head, "No." This was as far as my plan had gone. Next, I would need to find some way to intercept Anthony Warner as he left the press conference. But how?

"They said they already had invited someone from the Tribune. But I know who's in there." He scoffed, "Celeste Norman, political analyst. Barely! She is practically the head of the Warner Fan Club. Been in his back pocket since his first term."

Leaning forward, as if he had heard my thoughts, Tim added, "But I've got a plan to intercept good ol' Tony on his way out and ask him the tough questions that no one in that room is going to ask."

Intrigued, I leaned forward too. Nodding toward the group in the lobby Tim explained, "Most of those folks are just supporters that showed up to be around the excitement, maybe shake the hand of Governor Warner, congratulate him on the election. But a few, like Josie over there for Channel 6", he smiled fondly and pointed toward a young lady in a tan skirt and coat, with a messy bun on top of her head and scuffed high heeled shoes, peering impatiently through the crowd at the closed door, "they're like me. We're old school, we still abide by the Journalists Code of Ethics, even though most journalists now have completely abandoned *that* idea. But that's what makes journalism so beautiful; to seek the truth and report it. We are just crazy enough to believe what we were taught: that 'public enlightenment is the forerunner of justice and the foundation of democracy,'" Tim stated proudly. He laughed and gave a sideways glance at me, "Doesn't make us very popular though."

I laughed too. I liked this Tim Calloway. His passion for seeking the truth, the quick way he moved, his honorable ambition and his peppy attitude made me smile.

"So why aren't you over there with Josie and the others by the door if you are trying to talk to Mr. Warner as he leaves?" I asked, wondering why Tim chose this position so far away from the crowd.

"Because" smiled Tim proudly, "I know the layout of the hotel better than they do." He leaned back again and crossed his arms over his chest trying to look casual, and very slightly tilted his head pointing over his shoulder, "See that door behind us?"

I turned and saw a door tucked in the corner of the small empty lounge, "Yes?" I nodded curiously looking back to Tim.

"Well," he continued, "when this press conference is over the last thing that the Governor is going to want to do is fight his way through all of that." He pointed again toward the crowd of people who were starting to get restless by that point. They had all edged closer to the guards at the door.

"So, what are his other options?" Tim questioned hypothetically then answered himself. "There *is* a back exit to the conference room that *would* bring him to a hallway and to the service elevators that the hotel staff use." Tim smirked, "But fun fact about Mr. Anthony Warner, he *hates* elevators. An old superstition he has. So, he avoids them whenever possible. Which gives him only one possible option that bypasses both the horde and the elevators." He raised his eyebrows inviting me to guess.

"Oh!", I smiled, understanding what he meant and that we were perfectly positioned to receive the Governor as he made his exit through this lounge. Then all we had to do was wait for the press conference to conclude.

Several quiet minutes passed before Tim sheepishly turned to me. "Say, I apologize for prying earlier. Your reasons for wanting to talk with Mr. Warner are your own. I guess it's just the investigative reporter in me that *needed* to know."

I placed my hand on top of my bag which was resting on the chair beside me, relieving the weight of it from my shoulders for the moment, "That's alright Tim Calloway. I guess I have become very protective of the message I've been sent here to deliver. It is not meant for just anybody. There is *someone* I am looking for. I'm here to find out if that someone is Governor Warner."

"But how will you know?" Tim exclaimed, then cringed at himself. He quickly added apologetically, "Sorry! You don't have to answer that!"

I giggled at Tim's battle with his curiosity, and now that I trusted him, I shared, "Well there are several qualities that he will have to possess, but I think the most important one is that he must be *willing* to receive the message, and that his desire will be to use it to give hope to the people of this land. Then his actions will glorify the one who sent me."

Thoughtfully taking in my words, Tim responded prudently, "You may be disappointed by Anthony Warner then. He is not known for sharing his glory."

At that moment, a frenzy broke out in the lobby across from us as applause and cheers inside announced that the press conference was ending.

"You ready?" Tim breathed, standing, and moving to the stairs. He pressed several buttons on the flashing box that he wore and pulled a small device from his pocket that he held close to his face and pressed a button with his thumb. Speaking quietly into the device he stated, "Wednesday November 8th. At the conclusion of the post-election press conference of Governor Anthony Warner. Tim Calloway reporting."

Several moments passed in a tense cloud of anticipation, and as the people filling the lobby fixed their eyes on the conference room doors, we were watching the single door in the corner of the lounge. Tim's hunch paid off. The silence was broken as the door flew open and a tall man in a gray suit with shiny black hair slicked back on his head, busted through it followed by several other men. The men all moved quickly and purposefully. I recognized one as Kimmy's father, the other was a mousy looking man in glasses carrying a brown case.

He was the first one to notice us and hissing under his breath, he looked to Kimmy's father, "I told you we should wait for the security men."

Anthony Warner looked up and saw us blocking his escape route, he groaned disdainfully before engaging Tim. "Calloway," he addressed him with a sneer, "Isn't there a spelling bee that's missing their two-bit reporter?" Tim was not fazed by the jab. The politician's lip curled into a cruel smile as he tried again to cut Tim down, "Couldn't help but notice that you were not *inside* the press conference today with the *respected* members of the press."

"Good morning to you as well, Governor Warner. Seems I was not invited, sir. Just wondering if I could have a couple of minutes of your time." Tim began in a friendly, yet pointed, tone that carried throughout the space, intentionally attracting the attention of the lobby full of people who were also hoping to gain access to the governor. They gathered around the gilded railings and down the staircases eagerly with flash boxes in hand making pops of light fill the space.

With an exasperated sigh, he glared down the stairs at us, "The election is over, Callaway. I don't have to prove anything to you or anyone else. I won!" Governor Warner moved to go around us and continue his hasty exit. "Now if you will GET OUT OF MY WAY, I have a government to serve."

Tim stepped in front of him boldly "And I have the citizens of this city to serve, Mr. Warner." And quickly adding, "Speaking of which, this young lady has been waiting to meet you, sir."

As soon as Tim stepped to the side and invited me to come forward, a wave of flashes erupted from the stairs and balcony.

Realizing now that this audience could not be avoided, the Governor replied amiably through a huge, forced smile, "Of course, it would be my pleasure to meet a future voter of our fine state."

Bowing politely, I began, "Your Governorship." Another eruption of flashes.

"Well, um . . .", he fumbled for his words, "Well, hello young lady." The Governor tried to conceal his shock at suddenly being presented with a rumpled looking child with tattered clothing and wet, stringy hair hanging over her grubby, unwashed face. This was obviously not what he was expecting or prepared to encounter.

Sizing me up quickly, he addressed the crowd and announced, "Over my last term in office I have worked hard to improve the educational outlook for the children of this state. And will continue to do so,", placing a hand on my shoulder he declared self-righteously, "as well as provide more secondary opportunities for *underprivileged* youth."

Many of the people hanging over the railings clapped and cheered at his boast. The Governor posed and smiled at them. I stared incredulously at this pompous man, and filled with conviction, I brushed his hand off my shoulder, "Anthony Warner, it is not a better education that I seek. I am looking for a leader among men who will inspire his people. Are you willing to receive the responsibility of spreading a message of hope across this land and giving glory to the King who sent me?"

From the lounge door behind Mr. Warner, the two security men, who had been guarding the entry earlier, arrived, breathless, having pushed their way hurriedly through the crowd that was still filing out of the conference room to assist the governor's foiled exit.

Looking relieved, the Governor glanced down at me dismissively, shaking his head, "We are the government, young lady, we don't have time for *hope*."

Smiling and waving to the crowd, Anthony Warner was led down the stairs by his guards. For a moment, Kimmy's father stopped on the stairs and looked back at me with a faint light of recognition in his eye, before turning and following along.

That was it, Anthony Warner was gone. Honestly, I was not one bit sorry for it. The crowd was already dispersing, but Tim stood still watching me, "I'm sorry I couldn't buy you more time to find out if Governor Warner was the one you have been looking for."

"It was plenty of time, thank you. I found out all I needed to know," I assured him, shaking my head. "I'm sorry you didn't get to ask him *your* questions."

He chuckled, "Oh don't worry about me, I got exactly what I came here for. Do you know where you will look next? I mean, to find the one your message is for."

"No, not yet, but Pari and I will find them. He will know what to do next. I had best get back to him." Sincerely, I bid the young reporter farewell, "Goodbye Tim Calloway, and thank you!"

I turned and bounded down the stairs. Sure, Anthony Warner was not who I was seeking, but I was proud and excited to tell Pari all that had happened. At just the right moment I knew exactly what to say! It felt like Pari really was there with me the whole time, just like he had told me he would be. Once outside of the glass door, I turned and headed toward the benches, calling out, "Pari, Pari, I met Anthony Warner, and. . . ." my words stopped short. Pari was not where I left him. Out of the corner of my eye I caught a bright strip of fabric hanging out of one of the bins for trash. As I approached, my heart sank, it was the vest Pari had been wearing. It had been torn and hastily shoved in the bin.

19

Nobody's Hero

THE SKY WAS AS gray as I felt. The clouds churned ominously above me as I wandered through the city streets. Aimlessly I peered down alleyways, around buildings and behind every parked carriage, desperately calling out for him again and again, "Pari, Pari!"

The city had lost the glamor or enchantment it may have held for me when we first arrived. Now it looked dirty and hopeless. I felt so defeated; I had not found the one who I was seeking; not with the king of Chicago, not with Zahara and her clamoring fans, and certainly not with Anthony Warner. Every time I had felt that this *could* be the one who would influence their world with the King's message, my hopes had been crushed.

This time I had no more ideas, and no Pari; I was without a guide. I was without a protector.

Surrounded by a busy, noisy world, thousands of people rushed here and there on the walkways, zooming past in carriages, and moving in and out of buildings. No one noticed me. I was completely alone. Only the buildings, looming above my head seemed to encroach above me to stare down and mock my small presence in their mighty city.

Too numb to cry, I continued, with my head down and my shoulders slumped. Hours passed and I abandoned calling for Pari. My throat hurt from yelling and the cough had returned. My eyes stung and watered as I squinted into the wind.

I didn't notice my path had begun to slope downward. It was not until I heard a cold voice that I finally looked up, "You don't have your stupid mutt to defend you this time." I suddenly realized that I had walked under the streets and buildings. I was in the shadowy underworld of the city. Empty carriages lined the dimly lit alleys and dusty stairways led back up to the light. Bottles and refuse littered the ground and the stale air reeked of garbage and urine.

In nooks and crannies and on tucked away ledges people had arranged blankets and boxes into make-shift dwellings. A few bodies lay huddled up under heaps of filthy blankets against the walls, with their backs to the dark world around them. Others, still awake, wandered about, or sat, slumped on the ground, eating a meager meal or puffing smoke from a stick. I had found the homeless of the city. None of them looked like they had made it to Zahara's concert the night before.

The voice rang out even louder this time, "Hey! Didn't you hear me? I said *no one* is here to protect you this time. Too bad someone called the pound on your dumb dog." Danny and the boys from the day before laughed mockingly.

"What? Do you know where Pari is?" I gasped hopefully.

"Yeah, I know where he is. Animal Control picked him up." Danny smirked cruelly, "Seems they got a call that there was a *vicious* dog lurking around outside of one of the fancy hotels."

The tears that had been held at bay finally let loose, "*You* had Pari taken away!" I gasped.

Ignoring my accusation, Danny stood up and so did the rest of his crew and they started down the steps toward me, fanning out and blocking me from escape. "So, about that money you owe me."

Backing away I cried, "I owe you *nothing*. Where is Pari?" My back hit the cold wall behind me as the boys crept in closer and closer.

"Let's just have a look in that bag of yours and see what you *do* have." Danny reached out to make a grab for my bag.

"No, don't touch that!" I shrieked, pinned against the wall clutching the King's gift to my chest. "It is mine to deliver! Leave me alone!"

Suddenly, a deep, mighty voice echoed like a roar around us amplified by the stone enclosure, "You heard the lady, leave her alone!"

The boys all spun around to see a man in a worn, dirty green coat and a black knit hat standing unsteadily behind them. Danny quickly put his hand into his pocket and when he drew it out there was a metallic click and the glint of a blade in the dim light.

Trying to sound brave and cover the quavering in his voice, Danny squeaked, "Oh yeah? Why don't you mind your own business? I don't have to listen to a drunk bum like you!"

The 'drunk bum' stumbled forward. Danny widened his stance and brandished his knife shakily.

Holding his empty hands up in front of him, the man slurred, "Whoh Killer! I'm not tryin' to get into your business . . .", all the while taking a few calculated steps closer to Danny. Once he was close enough, Danny lunged forward, and the man, with surprisingly swift and smooth precision, grasped Danny's wrist and spun him to the ground where Danny landed with his arm uncomfortably bent behind his back and the knife held securely by the man. Subduing Danny the man finished, ". . . but that's not how you treat a lady."

The boys slowly backed away, and in the panicked whispers I could barely make out, "Holy crap!", "It's him!", "It's the Shepherd!"

Folding the knife blade into the handle with one hand, the man pulled Danny to his feet with the other.

"Being a bully will never make you a man. Look, Killer, we can be friends if you don't ever pull a stupid stunt like that again. Do you hear me, son?"

Releasing Danny, he extended the closed knife back to him, "Now get out of here. If I ever catch you threatening a woman again, you won't get off so easy." The 'Shepherd' spoke slowly and the quaver in his voice was the only thing that revealed the fire beneath the surface of his cool aloof demeanor.

Reluctantly nodding, Danny reached out and snatched the knife. Backing away slowly, he glared at my defender until he was a safe distance away. Then dropping his eyes to the ground, he ran out of sight. His friends were long gone. They had abandoned him at the first sign of trouble.

I held my breath still pressed against the wall; I had never witnessed a fight before. I looked back to the man who had saved me. Clearly shaken, he retrieved a small brown paper bag from his coat pocket. He removed the cover from the bottle and raised it to his trembling lips. He took a generous swig, recapped it, and shoved the bag back into his pocket.

Catching his breath, he looked over at me, "What are you standin here lookin at? Get out of here kid! You don't belong down here." He turned and stumbled up toward the light of the streets above.

Unfrozen, I followed him. I wanted to thank him for defending me.

"Hey wait!" I called, catching up with him. "Thank you! That was amazing! You're a hero!" I stammered.

He scoffed gruffly, "I ain't nobody's hero." A pungent aroma of strong liquor tainted his breath. I stayed by his side, determined for him to accept my appreciation for his bravery.

"How did you do that?" I said in admiration.

He shook his head, trying to ignore me. "Are you the 'Shepherd'?" I said, repeating what I had heard the boys call him.

Closing his eyes as he walked, he mumbled, "Just a dumb sheep dog, who can't forget his training." He turned to amble down another street.

I quickened to keep pace with him; I had nowhere else to go. Glancing up, I noticed the deep lines etched into his unkempt face. It made him look much older and worn than I would have guessed from his heroics. A scar ran through one eyebrow leaving a gap where the hair never grew back. This weathered man had clearly seen some battles.

I continued to try to engage my rescuer, "My name is Anya. What is your name, is it Shepherd?"

"Joe.", he spat, quickly jabbing at a button on a pole, eager to get away from me. It took me a second to realize that would be his whole response.

"Are you a soldier of this city, Joe?" I stepped down from the ledge that we were standing on to circle around in front of Joe to get his attention.

On instinct, Joe's arm shot out pushing me back up onto the ledge just as a bright yellow carriage whizzed by within inches of where I had been standing.

Exhaling sharply, Joe glared down at me.

"Do you rescue people often?", I innocently inquired. He said nothing, but clenching his jaw stared up at the lights on the pole.

One of the lights changed to show a white figure of a person walking. The carriages all stopped, and Joe began to cross the street with me trailing after him. "Oh! I think I understand now!" I exclaimed. "That's a signal that it is safe to go across!"

Catching up with him again, I continued, "I'm so grateful you arrived when you did! You see, I was looking for my companion, Pari. He has been taken away. I didn't realize that I was in any danger; Pari usually keeps me safe. But then you came to my rescue!"

He pressed on determinedly, obviously hoping I would just go away if he ignored me. But honestly, at that moment, Joe was all I had, so I persisted, "Are there others like you?"

Turning down a small gap between buildings, he came to a stop and leaned up against a wall next to a huge foul-smelling bin of refuse. He pulled the brown bag out of his pocket again and uncapped it. He drank deeply of the contents, draining the vessel, then throwing it roughly into the open top of the bin. Out of breath, he slumped down against the wall and clenched his eyes closed taking deep breaths.

I slumped down next to him, silently waiting for him to respond. He did not. So, after a few minutes I offered, "Is there *anything* that I can do to thank you?"

Eyes still closed, he leaned his head back against the wall with a thump and an irritated grumble. He resigned himself to the fact that I was not going away, "Fine!" Joe turned to me, "You hungry?"

I nodded adamantly, "Yes!"

"Then here's what you do." He pulled a thin white bag from his pocket and shook it out. It was a small sack with blue writing on it that said, "Thank You!" He handed it to me, "You can get us some apples, the big, juicy red ones. That store over there keeps them back by the hotdogs and coffee. Just walk in and put 5 or 6 in the bag then bring them back out here and then we're even, ok?"

That seemed like much too small a request in exchange for saving my life, especially when I found the apples he was talking about. They were tiny and dull compared to the apples from the King's orchard. I stood staring at them for several minutes near the back of the establishment, before reaching out and taking one. Slightly offended at the puny offering, I placed six of them in the bag and turned to head toward the door.

Bypassing several long lines of people, I was almost back to the doors. I had to shake my head. These people and their love for waiting in lines astounded me! They seemed to do it everywhere! I approached the same door I had entered on the way into the market. I was fascinated at how it had bewitchingly opened on its own allowing me to enter. However, when I attempted to leave, I pressed my hands on the unyielding glass, unsuccessful in causing it to open for me. Behind me an angry shout caused me to jump.

"Hey! You lousy thief! I've been watching you. Where do you think you're going with those apples?" A large, bald man wearing an apron bounded toward me from behind a row of shelves.

The encounter with Danny and his gang was fresh in my mind, so my first instinct was to run away when I saw the man lumbering toward me. Frantically, I searched for a knob or handle, anything to make the door open to escape. A woman approached from the outside causing the magical door to open. I pushed past her and ran, without looking back, all the way to the alley where Joe was waiting. I hid myself behind the bin and listened for the sound of anyone approaching. Only the sound of my shaking breath and the carriages moving along the road persisted. The man never came, he had given up chasing me.

Breathlessly, I gasped, "The man at that shop was angry with me! Why?"

Joe, who seemed a bit surprised to see me again, laughed, finding enjoyment in my bewildered state, "You shoplifted from his store! Of course, he's gonna be angry!"

"Shoplifted?" I questioned, "What is *that*?"

Puzzled, he stopped laughing and scoffed, still amused, "Are you serious? You ain't been out here long have ya? It means you stole his apples."

That realization made my heart drop like a rock into my stomach. "That's why he called me a thief." I groaned. Joe burst out laughing again.

Feeling my face get red and I turned sharply toward Joe, "Stealing is not an act of the Kingdom.", I lamented. "No citizen of the Kingdom has to be reduced to thievery; the King provides for all our needs!"

Falling to my knees I whimpered, "What have I done?" I let the bag of ill-gotten apples fall. Burying my head in my hands, my cold fingers pressed against my unusually hot forehead. I felt so hopeless and fallen, unworthy, unable to deliver the King's message, and now I was a common thief. "Please, forgive your servant." I whispered my plea.

I was utterly alone in the world, except for Joe. He had gallantly come to my rescue, yet he had proved to be a deficient guide. Intrigued by my deep sorrow and repentance, he attempted to minimize my offense, "It was just a few apples, kid. Besides, you said it yourself, 'the king provides', and he provided." Eagerly he snatched up the bag and pulled an apple out of it. He held it out to me as a weak peace offering, but I slowly shook my head. My stomach was empty, but the apples disgusted me.

"There is a difference between being provided for and taking what belongs to someone else." I said, with anger lingering in my voice.

"That's easy for you to say, you've never had to survive on your own. Having some 'king' just give you everything is a fantasy. It doesn't work like that, kid. There is too much greed and lack in the world. You've got to take what you can get before someone else takes it away from you." The deep lines on Joe's face creased and he patted his pockets. Obviously looking for another bottle to drink away whatever painful thought that had just been stirred up. Finding none, he sighed and leaned back against the wall clutching the apple, he sharply inhaled, "Fat and lazy. That's why I'd be, living off someone else's dime. I'd take it easy and eat my fill, drink away my troubles and be happy."

I was appalled, "That is *not* how the Kingdom works at all. Those who choose to be lazy or sluggards, murderers, or *thieves*," I stressed, "are cast out."

Reflecting on my life in the Kingdom, I affirmed, with affection and longing, "I am happy to serve my King in whatever task he asks me to do. My work is to clean the dishes and scrub the floors. It would be my honor to do so all of my days if it pleases the King. But it pleased Him to send me *here* to *your* land."

Not quite following me, Joe dismissed me with an unsteady shake of his head, "More for me." and took a satisfyingly loud crunch out of one of the small, dull apples. However, his satisfaction was short-lived. Almost immediately, Joe started to cough and spit the apple on the ground.

"Bitter?" I questioned with some satisfaction.

Joe glared up at me as he spit out the remnants of his triumphant bite. In frustration he threw the apple angrily at the wall on the other side of the alley. It exploded into pieces that scattered across the ground and landed among the papers and leaves and other debris. One larger chunk bounced back and landed at my feet revealing the black rotted core. Joe shoved the rest of the bag away from him.

"Figures." He grumbled, his face falling slack in defeat, he stared blankly down at the ground, arms propped on his knees, his face, head, and hands hanging limply. He looked so despondent, sad, and hopeless. I felt a wave of pity for his state of despair and remorse for my feeling vindicated by his thwarted plan. He thought he was trying to help me.

I crawled over and sat beside him with a sigh, affirming, "The King *does* provide, but in *His* ways, and *His* timing. You'll see. An honest servant will not go hungry." Joe didn't look up, he just snorted weakly, and his body slumped further down.

My own grumbling stomach was trying to convince me my words were false. I rationalized, "My King has *never* let me down, why would He start now?"

We sat in silence for a time. The noises from the street faded in and out as I battled my own fears and doubts.

Joe was now snoring softly, still slumped over his knees, occasionally whimpering "Joanna, Joanna, I was too late. I'm so sorry . . ." as if some ghost of a memory haunted his slumbering mind.

A berating narrative haunted mine, "Is the King disappointed in me? Has He forgotten about me? Does He even know where I am? Who was I to think *I* was worthy?"

I hung my head just as Joe had done, and whispered, "After all I am just a lowly servant . . ."

"A servant I have chosen."

The deep, clarion voice broke through my clouded mind. I jumped to my feet and knelt at the sound of His voice. "My King!" I gasped.

After a moment of silence, I looked around. It was still just Joe and I in the alley. Joe, however, had snapped to attention and his eyes were wide, "You heard the King too, didn't you?", I said, locking eyes with Joe.

Before Joe could answer, I heard a woman's friendly voice call out on the walkway. "How about over here?" Her smiling face appeared at the entrance of the alley, "Oh, hello there!" She took a step toward us, "Um, my name is Molly. Are ya hungry?" The woman held up a white container. "We've brought some food and warm blankets for you if you need them."

Joe was now fully awake and was looking from the woman to me, then back to the woman. When he realized that I was frozen in shock, he motioned for the woman to come over.

Molly looked back down the walkway and called to someone out of sight, "Luke, grab another dinner and a few blankets." In a moment a tall man joined her, and they approached us. "Like I said, my name is Molly. This is my husband, Luke."

"Hey" Luke said in greeting with a huge smile and a nod of his head since his arms were full. He wore a funny shaped hat with a wide brim. "Friends call me Cowboy." I'd never seen a hat like that before, and I looked at him curiously.

Molly explained, "We are volunteers from our church out in Grant Park. We come into the city to help with Trinity Outreach up on 16th on Wednesdays, just bringing some supplies and dinner to those who may be without a place to go tonight."

Luke piped up, "Would you mind if we visited with you and your daughter for a minute?"

"What have you got?" Joe said in a gruff voice, nodding toward the white box in Luke's hand.

Luke smiled, "Best meatloaf and mashed potatoes in the state if you ask me!" Luke gave Molly a quick wink, Molly smiled at the complement that must have been directed at her.

Luke handed Joe the box he was holding and reached into his jacket pocket and pulled out a packet containing a forklike object and napkin. He offered it to Joe. Joe slowly accepted it. I am sure he was wondering if he was still asleep and dreaming. The smell of the meatloaf reached his nose; that was enough to make him believe, and he flipped open the box and began to devour the feast.

Pausing he wrinkled his nose, "It's under seasoned. Needs cumin, and more salt.", he critiqued, then continued to eat it anyway.

Molly shook off the criticism and turned her attention to me, "And what's your name?" Molly began, taking a step toward me, holding out the white box. I had been frozen in awe of the King's goodness.

I looked up and found my voice, "I, I'm Anya." Her smile was filled with such warmth, I could not help but smile back!

"Well, hello, Anya. You hungry?" I nodded and accepted the box from her as she reached over and snagged a fork thing from Luke's jacket pocket and unwrapped it for me.

Warm food tasted so good. I had two bites finished before I stopped, swallowed, and said, "Thank you, Molly!"

She smiled again, "You are so very welcome, Anya! But we are simply faithful servants, set about doing what we have been asked to do! I just want you to know that the King of all Kings cares for you, He sees you, He knows you and you are *worthy* of His love!"

I stared at her wide eyed, drinking in every word. My mind reeled, I thought, "A servant? A servant! Like me, she was sent on a task! The King really did provide!! He sees me! He *still* sees me!" My heart leapt! Unable to speak, joyful tears rimmed my eyes.

"Anya, is this all you have to wear?" I was so overjoyed; I had to shake my head and refocus to hear what Molly had said.

I stared up at her blankly, "Is this all you have to wear?" Molly repeated.

"Oh, well yes." I replied looking down at my, now tattered, clothing from the Kingdom.

"It's set to get pretty nasty tonight. We've got some winter gear back in the truck." She motioned, holding one finger up, "Hang on one sec."

She stepped over to where Luke had been crouched down talking with Joe as he continued to spoon mashed potatoes into his mouth and occasionally nod in Luke's direction.

Luke made introductions, "Molly, this is Joe."

"Hey Joe," Molly began sweetly, "Say, we do have some winter jackets that we've brought out. They are in our pickup, right there in the parking ramp." She said, pointing into the brick enclosure across from us. "You and Anya can come with us if you want, and we could find something to fit her?"

"Who?" Joe questioned. Luke and Molly looked at each other, then at me.

Joe realized they were talking about me and muttered, "Oh, yeah, sure, whatever. You go ahead, I'll stay here." He went back to finishing his meal and using his finger he hurriedly swiped the last bits of potato and gravy from the corners of the container.

Luke set the blankets down next to Joe. He left a folded paper laying on top, "I'll just set these here for you guys. It was nice meeting you Joe. Thanks for chatting with me, and God bless you."

Joe seemed to have a new clarity of mind, and his words were clear. Soberly, he wiped his face and grunted, "Yeah, thanks. You too.", glancing up at them only briefly, then looked directly at me, "Take care." He dropped his gaze to the container in his lap.

I set the box of food down and followed Luke and Molly out toward the street and around a wall into an enclosure of carriages.

Going to a strangely shaped carriage parked in the first row, Luke opened the back storage compartment. I had not seen many like it on the streets of the city. A *pickup*, that is what Molly had called it. Molly pulled a large blue container to the edge and removed the lid. Sorting through the contents she pulled out a red, puffy garment. It looked like red clouds.

"Most of the things we bring out are all about function, but I thought I saw something cuter down in here somewhere. . . ." Molly chatted, setting the puffy coat on the tailgate and continuing to rummage through the box.

"I love it!" I said and reached out to push down on the soft, red puffs.

"Oh, this one?" Molly stopped looking in the box. She tilted her head thoughtfully, "Well, yeah. This one IS really warm, it's down-filled. It was mine when I was younger. But it may be a little big on yo . . ." Her voice trailed off; she was looking down at me with a look of concern.

Now that we were out of the sheltered alley, the wind was finding its way into the enclosure and sent a chill up my back. Without thinking about it I had crossed my arms around each other to warm them and my bottom lip had started trembling.

"How about we try it on." Molly said quickly, grabbing the red jacket and wrapping it around my shoulders. "There!" She said with a smile, and with a mother's instinct, she fastened it around me.

"Oh, wait! I've got the perfect thing!" She went to the cab of the truck and grabbed something from inside a bag and pulled some tags off. She came back with a black band with a red fabric flower attached. "Here, this one even matches the coat." She slid the band over my head covering my ears and brushed my hair back, "There! How does that feel?"

"Wonderful!" I sighed.

Luke had retrieved two more containers of food from the front of the truck and prompted, "Well, I guess we better go see if anyone else is hungry today. We'll have to head back home before this weather hits. Hey Molls, you want to grab a few more blankets and water from the back?"

"Sure thing, just one second." Turning back to me, she said sincerely, "Anya, I am so glad that we met you. Is there *anything* else that Luke and I can help you with?"

Sparked by her invitation, I eagerly asked, "Do you know of a place called Animal Control? My friend Pari has been taken there."

"Oh no! I'm sorry, I don't know the address. But just hold on! Watch this." she smirked with a wink. Molly called to Luke who was waiting for her at the front of their carriage, "Luke, do you know what street Animal Control is on?"

Closing his eyes, and thinking for a moment, he slowly recollected as if searching a map in his mind, "Western and . . . 28th"

"That is amazing!", I commented.

"Not really," he admitted, "this country boy rode the bus right past there every day for the first two years I lived here. I could never find a parking spot for this big beast downtown," he nodded his head and patted his pickup carriage. "and besides, back then I was terrified of driving in the city!"

"He's being modest. I call it one of his spiritual gifts! He has a mental map of the city of Chicago!" Molly explained jokingly.

Hopeful, I asked, "And the *bus* goes to that place?"

"Sure does!" looking down he traced an imaginary path with his finger in the as he recalled, "Get on the blue line over here at Lake and Clark, and ride that over to Western Station and take the transfer to bus 49 southbound. Take that for," he counted, "seven, eight, nine blocks? And, BAM! There you are! Animal Control is on the corner to the right!" He looked up triumphantly and smiled over at me. When Luke noticed the befuddled expression on my face, he shook his head and added, "Just get on the bus here at the corner and tell the driver where you're going, they'll usually point you in the right direction."

"Thank you, I will do that." I replied gratefully. Tipping his large, brimmed hat, 'Cowboy' nodded a good-bye.

Molly had retrieved an armful of water bottles from the truck and handing one to me said, "Good luck finding Pari. But you and Joe may want to think about heading over to the mission or to the mercy house for tonight. It's going to get pretty bad out here." She warned kindly, shuddering from the wind and the cold of the bottles she was cradling.

Luke had started making his way down the ramp with meal boxes in hand and Molly called after him playfully, "Woah there, Cowboy! Wait for me!" Looking back at me, she smiled before following Luke down the ramp. "God be with you, Anya! Hope you find your friend."

I made my way back to where Joe had been sitting and found nothing, except my white food container and a blanket neatly tucked next to the wall. I had kind of expected Joe to be gone with the way he had said goodbye. None of us noticed him slip away.

"It is for the best anyway.", I reasoned out loud. Joe had rescued me in my time of need, and I was thankful, but I had a feeling that he was fighting a war I did not understand. As I stood in the cold, lonely alley I hoped that someone would rescue Joe from the battle inside of him, like he had rescued me.

I turned to leave, and my foot kicked a broken piece of the rotten, shattered apple, a reminder of the brokenness and decay of this land. As it skittered to a stop, it landed on top of the glossy folded paper that Luke had left with the blankets. Joe must not have wanted that and left it behind too. Picking it up I read the words: "Have you found what you're searching for?"

20

Rescue Mission

THE APPLE AND THE pamphlet brought me back to the great crisis of this land and the importance of the gift I carried. I realized I had grown accustomed to the heavy weight of my burden, so much that I had nearly forgotten about it. I had been caught in the trap of focusing on my own afflictions and discomforts rather than my purpose.

Looking down at the pamphlet in my hand I answered the question it posed, 'Have you found what you're searching for?'

"No, not yet" I admitted, and although my body ached, and my feverish head pounded, I promised desperately, "but I will find them." My voice sounded weak, but I resolved to see my mission through. The King had proven that He had not forgotten about me, and I would not forget about Him and His love for the people of this land. First, I had to find Pari.

"Western and 28th" I repeated several times to myself to make sure that I still remembered the location Luke had given for the place called Animal Control. My search for the recipient of the Kings message *would* continue but reuniting with my guide was *most* imperative. I could not bear to think of continuing in this land without him.

I left the alley and began toward the corner where I could see a sign posted for the bus carriage. I hesitated. As urgent as finding Pari was, I knew I must not leave without making things right with the man whose apples I had stolen.

I entered the shop once more. There were only a few people lined up at the front now. No one noticed me as I hurried between the rows and scanned past the shelves for the bald man. It did not take long before *he* found me.

"Dared to come back again? You are bold!", a deep voice boomed behind me.

I turned, startled, to see the man standing there with arms crossed and a stern look on his face. Plucking up my courage, I addressed him, "My sincerest apologies, sir, I did not intend to steal from you. I am not familiar with the ways of your land. I have come to make things right." Reaching into my bag I pulled out all the crumpled papers that Jen had given me and deposited the pile into his hands. "I hope this is enough to cover my debt."

The man's expression softened and with a confused nod, he received them. I turned without waiting for his response and hurried to the door, leaving him standing speechless staring down and the untidy jumble of papers. Having learned from my earlier troubles, I found a different door that was agreeable to allow me to leave the shop.

As the door closed itself behind me, I heard the man's voice calling urgently, "Wait, this is way too much . . ." But I had no time to stop, I had given him all I had and could pause no longer.

At the corner, a bus carriage with a blue band above the door screeched to a stop and people were streaming out of it. I ran toward it waving my arms stopping the man inside from pulling the lever to close the door. It was only a short distance but by the time I climbed inside, I was out of breath and wheezing. Fumbling for the card in my bag I managed to gasp, "Western and 28th . . . . Animal Control?"

"I can get you as far as Western, but you'll have to take a transfer to the 49th from there."

I nodded, trying to catch my breath, Luke was right, they knew the way. I was encouraged as I searched for an open seat on the crowded carriage. I was finally on the right path to finding Pari. It felt good to sit, but I was anxious to keep moving.

After several stops the driver motioned for me, "This is the Western Blue Line Station, Miss" Jumping up, I hastily made my way to the front of the carriage, then he added, "Animal Control closes in a half hour so you're cutting it pretty close. The 49 bus will pull up right over there in about two minutes." He pointed across the platform to a small group of people that were huddled together under an awning trying to get out of the misty rain that had returned.

I nodded gratefully and exited the bus. Making my way across the wet platform I was very thankful for the warm coat. The bitterly cold wind and rain would have soaked my tunic and chilled me to the bone if it were not for the puffs of red cloud surrounding me. Even then, my head and face were soon wet with icy drops. I hardly paid any attention to the rain, my focus was on getting to Pari. Time was of the essence! From what the driver had said, whatever this place called Animal Control was, it would not stay open much longer.

The two minutes of waiting seemed to drag on and on, as if time had purposely slowed to a crawl just to spite me. Finally, the carriage arrived exactly as scheduled and the people waiting scurried to get on board and out of the rain which had started coming down harder, driven sideways by the wind. I was the last one on the platform to enter the carriage and by then my stingy hair was dripping beads of water onto the floor. I used the card again on the box that made a chiming noise. What purpose this strange ritual had to the people of this land is still beyond my understanding, only that it was very important that each person entering made the box chime before they were admitted.

"Western and 28th . . . Animal Control?" I repeated to the silver-haired lady who sat behind the huge wheel.

She nodded and replied gruffly, "Take a seat."

I said nothing in reply but obeyed her command and found a seat nearby. It hurt to speak so the less words I could use the better. The bus bumped down the road, screeching to a stop every minute or so to let some passengers get off and others get on. With each stop the carriage emptied as more and more people were getting off and less and less were waiting at the stops to enter. Each time we stopped, I leaned forward eagerly, about to rise, hoping this was the place I was waiting for, but each time the driver looked back in the mirror, scowled, and shook her head. Disappointed, I would sit back until finally I stopped trying to rise at all and just stared up at the driver impatiently.

Was I going to be too late? Would I even find Pari at this Animal Control place? What would they have done to him there? My legs were restless with nervous energy and worry. Finally, the bus screeched and lurched to a stop and the driver rolled her eyes and nodded at me. Jumping up I nearly tripped over the bag of a person sitting in front of me in my haste to get off the bus. "Excuse me." I mumbled weakly. Passing the driver, I managed a "Thank you.", in a hoarse whisper and bounded down the steps.

It was much quieter here than in the heart of the city; things were more spread out with expanses of brown grass separating the wide low buildings. There were no tall towers to be seen. The bus pulled away and my eyes frantically scanned my surroundings to find a clue to my next move. Eventually, I spied the words, 'Animal Care and Control' on the side of a building across a quiet street and a large stretch of grass. I started running towards it not even looking to see if any carriages were approaching. I flew over the street and stumbled across the uneven grass towards the doors.

I arrived at a set of glass doors and startled a young woman who stood just on the other side with a key in her hand about to engage the lock. Boldly I pulled the door open, so she could not lock me out, and gasped, "I'm here to find Pari!"

Perhaps moved by my soggy, desperate state, the young woman glanced down at a bracelet on her wrist then conceded, "Ok, come on in." She stood back, inviting me inside, then locked the door behind us.

Leading me through another set of doors, we entered an open area with a few large desks and a market of some sort covering a large section of one of the corners. It was filled with colorful ropes and large boxes and many bags of various sizes and colors, among other strange items. I paid little attention to this area; I was looking around for any sign of Pari. The room was very clean and had a strong sterile smell mixed with the smell of wet fur.

One of the doors at the back of the room burst open and a young man and a very pregnant woman walked out, chatting happily, obviously preparing to leave for the day. From behind them I could hear barking, and my heart leapt. Hopeful to see Pari I strained to try to see behind them into the next room before the door snapped shut.

The man had a big pack of some sort slung over his shoulder and coat draped over the other arm and the woman carried a tote bag. I noticed that they all wore a similar kind of uniform; it reminded me of the uniform that I wore to do my daily chores back in the Kingdom. It looked very comfortable to move in and durable. Theirs varied in color and pattern and went down to their ankles, while mine was very simple canvas cloth and stopped at the calf. The woman's shirt was covered with pictures of cats, while the mans was solid navy blue and the young lady who let me in had a shirt covered with a rainbow of hearts and paw prints.

The man hurried toward the door, but the woman paused at one of the desks to search in her bag for something before she turned to talk to us, "Hey Jamie, everybody is all taken care of back there except for the dogs in pavilion G. There are a couple of potential biters that came in today, so Bryson's gonna need an assist to bring them outside once more before you leave . . ." she looked up from her bag and noticed me with 'Jamie', "Oh, well hello! I didn't realize we still had a guest."

"She got here right when I was locking up." Jamie explained, "I can help her, then I'll give Bryson a hand. You go ahead."

"Thanks," the woman sighed pulling a ring of jangling metal keys out of the bag and pausing to lean on the desk a moment for support, "I've got to go pick up Emma from basketball practice. So I've gotta run," she chuckled to herself, "well I guess I mean waddle. Not much running happening these days." She patted her bulging tummy gently.

"Only three weeks left to go." Jamie assured her.

"Yup, almost there!" the woman replied tiredly, and smiled before hoisting her tote to her shoulder and waddling towards the door. "See you tomorrow."

"Good night," Jamie called before focusing her attention back to me. "Sorry about that! So, *who* are we looking for today?"

Shaking with anticipation, I deliriously blurted out my story, "Pari, I'm looking for Pari! He's my guide. I had left him out at a bench this morning when I went to meet the governor and when I got back someone had torn his vest and he was gone. I looked and looked for him until I ended up under the street and then this boy, Danny, told me that he had summoned the Animal Control and they had picked up Pari. Then Danny tried to take the King's gift from me, but thankfully a street soldier saved me. But then the soldier tricked me into stealing apples for him, only they were rotten. Then Cowboy and this lady, Molly, showed up with food and they gave me this jacket and told me how to get here."

I realized how crazy I was sounding, and by the look on Jamie's face, I could tell she thought so as well. I took a deep breath trying to collect myself, and with tears brimming my eyes I pleaded, "Please help me find Pari. Do you have him here?"

Bewildered, Jamie compassionately placed her hand on mine, "Hey, it's gonna be ok." she assured, "If Pari is here, we'll find him. Usually, I would have you search our database first, but the computers are already shut down for the day, so why don't you come with me, I'll walk you through and we can take a look, ok?"

She stood up and I followed her to one of the desks, where she had me write my name in a 'Visitor Log', then she gave me a blue badge of some sort on which she had written my name. We continued to the door the man and woman had used earlier. As she opened it, I could hear a chorus of barks and yips coming from a long hallway. None of them sounded familiar.

We entered a long room filled with cages; I shuddered, horrified that Pari could possibly be locked up as a prisoner like this! As we passed each one, a dog inside barked or whimpered at us from behind the bars.

"Do any of these dogs look familiar?" Jamie gently questioned. I shook my head.

Jamie pried, trying to help, "Well can you describe Pari for me?"

"He's big and white with long fur, he's very patient and calm and kind." I said feeling more and more discouraged, none that we had seen were anything like Pari.

"Hmm," Jamie paused with a concerned look, "there is *one* other place we can check." She didn't sound very hopeful.

She led me around a corner to another hallway and paused before a glass case, "These are pictures of some of the animals that have come in recently who have not yet passed their screening, or are deemed as," She paused searching for the right word, "*aggressive*, so they have not been released for viewing yet. None of these look like your Pari, do they?"

I squinted, scanning the small images in the case and my eyes fell on a picture that shattered me, "Pari . . . ," I lamented, placing my hand on the glass, happy to see that he was here, but devastated by the image before me. My gentle guide and comforter muzzled, confined, and labeled with a sign that said "Beware: Use Extreme Caution".

Reaching into the case Jamie pulled the picture down and held it closer for me to confirm, "*This* one looks like Pari?"

I shut my eyes and nodded; I couldn't look at it any longer.

Rubbing her ear nervously, she explained, "Um, I'll be right back. I'm going to go talk to Bryson, he's our vet who's been on duty since this afternoon and he would have done Pari's screening. I'll go see what the scoop is. It might take a few minutes. He has," She fidgeted uncomfortably before continuing, trying to put it delicately "*other* duties that he may be in the middle of. Are you alright waiting right here while I go check it out?" she waved her hand to a few chairs against the wall.

I didn't really like the sound of the 'other duties' that may be going on. And the way it made Jamie squirm to even talk about it, did not help! Just the same, I didn't really have a choice, so I nodded my consent and retreated to the chairs.

Jamie hurried to the doors at the end of the hall marked with a big letter G. A sign on the door read: Caution: Authorized Personnel Only. She pulled a key from around her neck and used it to unlock the door. As it opened, loud snarling and snapping caused Jamie to stay close to the wall as she advanced further into the room. I could hear her calming voice cooing, "Hey big guy, you're all right. I'm just passing through.", before the heavy door slowly closed and clicked, reengaging the lock.

I lowered myself pensively onto the edge of the first chair, unwilling to get comfortable while I knew Pari was somewhere beyond the locked door being held captive. I could sense that Jamie was a very good person and by the way she had spoken to the dog that was snarling at her, I could tell that she cared for them. However, why they kept all these animals confined in cages was beyond my understanding.

Several minutes passed slowly. The dogs in the pavilion had settled down and were quiet now that they thought everyone had gone. No one was there to listen to their plea.

In the lonely, washed-out light of the hallway I slowly pulled the messenger bag onto my lap and opened the flap. Laboriously, I lifted the heavy pearl into view. Partially transparent now, there was only a faint glow from within. The mist inside swirled ever so slightly, revealing my hand below it.

I lowered the pearl back into the bag with a sigh of discouragement.

The angry barking on the other side of the door resumed just before the door opened and Jamie slipped back out to join me in the hallway. As she approached, I stood up expectantly, "Did you find Pari?"

"Well, maybe." She admitted more hopefully, "we do have a big, white sheepdog that was brought in here late this morning. He fits your description, but we will still need you to verify whether he is your dog or not. So that will be the *first* step, ok?"

I nodded anxiously. We walked toward the door to pavilion G. Jamie was explaining that this was where they kept the dogs that were either aggressive or were not otherwise able to be out in the viewing pavilion. She warned that I needed to stay close to her and not go near any of the cages until directed. I nodded at her, but hardly listened to a word she was saying. I was so fixated on getting behind that door and closer to Pari. By the time we had gotten to the door, and she had unlocked it, I had quite forgotten everything she had said.

The sudden snarling and barking made me jump when we entered the room. I saw a ferocious black beast throwing itself against the bars and snapping at us, saliva flying from his frothy jowls.

Jamie urged me gently to keep moving past the first few cages, each separated by a wall of solid blocks, and paused next to the third. There inside waiting, with his usual expression of patience and calm sat my Kingdom guide!

The sleek black dog from the first cell continued to viciously attack the bars in vain. His wild barking echoed off the walls. Pari, seeing Jamie and I pressed against the wall, and the atmosphere of chaos that the other dog was creating, gave one sharp rebuking bark. The other dog responded, dropping down from the bars onto his paws, whining and licking his jowls apologetically, before turning in a circle and settling himself attentively near the door, suddenly peaceful and obedient. Jamie's jaw dropped. This seemed more shocking to her than the mad, threatening dog that had been there moments before.

"That's my Pari!" I murmured appreciatively, kneeling at the door of the cage that held him, I reached through the bars to caress his beautiful shaggy face. I was not shocked in the least.

"I've never seen *that* before!" Jamie mused, shaking her head, still dumbfounded, she did not stop me from greeting Pari. "What just happened?"

"Pari spoke to him," I smiled, relieved to be reunited with my guide.

Humoring me, Jamie chuckled and asked, "And what did he say?"

I looked up at her and translated Pari's gentle command, "Peace, brother wolf."

Jamie's face went slack, as though something long forgotten had just been brought to memory. "St. Francis and the Wolf", she whispered to herself, gazing at Pari.

Pari responded to her with a soft affirming yip and a nod of his head. Her assessment must have been correct, though I had never heard of this story before. "What is St. Francis and the wolf?" I questioned.

"Oh, it's an old story my grandmother used to tell me." Jaime began, "The legend tells of a peaceful monk named St. Francis and how he saved the village of Gubbio from a ferocious wolf. The wolf was hurt and could no longer hunt so had turned to easier prey like the townsfolk and their live-stock. Moved with compassion for the injured animal, St. Francis cared for the wolf and tamed it. The people of Gubbio forgave their enemy and they lived in peace for the rest of its days. Upon the death of the wolf years later the entire village mourned the loss of their friend, Brother Wolf. It's a great story of forgiveness and peace." Jamie turned her gaze to the black dog who was staring desperately back at her. "I wonder . . ." she murmured.

Suddenly the door leading to rooms further back opened and a man wearing a white coat entered staring down at a larger version of the black boxes I'd seen others obsessively gazing at.

Looking up from the box, he paused, noticing the unusual quiet in the room. With a puzzled expression he looked over at the black dog, then at Jamie, "What happened to him?"

Unsure of how she could possibly explain what really happened, she shrugged instead and inquired, "Bryson, do you think it's possible that he may be injured or sick?"

Bryson responded, nodding, "It's *very* probable, it's just that no one could get close enough to check him out. His owners surrendered him. The guys who picked him up this afternoon had a heck of a time even getting him here. He's on the docket tomorrow to be sedated so we could see if there is an issue, but from what it *was* looking like, he is probably going to have to be euthanized."

I didn't know what that word meant, but in unison, both Pari and the dog responded with a whimpering plea at hearing the assessment. The black dog lay down and placed his head on his paws looking up with sad eyes, as the man, called Bryson, curiously stepped closer, intrigued by the sudden change.

"But maybe there is hope for you yet." Bryson pondered out loud. The black dog stood, beseeching the man's mercy, he limped closer to the door before sitting attentively again.

"Hmm. Interesting." The man, still careful to remain several feet from the cage, crouched down to look closer. The dog submissively lowered to his belly and pawed at the ground. "When the night crew gets in, we'll come back and check this guy out."

Standing and turning back toward us, using the black box to point, Bryson redirected his focus, "But he's not why you asked me to come up here, is he?"

"No." Jamie admitted, "I was hoping we could ask you about this dog. She calls him Pari. Obviously, they know each other, but what can you tell us about him? Why isn't he out in the viewing pavilion?"

Referring to the black box he held in his hand, he breathed out a loud exasperated sigh, "That's where this gets a bit tricky. So, this dog was brought in as a potential biter and was reported for viciously attacking a group of young men. But nothing I have observed with this animal indicates *any* aggressive behavior. He's been a complete gentleman." Looking up from the box in his hands, "The only issue that we are coming across is that upon intake when we *tried* to administer vaccinations, we couldn't."

"He wouldn't let you?" Jamie inquired.

"No, it's not that! He let us try just fine. But nothing would penetrate, even the vaccinations administered nasally just dripped right out! It's like his body repelled them." He sighed throwing his hand up, "Without the required vaccinations we are not able to release him."

I had no understanding of what they were talking about, but the last part caught my attention, and I stood up, concerned, "What do you mean not able to release him?"

Tenderly trying to explain, Bryson lowered the black box, and looked very seriously at me, "Well, until we can be assured that an animal has had all the required vaccinations and is properly registered, we cannot allow them to leave the shelter. But tomorrow if your parents or guardians bring in his vaccination record and registration . . ."

I interrupted, "But Pari *is* my guardian."

Bryson and Jamie exchanged a concerned look before Jamie took over. "Why don't you go home tonight. Pari is safe here, and now you know where he is.", she tried to assure me. "Tomorrow morning you and your mom or dad or *whoever* takes care of you can come back and we can talk it over with the director, ok?"

There was no use arguing with them, and I did not know *what* else to do. They let me say goodbye to Pari and Jamie led me toward the door. She called over her shoulder, "We still need to bring these two outside, are you able to handle it on your own now?"

"Na, we still have to follow procedure. I'll grab the control poles and meet you back here?" Bryson responded.

"Sounds like a date." Jamie joked back. I could not help but notice Bryson blush as he turned to leave the room.

I looked back at Pari's calm face behind the bars before being ushered out and back through the hallways to the entrance. Jamie grabbed a pamphlet from her desk and with a pen she circled a set of numbers on the back and wrote her name next to it before handing it to me. "Your parents can just call this number and ask for Jamie, and I can get things set up. We open at 8 o'clock tomorrow morning."

I took the papers from her, but I knew I did not have time to wait. "I have to get Pari out of here tonight, but how?" I thought out loud to myself as the doors were locked securely behind me with a loud click and Jamie disappeared again to go help Bryson.

I walked along the perimeter of the building looking desperately for another entrance. Finding none, I was following alongside the high fence that continued around a large open yard hoping there would be a break at some point. When a door inside the fenced off area opened, Jamie and Bryson emerged leading Pari. Each of them held a long pole with a loop on the end that was loosely draped around his neck.

"Pari!" I shouted, happy to see him outside of the building. Suddenly pulling the poles out of the hands of the workers, Pari bolted towards me with the poles trailing behind him. Bryson and Jamie, caught off guard, scrambled to catch up with him. It was no use. He shook the poles free, and they were left behind. With a sudden burst of speed Pari streaked toward the fence where I stood. Not slowing down, he leapt and defying the existence of the chain fence between us, he passed through it and gracefully landed at my side.

Jamie and Bryson had almost made it to the fence when they stopped short in shock at the unlikely phenomenon they had just witnessed. For a moment I locked eyes with Jamie, while Bryson shook the fence looking for an unseen hole or opening. Pari and I turned and took flight.

We soon found ourselves back at the bus stop just as the bus carriage was arriving and we scrambled on board. The same woman that had let me off earlier still sat behind the big wheel and looked curiously at Pari and I.

Grasping in my bag for the card, I performed the ritual of tapping the box and flopped into the nearest seat. The driver looked back at us in her mirror about to say something, but then shook her head and decided against it. To my relief she reached over and pulled the door closed instead.

21

Flight of the Fugitives

As THE BUS PULLED away from the side of the road, Pari and I watched out the window as Jamie and Bryson burst through the front doors of Animal Control frantically looking around and calling out for Pari and me, unaware that we were watching them from inside the bus that was rolling away.

For a moment I felt a tinge of guilt for running, but now that Pari was an escaped prisoner I knew we would have to keep running. Being back with Pari was worth the fugitive status and I wrapped my arms around him and silently sobbed grateful tears into his thick fur.

When I finally lifted my head, in response to a gentle nudge from his cold, wet nose, the bus had pulled up to a landing and had stopped. Pari stood and I followed him down the stairs and out into the cold evening air. Thankfully, the rain had stopped for the moment, but strong gusts of wind remained, and the air felt heavy.

We stopped in front of a wall that displayed a large map. I tried looking up at it, but my head throbbed, and my eyes hurt trying to focus, so I wearily let them close while Pari studied its many-colored lines to determine our next move. The bus we had been on pulled away and began heading back toward the heart of the city. Pari led me to a carriage that was waiting nearby in an open arbor. I was relieved when it pointed *away* from the city and the sea of Lake Michigan. I felt no resistance to us leaving its shadows behind us.

In the dying light of the day as the bus pulled away from the arbor, I pulled the journal from my pack and wrote:

> This crooked place seems bent to separate
>
> The guide from the messenger to seal our fate.
>
> Where bloated pride leads the shallow of
>
> heart,
>
> And faith and hope are given no part.
>
> Wicked doubts whisper and addictions taint.
>
> The need screams louder, yet the message
>
> grows faint.
>
> Urgency guides my weary steps,
>
> Weighted by promises I have not yet kept...

Slipping the journal and writing stick back into my bag I pulled it securely between Pari and I. Curling into a ball I leaned into him, and blissful sleep overtook me. Time passed. Unaware of what direction we traveled or how long we rode, I awakened to Pari's wet nose nuzzling my cheek.

In a dreamy trance I followed him off one carriage and onto another. Performing the card ritual out of sheer memory, Pari and I moved to a seat at the back of the nearly empty carriage and resumed my position, dropping off again into slumber. The carriage rumbled further and further away from the city, as a compelling force pulled us away from the monstrous buildings and glaring lights.

22

At the Crossroads

ROUSING, I BLINKED MY heavy eyelids awake and stretched my aching limbs. Pari still sat attentively beside me gazing out the window at the darkening fields being dusted with white snow that had replaced the earlier rain. The carriage was now empty except for the driver, Pari and I. It screeched to a halt before a dimly lit brick building in what appeared to be a village. Pari leapt from the seat and led me down the aisle to the front of the bus. We stepped down onto a quiet walkway.

Several ornate black streetlamps illuminated the snowflakes as they whirled around the short pole and were whisked away out of sight by the wind. The driver of the bus carriage made a wide turn and went back the way he had come. This must have been the furthest they went and now they were returning to the city, leaving us, the last passengers, at the furthest reaches of the route. The sound of the carriage's screeching and purring faded, and stillness dropped around us like the blanket of snow covering this quiet village.

The lamps trailing away from us lit the fronts of darkened shops that lined the quaint street, and their glow appeared to flicker in the swirling snow. Nothing else stirred. The empty carriages that had been left alongside the street were silently sleeping under their snowy sheets. What a contrast to the bustling, crowded city we had left behind. But even in the quiet of the village, I was unsettled; the urge to flee remained. I felt that we were not yet far enough away from the perceived danger, nor did I have the clarity of mind to stop and plan our next move. So, we continued our escape, away from the lights of the village and into the approaching darkness.

The last shreds of light faded from the sky and, in its absence, the air around me began to take on the piercing chill of the winter night. We trudged on. I looked down at Pari, obediently trudging beside me and out loud I tried to reassure both of us, "We will find someone, Pari, but we cannot go back there." I shook my head, glancing over my shoulder and let out a sigh of frustration. Pari sniffed and shook his shaggy head in agreement. I guess he had had enough of the city too.

We marched, staying close to the edge of the road where the hard pavement gave way to a small strip of gravel that made a soft crunch with every step.

Pari padded along quietly, but the whistling of the wind and the crunch, crunch, crunch, of my steps echoed in my ears. Mesmerized by the sound for a long time, I began counting them, one to ten, then starting my count at one again. I am unsure of how long we walked through the dark countryside. Eventually, all I could focus on was the decision to take ten more steps.

After many, many sets of ten, I noticed my bottom lip was trembling uncontrollably. I wrapped my arms around myself, and my whole body shuddered. So cold! A wicked wind had picked up and swirled my hair around my head and stung my cheeks with icy shards of a furious blizzard.

Tucking my chin into the collar of the coat, I pulled the red hood up over my head to try and shield my face from the snow that was being pelted relentlessly against me by the angry wind. The temperature plummeted even further.

We walked on. Pari and I pressed into the cold night, and I reached out my hand to find warmth within his shaggy fur. The darkness clung so close that I could barely see, so I kept my eyes nearly shut, relying on my other senses. Only the sound of the crunching gravel beneath my feet, and feeling Pari's body pressing against me, let me know that I was still on the edge of the road.

Every so often, in a moment of icy clarity, questions plagued my mind, "How long have we been running away?", "Where are we running to?", "Should we turn back?", and "How far is it to get back to the city?" I knew none of the answers. Pari tugging at my hand, still buried in his fur, urging me to keep moving into the unknown. He was right, even if we did turn back, we had no place to go?

Step after step, inch after inch my faithful guide and I did the only thing we could do, which was take one step, and then another, and then another.

The rhythmic crunch, crunch eventually changed to kicking through small drifts of snow that had started to form on the side of the road. The wind wrapped around my ankles and the snow it carried stuck to my skin.

My knees were trembling so badly I was finding it hard to remain on the edge of the road and several times my foot slipped onto the steep snow-covered grass, and I started to slide down into the ditch next to the road. Catching myself, it took all my strength to crawl and claw on my hands and knees back up onto the shoulder of the road.

Finally, we approached a crossroad, the path no longer went straight. To continue we would have to choose which direction to take, to the left or to the right. I was unsure where either of them would lead us. I slowed down, disoriented, and lost in indecision, when my feet stumbled for the third time and my knees buckled, no longer willing to hold me up. I lay in a crumpled heap at the crossroads, unable to go any further, my strength had been fully spent.

Pari circled around behind me and lay down whimpering softly, and I felt a strange comfort and warmth wrap around me. Half on the grass and half on the gravel, Pari's warm fur pressed up against me as he tried to wrap his body around mine shielding me from the wind. I do not know how much time passed. But eventually the shivering stopped. The sound of the wind, and the sound of Pari's breath beside me grew quieter, as a strange sleep began to overtake me.

Just before I was about to succumb, I noticed a brightness begin to surround us through my closed eyelids, even before I heard something approaching, I felt Pari's head raise. A wave of snow blew over us as something large moved past us. It was the sudden screeching sound, then a soft crunching noise of it slowly returning that awoke me out of my trancelike state. I could not move. Through my closed eyelids I could sense that the brightness had returned. There was a creaking sound like a door opening and then another.

Above the wind I heard a woman's voice yell, "What is it?", then another voice, a man's, but closer to us responded, "It's a dog and", he paused, "and something else."

Footsteps approached, crunching through the snow, "O my gosh, Mol, come here!" he yelled back over his shoulder, calling for the woman, panic and concern entering his voice, "It's a person!" The sound of the footsteps quickened. Pari was now standing above me, growling softly as a warning, maintaining his vow as my protector.

"It's OK boy, we are here to help.", the man's voice pleaded. I could not move to look and see, but there was something familiar about the drawl in his voice.

Another set of footsteps approached, and another familiar voice gasped, "Oh my gosh, Luke, I think it's a kid!" I felt Pari lower his head closer to my body and his growl get deeper.

"Let me help, please.", the man had now crouched at the side of the road, speaking as softly as he could over the howl of the wind. My defender, convinced of the man's sincerity, whined softly and backed away letting the man approach.

"Oh, Luke, it's the girl from the alley! It's Anya! That's my old coat I gave her." Horror filled the woman's voice, "Is she . . . ?", her voice trailed off.

I felt him gently roll me over, and a warm hand brush the hair from my face. Recognizing the voices from earlier in the alleyway with Joe, I tried to speak, but could only manage a soft moan. Relieved, the man replied, "No, but she's freezing. We need to get her into the truck!"

I felt strong arms surround me and lift me from the freezing ground, "You too boy. Come on." He called to Pari as he ran back toward the truck holding me tightly. A creaking door opened, and the woman's voice came from inside the truck, "Here give her to me." I felt myself being gently lowered into the woman's waiting arms as she pulled me into the warmth of the compartment, making room for Pari to scramble up beside me before the man jumped in and closed the door shutting out the wind and snow.

There was a moment of silence as the warmth melted around us and Luke and Molly caught their breath. I had remembered their names, but I still could not move or say anything.

"How did she get all the way out here?" Molly finally asked, taking my icy hands in hers and trying to warm them.

"I have no idea?" Luke added. "And where did this dog come from?"

"Don't you remember? *You* gave her the directions to Animal Control. She must have found Pari there." Molly said, trying to piece the puzzle together.

"Pari?" Luke questioned. Pari whined appreciatively in response. Luke chucked despite the desperate situation. I could feel Pari's body move next to me as Luke ruffled his fur and asked, "What do we do now?"

"Should we try to make it back into the city and bring her to the hospital?" Molly pondered. Pari groaned and put his head down on my shoulder.

"Pari's right." Luke affirmed, "The expressway was already closed because of the storm, and with that wind picking up, it's going to be nearly impossible going back the way we came."

"He told you *all* that?" Molly challenged.

"Well, no, but *yes*." Luke stammered, trying to explain, "I mean, I just get the *feeling* that he doesn't want us to go back."

I felt Pari sit up and lean away from me and from Luke's reaction, he must have licked Luke's face to thank him, "Ok, OK your welcome!" Luke continued, "We're only a few miles from home Molly, let's bring Anya and Pari there and then we'll call the hospital and ask them what to do." I felt the carriage shift slightly, "Here wrap this around her." An extra layer was wrapped around me from the man's coat.

My mind was alert, and I could hear them, but I still could not open my eyes or move so I lay there draped across Molly's lap. Wave after wave of warmth started to blow over me, my world melted, and in relief I let myself drift to sleep. We could have been traveling for hours but I'm sure it was only a minute or two before we arrived at their home. I was carried inside.

Opening the door in front of us, Molly called out in an urgent whisper, "Nana, Nana Betty!"

An older voice came from a room nearby, "Molly, Luke? I'm so glad you made it back, I was beginning to worry when the weather took a turn. Oh my . . . .!" The older woman's voice did not conceal her shock as she entered the room where we were and saw my limp body being carried in.

"We found her out there on the side of the road, Ma." Luke explained quickly.

"Nana, could you please get the extra blankets out of the girl's closet? I'm calling the hospital to see what we should do." Molly's voice sounded muffled as she called from behind another wall.

I felt myself sinking into a soft, warm place. Moments later the older woman, who I guessed was Luke's mother, returned.

"Thanks Ma." Luke said softly as the old woman's motherly hands removed the wet jacket I wore and tucked the blankets around me. She gently unlaced and removed my boots and stockings.

"Luke, who is she and where did she come from?" Luke's 'Ma' murmured softly, gingerly wrapping her warm hands around my exposed toes.

"Actually, her name is Anya, and we met her earlier today when we were handing out meals in the city." Luke admitted, sheepishly answering her. "Molly gave her that old red jacket of hers, but I have no idea how she got all the way out here or why. We were the only ones crazy enough to be out traveling on old Highway 1 tonight."

"Well, praise the Lord that He made your paths cross again when He did!" the old woman whispered in awe, then added somberly, "She wouldn't have made it much longer out there in this storm. They said on the news that it wasn't going to let up for a few days!"

Starting to shiver under the blankets, I managed to control my eyelids long enough to begin to open them and see the woman's kind, plump face gazing down at me along with the man's familiar face next to her still wearing the worn hat on his head.

"Cowboy" I whispered weakly in greeting. And as my vision faded and I fell into a deep sleep, a relieved smile passed over the cowboys face, and 'Nana Betty' smiled proudly at her son.

23

Slumber & Snow, Soup & Shampoo

SOMETIME DURING THE NIGHT, a sound, which was completely foreign to *my* ears, woke me from my deep slumber. My body, warm under the pile of blankets, did not yet dare move, but through my barely opened eyes I could see the cozy chamber. The flickering golden light of a fireplace nearby illuminated the sitting room and a flaxen haired child in a long nightgown stumbled sleepily across the room in search of her mother who had fallen asleep, curled up in a stuffed chair, keeping vigil over me through the night.

"Mama?" she whispered again sweetly, climbing up next to her mother. Molly pulled her in close, draping a blanket around them both. The child snuggled into her mother's arms, and they both drifted back into slumber with a contented sigh.

Witnessing the tender moment, bathed in the glow of the fire made me smile dreamily and with a similar contented sigh my weary mind drifted away as well, as if I too had been drawn safely into a mother's soft, warm embrace. I slept deeply.

I had never known nor seen what a *family* was like, other than Marita and I and the other servants who worked with me in the palace. The beautiful image of mother and child nestled together had struck a chord and when I opened my eyes again hours later, I searched the room for them. However, many, many hours had passed, and it was already midday by the time I had emerged from my restorative slumber. Muffled sounds of people moving about and talking came from an adjacent room, along with several light, sweet voices giggling from somewhere above. Someone had draped a cool rag across my forehead and the blankets had been re-tucked around me with care.

My body ached as I slowly sat up, pulling the rag from my head, and looked around. The couch where I had been laid was in a small cozy chamber with a sitting area. Several chairs and small tables were arranged throughout the room and although the fire in the fireplace had died down, the room was still pleasantly warm.

Through the windows I could see that outside the wind still howled and snow swirled furiously as the storm continued to rage on. By some unlikely circumstance, miraculously, there I was, safe, warm and being cared for.

Pari, who had been loyally lying alongside the couch, sat up when I did and looked attentively up at me. Beside him was a bowl of water and a plate that held a large ham bone, untouched.

The homey familiar smell of bread baking and a savory chicken and roasted garlic aroma awakened my senses and I tried to breathe in deeply, but with the conditions of past few days still affecting me, a powerful sneeze propelled me back into the couch, where I sat dizzily for a few moments trying to regain my bearings.

Drawn by the sound of my stirring, three figures peered in at me from the next room. Above me, on an upper level, I could hear the pattering of children's footsteps running across the floor and then down the stairs into the room I was in. Two rosy cheeked faces peeked through the old wooden railings on the stairs.

Plucking a thin paper handkerchief from a nearby table, Molly cheerfully approached, "You're finally awake!" She looked relieved as she sat on the edge of the chair nearest me and held it out. "Hi Anya, it's me, Molly. Luke and I met you and Joe yesterday in the alley?", she tentatively asked, seeing how much I recalled.

Gratefully taking the handkerchief and wiping my nose, I nodded, and weakly clearing my throat, responded hoarsely, "Yes, I remember you."

Smiling, she acknowledged the progress, "Ok, good!" and then continuing she introduced the rest of the family, "This is Luke's mom, Betty. We call her Nana Betty."

Nana Betty stepped into the room, with a gentle, sage-like smile, wiping her hands on a kitchen towel. "It is a pleasure to meet you, Miss Anya." She said with a pleasant drawl to her words.

Motioning toward the stairs, Luke summoned the two small figures who were crouched there, anxiously peering through the rails. "You can come on down now, girls." They looked as though they had been reminded several times to stay upstairs and let me rest. Now, finally able to meet the curious guest in their home, they scrambled down the stairs and joined their parents. The slightly taller one hid sheepishly behind her mother and the smaller one leaped into her father's arms. I recognized the smaller girl as the sleepy flaxen haired child from the previous night.

"These are our girls, Lauren and Callie." Luke introduced proudly, first ruffling the hair of the girl peeking out from behind her mother and then looking to the girl in his arms. "They couldn't wait to meet you!"

"Hi, Anya." Lauren beamed, a bit more bravely, but still clinging to her mother's arm.

"I'm four!" Callie blurted out excitedly holding out four fingers, "I like your dog! Can I pet 'im?"

I laughed with them all, and gladly complied, "Hello Lauren. And thank you Callie, of course you can."

Luke set Callie down and she and Lauren knelt near Pari and he happily rose to meet them and lapped their faces. It seemed that children were naturally drawn to Pari, and he to them. The bond was immediate and affectionate.

"Are you hungry, Anya?" Nana Betty offered, "I've got some chicken noodle soup I'm just finishin' up and some fresh baked bread."

I nodded eagerly and attempted shakily to get up. Nana Betty raised her hand to stop me, "You just stay put right there, little missy. I'll get it for you."

Nana Betty headed into the next room accompanied by Luke and the girls happily lay on the floor petting Pari, and Pari happily let them!

Molly gathered a few items from a nearby table and sat down next to me, "Now that you're awake, let's check your temp again. You were burning up this morning."

Scanning a device across my forehead she murmured "This will just take a second." The device made a sharp tweet. Molly glanced down at it, read the numbers it posted, and looking pleased, she placed her other hand on my forehead lingering for a moment before she happily sighed, "Praise God! Looks like your fever broke! How are you feeling?"

Honestly assessing how I felt, I responded, "Tired, but thankful."

"Ok," Molly chuckled, "good." She continued her examination, taking my hands in hers and looking them over front and back. She noted the scratches that were left when I clawed my way out of the ditch. With a slight frown she moved on to my fingertips, squeezing them gently, "Can you feel this?"

"Yes."

"Does it hurt?"

"No."

Molly reached up and brushed my tangled hair away from my ears. "No red or white patches.", she noted. "Are they tender at all?" she asked, gently touching the tops of my earlobes.

"No." I answered again.

"Hmm. Good." with each part of the examination, her concerned expression softened a bit and was replaced with relief.

"How about your toes, any numbness or pain?"

I looked down at my bare toes and wiggled them. I shook my head, "My feet *are* sore, but that's from all the walking I've done since I arrived. My toes feel fine."

"Well, I kind of expected that, actually. Nana said that even when she took your boots and stockings off last night, your feet were still warm. Those must be some well insulated boots! You'll have to tell me where you got them, I could use a pair like that!" she jested.

Nana returned carrying a tray with a steaming bowl of soup and a small plate of fresh sliced bread, spread thickly with melting butter and a glass of milk on it. My eyes widened with excitement over the comforting sight for an empty stomach.

"You go ahead and eat. Then how about a warm bath?" Molly invited. "We installed a great classic soaker tub in Nana's bathroom!"

"That would probably be a good idea." I said, feeling slightly embarrassed glancing down at my stringy hair and dirty fingernails.

Standing up to leave, Molly put her hand on my shoulder, and smiled assuredly, "I'll go get things ready for you. You'll feel much better after some of Nana's special chicken noodle soup and a warm bath."

Molly headed up the stairs as Nana came over and set up a tray in front of me.

The girls had moved the dish of water and ham bone in front of Pari, and kissing his shaggy face, they had gotten up and made their way into the kitchen at the sound of their father calling them. Through the doorway I could see Luke setting small bowls of soup on a long dining table for them.

Now that I had food as well, Pari settled down next to the ham bone that had been left for him and started to gnaw on it contentedly.

I slowly relished the first few spoonsful of soup, letting the savory garlic and dill in the broth trickle across my tongue. Next, I enjoyed the soft, sweetness of the carrots with the slight crunch of the diced onion and the chewy noodles and chicken. I closed my eyes as the tastes mingled together.

Maybe it was my hunger, but since my arrival, it was the closest to the food of the Kingdom I had tasted yet. The rest of the bowl of soup went quickly and soon I had sopped up the last of the broth with the crisp crusts of the warm, soft bread.

Nana Betty peeked out from the kitchen, smiling, she emerged with another bowl, "How about another round?"

I nodded, and gratefully accepted. It had been since the previous morning at Lulu's that we had eaten a meal, plus the soup was delicious, so a second helping was a welcome sight. She set the bowl and another slice of buttered bread down on the tray in front of me. Taking the empty bowl away, she paused and leaned over to rub Pari's fur, "You all were hungry, huh?"

Pari responded with a huff that sent the fur on his muzzle fluttering and went back to gnawing contentedly. Chuckling at Pari's reaction, Nana Betty turned to me and asked, "Mind if I join you?"

Forgetting my manners, I mumbled over a mouthful of bread, "I would like that."

"Alright," she smiled warmly. "I'll grab a bowl myself and be right back." Nana headed back into the kitchen where Luke had the girls giggling at him slurping up noodles noisily, seeing his mother enter he playfully straightened up and exaggeratedly wiped his mouth. Nana Betty played along, giving him a playful stern look and wagged her finger at him. The girls nearly fell off their chairs giggling.

"You got in trouble from Nana!!" Callie squealed.

"Remember your manners, Daddy." Lauren scolded, composing herself very ladylike. Grinning, she shook her head, "That's not how to eat in a fancy restaurant like this!"

Copying her big sister, Callie nodded and followed suit sitting up rigidly, trying hard not to giggle.

Raising his eyebrows Luke replied very formally, using a stuffy accent, "Oh! Is that so? Many apologies, my dear ladies!" He daintily held his spoon with his pinkie out. "How's this?"

This was too much for Callie and Lauren and they collapsed into a fit of giggles. Callie toppled her spoon and half full soup bowl into her lap.

"Waiter, waiter? Clean up at table one, please!" Luke joked, then seeing Callie's downcast expression, he dropped the act, "Comon' Peanut, let's get you cleaned up." She lifted her arms to her father, and he scooped her up into his embrace. Something deep within my heart stirred.

Nana Betty emerged from the kitchen again, carrying a bowl of soup and sat down on a chair next to me. "How's the soup?"

Fascinated by the playful scene from the kitchen, I was determined to show better manners myself and wiped my mouth on a paper napkin before responding to Nana Betty's question. My ravenous hunger was subsiding and with another bowl of soup to enjoy, more slowly this time, I was truly looking forward to spending a few minutes with her. She reminded me, in many ways, of Marita, whom I missed terribly.

"It is delicious! The garlic and dill made the broth especially tasty. And the tarragon was a very nice touch." I complimented her. "And there is something tangy that I just can't figure out."

"Oh, it's a squeeze of fresh lemon." She winked, letting me in on her secret ingredient. "I'm impressed you could identify those herbs and spices though!"

"Well, I've grown up in the kitchen watching the chef.", I modestly explained, stirring my soup, thinking fondly of the jolly face of the chef in the Kingdom, delicately tasting a dish and joyfully announcing the name of the spice it still needed. When I was not busy with my other duties, I would run and fetch them for him from the rack in the pantry, so I had become quite familiar with their subtle smells and flavors. "I will have to tell him about adding lemon to his soup when I get back." I smiled at her.

"Are you from Chicago then?" she casually inquired, blowing on her hot soup.

"Oh no, Pari and I arrived in the city only a few days ago. We uh . . ." I answered quickly, then grew silent, unsure of what to say next.

Nana Betty was in no hurry and sat relaxed, yet attentive sipping her soup, giving me ample time to answer.

Hesitantly, I continued, "We were dropped off on the pier several days ago. We have been sent to deliver a . . ." I gasped and a sickening feeling came over me and my voice dropped to a desperate whisper, ". . . message."

Frantically I searched the couch where I had been laying, "My bag! Where is the King's gift!?"

In her eyes I could see that she was alarmed by my sudden frantic behavior, but very calmly Nana Betty set down her bowl of soup on an end table and when Luke and Molly appeared from the kitchen and from the upstairs, drawn by my panicked, raised voice, Nana Betty raised her hand calmly and they slowed and paused at the fringes of the room.

My trembling hand reached for my shoulder and rubbed against the painful raw patch of flesh on which the bag no longer hung. I felt sick to my stomach, where could it be? Out in the snow? Perhaps when I fell it had dropped and been left behind?

"I've lost it *again!*" I moaned to myself, then turning to Luke and Molly, "Thank you for your kindness," I began, wiping away the large tears that were beginning to well in my eyes, "but I must go now. I must find my bag!"

I was struggling to rise, when Nana Betty's hand pressed down on mine, calming me, "Anya, you were wearing your bag under you coat when you got here last night and after I took off your coat, I set your bag *right here* next to you and it's been safe ever since." She quietly explained, and never taking her eyes off me, she reached down next to the couch with the other hand and lifted the messenger bag into view.

My heart throbbed with relief as the kind old woman set the bag lightly into my lap. Grasping it, I hugged it close to my chest for several moments gulping back my sobs, while the family looked on and exchanged perplexed glances. Catching my breath, I sat up and decidedly draped the bag back over my shoulder, wincing as the strap dug into its familiar place; I was so thankful that I had not lost it out in the storm that I did not mind the pain. I still did not know what I was going to do next, but at least I was not having to go back out into the snow and retrace my steps to retrieve the King's gift this time.

Slowly approaching, Molly held a large towel and some clothing in her hands. "How about that bath?", she proposed gently.

Nodding, I agreed, "Thank you Molly, I think that is just what I need." I was anxious to wash the grime of the past days' trials from me and make a fresh start.

Slowly, with Molly's help I rose to my feet, and we left the sitting room, went through a kitchen and into a large room that held a red stuffed chair, a bed neatly made with a beautiful, flowered pink and white quilt, and a stand that held a large box with a black window on the front of it.

Molly was explaining, "This used to be the old dining room, but when Nana Betty had her knee replacement surgery a little over a year ago, we converted this and the attached bathroom into a 'mother-in-law' suite while she recovered. But we found we really enjoyed having her close and she loved the extra time with the girls that it just made sense to make it permanent. That is when we installed this tub for her! It really fits this old house anyway!", she laughed, opening a door that led to a smaller room.

The crisp white room we entered was elegant and simple with a window that was draped with lace curtains and near it a large clawfoot bathtub that was already waiting, luxuriously filled with steaming water, and loaded with bubbles. Splashes of color added a cheerful warmth to the room that betrayed the wintery conditions outside with a vase of sunny yellow flowers and yellow towels draped on the racks.

"I was able to find some old sweats and sweatshirts from back in my college days. You'll still swim in them, but they should work if you cinch up the waistband." Molly shrugged, "Then I can get your clothes washed up for you. How does that sound?"

Not sure how to thank Molly, I just nodded and smiled gratefully at her. She showed me where to find the soap and something she called shampoo. Finding a brush in a small vanity, she left the brush, the towel, and the clothing on a small white wooden chair near the door. Preparing to leave the room, she added, "Take your time, I will be right out here in Nana's room if there is anything you need.", then she slipped out the door and closed it behind her, leaving me alone.

Slowly I removed the weight of the bag from my shoulder and draped it over the back of the wooden chair and turning around saw my sad reflection in the looking glass. My now tattered clothing and my face were smeared with dirt and my tunic, new only a few days before, looked dingy and old. The knees of my leggings had been torn when I fell and were speckled by the blood from my skinned knees. My hair hung completely disheveled into unkept matted locks. Oh, the things Marita would have said had she seen me then!

I quickly peeled away the soiled layers and settled into the soothing bubbly water and let the filth and tension be washed away. When I emerged from the bath sometime later, I was feeling fresh and renewed.

Using the brush, I painstakingly untangled and unmatted each rope of hair until it was smooth and manageable. I was still unable to recreate the double-braided crown that Marita had done before I left the palace, so I had opted for a single long braid that draped neatly over one shoulder.

Molly had been right about the clothing she had left, it hung on me loosely, but they were clean, comfortable, and warm. I was thankful to have them. After getting dressed, I gingerly slung the bag over my shoulder and prepared to leave the bathing room.

As I began gathering up my soiled clothing, I heard Molly and Nana Betty's hushed voices talking on the other side of the door.

"What do you think could be in it?" Molly was pondering.

"It couldn't be much, the bag weighed hardly anything. But Anya seemed absolutely grief-stricken when she thought it was lost." Nana Betty too, seemed to be trying to understand this mystery. The pearl, meanwhile, seemed to grow heavier with each passing hour and my legs strained under the weight as I moved closer to the door, leaning in to hear better.

"She was so relieved when she saw it!" Molly's voice grew more concerned. "But did you see that when she put the bag over her shoulder she winced, like it was painful to carry?"

"Hmm," I could hear Nana Betty sigh, "First we need to find out where she even came from."

"And why she was running." Molly finished.

"Well, we will have plenty of time to figure that out! From what the news report said, it sounded like this storm may not blow over till tomorrow night, and then it could take a few more days just to clear the roads." I could hear Nana Betty's voice retreating into the kitchen.

A few more days? My heart which had been lightened by my refreshing bath was now brought low again. How would I ever find the one I was looking for if I was stuck there at the house! Don't misunderstand, I was very grateful to be with such nice people. But I feared that I had made a huge mistake running away from the city! Silently, I dropped to my knees before the throne, drawn there by the weight of the pearl, the burden that I carried.

24

Healing Bridges

MOLLY WAS PATIENTLY WAITING in Nana Betty's plush red chair when I finally emerged from the bathing room. Though I was dismayed by the thought that I was now stranded with no way to search for the recipient of the King's gift, there was also a strange peace about being surrounded by and sequestered with this sweet family. I had decided to enjoy their warm hospitality for the time being, besides, maybe by asking them some questions I could identify someone who matched the description given to me by the King.

My opportunity to ask questions would have to wait, however, Molly had plenty of questions for me first. Rising she smiled, "Feeling better?"

"Yes, very much!" I could not help but smile too, it really felt quite wonderful to be clean, warm and fed.

"Here, let me take those for you and put them in the wash." Molly extended her arms to receive the clothing and the used towel and dropped them into a wicker basket near the door.

Inviting me to join her, Molly sat down on the edge of Nana Betty's bed next to a white box with a red cross on it that lay open there. "Now that you're all cleaned up, let's take care of those scratches and scrapes, ok?"

I looked down at my freshly clean hands and noted the long, shallow gashes that I must have gotten when I fell and slid down the steep embankment. My hands had been so cold and numb that I had not even felt the twigs and jagged rocks tearing into my flesh as I desperately clung to whatever I could grasp to pull myself back up to the roadside.

I sat down next to Molly on the delicate flowered quilt and with considerable effort pulled the bag containing the King's gift up onto my lap, then held out my hands to her. Gently she began to tend to my wounds.

"You did a lovely job on your braid." Molly complemented, breaking the silence as she used a tweezer to pick out bits of dirt and pebbles that the bath had not washed away.

"Thank you," I replied sheepishly, tugging on the braid gently with my free hand. "It's not as good as the ones that Marita does."

"Who is Marita?", Molly asked, trying to sound casual and busying herself with wetting a cotton pad with some clear liquid from a brown bottle.

"Marita manages the household at the palace, that's where I live. She oversees *all* of the servants, but mainly she watches over me." Shrugging, I looked down and smiled sadly at the thought of her.

Furrowing her brow, Molly seemed concerned somehow about what I had said, and decidedly brought the focus back to the task at hand. "This may sting a little." She warned before gently dabbing at the abrasions on my palms with the cotton pad. I bit my lip and tried to sit still; it *did* sting, leaving a ring of fizzing white bubbles on the edges of the cuts.

Discarding the cotton pad and uncapping a tube of salve, she was ready to press further, "So, where is this *palace*?"

"It's on the other side of the sea of Lake Michigan." I told her matter-of-factly.

"So, like *in* Michigan the state?" she suggested.

"No, I don't think so. I have never heard of the land of 'Michigan the state' before." Perhaps that was near the land north of the Dakota where the real Annie had hailed from, I considered.

I thought that maybe it would help if I tried to explain how we had arrived, "We set sail from the shores of our Kingdom and journeyed through the sunset. Our ship, the Shama, came through the sun. And when we arrived at the pier we were on the other side of the sunrise."

Molly inhaled sharply and froze, as if someone had doused her with icy water, and simply said, "O.K," After a moment, she returned to applying the salve, collecting her thoughts and when she had finished, she put the cap back on the salve and setting it down, took both my hands gently in hers and chose her words very carefully. "Anya, were you running away from the 'palace' because you were in danger?", she solemnly asked, watching closely for my reaction.

"Oh, no! I was not in danger. I only left the Kingdom because I've been *sent* to deliver a message for the King." I adamantly replied. "And from all I have seen since I arrived, it seems a gift from the King is desperately needed here."

"I see." Molly muttered, not really seeing. She set my hands down and searched the box for cotton pads. She placed them on my palms before wrapping each of my hands with a long bandage. The conflicted look on her face told me that while she believed I was *telling* her the truth, she was having trouble *believing* what I said.

Pari meandered into the room, yawned loudly, and settled down on the rug by our feet. Looking at him, I thought that if I explained the purpose of our journey, maybe I could bridge the gap for Molly, "We, Pari and I, come from a land very different from yours, more vibrant and clearer, but connected somehow to your land. The King, whom I serve, loves the people here very much and has sent me with a gift for your people as a reminder of the love He has for you."

Something about what I had said, and perhaps Pari's presence, set her strangely at ease and she laughed softly and shook her head.

Shifting the discussion, she commanded in a very Marita-like way, "Now we need to take care of those skinned knees, too. Here, let me take that bag and I'll set it down right here on this chair.", she referred to a white chair next to the bed that matched the chair in the bathing room. Sensing my hesitation to set the bag down, she assured, "It will be safe here, I promise."

Convinced, I strained to lift the messenger bag, with both hands, up to her but when she took it, she seemed rather surprised that she could lift it easily with one hand. When I turned toward her the large collar of the bulky shirt I was wearing slid down to reveal one red and blistered shoulder. Molly looked back to me, and seeing it, gasped, "That couldn't possibly be from *this* bag could it?"

Nodding, I moved my braid and revealed the other shoulder. That one was even more irritated from the strap of the bag digging and rubbing against it for days, as I had switched it from one shoulder to the other.

"But it barely weighs a thing!" Molly reasoned.

"In the beginning, that's how it felt for me too." I admitted. "At first the King's charge was lighter than a feather. I feared that it would blow away if I did not hold on to it tight enough. But as time passed and the need seemed so great, I've allowed the burden of it to weigh down on me. Now it is nearly unbearable to carry. I've been sent to deliver it to someone who can use it. I think they may be waiting for it, but I don't know who it is, and I don't know how I can even find them now that we've left the city," I finished with a disappointed quaver in my voice.

Molly set the bag down softly on the chair and went back to tending first to my knees and then to my shoulders, and I took this as my chance to find some answers of my own, "Molly? Can I ask you a question?"

"Sure! Why not? Ask away.", Molly sighed, with a wary smile, still trying to make sense of our conversation. She seemed content to deviate from
that topic, at least for the time being.

"Do you know any people of influence in the city?" I got straight to
the point.

Taken aback by my very specific question, Molly pondered for a moment, "Well, I guess I know some. I lived in the city for about five years after
I graduated from college, and I worked downtown in one of largest buildings as a receptionist to a very successful businessman. He could definitely
be considered influential."

"The king of Chicago?" I questioned blandly.

Slightly shocked, Molly exclaimed, "Yes, Steve Talon! How did you
know?"

"I already met him." I shrugged my bandaged shoulders.

"You did?", she questioned suspiciously.

"Yes, and did you know that he is not *really* a king?" I asked in
consternation.

Molly laughed, "Yeah, he's just *called* the king of Chicago, because his
family has owned or donated half the city."

"Mrs. Kelly and I agreed that Stephen Talon was not the one I was
seeking.", I affirmed.

Molly's eyes widened a bit and she looked up from the white box where
she was packing away the supplies. "You know Mrs. Kelly?"

I nodded, "She has a big desk right where the golden doors open. She
took care of Pari for me while I met with Mr. Talon, because he is.um er . . .
eller . . ." I stumbled, trying to recall the word, as I had only heard it once,
"aller . . ."

"Allergic to dogs." Molly finished for me with awe in her voice.

25

Llama Laughs & Lingering Hope

LAUREN BURST INTO THE room excitedly, "Mom! Mom! Dad said we can finally play that game that Uncle Bennie sent me for my birthday! The one with the singing llama!" She squealed with excitement, as she ran off to find her sister and tell her the big news.

Luke appeared in the doorway, holding a colorful box, with a guilty grin on his face. "She talked me into it, Mols! Besides, it's a snow day; there's no better time to be tortured by a llama wearing a tiara!" He tilted his head toward the kitchen and beckoned us, "Come on ladies, I can't go into this battle alone!"

Molly groaned, "I guess it's time for Princess Lala's Birthday Tea Party then. Care to join us?"

"I'd be delighted." I replied, intrigued by the opposing reactions from Lauren and her parents to this activity, I gathered my bag and followed Molly into the kitchen to see what this singing llama was all about.

I soon found out, as we spent the next hour wearing silly cone-shaped 'birthday' hats and following the directions of 'Princess Lala'. The disembodied, animated, singing llama head sitting in the middle of the table was as terrifying as it was ridiculous. We served each other pretend tea and collected inedible fake cookies until someone was declared the winner and awarded them with Princess Lala's crown.

Seeing the girls enjoying the game brought their parents and I joy and laughter, although by the end we all would groan when it was time to sing 'Princess Lala's Birthday' song again. Somehow, Princess Lala sounded strangely familiar. To everyone's delight, Luke was the first winner, and the girls gladly crowned him.

"How old is Bennie's son, Grayson?" he asked, scowling up at the tiara.

"Six weeks, why?." Molly answered suspiciously.

"Excellent." Luke maniacally responded, drumming his fingers together, "Your day for annoying children's toys is coming, dear brother-in-law," he threatened mischievously to the absent 'Bennie'. We all laughed, even Nana who had come to the doorway to watch the action. We played the game over and over until each member of the family, including me, had been crowned as a winner.

"One more game, paaaalllleeeeeezzzeeee!" Callie insisted when Molly started to pack the game back into its colorful box.

Plucking the tiara off her head, Molly declared, "I think we've had enough of this game for today."

Under his breath, Luke muttered, "For the year."

"For the decade." Molly agreed, and laughing, handed him the box. He whisked it away to be hidden in the back of some closet, but I had a feeling that it would not be long before the girls would convince them to play it again.

"Come on, Callie Girl, you can help me put the soap in the washing machine, ok?" Molly encouraged the pouting Callie, who had slumped down on her chair with arms crossed.

Perking up, Callie hopped down and left with her mother to gather up the wicker basket of soiled clothing and together they left for another part of the house. Lauren and Nana Betty remained and began playing a game with white tiles that Lauren told me were called dominos.

As the tiles clicked on the table and Lauren and Nana Betty chatted, fatigue started setting in again and my mind wandered back to 'Princess Lala'. I pondered sleepily aloud, "That llama sounded kind of familiar; I've heard that voice somewhere before."

The ladies paused their game and Lauren said knowingly, "Oh, that's Zahara, she does the voice for Princess Lala in all the movies."

"Movies?", I questioned, I had not heard this term before.

"Yeah, I was totally into the Princess Lala movies when I was little." She stated, in a very grown-up tone.

Nana Betty chuckled and whispered to me, "Last week."

Seeing her grandmother outing her, Lauren defended, "I'm eight now, I don't watch little kids' movies anymore!"

Smiling at this sweet little girl, trying to grow up so fast, I shared, "I met Zahara the other day."

"Did you?" Nana Betty asked with raised eyebrows.

"Yes, I met her before her performance at the big pavilion in the park.", I admitted.

Nana Betty remained quiet, but Lauren was wide eyed and seemed impressed, "Really? You met Princess La. I mean, Zahara! What was she like?"

I tried to field the question as best I could, "Uh, she is very beautiful, dramatic, and very bold. It's just an act, it's like she is always putting on a performance; underneath she's frightened and lonely. She is too afraid to show anyone who she *really* is. She feels she is not good enough just being herself."

"Zahara *told* you that?" Nana Betty questioned.

"No, not with words anyway." I struggled to explain, "When I looked into her eyes, I could just see it. She knew I did too, and it scared her. I tried to comfort her and tell her about the King's gift, but the guards told me to go away. When she was singing at the pavilion, I could hear in her voice that she didn't really believe what she was saying. She was just saying what she thought people would want to hear. Hollow, empty words."

"Hmm," Nana Betty breathed leaning back thoughtfully.

"I'm sorry." I began, as a wave of drowsiness came over me. "Maybe it's just me. I must still be tired."

"No, that sounds like a pretty *accurate* assessment of Zahara, if you ask me. I just don't hear many *your* age who think that." she affirmed, sounding surprised. "But you *should* probably get some rest, Anya. You're still recovering. The couch is still made up for you if you want to lie down."

Nodding sleepily, I struggled to pick up the bag that had been sitting on the bench next to me and dragged myself and it into the sitting room where within moments of snuggling up under a fluffy blanket, I had drifted away with my hand draped over the bag as it lay on the floor next to the couch.

When I awoke, the room was dark except for the flickering fire that was once again kindled in the fireplace. The rest of the day had escaped into the darkness, and it was now night again. Groggily I sat up and glanced out the window. After a full day, the storm outside was finally losing momentum, but great gusts of wind still tossed the loose snow into white clouds that swirled around the yard. Enormous piles of snow had covered everything and were blown into huge mounds against anything that blocked its way.

Instead of Molly asleep in the chair it was Nana Betty this time, with her feet propped up on an ottoman and her hands folded over her stomach. Her chin dropped to her chest; she was snoring softly.

A small table had been pulled up next to the couch and on it was a plate holding a sandwich in a clear bag, a banana, and a bottle of water, thoughtfully left out for me since I had obviously slept through dinner.

Pari was curled up on a rug before the fire. Gathering the plate, I slipped off the couch and joined him on the floor. He raised his head sleepily and placed it on my knee and we both watched the fire dance as I enjoyed the cool sweetness of the fruit preserves and the earthy goodness of the peanut spread. 'Peanut butter and jelly sandwich', that is what Rita had called it back in the park; I decided I would have to introduce this comforting delicacy to those back home in the Kingdom.

In a quiet voice I confided to Pari as we watched the flickering, crackling flames. "I have *tried* to deliver the King's message, haven't I?" Hanging my head, I sighed, "I'm not a messenger, just a lowly kitchen servant. Considering the trials we have endured, and the fact that we are stranded here now, surely the King will understand that the task was simply *impossible*, right? Who is even worthy of a gift from the King?"

Interrupting my justification, Pari pawed the rug in front of me and gave a soft whine. He had heard enough, and in his gentle way he raised his shaggy eyebrows and cocked his head to the side, telling me just what I needed to hear. A wave of clarity hit me, and I knew deep down that giving up was not the answer.

"You're right, of course." I admitted. "We cannot just quit. We still have two more days to deliver the King's message."

With a gentle growl Pari corrected me again. "I know." I conceded, stroking his soft fur. "The King made no mention of anyone needing to be *worthy* enough to receive His gift, only that they would be a leader among men, inspire others to take action, influence a generation and be willing to receive the message." I listed the qualities I had been searching for.

"I *will* make the King proud that he sent me to do this task. Someone is waiting for this message, Pari, and we are going to find them. We must keep searching, *somehow*."

My hunger satisfied, I returned the empty plate to the table and retrieved my journal and writing stick from the messenger bag. I lay with Pari on the rug in the warm glow and began to write.

Compelled I fled. Repelled or drawn,
Beyond the city into the unknown.
To a seemingly forsaken path.
Cast into the storm's frigid wrath.
By chance? Or some predestined luck?
Was I from icy death's door plucked?
I sense Your hand not far from me.
Lord, my heart yearns to bring You glory.
But the storm reminds with icy blasts,
The disappointments of hours gone past.

Closing the journal, I rested my chin on folded hands over its leatherbound cover. Pari shifted closer to me and together we slept soundly the rest of the night.

What I hadn't noticed was that the snoring had stopped as soon as I had started talking to Pari, nor had I perceived that Nana Betty had adjusted in her chair to better watch and listen to us.

26

Warming Up

I AWOKE AS THE sun peeked through the windows and draped the orange light of a newborn day across the room. A blanket had been laid over me at some time in the night and Nana Betty had retired to her room where I could hear her soft snores across the quiet house. I sat up and stretched, completely rested, and rubbed the sleep from my eyes.

Hushed voices filtered down from upstairs, "Honey, you can go back to bed. Preschool is canceled today." Luke's sleepy voice murmured.

"But Daddy, it's morning time and the sun is shining! It's time to get up for school!" Callie cheerfully reasoned.

"Ah, sorry pumpkin. No one can get through all this snow. If we are lucky the roads will be cleared in time for school on Monday, ok?"

"Ok Daddy." Callie complied sweetly.

Several minutes passed before the very awake little voice piped up again, "Mommy, can I have some breakfast?

Giving in to the fact that sleeping in today was not going to be an option, Molly's groggy voice mumbled back, "Sure, honey, I'll be right down."

Light footsteps scampered across the hall above my head and down the stairs and Callie's face lit up when she saw that I was already awake. She bounded across the room and threw her little arms around my neck, "Good morning, Anya!" she chirped.

"Good morning, Callie!" I giggled and hugged my little friend back.

Lauren, who had been awakened by her sister, had made her way down the stairs as well and smiled a sleepy half-grin brushing her bed-tousled hair from her face. "Mornin'," she yawned.

"Mornin'," I echoed back, impulsively inviting her in for a hug as well. She stumbled across the room and slumped down next to me and snuggled in.

Callie let go of my neck and picked up my writing stick that lay next to my journal. "What's this?" she asked holding up the worn wooden stick that held a piece of a writing stone fastened in place by a sliding silver ring.

"Oh, that's my writing stick. See?" I picked up my journal and flipped to a blank page and drew a dainty little flower.

"Cool! It's like a fancy pencil." Lauren sat up, "Can I try?"

"Sure." I said, extending the journal and writing stick 'pencil' to her. She easily copied my flower exactly and beamed up at me.

"Well done, Lauren." I assured her. "Here, try this one!"

Retrieving the writing stick I drew another flower, this time a drooping bell shaped one with more details. I handed the journal back to Lauren who eagerly lay the journal on the floor in front of her and biting her lip focused on duplicating the delicate petals. She was a very good artist for such a young girl.

I watched her intently, thinking of the quiet evenings back in the palace kitchens, when Marita and I had finished our work and my studies. By lamp light I would often busy myself with sketching flowers or animals that I had read about in the books from the palace library, while Marita was busy with sewing or mending. Lauren and I both enjoyed our game immensely! Within minutes, we had filled the whole page with a garden of matching flowers.

Molly and Luke slowly made their way downstairs with slippers on their feet, tying cozy robes over their night clothes. They paused on the landing for a moment and watched us as Lauren and I drew, and Callie whispered secrets in Pari's floppy ear. They exchanged smiles at the sight of the four of us huddled together on the floor. It was quite a pleasant way to start the day!

Still groggy, Luke headed into the kitchen to get breakfast started; scrambled eggs and toast were on the menu. Molly trudged upstairs with the girls in tow to get dressed.

Alone in the sitting room, I folded the blanket and lay it over the arm of the faded couch.

I picked up my journal and writing stick and smiled proudly at our field of flowers before closing the leather cover and moving to my bag to slip them inside. I peered briefly at the dimmed contents it contained; the glow of the pearl had diminished even more. I did not linger, but quickly closed the flap. It was too discouraging to look at the gift, fading as I sat there unsure of my next step.

I did not even attempt to lift the bag from the floor, the weight of it had surpassed the strength in my arms. I just let the strap fall from my hand and lowered to a knee in the beam of morning sunlight for a few steadying breaths, honoring my King who had sent me. Pari came alongside me and affectionately nuzzled my arm. Lifting my head, I looked into his soft brown eyes. "How about some breakfast?" I suggested to my shaggy companion who obliged and walked with me out of the sitting room, leaving the bag and the King's gift sitting on the floor.

We entered the kitchen where Luke had been talking quietly with Nana Betty near a long counter cracking eggs into a bowl. When they saw us, their conversation ceased abruptly and Nana Betty smiled and greeted us warmly, "Good mornin' darlin'! And good morning to you too Pari!", she added fondly, scratching his head as she passed. Heading back into her room, she left Luke and I in the kitchen. Pari settled on the rug under the table and went back to snoozing.

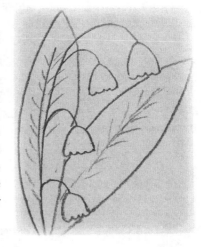

"Can I help with anything?" I offered. I felt right at home in a kitchen, so it was natural for me to look for work to do.

"Sure! Here, you can make the toast!" Luke said, pointing to a loaf of Nana's bread thinly sliced on the cutting board.

"Alright!" I agreed enthusiastically; I had made toast hundreds of times. I looked around for the fireplace in the kitchen that would heat the ovens like the ones back home. Not seeing one, I figured they must use the sitting room fireplace for their cooking. A bit primitive, but it would work.

"Should I get the fire started first?" I asked, pointing to the sitting room.

Luke laughed, thinking I was joking, "You want to toast them like a marshmallow? We'll just use the toaster this time."

"Toaster?" I questioned.

He paused in his beating the eggs and looked at my genuinely perplexed expression. "Yeah, the toaster, right here." He motioned to a white box on the counter in front of me with two metal openings on the top and a cable that was attached to the wall.

Fascinated, I leaned in to see it closer, "How does it work?"

Reluctantly, he explained, "You put two pieces of bread inside," he dropped a slice of bread into each of the slots, "and you push the lever down, and when the bread is toasted it pops up. Go ahead," he encouraged, "give it a try."

Timidly I reached out and pushed the lever down, a red light appeared on the front of the box and a soft hum came from within. I peered into the top and saw glowing red lines heating up to toast the outside of the bread.

"Amazing!" I admired the marvelous 'toaster'.

"Yeah, I guess it is!" Luke had to agree, and with a chuckle he went back to beating the eggs.

While I patiently watched the toaster and smelled the warm bread slowly browning, Luke brought up the subject of going back to the city.

"So, Anya, as soon as the roads are cleared and it's safe to go out, we'll bring you back into the city and find your dad. He is probably really worried about you."

"Dad?" I asked, puzzled at the meaning of the word.

Luke had just poured the eggs into a pan where they sizzled and bubbled even though there was no visible fire beneath them. He paused, frozen with his spatula in hand, "Yeah, your father. You were with him in the alley when we met you yesterday."

"Oh! You mean Joe?" I exclaimed in recognition, "No, he's not my father. I had just met him right before I met you. He came to my rescue when some hooligans were trying to take my bag and saved me again when I stepped out into the street. One of those fast yellow carriages would have struck me if Joe hadn't pulled me out of the way." I casually explained while watching the red filaments inside of the toaster.

Suddenly, the toasted bread flew up with a snap, and I jumped back, startled, and wide eyed at this wonderous tool!

Luke shook his head, amused, and pushed a plate of butter and a knife toward me. I took the hint and pulled the hot toast to the counter and began to spread the butter on it with a dull knife.

Luke stirred the eggs around in the pan. "So why *were* you in the alley with Joe?" He asked, looking perplexed.

"Well," I pondered, "After my encounter with the hooligans, I figured I'd be safer with Joe than alone. At least until I could find Pari, that is. And thanks to you, I found him!"

"At Animal Control." Luke deduced.

Placing another two pieces of bread into the magical device, I pressed down the lever delightedly, before responding.

"Yes! Praise the King! He was there! But they had him locked up and would not let him go, so he ended up jumping through the fence to escape. Jamie and Bryson seemed pretty upset about it. They take care of the animals there, and they came looking for us. That is when we ran away from the city. I was not going to let them put Pari back into prison! So, we just rode on the bus carriages as far as they would take us, then we kept walking after that." At that moment, the toast springing from the toaster punctuated my rambling and made me jump again. I could not help but laugh in embarrassment that it had caught me off guard!

"Simply marvelous!" I giggled, then looking at Luke, my joyful expression faded when I saw the somber look he wore.

"Anya where are your parents?" he asked pointedly. I could tell he was very serious this time.

I swallowed hard, being put on the spot, "I, I don't have any." I stammered, looking Luke square in the eye, hoping he could tell I was being honest with him. "Marita, the head of the palace household, watches over me. I think," I paused with the many years of frustration at not knowing my past welling up all at once, "I *think* I am an orphan.", I explained quietly, dropping my head in shame.

Using the sleeve of the old shirt that I wore, I quickly wiped the tears away from the corners of my eyes, "I am sorry, I don't know much about my past." I spoke nearly in a whisper.

Luke softened his expression but remained emphatic, "I'm sorry to upset you Anya, but I bet someone at home is worried sick for you. How can I get ahold of Marita to let her know where you are and that your safe?"

Going back to buttering the toast, I thoughtfully answered his questions, "I'm not sure *how* you would get a message to anyone in the Kingdom. Sometimes," I admitted, "I think that maybe the King can just hear me. He always seems to send help right when I ask for it. Like you and Molly, twice!" I looked up at Luke and smiled appreciatively, then continued with the toast, "Besides, Marita *knows* where I am. She prepared me for my journey and took me down to the harbor to meet the ship to sail to this land. They are expecting my return in a few days."

This conversation had not gone *at all* the way Luke had expected, and I could tell he was not sure where to go from here, so we worked in silence as he sprinkled the eggs with cheese and placed a cover over his pan.

I toasted and buttered several more rounds of bread and put them on a plate that Luke had gotten down out of the cabinet.

Eventually, Nana returned to the room dressed in light purple pants and a matching jacket. Her hair was neatly tied back with a lavender and pink kerchief like she was ready to start a big task.

Luke laughed and jested with his mother, "Ya' gonna go for a jog ma?"

"Maybe I am!" she shot back with a sly grin. "I do have to do my exercises after breakfast, then maybe I'll work up a sweat making a few batches of banana bread with the girls."

"Now *that's* my kind of workout!" Molly jumped in, coming in from the sitting room. "Mornin' Mama!" she gave her mother-in-law a quick hug and a peck on the cheek, "Mornin again Anya! Breakfast ready, Hon?"

Luke lifted the lid of the pan and a puff of steam rose into the room. "Just about!"

"I'll go get the girls then," Molly said as she spun around to leave the room.

Nana Betty had stopped at a small hutch between the sitting room and the door to her room and switched a lever on a small box and it started to play music and sing loudly! I was amazed! The box was much too small to hold musicians, yet it produced the sound of them as if they were in the room! Nana Betty somehow made the musicians play quieter, then turned to Luke. "You going to work with Henry today?" she asked with raised eyebrows as she moved to the counter next to me and poured some coffee into a mug. I was familiar with the smell of coffee as many of the servants in the Kingdom seemed to enjoy it as well.

"Yeah, I'll give him a call after breakfast and find out, but if I know old Henry, a little snow won't stop him. He's too stubborn for that!" Luke smiled fondly. "It's like a playground out there for him today, he gets to take out his big toys!"

Luke chuckled then explained, "Henry is a retired farmer who doesn't understand the meaning of the word 'retired'. He owns this section of farmland between our house and the church that I pastor. Henry was one of the first members of the congregation, and happy to see his childhood church being used again. He said we were an answer to prayer, but really, he's been an answer to ours in so many ways."

"He's been a champion of what we've been trying to establish out here at 'Simple Faith Country Church' and when things have gotten tight these past few years, he's hired me on to help him out at his place part time to fill the gap. He helps me with upkeep of the church and grounds too, and helped me with some of the building updates, at least the ones we could tackle on our own. Basically, Henry feels like one of the family. Huh, ma?"

Luke, glanced over at Nana Betty whose cheeks flushed slightly when she added "And he is one of the most stubborn, opinionated, kind, and generous, faith filled men I've met since Luke's dad passed away ten years ago!"

Looking to me and ignoring the smirk on her son's face, Nana continued, "You'll probably meet him tomorrow morning when he comes to pick Luke up for Saturday Men's Bible study. He likes to give Luke a ride."

Luke contradicted her, "You know full well that its not to give me a ride, he just knows *you're* going to invite him in for some of your blueberry buttermilk pancakes!"

With a scowl Nana Betty shushed him and pretended to be very interested in the monotone voice that had taken over for the music coming from the box on the hutch. Touching the box, she made the voice speak louder,

"Early this morning Governor Warner declared a disaster proclamation for the state of Illanois, after a winter storm blanketed wide sections of the state with snow and caused power outages for over 7000 homes. High winds and drifting snow are still making travel unadvised and snow removal crews have been urged to focus on main and emergency routes first. Supplemental snow removal equipment, such as garbage trucks fitted with temporary plows, are being dispatched to assist in snow removal. So, get comfortable and stay warm, it's going to take a few days to dig this city out, folks!"

Nana Betty made the box quieter again, and started to gather some plates, cups, and silverware. I helped her carry them to the table.

As I put the plate of toast on the table I blandly mentioned, "I met him too.", pointing to the box.

Looking at the box then back at me, Nana Betty questioned, "Who's that honey? The radio announcer?"

"No, Anthony Warner, you know, Governor 'Tony'." I said with a slight scowl on my face.

"You met the *governor*?" Nana Betty asked dubiously.

"Yes, Tim Calloway helped me, he is a reporter of truth," I stated factually.

"Tim Calloway? That kooky guy from the Tribune that does special interest pieces?" Luke seemed doubtful as he transferred eggs from the pan onto plates around the table.

"He is very clever and passionate for the truth," I defended. "The guards would not let him into the press conference either, so he devised a way for us to catch Tony before he left through a secret door, because the governor is afraid of elevators."

Agitated, Luke let the metal spatula fall into the empty pan with a clang and left the table to bring the pan to a basin where they clean the dishes.

Nana Betty also seemed uneasy, but pried for more answers, "Anya, where was this press conference?"

I strained to remember, "At a kind of palace. It had flags hanging over the entrance, glass doors and a huge marble staircase. Geoffrey, a servant at the palace, was kind, but he would not let Pari come in. Pari had to wait outside; that's when the Animal Control imprisoned him."

Returning to the table Luke sternly stated, "That's enough!"

Shocked by his abrupt interruption, Nana Betty looked at him questioningly, "Luke?"

"Breakfast is ready. It's time to eat." He mumbled, clearly flustered.

Molly and the girls had returned, and we all settled in around the table. The girls chattered and Molly and I laughed with them. And when their mother was not looking, the girls would give Pari bits of their eggs under the table, which he licked out of their hands. Luke remained very quiet as he pushed his eggs around his plate, staring down at them with a furrowed brow. Nana Betty watched her son with concern.

Oblivious to the tension that was in the room, Molly grabbed a piece of toast and pointing outside with it, she commented before taking a bite, "They were saying on the news last night that this storm may be the second or third highest snowfall ever recorded for a single winter storm for this area. And that's saying something! We get a fair amount of snow every year!"

Molly turned to Luke, "After breakfast you want me to come out and help you dig the truck out of the garage?" Not getting any response from her husband, she raised her voice, "Hon? Hello?"

Shaking himself out of a daze, Luke finally looked up, "Sorry. What?"

Laughing, Molly repeated herself, "You want me to help dig out the truck?"

"Oh, no. Not yet. Even if we got the garage open, we couldn't even get out of the driveway."

"Really!?" the girls exclaimed and scrambled to look out of the window.

Luke continued, "Let me call Henry and see if I'll be working with him today. Chances are good we're going to be moving snow all day. We can make our way over here with the snowplows when we're done and clear out the driveway." Luke said, still distracted. He gathered up his plate of uneaten eggs, he got up from the table.

Just then the sound of a tinkling bell from the next room got his attention, "I should get that. It's probably him now."

Luke left the room toward the sound of the bell, and I helped Molly and the girls clean the table, putting the plates, silverware, and cups near a metal basin. Molly turned a knob and water flowed from a spout into the basin and soon steam rose from the water. There were many amazing things in this kitchen!

Molly squeezed some green liquid into the water and soon the sink was filled to the brim with bubbles. She gave me a towel with warm soapy water to wash the table and the girls pulled up chairs next to the empty side of the basin. Molly filled it with clear cool water then as she washed each dish, she would hand it to Callie who would dip it into the clear water to rinse off the bubbles then on to Lauren who would set it in a tray to dry.

Luke poked his head back into the room and called, "Hey Molly, have you seen my wool socks?"

"Have you checked your sock drawer?" Molly called back.

"Yeah, I didn't see them."

Molly smiled and sighed, wiping her hands on a towel that hung from the cabinet, "Ok, I'm coming."

"Why don't you girls go play. We can finish these in a bit." Molly dried the girl's hands then dismissed them from their task and they scampered from the room.

I was left in the kitchen wiping down the table. I returned to the basin and dipped the towel into the hot soapy water. I figured I could just as well wash the rest of these dishes for Molly. I had washed many, many dishes in the Kingdom and I made very quick work of the few plates, cups and forks that were left and stacked them neatly with the rest of the clean dishes in the tray.

Then I busied myself around the kitchen by wiping down all the counters and the outsides of the cabinets. Finding a broom in the corner I swept the kitchen and then sat down at the table next to Pari and stared out the windows. Pari rose and placed his head across my knees and my hands stroked the silky fur around his ears. "There must be a way back into the city." I murmured.

We sat in the quiet kitchen for some time watching the loose snow being blown down roofs of buildings, across the hills of snow and around into a white haze below a bright blue sunny expanse above it.

Eventually, a whining noise approached from outside, faint at first, it got progressively louder until I saw a strange vehicle approaching the house. It climbed and dipped over the mounds of snow, its bright eye bobbing in and out of sight. It was small and held only one passenger who was wearing a thick brown coat and pants and large boots. Seeing me in the window, he raised a hand in greeting. I smiled weakly and waved back, amazed, and fascinated by this strange appearance. Especially since I could not see his face; his entire head was covered by a large smooth globe. He drove right up to the door near the kitchen window. The vehicle stopped there and purred loudly.

Could the King have heard me and sent this person to transport us back to the city? The thought crossed my mind but was quickly dismissed when I heard Nana Betty holler up the stairs, "Luke, Henry is here for you."

Luke rushed down the stairs pulling on large boots and a heavy coat over his thick black overalls. His clothing looked similar to those of the person outside. He quickly pulled open a large closet and rummaging through a box inside he emerged with a black hood that covered his head and neck and a large pair of gloves.

Seeing me watching from the table, Luke paused with his hand on the knob about to open the door, and sighed, "Anya, I'm really sorry for raising my voice earlier. I shouldn't have done that, and I apologize. Will you forgive me?"

His humble and sincere apology was perfectly timed. I had just been pondering our conversation as well. "No apology needed. I know my story is hard to believe."

Nodding, but unsure how to respond, he smiled awkwardly, "I'll see ya later then," Luke opened the door to join the man on the snow vehicle and a rush of freezing air surged in through the open door. Luke had to pull the door behind him to make it close.

I watched through the window as the man, Henry, tossed Luke a globe like his. Luke put it on his head and sat on the back of the vehicle behind Henry. The strange vehicle whined loudly, and they moved away over the snow and out of sight.

27

Mended

MOLLY CAME BACK INTO the kitchen carrying a basket of folded laundry and found me staring across the snowy yard where the red lights on the back of the snow vehicle had disappeared into the white haze.

She set the basket down near the door to Nana Betty's room and picked up a bundle from the top and came to sit with me. Placing the bundle of clothing in front of me, she broke the silence of the kitchen gently, "They are all cleaned up. It took a little longer, but I was able to mend those tears too. Anya, I don't know where you get your clothing, but this fabric is like nothing I've seen or felt before!" Reaching out to touch the embroidery on the tunic she said with admiration. "They are very well made and these patterns," she mused as she ran her finger over them, "look like they were stitched by hand."

"There is a little merchant village outside of the palace gates. Marita and I went there the day before I left the Kingdom." I explained. "I got the boots there too." I added with a smile, remembering that she had compli-mented them the day before.

"I should have known it was from a boutique!" Molly laughed. "I also dug in the back of the closet and found a few other things from when I was younger. Not as nice as these, but it will give you a few options for now. Once the roads are cleared to get into town, we can go get you a few things that are new that will fit you better. It just might be a few days."

"Molly, thank you for mending these for me and for lending me the clothing, but in a few days, I will be gone. I will be returning to the Kingdom soon," I explained.

"Ok." She sat back and challenged me gently, "So let's say you are going back to the *kingdom*. Just how do you get there?"

"I don't know," I admitted. "I don't know the way back. The King just told me that I would have seven days in this land to deliver the message. I left the Kingdom six days ago. Maybe I am supposed to meet the ship at the pier?"

Molly reasoned, "Even if we could get you back to the city, Anya, there are no boats that would dare be out on Lake Michigan now."

At the mention of going back home, a flood of desperation welled up, displacing the peace and tranquility of the warm cozy kitchen. Molly had a good point. I *did not* know how to get back to the Kingdom and Pari was being of no use in this matter. He seemed perfectly content to lay by the fire, play with the girls and nap under the table, completely unconcerned with the passing of precious time.

"I at least have to try," I blurted. "Do you think that Hank could bring me back to the city on his snow vehicle?"

"On the snowmobile?" She asked doubtfully, "Oh Anya, I don't think so. It took Hank a half hour just to get here and that's less than a mile away. Besides, who knows how long they will be just clearing the driveway. I'm sorry, I know your feeling anxious to get back."

She reached over and squeezed my hand encouragingly then noticed that the bandages were wet. She glanced at the sink, then back to me, "Hey, you stinker! You finished the dishes," then noticing the rest of the kitchen, she slowly added in awe, "and cleaned the *whole kitchen*! Thank you! Wow! But we better change those wet bandages."

Molly got up from the table and opened one of the cabinets. She retrieved the white box she had used the day before and began to unpack new bandages and the ointment. Sitting back down with me, she begin to remove the soggy wrappings from my hands.

"So, Anya, that phone call that came in earlier," she struggled, deciding how to explain, "Well, it may not be as smooth or quick to get home as you think it will," Molly started, almost apologetically, "There are some people at the hospital that will be very interested to meet you when we get back into Chicago. You see, I called there for help the first night when we found you. We needed to know what we should do and what we *could* do to help you. That was the hospital social worker that called. They said they are going to want to do an examination to make sure you're ok. They're actually expecting us there on Monday morning."

She hesitated, then earnestly said, "And the social worker is going to have some questions for you about where you are from, and how you got to Chicago. She *is* going to need you to tell the truth, Anya. Ok?" Not sure what she meant by this, I said nothing, but watched her wetting a cotton pad with the liquid in the brown bottle again. "For now, let's just get those scrapes cleaned up and bandaged again," She stopped talking and was staring down at my hand in hers. Slowly she turned my hands over and searched the back sides. The scrapes had healed well and were gone. But Molly seemed shocked.

"What is wrong?" I asked innocently.

Molly stammered, "There is no way those could have healed that fast,"

I shrugged, "No one in the Kingdom has to remain wounded, Molly, does this surprise you?"

At a loss for words, Molly determined, "Let's check your shoulders and knees."

I let Molly gently peel the bandages from my shoulders and unwrap my knees and she seemed astonished to find them completely restored as well. This was not at all surprising to me, as afflictions did not last long in the presence of the King. And since Marita had said that the Kingdom is not a place that can be left, I reasoned within myself that the King could just as easily bring healing to His servants there as He did within His palace.

"Praise the Lord," Molly finally said in awe, unable to think of any other possible explanations, and began to pack away the supplies she had laid out on the table.

"Yes, praise Him indeed!" I agreed, thankfully rubbing my healed shoulder.

After that, Molly dropped the talk of meeting with anyone back in Chicago and spoke no more of taking me back there either but invited me to go with her upstairs and pick out something to wear for the day. She had laid out several outfits across the bed. I selected a blue jumper that buckled over the shoulders, Molly called them overalls, and a long-sleeved grey cotton shirt. I went down to Nana Betty's bathing room to clean up and change.

Nana Betty was in her room and pedaling a contraption that looked like the ones I had seen on the walkways by the pier, only this one stayed in one place. Using quite a bit of energy for not going anywhere, Nana Betty dabbed sweat from her forehead with a towel. As Molly and I entered she touched a panel in front of her and after several beeping noises her peddling slowed to a stop, and she dismounted.

"Looking strong, Ma!" Molly commented.

"Thank you, darlin," she replied breathlessly as she uncapped a bottle of water and took a sip. "Just keeping these old knees movin."

"Yeah, just don't overdo it. You're still recovering, remember?" Molly warned.

When I emerged from the bathroom, Nana Betty was sitting in her red chair with the legs of her pants rolled up above the knees. Molly was applying some strong-smelling ointment to her legs. I noticed two thin, long scars down the front of her knees.

Lauren and Callie bounded into the room and insisted that we must play something they called 'beauty shop'. It consisted mostly of them brushing my hair and tying it up with white ribbons that draped over each shoulder.

Nana Betty and Molly laughed that now I really looked like a 'country girl' wearing overalls and pigtails.

28

Something Missing

THE REST OF THE morning was spent in the kitchen with Nana Betty, Molly, and the girls. We stirred, mixed, and mashed while making what Nana Betty called 'banana bread' in the warm and cozy kitchen. Just as we were spreading melting butter onto the warm sweet bread Luke burst in through the door. He was covered in a layer of snow and stomped, shaking it off onto the rug, and peeled off the wet, snowy layers, "That isn't banana bread I smell, is it?"

"Yeah Daddy! We made it with Mama, Nana and Anya. You want some?" Callie offered, holding out the slice she was holding, melting butter dripping from the side.

"Do I ever!" He hurriedly removed his boots and gear and hung them on a hook by the door and joined us at the table, "Thanks Callie Girl!" he said, receiving the sopping bread and giving Callie a kiss on her forhead.

"Surprised to see you back so soon!" Molly returned from pulling the last two loaves of bread from the oven.

Through a mouthful of buttery bread Luke replied, "Yeah, we got Henry's driveway pretty much cleared up to the road, but that was as far as we could go. The wind was just blowing it right back in," He swallowed and continued, "Henry just had me take the snowmobile home. I should give him a call and let him know I got back alright."

"I'll give him a call and let him know," Nana Betty offered, getting up from the table and leaving for her room.

"Have any of the plows made it out this way yet?" Molly inquired.

"Nah, not yet. Henry checked with his buddy who drives snowplow over in Grant Park and they are clearing in town and the highways first, but they are having to go back around and do it again because of the wind, so *maybe* by tonight they'll be out our way?" Luke shrugged. "The wind is supposed to die down sometime this afternoon."

Luke was right, eventually the whirling white haze did settle down and the bright winter sunlight reflected off the clean white snow that covered everything. It made the once dull, brown world look fresh and crisp.

After a late lunch of ham sandwiches, carrot sticks and apple sauce, the girls were begging to go play outside in the snow. Molly rummaged through the closet pulling out coats and boots, Lauren turned to me and pleaded, "Anya, will you come out and play with us, please?"

"I could find you some snow gear if you would like to," Molly offered.

"Alright," I quickly accepted. I was curious what it meant to 'play outside', especially now that 'outside' was completely covered in snow. Back in the palace kitchens I mostly focused on my work and studies and there was little time for much else. For the most part, the concept of 'play' was new to me.

Molly hauled an armful of various bulky items to the living room and sorted them out into piles. With the help of their mother, the girls tugged and fastened into their snow pants, boots, coats, hats, and mittens. She found a pair of snow pants for me as well. They were long, thick and were cinched at the waist, but we had to pull them up to my armpits and tie them tightly, so they were not dragging on the ground. Like everything else they were too big and baggy, but in the end they worked.

Sitting on the floor, I pulled on my own boots again. I hadn't worn them for several days and it felt almost strange to hold something made in the Kingdom again. They felt softer and lighter than I had noticed before. I appreciated how fine and even the stitching was and how warm they made my feet feel.

Molly brought me the red coat she had given me, a thick wool hat, and her own mittens to use, "These should keep you nice and warm." She added setting the mittens on the couch next to me.

"I'm getting too hot, Mama!" Callie whined, draping herself dramatically over the arm of the couch. With flushed, red cheeks, Lauren looked like she was about to melt from heat too.

"Alright, then you two head on out!" Molly opened the heavy wood door and the two young girls hobbled in their bulky gear out onto the porch, followed eagerly by Pari. The outer door shut loudly behind them with a bang, as they bounded out across the white, wind-whipped dunes of snow and flopped onto the nearest one. We could hear their happy voices and giggles even through the closed doors.

Molly smiled at her girls, "Thanks for playing outside with them, Anya. Just come on in when you get too cold. I do not expect that they will last too long before they want to come back in. I'll get some hot cocoa ready."

"Mmmmm! I've had hot cocoa twice since I arrived, and I really liked it! Once with my friend Kimmy at the pavilion and once at Lulu's" I chatted while I hurriedly pulled on my puffy red coat.

"Oh gosh! I haven't been to Lulu's in ages!" Molly mused, making conversation while I was finishing getting ready. "I used to go there all the time when I worked downtown! Does that crabby lady still work there?"

"You mean the really thin one who rolls her eyes every time the bell on the door rings?" I laughed.

Molly chuckled along with me, "That would be her."

"Yes, she was there, but I didn't talk to her much."

Seeing my struggling with the coat, Molly stepped toward me, "Here, let me help you with that zipper."

As she did, I continued, "There was this other woman who was very nice though. She had this spiky red hair and lots of sparkle and buttons, her name was Caroline. *She* talked with me for a while; she wants to be a teacher," I paused in reflection, and smiled, "I really liked her."

Staring down at the pattern on the knit hat, Caroline's urgent whisper still rang in my ears, "Hurry Anya."

I pushed the thought away. I had nowhere to hurry to and, at present, no way to get there. Pulling the hat snuggly onto my head, I looked up at Molly, "I *am* really looking forward to having hot cocoa again!"

"Alright then, I'll get it started!" Molly replied cheerfully and leaving the big wooden door open for me, she started toward the kitchen, calling over her shoulder, "Have fun!"

I had opened the screened door before I realized that I had left Molly's mittens on the couch and thinking nothing of it, I let the door bang shut and went back to grab them.

As I entered the room again, I noticed that past the couch the double doors that had been closed before were now cracked open a few inches. Through the gap I could see bookshelves piled with books and a sliver of a desk and a light brown leather chair, worn with age and use. The desktop was littered with papers and books and a fresh notebook and pen. It looked like a sort of library or study.

I grabbed the mittens and was about to turn to go out when I heard Molly's voice from behind the doors enter the study. There must have been another entrance from the kitchen, I thought.

"Hey, what cha doing in here?" I froze, thinking at first that she was talking to me, then realized she thought I was outside already.

Luke replied quietly from somewhere within the study, "Ah, nothing Mol." there was just a hint of sadness in his voice, "I'm just trying to get some inspiration for this Sunday's sermon,"

"You haven't started on the sermon for *this* Sunday yet?!" Molly laughed.

"I know, right?" Luke agreed. "I've been trying all week, but nothing seems to click, there's something missing."

Molly walked across the room and as she passed the cracked door, I could see through the gap that she was holding two cups. "Here, maybe this will help," The smell of the fresh coffee grounds from the kitchen wafted through the house.

"Thanks babe." Luke spoke quietly, then there was a long pause. I did not intend to eavesdrop, really, but something drew me in and quietly, I took a step closer. I could see them standing, one arm wrapped around each other, looking out a bay window to the snowy line of trees that edged the yard of the old farmhouse.

After a long silence, Luke took a deep breath then looking deeply into his coffee cup he leveled with her, "Molly, things are not looking good. If anyone can even *make it* to the church at all on Sunday, it will probably be the same twenty folks who have been coming since we started here."

Taking a drink from the cup in his hand, Luke cleared his throat and continued, "Pastor Mike sent me a message yesterday that he had something he needed to talk to me about, so I called him while you were putting the girls to bed last night,"

Luke took a breath, then laboriously explained, "I guess there was a meeting of the district board on Monday. They are not sure, 'Simple Faith Country Church' is working out. Some of the people out here are just traveling into the city to one of the flashier churches, or worse yet, just not going to church at all. If the roads are cleared by Sunday, they will send Kevin from the district office to check out our service to see if he can offer some suggestions. And now I don't even know what I'm going to preach about. They are having second thoughts of letting us revive this old country church. And if I'm honest, they're not the only ones."

"Hey," Molly leaned in making Luke look up from his cup, "we *know* God called us here for a reason, right? 'Simple Faith' is genuine, Bible led, and faith filled; living in God's promises and teaching Jesus' love and believing in His miracles is our foundation. He has a purpose for us, and a purpose for that old church. Besides, the online attendance and podcasts are doing great. Don't lose hope, maybe now is the time for a miracle." She squeezed his arm encouragingly.

Luke sniffed, "All I want to do is to give people hope. But to do that, I've got to have some left to give, and right now I'm feeling tapped out, Mol. It's been 5 years and I really thought things would look different by now. There's something I'm missing, and I just can't seem to find it. It feels like I'm running out of time for that miracle."

Molly set her cup down and wrapped her arms around Luke's waist. With one arm around her and the other hand holding his coffee cup, he leaned his head on hers as she leaned against his chest, both staring out the window.

I had lingered too long eavesdropping on their conversation. Quietly I crept past the couch clutching the forgotten mittens and slipped out the back door, careful to shut both doors gently behind me.

29

Snow King

THE SUN'S GLARE OFF the snow blinded me for a few seconds until my eyes
adjusted to the brightness. Pari yipped and bounded happily through the
drifts towards me. It was good to be out in the fresh air and under a blue sky
again. I knew it was not the same brilliance as the sky back in the Kingdom,
but if I was honest, I could not quite recall the color of the sky back home.

"Anya!" the girls called to me from further into the yard. They were
climbing over a metal frame that was deeply planted in the snow. From one
end there was a small ladder leading up to a ramp that Callie was standing at
the top of. Lauren stood on a small platform that was suspended on chains
from the metal bar above, and another just like it swung gently next to her.

"Hurry!" Callie cried, "You're in the hot lava!"

With a puzzled expression I struggled through the snow toward them,
glancing around at the sea of white surrounding me. "But this is just snow,"
I reasoned.

Lauren cocked her head and whispered loudly, "It's just *pretend* lava!"

"Pretend?" I questioned, puzzled. I had no idea what she was saying, I
had never used nor heard the word before.

She eyed me curiously and explained. "Yeah, you know, *pretend*. *Make
believe*. Like we just make it up in our heads and imagine we see it. Didn't
you ever play pretend when you were little?"

Seriously trying to remember, I slumped into the swing next to her
and honestly replied, "I don't think so. How do you do it?"

"Well," my little teacher began her lesson, "First, you decide what you want to imagine. Like . . ." she paused thinking.

"Like hot lava?" I offered feebly.

"Yeah," she said tentatively, not convinced, then her eyes widened, "Or the jungle!"

Callie nodded approvingly.

Lauren continued, "Then you close your eyes and see what it would look like. Think of all the tall trees with vines hanging off them."

Lauren held on to the ropes of the swing and leaned back, closing her eyes. Callie sat down at the top of the ramp and squinched her eyes closed too. Reluctantly, I closed my eyes and took a breath and to my surprise it was easy. With my eyes closed, towering trees rose from the snow, like the ones I had seen in picture books from the palace library, draped with vines. Brightly colored birds flew overhead, "And birds," I murmured.

"Yeah! Parrots!" Lauren agreed approvingly.

"And Monkeys!" Callie exclaimed happily, starting to imitate monkey noises.

Giggling, I opened my eyes to see Callie puffing out her cheeks and dancing around with one mittened hands scratching the top of her hat and the other holding on to the metal bar beside her. Lauren and I burst into a fit of laughter.

Pleased that we thought she was so entertaining, Callie hooted louder and tried to jump up and down at the top of the ramp. But when her boots hit the slippery slide, she lost her grip on the bar and went zooming down and landing face first in the snow at the bottom.

Lauren and I stopped laughing and froze for a second unsure if Callie was injured. Raising from the snow, the stunned Callie huffed a stream of breath up the side of her face and blew snow and wet hair from her eyes before exclaiming, "That. Was. Awesome!"

Relieved, Lauren and I rolled with laughter again. Then, seizing the opportunity Lauren added some drama to our imagined scene, "But then a baby monkey fell into the raging river!"

Catching on, I proclaimed, "We have to rescue her!"

Happy to play the unfortunate baby monkey in parrel, Callie smiled and began frantically thrashing in the snow, pitifully calling out, "Oo oo! Ah ah! Help! Help!"

With pretend urgency Lauren and I made our way across the 'vine' swings to the 'waterfall' slide and devised a plan to save the poor monkey and pull her up the slide to safety.

Our adventures continued with dinosaur encounters, searching for buried treasure, sailing on a pirate ship, performing in a circus, and taking care of animals in a zoo, which were made mostly out of snow and twigs. Each time we closed our eyes and imagined our way into a new place until the girls were completely out of ideas. Playing the mental game of making the imaginary come alive was exhilarating, not to mention, just plain fun! It seemed so familiar to play and imagine, yet so distant. How is it that I could not recall having done it before?

The afternoon joyfully slipped away, and the sun was just starting to dip from the sky when Callie looked to me, still breathless from chasing Pari and the other 'rhinoceros' back into their pretend pen. "Where should we go next, Anya? What places do you know?"

Thoughtfully I explained, "I guess the only place I really *know* is the palace where I live."

"Wait! You *live* in a *palace*?" Lauren stopped patting snow onto her snow lion she was making, and looked at me, awestruck.

"Well, mainly the *kitchen* of the palace, but I do help clean many of the corridors and windows as well, and sometimes even the throne room." I said, rather wistfully, trying to remember the feeling of being in the throne room. Had it truly been only six days since I had last been there? It had started to feel like it had been much longer.

Callie and Lauren gathered close to where I sat in the snow, having abandoned the snow animals that they had been building, and hung on my every word, "Tell us about it," Lauren pleaded.

"Alright!" I eagerly accepted and began to describe the splendor of the throne room. "The walls and floor are glorious white marble, swirled with gold and there are pillars that reach all the way up to the ceiling. Enormous windows fill the room with light, so much light! And under each window the wall is adorned with precious stones."

By then I could see it all so vividly in my mind that I got up and lead the girls, "See this diamond shape inlaid under the window? This is my place in the assembly. Here under this window is where I kneel before the King." Kneeling, I showed them how we honored our King each morning. Callie and Lauren tried it too, attempting to keep their balance in their bulky snow clothes.

"What is he the king of?" Callie asked innocently.

"Well, He *is* the High King. He rules over the people of the Kingdom and over the seven realms, so I guess that would make him the King of *everything*. He sent me here to your land to bring an important message, although, I don't seem to be doing a very good job delivering it."

"Where does the King sit?" Lauren inquired.

"The throne is right up here," I stood and crossed the yard and stopped in a large open area. "He stands here in front of the throne and addresses us, encourages us, and instructs us. Then once we have heard from Him, we sing to Him and then go about our duties for His good pleasure."

Pushing a ball of snow toward me, Lauren decided, "Then we will put the King here. She made the ball bigger and bigger by rolling it through the snow, until she needed help from both Callie and Ito roll it into place. Making two smaller balls, we piled them on top, then we decorated the 'king' with arms made of sticks and rocks for eyes and a smiling mouth. Callie found some short twigs that Lauren arranged into a crown. I cringed as she pressed the sharp points firmly into the snow king's head.

We stood back to admire our tribute to the King. Callie piped up, "And now we sing, right?" she prompted.

"That's right!" exclaimed Lauren, "What do you sing to the King, Anya?"

A little timid to sing in front of them, I stammered, "I, I'm sure the King would like whatever you would like to sing." But they would not let me get out of it that easily.

"No, Anya! What do *you* sing to the King?" Lauren insisted.

"Yeah," Callie exclaimed, "teach us *that* song!"

Blushing, I complied, and standing before the 'throne' I quietly began teaching them the words and melody of the Kings song. It felt very good to sing it again, even though most of my focus was on instructing the girls. They learned it very easily and soon both sang out bold and loud; proudly I smiled listening to them.

Then Callie turned to me, "Then what? What do you do after you sing?"

"Then we set about doing what pleases the King. My work is helping with the cooking for the other household servants and taking care of His palace," I instructed as I lead my pupils toward the side of the porch, "Like these windows," I pointed out, using my best Marita voice, "They could certainly use a good washing!"

Giggling, Lauren asked eagerly, "How do we wash them?"

I thought out loud, "Well I suppose that first, we will need a bucket."

It only took a moment for Lauren to light up, "I know where we can get one!" She trudged up the steps and opened the porch door and vanished inside for a few seconds then emerged carrying a small red bucket and blue shovel.

"Next, we need to fill it with soap and water. But just for pretend, of course!" I added hastily to clarify.

"How about snow? Lauren offered.

"That will do." I nodded.

Callie held the bucket while Lauren filled it with clumps of dense, wet snow. Proudly Callie held up the filled bucket, "Now what?"

"Now we wash the windows!" I announced, taking a mitten full of snow I rubbed it across the window. It didn't so much clean as it did grind snow into the mesh covering and get lodged against the glass, but the girls seemed delighted by this and followed suit happily coating each window in snow.

Eventually, Callie's bottom lip had started to shake from shivering and her cheeks were red from the cold when Molly finally opened the porch door and peeked her head out, "Anyone out here ready for some hot cocoa?" The girls and I eagerly agreed and began heading toward the door.

Then Lauren stopped, "One last thing!" She said wading through the snow back to where the snow king stood. Taking her mittens off her hands, she carefully draped them over the ends of the snow king's stick arms, then playfully tapped the king's 'hand' with hers.

"Hey, I want to give the king a high five too!!" Callie whined. Lauren rolled her eyes and motioned for her to come across the yard. Callie bounded across the snow with Pari pouncing beside her to give the king a 'high five'.

We made our way back to the porch where Molly met us and helped brush the snow off our jackets and hats. Pari shook the snow from his fur and licked his paws to clean and warm them.

"Momma, did you see our snowman?"

Looking through the screen door window, Molly smiled, "First snowman of the year! He looks awesome, Callie girl!" she said, crouching to brush strands of hair off Callie's cold cheeks, and help her out of her snow pants.

"He's the King!" Callie proclaimed excitedly.

"Oh! Is he?" Molly teased, "What is he the king of? The swing set?"

"Anya told us he is the King over everything! He sent her here on a mission! She has a message to deliver. We played that we were in her Kingdom, and we sang to the King!" Lauren explained very matter of factually.

"And then we washed the windows!" Callie added exuberantly pointing to the porch windows that were now smeared with slush and snow where the girls had "washed" them.

"Okay? I think that's enough *make-believe* for today." Molly said haltingly, then looked over at me with a curious sort of expression on her face.

"Sorry about the windows. We were "imagining" that the snow was soap and water." I apologized quickly. I had been having so much fun with the girls teaching me how to pretend that I had not noticed what a mess we had made.

"Oh, the windows are fine, Anya!" Molly laughed nervously, "There will be plenty more snow that hits them before this winter will be over!" she said, crinkling her nose. As the girls headed into the house, I helped Molly hang up the wet snow gear to dry on the hooks in the porch and pull out the boot liners to dry as well.

We were about to go back into the house when Molly put her hand on my shoulder, with a concerned look, she said, "Anya, I'd like to hear more about your *King* and what he has sent you to do. But let's talk more about it later," Then she stressed, "when it's just the two of us, ok?" I could tell she was cautious of me telling the girls more about the Kingdom.

30

Marshmallows & Fairytales

WHEN I ENTERED THE kitchen, Lauren and Callie were sitting at the table delightedly plopping little white puffs into their steaming cups of hot cocoa.

Entering the room behind me, Molly picked up two mugs and handed one to me. It was filled with sweet, hot, chocolate happiness. Breathing it in, I thanked her and slid onto the bench by the window beside Callie who eagerly thrust the bag of white puffs toward me.

"Mauf-mowwow?", she questioned while shoving a handful of them into her mouth.

"Thank you." I cautiously responded reaching into the bag and retrieving one of the small squishy treats. It was soft and pillowy and extremely sweet.

"Hey!" Molly intervened as Callie reached her hand back into the bag to pull out another handful and slyly dropped them all into her cup before her mother could get out, "That's enough, young lady, you'll spoil your dinner!"

With a tilt of her head, and that look that I had only seen perfected by Marita, Molly held out her hand and Callie obediently handed the bag over still grinning a sticky grin.

Soon the girls had finished their hot cocoa, or at least the layer of floating 'marshmallows', as they called them, and went with Molly upstairs to take a bath before supper. This left me alone in the kitchen peeking over the top of my cup into the next room where my eyes fell on my bag still slumped against the couch.

I slumped too; I was running out of time. I had spent all afternoon with the girls and had not even thought about the gift or my mission. Something Molly had said kept haunting me. She had said that we had 'played enough *make believe* for today'. But I wasn't really *playing* make-believe about the Kingdom. I was just *remembering*. Wasn't I?

The sun dipped behind the horizon and the room darkened quickly. My mood followed. I thought about the brightness of the Kingdom; it seemed so distant and hazy and the darkness, doubt, and fear that I had begun to feel since I had arrived seemed so poignant, piercing, and real.

"No wonder it's hard for Molly to believe me," I muttered out loud to the empty room. If I was honest, in that moment, it was starting to seem easier in my mind to believe that the Kingdom *was* all make-believe too, even though I was sure that I had only left it a few days ago.

I set down my cup and entered the quiet sitting room where my bag lay. As an act of defiance against my unbelief I attempted to lift the bag. It was still firmly rooted to the floor by the weight of the pearl.

With a relieved sigh I lowered to the ground and moved back the flap. In the dim light that still filtered through the windows from outside, I peered down into the depths. I could see the blanket from the sailor. I pulled it out and set it on the couch. I could see the crumpled map of the city of Chicago crammed into one corner and several other items I had collected from my journey, pressed unnaturally away from the center of the bag: my transit card, the coin from Talon Tower, Zahara's poster, the business card from Kimmy's father, the slip of paper with Rita's numbers, Caroline's Learning Center brochure, and the pamphlet from Animal Control.

To the eye, there was *nothing* else filling the empty place between them. No glowing, no swirling white mist, no iridescent pearl. Just heaviness and an invisible weight that I could no longer carry on my own.

Groping into the bag, I willed my hand to feel *something* and thankfully my fingers brushed the cool hard surface of the orb. I felt ashamed for a moment. Who was I to have doubted for a second that my mission was still real? But my dilemma remained; what good could I possibly do with it now? I had no idea.

"Tomorrow will be the seventh day, Pari." I said quietly, closing the flap over the top of the bag. Pari was curled up napping on the rug by the fireplace and opened one eye in response before closing it again and resuming his nap. He couldn't have been less concerned; he was a picture of perfect peace. Meanwhile, I was eaten up with anxious thoughts and my stomach churned uneasily with worry.

At dinner I hardly ate, but just picked at the pot roast, roasted potatoes and carrots. I'm sure it was delicious; Molly made it herself, but I had no appetite.

Just as the family was finishing the meal, strange lights and vehicles were slowly making their way down the road past the house. We could hear the beeping and grinding sounds as they painstakingly moved snow off the roadway. The girls and I watched, fascinated.

Luke stood up, starting to clear the table, "Well, looks like Henry and I will be out bright and early to clear the driveway and the church parking lot for Bible study tomorrow."

The girls jumped up and were about to trot out of the room, "Ladies?" their father said in a low commanding voice, clearing his throat, "are you forgetting something?"

They stopped in their tracks and turned around smiling sheepishly, Callie mumbled in a sing-song voice, "We forgot da dishes!"

The girls and Luke worked together to gather and clear away all the dishes from the meal and by the time they had them neatly stacked next to the sink Callie was rubbing her tired eyes. Our adventures that day had certainly tuckered her out.

Molly sent the girls up to their room to pick some 'bedtime' stories and Luke went to the study to get some work done (whatever that meant) and Molly and I washed and dried the dishes quickly while Nana Betty put them away.

Nana Betty was moving a bit more slowly and gingerly than she had been earlier, and finally she leaned over to gently rub her knees, "Oof, you may have been right about me overdoing it on the bike this morning. It just felt good to get moving again, but my stubborn streak gets me in trouble. I probably pushed myself a little harder than my body was ready for."

"Why don't you take a load off, Ma? I'm sure Anya and I can finish the rest," Molly looked to me, and I nodded in agreement. "When I get down from putting the girls to bed, I'll put more of your medicated ointment on your knees. That should help."

"Thank you, dears," Nana Betty said gratefully patting me on my shoulder before hobbling toward her room.

Molly and I quickly finished the dishes and as she put the last of the clean plates away, Callie appeared in the doorway with her arms loaded with books, "You ready Mama?"

Molly scanned the pile of books, "Great choice Callie girl," she commented, half to herself. Turning to me, with a suspicious smile on her face, she invited, "Anya, why don't you join us for story time tonight?"

Unaware of Molly's plans, I gladly accepted; I didn't want to be left alone with my own thoughts and worries swirling around in my head anyhow. I followed them up the stairs and to the bedroom that Callie and Lauren shared. While Molly brought the girls to brush their teeth, I sat down on the edge of one of the two small beds that flanked a table with a glowing lamp on it. Looking up at the walls of the cozy chamber, I could see that half the room was painted pink with gold crowns decorating the walls and the other half was painted purple with silver unicorns. On the wall in between was a large plaque that was hand painted with beautiful looping letters,

> "Little One, you are loved and cherished, one of a kind, uniquely made for a special purpose to serve the Lord and shine for Him."

Surrounding the large plaque were several small frames each holding a quote of some sort that seemed to tie into the message of the plaque. As I whispered the words that they held, a strange peaceful feeling came over me. The words resonated as reassuring truth. Although I could not remember ever seeing or hearing them spoken before, they were familiar and deeply comforting.

> "For God so loved the world, that He gave His only begotten Son, that whosoever believeth in Him should not perish, but have everlasting life.
> ~John 3:16"

> "I will praise thee; for I am fearfully and wonderfully made; marvelous are thy works; and that my soul knoweth right well.
> ~Psalm 139:14"

> "Being confident of this very thing, that He which hath begun a good work in you will perform it until the day of Jesus Christ.
> ~Philippians 1:6"

> "Let your light so shine before men, that they may see your good works, and glorify your Father in heaven.
> ~Matthew 5:16"

Molly and the girls returned, and Lauren sleepily crawled under her pink blankets. Callie flopped onto the bed next to me, then climbed up onto my lap, "Anya, sit with me!", she murmured, taking my arms, she pulled them around her as she leaned back against me. I quickly complied and hugged her close.

Sitting down on the edge of Lauren's bed, Molly smiled fondly at her sleepy girls and taking the pile of books that Callie had picked out, she pulled one of them from the top of the pile into her lap.

On the front of the book were the words, 'Fairy Tales'. Lauren piped up from her snug little borough, "Mama, read the one about the princess and the frog! And do the froggie voice, pleeeeese?"

"Yes, mama!" Callie squealed, bouncing excitedly. "And the mermaid one too!"

"Ok, ok, OK!" their mother complied, "But you need to get all snug in your bed first."

Callie climbed off my lap and slid under her plush purple blanket, and then her mother began to read. She read all sorts of short stories from the Fairy Tale book; many of them about kings and kingdoms and princesses locked in towers, tiny little people who were born out of a flower and many more fantastical things. There was one story that I found especially intriguing about a servant girl, Cinderella, who became a princess. Occasionally, Molly would look up from her reading to study my reactions.

Finally, Molly closed the book. The girls' eyelids were drooping heavily. "I think that's enough for tonight."

"No," Callie weakly protested, "One more please!"

"Maybe tomorrow night, sweet girl! It's time for bed." Looking at me she added, "Anya, would you like to join us for prayers?"

"Prayers?" I questioned; I had not heard this word before.

Lauren wisely offered an explanation, "Yeah, it's when we talk to God and thank Him for everything He has given us. Then we tell Him about our day and ask for His blessings and stuff."

"Oh, alright," I was curious what this was all about.

Callie and Lauren slipped out of their beds and knelt beside them with their elbows propped up and little hands clasped together. They closed their eyes and drooped their heads, and Lauren began.

"Thank you, God, for a great day. We really liked playing outside with Anya today. Thank you for making the sunshine and for sending the snow so we didn't have to go to school!" She opened one eye and peeked at her mother slyly before continuing. "Thank you for my family and for loving me. Grant me wisdom. Amen."

Callie picked up as soon as Lauren was done, "Thank you God for food and stuff. Thank you for this day and giving us snow to make a snowman. Thank you for sending us Anya, please let her stay with us forever. I love you! Amen."

With a big yawn Callie climbed slowly back under her blankets and Lauren's eyelids were nearly closed as she settled into her bed. Molly gave them each a hug and a kiss and tucked the blankets around them; quietly I slipped out of the room.

I was struck with how their simple prayers sounded a lot like how I would write to the King or call out to Him, somehow knowing that He could hear me. They must know that the one they called God, could hear them and was listening to them too.

I stood in the stairway for several seconds trying to wrap my mind around this when something drew my eye. It was another large frame with a picture of a simple dirt road which met the sunrise in the distance. There were two ruts that were well worn from use and grass growing up in the middle. The fields on either side were ready for harvest and glowing golden in the morning light. The sky above was painted with soft hues. My eyes followed the path until it touched the sunrise and disappeared. Below it was written:

> "Trust in the Lord with all your heart and lean not on your own understanding. In all your ways acknowledge Him, and He will make straight your paths.
> ~Proverbs 3:5–6"

31

The Word

As I entered the dark sitting room, I pondered the meaning of the messages on the walls. What were they all about?

"Trust in the Lord," I murmured quietly. Well, in the Kingdom, we often referred to the King as 'Lord'. So that made complete sense to me. But who was *this* 'Lord'? Could it possibly be referring to *my* King? It seemed to me that not many people here knew anything of the Kingdom I was a citizen of.

Deeply lost in thought, I paused at the bottom of the stairs, more confused than ever.

Who is God? And that name, Jesus? There was something special about that name, but I couldn't quite figure it out. What did it all mean?

In a daze, I stood there while these questions bounced around my mind for several minutes before I noticed that Pari was not curled up on the rug where I last saw him.

"Pari?" I called out softly.

From the open door to her room, I heard Nana Betty answer for him, "He is in here with me Anya. He's been keeping me company while I do my Bible study and wait for Molly to get the girls to bed. She was going to come down and help me put some more ointment on my knees, they are killing me!"

I entered the room shocked, "They are doing what?!" I stammered, taking her words quite literally.

She laughed, "Oh Anya, it's a figure of speech. I only mean they are hurtin' something awful since I did my exercises this morning."

"Oh yes!" I laughed sheepishly, feeling rather embarrassed that I over-reacted, "I am sorry, I guess I have a lot on my mind."

Pari was sitting attentively next to Nana Betty's chair where she had a large well-worn book open on her lap. She closed her book carefully, marking her page with a crimson ribbon, and patted the white chair that had been pulled up near hers. "Well, my friend, why don't you come on in and tell me about it."

Set at ease by the old woman's inviting smile, I settled into the chair beside her attempting to pull my thoughts together. Not really knowing where to start, I opted for a question instead.

"I read the messages on the walls upstairs. What do they mean?"

"The messages on the walls?" Nana Betty repeated. Recognizing what I meant, she continued, "Oh you're talking about the scripture verses. Molly and I put those up last year when we repainted the girls' room."

"And the one at the top of the stairs?"

Nana Betty closed her eyes trying to recollect in her mind an image of what was at the top of the stairs. Her eyes stayed closed, but a soft smile played across her thin lips, "Trust in the Lord with all your heart, and lean not on your own understanding. In all your ways acknowledge Him and He will make your paths straight. Proverbs 3:5–6," she murmured.

She opened her eyes and turned to me with a sad kind of smile, "My late husband, Luke's father, made that as a gift for Luke when he was about to leave home. Luke was bound and determined he was going to move to Chicago for school and go into ministry. Of course, we were so proud of him, but also a bit unsure about where this path was going to take him. Luke's been a country boy his whole life," she explained, "and his father was nervous about him moving to such a big city."

"But that next morning, Michael, Luke's father, was out for a walk on our ranch and he took that photo. It's leading out of our driveway back home and looking toward the sunrise. We didn't know what God had planned for our son. Michael was reassured that morning that Luke was following God's plan and took that as a promise that the Lord would be with Luke wherever that path may lead. Thank the Lord, He has been faithful! He eventually led Luke back to the country!"

Reflecting, Nana Betty fell silent. And to clarify I asked, "So those words are from Luke's father?"

"Oh no!" she assured me, patting the book on her lap, "Those are straight from the Word of God!"

Slowly, I repeated her words back to her, "Word of God?" then asked, "Who *is* God? Are they a king or something?"

Nana Betty leaned back and studied my expression, to see if I was joking with her. When she saw that I was sincere in my question, she earnestly and patiently tried to answer.

"Well, Anya, that *is* the big question, isn't it? Who is God?" She smiled at me and patted my leg reassuringly, "Whenever I am faced with a big question like that I always turn to His Word," she said placing her weathered hand gently on the cover of the well-used book, "and the Lord shows me the answer."

Opening the leather cover of her book, Nana Betty adjusted her glasses as she turned the first few pages "I think the best place to start, will be at the beginning,"

She smiled sagely at me, then began to read. As she did, a tingle surged up my spine to the base of my neck and awakened all my senses. The mental cobwebs that had cluttered my thoughts were instantly cleared away and a feeling like warm honey melted over my head and down my shoulders relaxing all the tension I was holding from my worry. Surprised that I instantly felt more at peace, I leaned in reading the words off the page as the soft timbre and gentle sound of her voice brought each word to life, like a long-forgotten story suddenly being recollected again.

"In the beginning God created the heavens and the earth. The earth was without form, and void; and darkness was on the face of the deep. And the Spirit of God was hovering over the face of the waters."

"Then God said, 'Let there be light'; and there was light. And God saw the light, that it was good; and God divided the light from the darkness."

She continued reading and the words painted an amazing and beautiful picture of all creation coming into being as God commanded existence to take form.

Putting my newfound skills of imagination to work, I could vividly 'see' God's breath of life entering man, the plants and trees springing forth from the ground, and the sun, moon and stars being placed in the sky.

Nana Betty paused for a moment to observe my enraptured expression, "Does that start to give you an answer to your question?" she gently prodded.

"I think so . . . so God is the creator, and He has a Spirit and through His Word He created all things . . ." I tentatively offered. Nana Betty nodded encouragingly as I was tentatively stepping into a new understanding as if I were crossing a stream by stepping cautiously from one rock to another.

Pausing mid-thought stream, I found myself with no more rocks only more questions, "But what about God's Word? Where did it come from?

And what about His Son? Who is He?" The questions came quickly as I thought back to the messages on the girls' wall about God sending His Son to save people.

By the expression on the old woman's face, I could see that Nana Betty was pleased by these questions. "Very good, Anya! Let's see if God's Word has the answer for that as well."

Her aged fingers nimbly flipped through the book and by the grin on her face and the way she stopped abruptly on just the right page, I could tell that she already knew that it did.

"In the beginning was the Word, and the Word was with God, and the Word was God. He was in the beginning with God. All things were made through Him, and without Him was not any thing made that was made. In Him was life, and the life was the light of men. The light shines in the darkness, and the darkness has not overcome it."

"The *darkness?*" I uttered quietly, that struck a chord, "My King, He talked about the *darkness* too. My gift is supposed to remind people of something that will help push back the darkness." My eyes scanned the pages frantically searching for the meaning of this, but then I remembered my other question, "But what about God's son?"

"That is who we have been talking about. Here," she offered, tracing ahead with her finger, "And the Word became flesh and dwelt among us, and we have seen His glory, glory as the only Son from the Father, full of grace and truth. For from His fullness we have all received, grace upon grace. For the law was given through Moses; grace and truth came through Jesus Christ."

"Do you understand that, Anya?"

"The Word become *flesh* . . . does that mean a man?" I was slowly putting the pieces of this puzzle together.

"Yes Anya, very good! And that man is the Son of God, Jesus Christ! Because of God's great love for us, for you, for me, for everyone, He sent His Son Jesus to save us from our sins."

"Sins?" I questioned, another thing that I had never heard of. "What is a sin?"

"Well, a sin is something that we do that is wrong, that hurts God's heart and displeases Him. God is perfect and holy, and sin cannot be around God, so that sin separates us from Him."

"Oh." I said quietly, looking down at my feet, shamefully remembering the stolen apples, the harsh words, and the bad attitude I'd had and how I had run away from the city where the King had sent me.

Placing her hand on mine Nana Betty assured me, "We have all sinned, but that is why we *need* Jesus. It is through Him that our sins are forgiven and our relationship with God is restored!"

I took a deep breath, not sure if I could let myself believe that it could be that simple. Turning to Nana Betty, my confession spilled like water from a dam breaking, my words gushed out and I could not hold them back.

"When I first arrived in this land, I thought I was going to make the King so pleased and accomplish this mission for Him so easily. And I tried; I really did!"

Adamantly, I continued, "For three days I met with the wealthy, the influencers and the powerful of this land. But every time I failed."

Making the connection, Nana Betty leaned back astonished, "You mean like Zahara and Anthony Warner?"

I nodded, "And the King of Chicago."

"Oh, yes! Molly told me about that." She confirmed.

Staring down at my feet, I continued, "But none of them were who I was seeking. Even so, I remained hopeful that Pari and I could still find them. But as time went on things got worse and worse. I started to doubt myself, and then," my voice caught for a moment, "then I thought I had lost Pari. Without my guide, I didn't know what to do."

I shrugged my shoulders, recalling my downtrodden state, "I just wandered the streets calling for him. I went into a dark place and was attacked by some boys. A man saved me from them but then he tricked me into doing something that would displease the King."

I didn't look up but heard Nana Betty inhaling sharply. She cradled my trembling hands in hers. My bottom lip began to quiver, and fresh tears gathered in my eyes, "I was just so confused, discouraged, and sad. I felt alone and tired and cold."

"Oh, Anya!" she whispered sympathetically.

"Then I heard the Kings voice and I first met Luke and Molly. They helped me with food and warm clothing, and they told me how to find Pari. Once I got Pari back, I was afraid someone would come after us and try to separate us again, so we just got as far away from the city as we could. We rode on bus after bus, until the city was far behind us. That's how I ended up where Luke and Molly found me."

"I have shown how weak and useless I really am. At every turn I've needed the help of others just to survive. I'm near the end of my time here and I feel like I've done very little to make anything better. Now I'm stuck, I've made a wrong turn and I can't get back!"

Taking a shuddering breath I continued, "I'm not where I am supposed to be, and I've done things and acted in ways I am not proud of. I don't know how I can possibly deliver the Kings message in time or if I'll ever be allowed back into the Kingdom! What if I can *never* be forgiven?" I blurted, "I've failed."

In a soothing voice, Nana Betty tried to calm me, "You are never too far from God's grace to be forgiven, child! It's ok! There is nothing you could have done that cannot be laid down at the foot of the cross. Anya it does you no good to wish you were anywhere else than where you are right in this moment. How do you know you are not right where your King wants you to be?"

My tears flowed like rivers down my cheeks as I tried to hold back my sobs.

Pari put his paw on Nana Betty's leg and groaned softly. She looked at him with a shocked and perplexed expression, then nodded decidedly and turned to me and reiterated, "How do you know you're not right where the King wants you to be, Anya? Instead of wishing you were someplace else or fearing that you've missed His mission, be His ambassador right where you are at. Don't spend so much time worrying about yesterday that you miss what is before you today. The answer is closer than you think, Anya."

Sniffling, I blinked and wiped away my tears, "How do you know?"

Smiling, she turned to Pari, and gently scratched his hairy chin, "I don't. But Pari does."

I looked from Pari to Nana Betty then back again. I didn't know that anyone else there could 'hear' him like I could.

32

In the Name of the King

SQUINTING UP AT A large clock on the wall, Nana Betty yawned, "I'll bet Molly fell asleep putting the girls down to bed. That girl works so hard to take care of all of us. I can go without this stuff for tonight."

She started to put the cap back on the canister of ointment that I had seen Molly using on Nana Betty's legs earlier.

"Can *I* help you with it?" I offered, eager to be useful.

Nana Betty cocked her head. "You would do that for me?"

"Of course. It's the least I can do to repay the kindness you and your family have shown me."

I opened the canister and knelt on the floor in front of Nana Betty. Scooping some of the pungent ointment onto my fingertips I inquired, "How long have you had this ailment?"

"You mean how long have my knees been giving me trouble? Oh, years and years, that's why I had the surgery. It helped, but they still give me *some* pain nearly every day." Straightening her leg she exhaled slowly, wincing from the pain, "Ooh. Then on days like today when I get a bit too ambitious, they still remind me that I'm not as young as I used to be."

"You have been in pain for *years*?" I was shocked! It's not that we are unfamiliar with pain or affliction as citizens of the Kingdom, just that the afflictions are made low in the presence of the King. When we bring Him our hurts, He is faithful to ease our burdens.

I reached out and began to smooth the ointment over Nana Betty's knee, and was filled with compassion for her pain, "In the name of the King, be healed."

I felt her hand touch my shoulder, "What did you just say?" Nana Betty murmured; her voice filled with wonder.

"Oh, that is just something we say in the Kingdom. When we are with the King, He takes away our hurts, but when we are not in His presence physically, we will still say to one another. 'In the name of the King, be healed!' and we are!"

Pari stood up and came beside me. I looked up at Nana Betty, my hands still placed on her knees, and repeated, "In the name of the King, be healed!" The same tingle as earlier went up my spine and from the look on Nana Betty's face she felt it too.

She reached down to touch her knee and began bending it back and forth. With a tear in her eye she breathed, "Anya, I think He has!"

33

The Distance from Home

SUDDENLY, VERY EXHAUSTED FROM the day's activities both physically and emotionally, I excused myself to prepare for bed. After changing into night clothes and washing up I stumbled to the couch. My bag was still sitting on the floor, and I forced myself to get the book and writing stick from it before I sat down.

What to write about this day? I thought to myself. I had no idea where to start.

I wrote longingly at the top of the page. At a loss for words, I began to mindlessly draw long curving lines down the edge of the page. With a sigh, I leaned back to try to think. It was not long before my head nodded with weariness and my eyelids drooped heavily, and I fell into a deep sleep.

At some point in the night, though my body remained slumped on the couch, my mind awakened and wandered into the unfamiliar realm of dreams. In my fourteen years, up to that point, I do not remember ever having a dream. However, that day something had been unlocked by the discovery of imagination and dreams. What started as a doodle on the page of my journal took on a life of its own. The curved line gained dimension and color and soon I found myself on the page as a part of the drawing. The

drawing had become the path. Looking behind me, I could see that the
path lead from the harbor in the
Kingdom up to the palace.

The surroundings took on sub-
stance and color. I began to walk up
the path toward the palace. There was
a watery slowness and weightlessness
to each step I took.

Before me was the palace, sil-
houetted by the light of the rising
sun and beams of light gloriously
streamed out from behind it. I was
overjoyed! I was home!

I tried to run to the palace, but
my legs would not respond to my urgent request. With each step I managed to take, the path got steeper and
began to crumble beneath my feet.
Soon, I found myself sliding backwards. Panicking, I tried harder, but
something was pulling me. I looked
down. Hanging from my side was the
messenger bag and the pearl inside
had grown and was now ripping the
bag apart at the seams. The weight of
it was making me sink.

The earth began to swallow me
up. I desperately wanted to cry out
for help but was silenced by some invisible force. The palace was getting
further and further away from me
as I sank down, down, down; pulled
by the heaviness of my unfinished
mission.

I reached for the Kingdom as I
sank deeper into the pit. Finally, my
voice responded faintly, "My Lord,
help me, please!" as the smothering
darkness closed in around me.

Suddenly, a strong hand clasped my outstretched arm, and I felt a great tug pulling me up out of the pit. With a gasp my eyes flew open and my book and writing stick tumbled to the floor revealing the moment captured in the margin of the page.

34

Decided

EARLY MORNING SUNLIGHT FILTERED into the room. Slowly I realized that I was not back in the Kingdom at all; I was still in Luke and Molly's sitting room. My pounding heart was echoing in my ears. I sat up on the couch unable to sleep any longer. My mind was spinning. My time there was nearly over, and the weight of the burden was heavy on my soul.

Pari, who was asleep on the rug by the fire, stretched his legs and yawned. He stood up, came over to me, and laid his head on my knees. He too, finally felt the urgency to arise and complete our mission. He got up from my side and pawed gently at the door to the backyard. Tucking the book and writing stick back into my bag, I arose to follow.

The sun had just peeked over the horizon, as we slipped out onto the porch where the girls and I had left the boots and outdoor clothing. Pulling on my boots and Molly's old red jacket, we quietly made our way outside.

The morning sun was shining through the trees and allowed a stream of warm glowing sunlight to spill over the "snow king" we had made. His long shadow draped across the yard. The air was crisp and exhilarating and awakened my senses, fully chasing any grogginess of the restless night away. My breath rose around me and hung as a cloud in the cold air.

Pari bounded through the snow playfully, enjoying this chance to run. Wading across the yard, I gave the king's mitten a "high-five" as the girls had done the previous day. I chuckled thinking of how strange this gesture would be in the Kingdom; to "high-five" the King!

Pushing my hands into the jacket pockets to conserve warmth, I stepped past him into a beam of sunlight that was twinkling off the snow. "My King." I sighed to myself at the thought of standing once more before Him. The sunrise marked the start of the seventh day since we had sailed away from the Kingdom. So far, my journey was a failure. I had not fulfilled my mission; I had run away from my responsibility and ended up stuck miles away from where I started.

"My King," I whispered, "show me what I should do." I had heard his voice in the alleyway a few days before and hoped I would hear it again. I did not; there was nothing but a happy 'yip' from Pari as he bounded over to me.

"I really miss home." I sighed. He whimpered sympathetically.

I put my hand on his shaggy head and gently ruffled his fur. "You ready to go back?" He sat down with a grumble. I knew what he meant; we were not done with our mission yet. We couldn't give up hope.

"I meant going inside. Are you ready to go back in the *house*?". He jumped up and started to bound across the yard back toward the house. Suddenly, Nana Betty's question came to mind, "How do you know you are not right where your King wants you to be?"

I turned toward the house; it was bathed in the morning sun. I saw Luke, still in the clothes he had on last night and Molly in her pajamas, both standing in the study window. Their heads were bowed, like the girls had done when they prayed the night before.

Suddenly, I knew what I was going to do. Of all the people I had met, Luke and Molly were the kind of people who should receive the King's gift. They didn't have the power of Governor Warner, the influence of Zahara, or the money like Mr. Talon, but they were *good* people. Good people who cared and were willing to reach out to those in need. I had no idea how they could use it to change their world, and maybe the King would be disappointed in me, but I had found no one more deserving than the cowboy and his wife.

35

The Pearl & the Call—Part Two

PARI AND I ENTERED the house quietly. The girls had woken up and as soon as Pari saw them he hurried over to nuzzle them playfully with his cold, snowy nose. They squealed and wrapped their arms around his shaggy neck.

"Good morning Pari," Lauren cooed.

Luke and Molly entered from the study, "Morning Anya! I hope you like blueberry pancakes, they are Nana's specialty on Saturday mornings."

Molly ushered the girls upstairs to get dressed and went to the kitchen. Nana headed to her room to get ready for the day. Luke returned to the study.

This was my chance to present the gift; I knew I could not hesitate. I attempted to pick up my bag, and to my surprise I was able to lift it to my shoulder. Nestled snuggly in the messenger bag, I could still feel the weight of the pearl, but I carried it into the study without struggle.

"Luke? Could I talk to you and Molly?" I began.

Luke looked up from the papers and books that were strewn across his desk, "Yea, of course Anya." He called into the kitchen, "Molly, ya got a minute?"

"Sure, be right there!" she called back.

"How is your project going?" I inquired.

"My sermon? Oh yeah, this is a sermon I've been working on since we moved out here and started our church. I just haven't been able to finish it. If its ever going to come together, today is the day for it," Luke shook his head, "There is just something missing. I've always had all these pieces but just can't find that one thing that could tie it all together. It's like it's right there

205

beyond the tips of my fingers. I think I have it, but then it's just out of grasp."
Luke sighed, "This world is a pretty broken place, Anya,"

I nodded in agreement. From all I had seen, I had realized that was true.

Luke continued, "People need hope. Real hope in something that
doesn't change; solid ground for them to place their faith. We tend to get
caught up in our fast-paced busy lives and we forget that there is a simple
truth that can bring true peace. We started Simple Faith Church to help
people get back to that, but for the life of me, I can't quite put it into words
the way it feels in my heart. I just," He stammered, "I just don't want to miss
it and fail Him, ya know?"

"I know exactly how you feel." I confided.

Molly had come from the kitchen and stood in the doorway, drying
her hands with a kitchen towel. With the girls upstairs, Pari joined me and
gently nudged the messenger bag I was holding.

I took a deep breath, and began, "It is almost time for me to go." I
paused to look up at them, feeling a lump forming in my throat. I swallowed
hard and looked down at the ground searching for the words to say next as
if they had fallen out of my mouth and I could somehow spot them scattered
on the wooden floorboards at my feet.

Luke and Molly looked at each other and nodded, knowing it was time
to bring up something that had been on *their* minds.

"You know Anya," Molly began as she stepped toward me. She took my
hands inviting me to sit next to her on the bench by the window, "Luke and
I have been talking about it," Luke pulled his desk chair next to Molly. "and
we thought that you could just stay here with us."

Luke joined in, "The girls, Molly and I and Nana, we all feel like you
are family; that God brought us all together for a reason. So, until we get
things sorted out with your parents or whoever, you're going to need a safe,
stable place to be. And we would like to be that place for you, for as long as
it takes."

They both looked at me, waiting for my answer.

Finding my voice again, I was moved by their love and concern for
me, "I really appreciate the hospitality that your family has shown me. You
have been so kind to me. You and Molly saved me and took care of me. Even
though I was a stranger, you treated me like part of your family. Callie and
Lauren are so precious and dear to me. They are a joy and a blessing. I have
learned so much from them about playing and imagining. Nana has been
so helpful, her presence brings peace, she reminds me of Marita who has
looked after me since I was young." I paused for a moment.

Suddenly, overcome by how much I missed Marita and my home in the Kingdom, tears began to till my eyes and I had to hold my breath to contain my sorrows. Luke and Molly exchanged a concerned look.

"I *have* to get home." I sobbed.

It took several moments to regain my composure, before I reached into the messenger bag and began to explain, "I have been sent here by the Most High King to deliver this gift." I lifted the pearl, letting the messenger bag drop to my feet. The weight of the orb was still there, but somehow it was now manageable. The pearl glowed with light again. The mist within it swirled fervently, expecting, anticipating.

Luke and Molly both gasped at the sight of it and the light of the King's gift shone on their faces.

Encouraged by the revived energy of the pearl, I continued, "I was told that I would find someone who could use this message to bring hope to this land and remind them of the victory that has already been won. I have searched and searched. I have talked to the kings of this land who were too confident in their towers, the influential who sought only to bring honor and glory to themselves, and the powerful who were concerned only with accumulating fruitless victories at any cost. But none were willing to provide hope to others and give glory to the one who sent me."

Very seriously, I met Luke's eyes, "My time here grows very short and perhaps my King *did* lead me here to you. For I have found no one else that possesses your willingness to bring hope to others. So, humbly I offer this gift to you. Will you use it to bring hope and healing to your land? Will you accept the call?

With awe and wonder, Luke replied breathlessly, "Yes, I will."

Standing up I stepped forward and gently placed the pearl into Luke's two hands. The light from within the orb suddenly lit the room with a blinding light and as it subsided, Luke, Molly and I leaned forward in amazement; for a brief second the image of the Kingdom appeared within the orb and then it was gone. Only Luke's open hands remained, completely empty.

It felt like my heart became wax and melted within me. My mouth went dry, and I thought I may be sick at any moment! The pearl was gone! Yet I remained. As the Kingdom faded from my eyes, my hope turned to dust. My time was up. I had failed.

36

Early Christmas

"Anya, I . . . ." Luke stammered; his empty hands still open on his lap. Both he and Molly sat frozen with an expression of shock on their faces.

Devastated, I snatched my messenger bag from the floor and ran from the room. Nana Betty was just emerging from her bedroom. "Good morning, Sweetheart!" She said brightly as I stumbled into her. Biting my lip to contain my tears, I pushed past her and retreated into the bathroom shutting the door firmly behind me.

Clutching the messenger bag, I collapsed to the floor and knelt there, willing myself back to the Kingdom. When my tears had subsided and I opened my eyes, I was still on the floor of Nana Betty's bathroom. "My mission has failed; it's over. Why am I still here?" I whispered to myself.

I don't know what I thought *should* have happened. Was I expecting the 'Shama' to suddenly sail up to Luke and Molly's front door to return me to the Kingdom? I guess I had just expected *something* to happen once the pearl had been delivered.

I considered that maybe the things of this world were holding me back. Turning my bag over, I shook the contents out. The gold coin from Talon tower clanked to the floor, followed by the crumpled map, bus pass, folded poster of Zahara, slip of paper from Rita, pamphlet from Caroline, card from Kimmy, papers from Animal Control, my journal and writing stone and the blanket from the sailor. I gathered up most of them and shoved them into a waste basket that was beside the sink. I returned the blanket to my bag; it was from the Kingdom, after all, and perhaps I would see the sailor again and could return it, I reasoned. I placed my writing stone and journal safely in the bag and fastened it.

Molly had left my mended and clean clothing folded on the chair in the bathroom and I quickly changed into them, leaving the baggy clothes Molly had loaned me on the chair in their place.

Breathing hard, I stood in the middle of the room, with the messenger bag slung across my shoulders. Ready. Waiting. "Any second," I thought. But seconds passed, then minutes, and I finally resigned to the fact that the 'Shama' was not coming back for me.

Pari pawed at the door, and I could hear Luke, Molly and Nana Betty talking urgently in the kitchen. I opened the door just enough for Pari to push his way in. He nuzzled me with his wet nose and licked my tearstained face. Comforting me, he groaned softly, telling me to be patient and that our time was not yet complete.

Taking a deep breath, I tried to compose myself. I stepped before the mirror and saw the pitiful look on my face with flushed cheeks and red eyes still wet with tears. I washed my face, brushed my hair, pulled it into two long braids and emerged from the bathroom. When I entered the kitchen, the three of them stopped talking and stared at me for a moment.

Luke gently broke the silence, "Hey Anya, you ok?"

Silently I nodded my head, still numb from the shock that the pearl was gone. I really *did* feel 'ok'; the weight of the burden was lifted but it left a strange emptiness. I felt like I was floating, just waiting for something to happen. So, when Molly invited me to help her make Nana Betty's 'famous' blueberry buttermilk pancakes I accepted and was glad to have something to do.

While we were mixing the batter, the door to the kitchen burst open, and an elderly man backed into the room pulling something wrapped in a huge white sack behind him.

At the sound of the door, Nana Betty turned and seeing him, chided, "Henry James Foster, what in heaven's name are you dragging in?"

Looking up with a playful twinkle in his lively blue eyes, he replied, "Just an early Christmas gift!" Frost still clung to his silver beard but could not hide the childlike grin on his face.

The girls must have sensed he had arrived, because at that moment they bounded down the stairs, "Henry! Henry!" and upon seeing him ran to embrace him.

"Is it a Christmas tree?" Lauren squealed excitedly.

"Sure is!" Henry affirmed, proud of his gift.

Nana Betty protested, "Henry! It is the beginning of November, that tree will be nothing but twigs by Christmas."

"Pshh! This is a fir tree! If ya keep it watered, it'll last ya till New Years!" he bantered back, then admitted, "Besides, I accidentally clipped it with the plow at the end of the driveway this morning and it seemed too perfect of a Christmas tree to waste!"

The girls looked to their mother, and Lauren begged, "Mama, can we put the tree up today?" "PLEEEASE?" Callie added, hands clasped expectantly in front of her.

"Of course," Molly conceded, "I love having a real tree for Christmas or at least Thanksgiving!" Turning to Henry she added, coming over and giving him a squeeze, "Thank you, Henry! It was sweet of you to bless us with it! You are staying for breakfast, right?" She winked at Nana Betty, having beaten her to the invite as she took Henry's coat for him and hung it on a hook by the door.

"Well, I suppose a few of Betty's pancakes couldn't hurt!" he said grinning sheepishly at Nana Betty who smirked as she sprinkled blueberries onto the batter and began to ladle it thickly into puddles on a hot griddle.

Having removed his wet boots, Henry turned to me, and offered his hand, "You must be Anya. Pleased to make your acquaintance."

Charmed, I put my hand in his and he shook it firmly before noticing that Pari had approached and sat calmly at my side. Kneeling, he put his hand out to Pari, "Hey there big guy!" he rumbled, in a deep voice, expecting him to sniff his hand. To Henry's surprise, Pari regally offered him his paw. Impressed, Henry chuckled, and shook it, "Pleased to make your acquaintance as well!"

We all laughed. It felt good to enjoy the moment. We settled around the table for a very pleasant breakfast of pancakes with blueberries topped with brown sugar and butter, eggs, bacon, milk, and orange juice.

As the meal ended, Henry and Nana Betty were deep into a conversation about winters gone by. Molly and the girls began to get up to clear away the empty plates.

Luke had been quietly staring down at the table lost in thought. "Hey Mol," he began, finally looking up, "I think I'm gonna just stay at the church after Bible study to work on stuff for tomorrow."

"Sure, let me know when you're done, I'll come pick you up. You want us to wait till your home to decorate the tree?" Molly offered.

"Na, you guys go ahead. Just save the star for me." Luke grinned reassuringly at her. There was a faraway look in his eyes, but a new energy about him as he gave her a quick peck on the cheek and went to gather an armload of books and papers from his study. He jumped into Henry's truck, and they headed down the driveway.

Nana Betty and I cleaned and put away dishes while Molly and the girls made trips up and down the stairs to the lower level of the house hauling up boxes containing shiny balls, bells, and glittery garlands.

"Phew!" Molly breathed, "That should be all the decorations. And I found the tree stand!" Molly held it up triumphantly.

It took us all morning, but with a few sawed off branches and a lot of effort, Molly, Nana Betty and I managed to prop the tree upright into the red and green stand and the girls filled it with water. "How strange," I thought, "to pluck a tree and put it in your house like a flower in a vase," however, when we removed the bag from the tree and I smelled the sharp, sweet aroma filling the room, I found a new appreciation for the custom.

That afternoon Molly and Nana Betty strung strands of tiny twinkling lights up and down the tree and the girls delighted in hanging all sorts of trinkets and shiny glass balls from its branches.

One ornament, a large star, was set aside to wait for Luke to get home.

The day drifted by, and it was already dark before Molly left and returned with Luke from the church. His dinner was waiting for him, cold on the table. The girls were in their night clothes and Nana Betty had found a small flat container and pulled a shiny disk from it. Somehow the disk made the box in the kitchen play music again and the house was filled with joyful songs about 'Christmas' and family.

Lauren and Callie were dancing around the sitting room when Luke arrived. Callie ran to him holding the star. Laughing, the family gathered around the tree while he secured it to the top and plugged a cord into the wall.

It was quite a sight to see the simple fir tree now adorned and glorious, illuminating the room with its glow. The girls resumed their dance and twirled around the room to the music. Nana Betty reclined sleepily in one of the worn chairs, watching her granddaughters fondly.

Luke and Molly stood back to admire the tree when Callie laced her tiny fingers into her father's hand and tugged him to the middle of the room, "Come dance with me, Daddy!"

"Why certainly, little lady. I'd be honored!" Luke replied gallantly. He did an elaborate bow before her and Callie, giggling, gave a quick curtsy. He suddenly swept her up in his arms and spun her around the room, the girl shrieking exuberantly.

The energy that I had seen bubbling under the surface at the breakfast table had fully released and there was a bounce in Luke's step and joy about him. He was changed; transformed, a man released from his sorrow. Tears glistened in the corners of his eyes as he set the giggling girl into her mother arms. Molly, receiving her daughter, sensed something had changed in her husband since their talk the previous day. He smiled at her assuredly.

Without exchanging a word, the emotion overtook her as well and she bit her lip blinking back tears of joy.

Turning, Luke offered his hand to Lauren. She put her small hand into his, grinned and curtseyed gracefully before him. They spun around the room. The tender golden moment, bathed in the soft light of the tree, etched itself into my memory. Seeing father and daughter, hand in hand, dancing together, made my heart long for such a relationship. What a blessing, to be cherished and protected as someone's child. Fondly looking down, he gently guided her, and with perfect trust she followed, looking up at him. As the song ended, he drew her in and kissed her sweetly on the forehead.

The music switched to a fast tune and the moment was over. Callie and Lauren ran over to me and pulled me to the middle of the room to dance with them. We spun, twirled, and laughed until the girls and I collapsed onto the couch breathless. Next, a slow crooning song about being 'home for Christmas' followed and Luke took Molly's hand and they slowly danced, the girls looked at each other and grinned, Lauren rolled her eyes and Callie copied her. They tried hard to suppress their giggles. Though they feigned disgust, I could tell that they cherished the love and honor their father and mother had for one another.

37

Golden Dreams

LATER THAT NIGHT, I sat alone in the quiet pondering the events of the day. The girls had sleepily made their way upstairs followed by their parents and Nana Betty had retreated to her room for the night. I picked up my bag, its natural weight felt strangely light as I drew it up on to my lap and retrieved my writing stone and journal.

I had been distracted enough by the day's activities to not think too deeply on my situation, but in the dim light of the tree and the warmth of a crackling fire, journal and writing stone in hand, I could not help but wonder:

> Why am I still here, Lord?
> The mission is over, the gift gone.
> Is there something left I have not done?
> Or... something I've done wrong?
> Your Kingdom is where I belong,
> My heart aches to return.
> Is the reason that I'm not there now
> Something else I've yet to learn?

I paused and closed my eyes, but the dream from the previous night was haunting me on the fringes of sleep and I shook myself, determined to stay awake. The nightmare of seeing the Kingdom slipping away from me again was more than I could stand.

Pari awoke from where he had been curled up by my feet and jumped up on the couch next to me, and together we watched the lights of the tree twinkle and the glow of the fire dance across the floor and walls. Willing my eyes to stay open, I replayed happier thoughts of Callie and Lauren as they danced around the room with their father. I remembered how they placed their innocent hands into their father's outstretched palm: fully trusting and without a care as he tenderly led them. I smiled at the thought, but it was the kind of smile that was filled with sweetness also held a twinge of sadness and longing. Nana Betty had worn a similar expression the night before as she thought of her late husband. I began writing in my journal again:

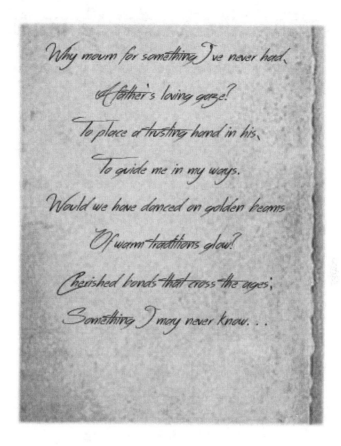

Why mourn for something I've never had,
A father's loving gaze?
To place a trusting hand in his,
To guide me in my ways.
Would we have danced on golden beams
Of warm traditions glow?
Cherished bonds that cross the ages,
Something I may never know. . .

"I wish I knew where *I* came from, Pari," I sighed longingly to my guide, voicing the things that I had never dared ask before. "Did I *ever* have a mother and father? Did *anyone* ever look at me the way Luke and Molly look at the girls?"

Lifting his head, he gazed lovingly at me, as if to answer my question. I shook my head and chuckled. Pari knew me so well. I wrapped my arms around his shaggy neck and leaned against my faithful companion.

Watching the flickering fire for a long while, I willed my eyes to remain open. I was determined to stay awake and keep the nightmares at bay. Lulled by the crackling of the burning logs and the dancing flames, eventually I was helpless to resist slumber's sweet embrace. With sleep came a dream.

It started as a never-ending expanse of brilliant golden light, like clouds saturated with the first light of dawn. Then a hand, the same bandaged hand that had caught me the night before, extended toward me, open and inviting. Drawn, I placed my hand within it, and was surprised by how small my hand looked. Guided by my unseen partner I was spun and twirled and moved through the clouds. Gliding effortlessly to music all our own, my joy was so profound, as if the very essence of love surrounded me. Finally, drawn into a gentle embrace, I remained safely nestled until the morning when Callie and Lauren tumbled happily down the stairs.

38

Finding the King

With eyes still closed, I delighted in their chirping little voices as they bounced into the room before hushing each other at the sight of Pari and I snuggled up together on the couch, seemingly asleep. I was fully awake, with my cheek gently pressed into Pari's soft fur but I was so peaceful and content I did not care to move. The heavenly glow from the dream was still draped all around me. It was such a lovely feeling to know that no matter what happened, I would be alright.

The girls had retreated into Nana Betty's room, where I could hear them chatting brightly with their grandmother in hushed tones and their grandmother cheerfully replying.

Eventually, the dreamy feeling faded a bit and I willed myself to sit up. Blinking my eyes awake, I yawned and stretched luxuriously; at peace with whatever the day was to bring.

Finding my journal and writing stick nearby on the floor I tucked them into the messenger bag and slung it easily over my shoulder. Breathing deeply, I stood to embrace the day!

I made my way into the kitchen and tapped on the open door that led to Nana Betty's room.

The girls looked up excitedly from their cozy perch on Nana Betty's lap where the three of them had been looking through a book together.

"Anya! You're awake!" Callie proclaimed, obviously relieved to not be whispering any longer.

"Yes! Good morning!" I replied serenely. I could not keep from grinning, I felt so good. "What are you three reading this morning?"

"It's grandma's favorite cookbook! She always gets her best recipes from here!" Lauren said with a raise of her eyebrows.

Nana Betty gave Lauren a squeeze then teased, "Don't give away all my secrets, now! You girls run along upstairs and get ready for church."

The girls slid off Nana Betty's lap and scurried past me, both giving me a sweet hug as they made their way back upstairs.

When they had gone, Nana Betty adjusted her glasses and propped up the book on her lap, "Now to look in my *secret* cookbook to find what we are making for supper tonight . . ."

As I entered the room, I noticed a face on the back of the cookbook that was strangely familiar! The man and woman were laughing merrily from behind a table set with a feast, arms around one another. I squinted and looked closer, "Joe?" I questioned, half to myself and half toward the man in the picture. It hardly seemed possible that this happy, clean-cut, neatly dressed man could ever be the same sad, disheveled man who I had met in the streets. But there was something unmistakable about the scar that ran through his eyebrow.

Barely hearing me, Nana Betty looked up at me over her glasses, "What was that dear?"

"That's Joe." I said blankly pointing to the back of the book.

Nana Betty closed the book to look at the back cover, "Ah, yes! Joe and Joanna Shepherd,"

"The Shepherd," I whispered in recognition remembering the name that the boys had called him.

"They were the hosts of this cute cooking show I really liked and had the most amazing story. This book came out right after they launched their restaurant downtown. They were the talk of Chicago until . . ." Nana Betty paused and sadly shook her head.

"Until what?" I implored her to continue.

Nana Betty sighed, "Anya, it's a sad story. You probably don't want to hear it."

"I think I *need* to hear what happened to them."

Looking down at the happy couple, Nana Betty complied and recounted their story "They had been high school sweethearts, Joe and Joanna, but when high school was over, he enlisted in the Navy and eventually became a Navy Seal traveling all over the world running dangerous missions. After going to school to be a chef, Joanna moved across the country to pursue her culinary career. Time passed and they just lost touch."

"Years went by and they never heard from one another, but after a serious injury on assignment in the Middle East Joe was medically discharged and sent to the Naval Hospital just north of here for treatment. One day he had come down to the city to see the sights. He was about to step onto a bus; the same bus that Joanna was just getting off. They found themselves standing there in the street, face to face again after so many years. From that moment on they were inseparable. She used cooking, the culinary arts and her faith in Jesus Christ to inspire and help Joe overcome the trauma that he had experienced during his career and their natural chemistry and fun-loving connection got the attention of the TV network and that's when they launched their show, 'Let's Get Cookin'. They got married along the way and eventually bought their own restaurant not far from the river in Chicago. They called it 'Jojo's Downtown'. Their style was unique, part exquisite and elevated and part downhome comfort food. They made an amazing team."

Nana Betty paused for a moment, then continued quietly, "One night, just a few years after they had opened, they had just closed the restaurant and Joanna went out the back door into the alley to go to the parking ramp while Joe was inside switching off the lights. By the time he followed her outside a minute later, he found her lying on the ground, dead. Security footage from the parking ramp just showed a shadowy figure attacking Joanna from behind and running off with her purse just moments before Joe came out the door. They found her purse emptied out in a dumpster a few blocks away, but they never did find the person who had killed her. After that Joe just flipped, Joanna had been his world."

An icy chill ran down my back as I stared blankly at the faces still smiling up at me from the book and thinking back to sitting with Joe in that alley with the memory of Joanna's death haunting him in his dreams.

Shaking her head, Nana continued, "When she was killed, Joe blamed God for what happened, and he blamed himself for not being there to protect her. The trauma from his military career all came flooding back and mixed with the loss of his wife, it drove him mad. He disappeared from the public eye but there are rumors that he is still in the city, wandering the streets exacting his own form of vigilante justice. Their restaurant still stands empty to this day."

"That explains a lot. Joe showed up and saved me when some boys were attacking me. They called him 'The Shepherd' and they were afraid of him. He was amazing. Joe protected me, but I could see that he was hurting and confused." I looked away ashamed, "He tricked me to do things that were wrong."

I could see Nana Betty's eyes widen and her back straighten. A look of extreme concern was on her face. "I went back and paid the shopkeeper back for the apples." I assured her quickly.

Her look of concern was replaced with a look of confusion, "Anya, what exactly did Joe trick you to do?"

"He told me to go into a shop and get some apples, but I didn't know that they were not for the taking and the man there got very angry with me when I tried to leave. I got scared and ran away. I was so mad at Joe for tricking me to do that. Stealing is not an act of the Kingdom, but Joe just laughed when I told him what happened. I went back later and gave the man at the shop some of those green papers in payment for them. I just hope the King will forgive me."

Looking extremely relieved, Nana Betty consoled me, "Anya, you made it right by going back and paying for them. That took a lot of courage."

Smiling hopefully at her I asked, "Do you really think so?"

She nodded, "Anya, I think you are a very brave girl. One of the bravest I've known."

My ear-to-ear grin returned.

The rest of the morning went quite quickly, getting everyone ready, including Pari. For the first time in days, we all left the house. Piling into Luke's pickup truck, we drove a short distance down the narrow snowy road to a serene white building nestled in a grove of pine trees. Wide steps lead up to a set of double doors and high above it a single spire housed a large bell. There was something inspiring about this simple building standing resolutely in the gleaming snow, something humbly divine.

We made our way inside the warm entryway and after hanging our coats on the racks, I got the sense that there was much to be done this morning.

Luke headed up a set of stairs past the rows and rows of benches to a low platform and began to take out some sort of equipment and set it up. Pari followed him and wandered freely among the rows. He seemed to enjoy the solemn reverence of the place.

"Luke has a Sunday morning podcast that he does before the service." Molly explained, "It's really become quite popular. I think there is something so sweet and special about this old church that really draws people in. Luke's messages on 'Simple Faith' really resonate in people's lives today." She smiled proudly at her husband. Then moving on she turned toward the stairs leading down, "We will leave him to that, but I thought it may be a good time for us girls to look in the storage rooms downstairs at some of the Christmas decorations that were left back there years ago. I think I saw an old Nativity set that I think we could use. Would you like to come help us?" Molly invited.

"Sure," I replied. I was up for anything, or so I thought.

We walked down a short flight of stairs to the lower level of the church.

"Mama, can we go play in the nursery for awhile instead?" Lauren asked hopefully.

Molly thought for a moment and then agreed, "Ok, but you'll have to clean up before the service starts. Anya and I will be right back here in the storage room by the kitchen."

The girls were relieved to be released from the task and made a beeline for a room off to the side of the stairs. Through a large window I could see a room with shelves of colorful toys and books and a few comfortable rocking chairs arranged along the sides of the room.

Leaving the girls to play, Molly led me away from the stairs to the back of the church. Taking some keys out of her pocket she searched through them and tried several before she found the one that would fit the lock. "Aha!" she said triumphantly when the door finally opened. We stepped inside the dusty over-packed room.

"I cannot believe that all this stuff just got left here. Some of the things in here must be as old as the church itself! I really need to take some time and go through all of it, but for now I thought I remembered seeing a Nativity set somewhere back here." Molly explained as she shifted a stack of folded chairs and a few boxes to the side to make a path.

Near the back of the room, she found what she had been looking for. "Here it is!" She exclaimed, lifting a small statue of a man in long robes holding a shepherd's staff for me to see.

"A lot of cleaning and maybe a little paint and these would really look great! Kind of nostalgic really," She mused, examining the figure. "I remember seeing one of these set up at church every Christmas when I was a kid. I wonder if all the pieces are here?"

Busily she began to dig around pulling small statues out of boxes. She handed them carefully to me to set out on a table nearby. A young boy holding a lamb in his arms, a sheep, an ox, a donkey, several old men wearing rich robes and crowns bowing down, a woman and man kneeling and even a figure with white flowing garments who had wings outstretched on her back. As more and more figures emerged, they all had one thing in common, they appeared to be looking with reverence at something that was lowly, down near the ground. I wondered what it could be that they were so fixated on.

Frantically, Molly continued her search, "He's got to be here someplace. We cannot have a Nativity scene without *Him*!"

"Without who?" I asked innocently.

"Without Him!" Molly exclaimed triumphantly, turning to show me what she held gently in her hands. "The baby Jesus!"

Cradled in her hands was an infant child lying in what appeared to be a feed trough for the animals. A halo of gold surrounded His head and His small hand was reaching up out of His lowly crib. In my mind flashed the hand that I had been seeing in my dreams, first catching me from falling into the pit and again inviting me to be guided and comforted. It confused me that the thought even occurred to me. How could this tiny infant and those bandaged hands be connected at all? But as Molly placed the child in my hands there was something so familiar that I began to get emotional.

"Jesus," I whispered, looking down with the same reverence that I saw in the faces of the statues.

Molly had already turned back to the stacks of old boxes again and determined, "Wouldn't it be great if I could find a little stable in here somewhere? That would be perfect!"

Shifting boxes and shoving towers of dust covered old chairs to the side she was able to locate what she was looking for, "Ah ha! Here it is! Anya, could you give me a hand with this?" she asked excitedly.

Hesitant to put the statue of the infant Jesus down, I moved to the table and placed Him gently in the center. Stepping over boxes to get to the back of the room, I joined Molly. Together we lifted a small shelter up into view. It was a simple, humble structure and we set it up on a stack of boxes. Molly busily began to pull years of accumulated cobwebs from the corners. I smiled at her excitement over the unpretentious building. I turned back toward the empty space that was left behind; my knees buckled, and I fell to the ground.

Hidden from view until we had moved the stable, an ornate cross lay propped on its side. Attached was a figure of a man. A cloth was loosely draped around Him but did not conceal His emaciated, battered, and bleeding body. Cruel metal spikes had been driven through his wrists and feet to secure him to the cross and a wreath of thorns had been wickedly pressed onto His head, piercing His flesh. Streams of crimson blood appeared to flow from his wounds. But it was not *what* I saw that brought me to my knees, but *who* I saw.

"My King!" I choked, horrified. Wanting to look away, I was unable to turn from the alarming sight, I could only shake my head and sob. Startled, Molly ran to my side.

"Who would do this to my King?" I demanded through my tears.

Clearly shaken, Molly replied quietly and compassionately, "It's ok Anya. It's only a statue."

"Then this did not *really* happen?" I gasped hopefully.

Gently Molly explained, "No Anya, it really *did* happen. Jesus really did die on the cross for our sins,"

Dismayed, I buried my face in my hands.

Molly continued, "But Anya, you don't have to be sad. The good news is that He didn't stay on the cross. He is risen! He had victory over death and now because of what *He did*, so do we!"

"How do you know?" I whispered in despair.

Taking my hands gently away from my face, Molly looked at me with compassion and a new understanding, "Because He is my King too."

39

The Way Back Home

IT TOOK A FEW minutes for me to calm my tears and I still did not understand what it all meant. But just like when Nana Betty read to me out of her book, what Molly said about this person named Jesus resonated within me. I could *feel* the truth in it and a strange peaceful feeling settled over me. That peace and having Molly's motherly arm around me as she patiently sat beside me on the floor of the dusty room helped. I began to catch my breath again.

Molly pulled a tissue out of her pocket and handed it to me, "You gonna be ok?"

I nodded, sniffling, and drying the tears from my eyes. Molly helped me to my feet and added casually, "You know, I can come back and get the nativity later, why don't we get out of here for now?"

Grateful, I followed her back to where the girls were playing. Nana Betty and Henry were settled into the rocking chairs with mugs of coffee in hand, chatting with the girls as they played. Molly looked down at the bracelet on her wrist and gasped, "Oh! It's almost time for Luke to start the podcast." She said to me in explanation.

Peeking her head into the room she instructed, "Girls, you know the routine. No running around or shouting while Daddy is on. You can come listen if you want but you'll have to stay in the foyer and sit quietly. Ok?"

Turning to Nana Betty, Molly mentioned, "I'm gonna go upstairs and watch for Kevin, he's coming in from the district office this morning." I noticed a flicker of nervousness in her voice.

Nana Betty picked up on this as well and reassured her, "I've got the girls Molly, you just take care of what you need to. We probably *will* try to come listen in, Luke was so excited about something this morning, I'm wondering what he has got up his sleeve."

"Thank you!" Molly whispered sincerely, then motioned for me to follow her up the stairs.

When we reached the landing by the door, Molly peered out the small window. "There he is! Oh! His wife, Sherri, came too!" Molly opened the door and greeted them warmly as the guests came up the steps into the church, "Hello! Welcome! Sherri, so good to see you! What a nice surprise!"

Having thoroughly inspected the upstairs, Pari had joined me near the entry wagging his tail happily.

A petite couple, fastidiously dressed in wool jackets, gloves and warm hats, stepped through the threshold and smiled politely at Molly and I, "Hello Molly dear! When Kevin told me he was coming all the way out here this morning I insisted on coming to see you!" She hugged Molly and then turned to Pari and I, "Well hello there! I'm Sherri. I don't believe we have met." Pulling off her dainty leather glove she extended a hand toward me, I extended my hand back to her and she took it in her two hands and shook it, smiling expectantly at me.

Molly came to my rescue and made introductions, "This is Anya, she is . . ." Molly paused then continued decidedly, "a family friend." Gesturing toward the visitors she added, "And Anya, this is Kevin and Sherri Noss. Kevin serves on the district board of our parent church in Chicago. Not to mention that they are longtime friends of ours." She exchanged a warm smile with Sherri, but Kevin only managed a tense smirk, it was obvious that something was on his mind. He glanced around, studying the interior of the building critically.

Pari circled around the ladies and sat down in front of Kevin looking up at him with his head tilted to the side, he groaned to get Kevin's attention. Startled, the man looked down and was pleasantly surprised to see the friendly face looking up at him.

"Oh! Hello there!" He said, pulling a glove off to stroke Pari's shaggy head.

"And this is Pari. He is with Anya." Molly tried to explain, "We didn't want to leave him alone at the house, and it's just too cold to leave him outside . . ."

Kevin didn't seem to mind at all, his gloves were draped over one knee, and he was kneeling next to Pari petting him gently. The tension released from his brow; he let out a deep sigh and looked up with a smile. "Where's Luke?"

Molly continued relieved, "Here, let me take your coats. Luke is about to get started any minute on the podcast, we can watch from the foyer."

"Anya, why don't you go on ahead." She shrugged, "Luke was pretty adamant about having you hear what he had to say this morning, just stay in the foyer just outside of the sanctuary and you should be able to hear him pretty well." she instructed.

Still in a bit of a daze from the events of the morning, I only half heard what she had said, but nodded my head and started to turn away.

"Anya?" Kevin said softly from behind me, "I'm glad to meet you and Pari." I looked back and smiled at him; I had grown accustomed to the soothing effect that Pari had on people. I have felt it many times myself.

I climbed a few stairs to a small receiving area just before a brightly lit hall with a lofted ceiling and colored glass in the windows. At the end of the hall was a low platform. Luke sat on a bench with his back turned to me, saying, "Check, check, mic check," then adjusted some of his equipment; it looked like he was about to start.

Behind me I could faintly hear Molly, Kevin and Sherri's voices carry up the stairs. They talked in hushed tones, but in the quiet foyer the stairway amplified them just enough for me to understand.

"I don't know how they could have gotten out there, but there she was lying on the side of the road . . . ."

"And the dog was with her?" Kevin asked, astonished.

"Yes, Pari was there with her, like he was watching over her and keeping her safe until we got there."

Sherri interjected, "I can't bear to imagine what would have happened if you hadn't come along."

"That's another funny thing," Molly confessed, "We don't normally travel on that road, especially during bad weather. We almost always take the expressway. But that night, for some reason, Luke felt like we *had* to go another way. I'm thankful that we've come to trust that quiet nudge and follow it."

I heard Kevin murmur, "Where did they come from?"

Curious to know how Molly would respond, I strained my ears to hear the story from her perspective. A wave of guilt came over me. I knew it was wrong to listen in; they didn't think I could hear them. But still, what did she really think? Did she believe I was sent from the Kingdom? Or did she still think that I was playing 'make believe'?

At that moment, Luke started to address a small box that was held up on a stand in front of him. "Good morning fellow Pilgrims. Welcome to Simple Faith Country Church. I am so glad to be on this journey with you today."

I decided to do the right thing and stepped forward into one of the open archways where I could clearly see Luke as he addressed the invisible 'Pilgrims'. His low voice resonated around the large room and rang through the dark wood beams across the ceiling.

There was something comforting and familiar about that old place that I could not quite describe, but only feel, like a reassuring embrace. Again, I felt that relaxing shiver down my spine. Flecks of dust drifting through the air were illuminated by shafts of morning sunlight peeking through the windows and gave the space a serene look. It was no wonder why Molly had called it a sanctuary.

In the center at the far end of the sanctuary was a large cross made of simple rough wood beams. The cross stood empty, draped with a pure white linen, a promise that the King *had* surely overcome. I still did not understand, but somehow the cross was the connection point from that land to the Kingdom.

Molly, Kevin and Sherri had moved to the foyer to listen to Luke too. Nana Betty, Henry and the girls arrived from downstairs and tried their best to greet Kevin and Sherri quietly.

"This morning I want to tell you all the story of how Simple Faith Country Church started and then I'm gonna share a special gift with you. The message of it has already blessed me so much and I hope it blesses you too. But let's start at the foot of the cross."

He bowed his head and closed his eyes and began to speak, "Lord Jesus, we come before you today." Out of reverence, I closed my eyes and bowed my head as well.

"Placing ourselves at the foot of the cross, a place that you have made for us. By your sacrifice you covered our sins and gave us access, through faith, to the Kingdom of Heaven. You made a way for us where there was no way, and you sent your Holy Spirit to guide us and comfort us. There is nothing we can do on our own, but through you, Jesus, all things are possible, and all things work together for good for those that love you, Lord, and are called according to your purpose. I pray for your blessing over every person who can hear this message of hope today and pray that you can use me, your humble servant, to deliver it well to your people."

Luke chuckled softly as he recounted, picking up his worn cowboy hat, "When I left home at eighteen I didn't have much more than my pickup truck, my Bible and this old hat. But I had some *big* city dreams of bringing glory to God by making a name for myself. I was bound and determined that I was gonna live *large* for Jesus! Well, I learned a few things along the way, but the one thing I had right was that I was willing to go wherever the good Lord told me to and do what He said to do. Everything seemed to be going according to *my* plan. I left our little country town in Oklahoma for the Windy City where I excelled at the Bible Institute, was a star on the soccer field, even landed an internship with the worship team of one of the most amazing churches in Chicago and through working with Pastor Mike, glory to God, I was offered a position as an associate pastor after graduation. I was leading the worship team on a regular basis and had the opportunity to preach on some Sunday's when Pastor Mike was away. I even got the chance to travel across the globe to places like New Zealand, Australia, and England and was introduced to influential people from all over the world. I'm still on the team in charge of urban outreach. It was exactly what I had been hoping for and more!"

"Along the way my best friend on the soccer team, Bennie, introduced me to his beautiful sister, Molly. She was sweet, spunky and loved Jesus and I knew I had found the love of my life. Who knew I'd fall for a city girl! Soon we were married and expecting our first child. My life was a picture of perfection! My big city dream was coming true! I had been blessed with an amazing wife and family on the way."

"So why did I feel like something was missing. Everything was dis-jointed somehow, misaligned. I went from feeling like I was on top of the world, to feeling like a puzzle piece sorted into the wrong box. So, I did what my daddy used to do when he needed some time alone with God to pray through an issue: I took my truck out for a drive in the country. Now, keep in mind I had to drive quite a ways out to find some 'country', but eventu-ally I lost myself in prayer and dirt roads. I didn't know where I was going, but God knew right where he was leading me. Right to the steps of this old country church. I sat in my truck and picked up the Bible on the seat next to me and God led me to Proverbs 3:5–6, 'Trust in the Lord with all your heart, and do not lean on your own understanding. In all your ways acknowledge Him and He will make your paths straight.'"

"I felt so jumbled up, so that sounded pretty good to me; a simple, straight path. So, I prayed that day for direction, 'Where do you want me to go God, what do you want me to do?' and He answered me, 'You don't need a fancy title or accolades or a large platform to bring me glory. I'm giving you everything you need right here to serve me. My Word and this old church.' Simple faith. That's all He was asking of me, to trust Him and follow Him."

"It was the hardest thing I've ever done, and everyone thought I was crazy for leaving my promising and secure position. Everyone but Pastor Mike and my wife Molly; they encouraged me, supported my vision, and helped plant Simple Faith Country Church right here in that old church that the Lord had led me to. We moved out to the country, back to a simple life and fell in love with this little community and its people."

"It wasn't *at all* what I had planned, but it was *exactly* what God had planned. The pieces finally fit, and I just knew it was the right thing to do. Even so, over the years since I still had doubt, I would think that maybe God had put us out here and forgot about us. But we just kept serving where He brought us and figured that if He'd changed His mind, He'd let us know."

Luke leaned forward and sincerely addressed the box, "I just want you to know that the Lord has never, ever, forgotten about you. He has never been late; His miracles are always right on time."

Slowly, with emotion in his voice he continued, "Don't you think for one second that He's not working miraculously in and through your life right now. His love is so deep for you, for me, that He was willing to go to any length and pay any price so that you and I could be with Him. In my life He has proven His love for me over and over and over."

Luke took a deep breath, and let it out slowly, "This has been a crazy few days, but I wouldn't trade them for anything. I just want to worship the King of heaven with you today and I believe that this song was a gift straight from the throne room. I can't explain it any other way, but I'm supposed to share it with you all today to bring you hope and to give God glory."

As he finished, he started to play several chords on the piano. Something stirred deep within me, and Marita's parting instructions came back to me, "Anya! Remember, enter his gates with thanksgiving and his courts with praise."

I began to walk up the side aisle; drawn closer to the cross, Pari close by my side. I knew in my heart that the Kingdom was real, even if no one else believed me. The King had saved me, and the King had sent me. Even if I never found the way to return to my home in the Kingdom, I would praise the King every day, just as I had when I stood before His throne in the assembly.

Placing my hand on the wall, beneath one of the windows halfway into the sanctuary, I fell to one knee, facing the cross as I had faced the King on the throne hundreds of times before. Luke's back was to me, so he had not seen me enter behind him and Molly and everyone else hadn't noticed me leave the foyer. Luke began to sing, and something in my spirit shifted. From the depths of my being a desperate cry of the Kings song arose, mixing perfectly with Luke's song.

He stopped suddenly and looked back at me, and a collective gasp came from the foyer behind me. But my eyes were fixed on the cross and I could not stop, even if I wanted to. Hot tears rolled down my face, and I squeezed my eyes shut and let the song take over.

Tentatively, Luke's piano joined in again and for a while I could hear Luke's voice singing with me. His part was different from mine, but we echoed and reflected and harmonized perfectly though we were not singing the exact same thing. I had never realized that the King's song could have more parts than the one I had learned. It was interesting and different. It was better and together we glorified the King!

I felt a warm light envelop me, and as the King's anthem swelled, all sound fell away but my voice crying out, echoing through a large expanse.

Breathless, I continued to sing even though I could no longer hear Luke or the piano. As I did, I became aware of myself again, my hand resting against the smooth hard stone and my knee pressing against the cool floor. Before I even opened my eyes, the thought occurred to me that the church sanctuary had neither stone walls nor stone floors and the song echoing back at me was not from the rafters of a quaint country church.

I opened my eyes and fell silent. I was back in the throne room, in my place under the window with my hand resting on the blue diamond on the wall. The King was standing at his throne smiling at me.

40

The Return

MY HEART GREW HEAVY as Pari and I approached the throne. I knelt before my King as I had done when I received the gift. I had no idea what to expect next. Certainly not a gift this time, I reasoned.

I had returned defeated. I had been sent to deliver the gift to the one who could share it with their world and be a powerful ambassador for my King. I had fallen short. The only willing person I found could not possibly have carried out the mission of hope for which the gift was intended. Or so I thought.

With a breaking heart, I thought fondly of Luke and Molly and the girls and the warmth of their home, the joy of their laughter, the goodness of Nana's cooking, their genuineness, their compassion, the strength of their character and I *knew* I had done the right thing, though I had squandered the gift.

How could I tell my King? He stood resplendent, with an expectant smile upon His face. I could not bear the look at Him knowing the disappointment that was sure to follow.

As I knelt, I was unable to contain myself and I blurted out, "My King. I have failed you." Choking back sobs I continued, "I'm sorry. Your gift was intended for one who could use it to bring a message of hope and healing to their land. But I have failed. I found none willing; only a humble preacher and his wife who cared for me."

The tears began to pour down my cheeks again as I knelt, staring down at the marbled floor, unable to lift my gaze.

"My child!" the King exclaimed gently. Quickly descending the stairs, He came near to me, and softly said, "Arise! You have not failed me." The joy in His voice was so unexpected, I turned my tear-streaked face to look up at my King and was frozen. How could this be?

"Arise, my child!" the King repeated, and lifting me, he set my feet upon the stone floor, "Come. Let me show you what your gift has done!"

"Anya, I will show you what I see." The King leaned forward with an outstretched arm inviting me to take his hand; the strong, familiar, bandaged hand that I had seen in my dreams. My tears were stilled by the wonder of it all and my hand felt so small in His, but so safe.

He led me to a hallway behind the throne. As we went, the marbled walls and floor gradually changed from sparking white to grey with swirls of black mixed in, then to mostly black and finally glossy black with white specks. Eventually the lines between the tiles were completely imperceptible.

For a long while we walked, hand in hand, down the long corridor. With no obvious source of light, you would have expected darkness, but even surrounded by the black walls, there was still light somehow.

I started to notice something else strange. At first, I thought it must just be the angle of the stone as we passed, but light seemed to be emanating from the pinpoints of white on the black walls, and as we continued some of the points of light twinkled as if from far away. The red and gold carpet that we walked upon had remained the same from the beginning of the hall and continued ahead of us. However, like a trick to my eyes, it now appeared as a path hovering in the midst of a great black expanse with far off points of light, some of them shining brighter, others dimmer, some seeming to twinkle and others, appearing closer, had a swirl of cloud with smaller points of light caught within.

Galaxies and stars! I recognized them from the books in the palace library! Could it be possible? The further we walked the more amazing our surroundings became! And the colors; stunning colors started to emerge. Fuchsias, purples, blues and oranges; cloudy nebula against the black of space. If I was not being led by the King, I would have been tempted to move off the path to where the wall *should be* to reach out and touch it to see if it was still there at all! As it was, I dared not step off the carpet for fear of falling off the edge, so I remained close to the King's side clinging to his arm.

As if to answer my unspoken questions, the King paused on our path and reached out into the void. At the King's touch a point of light was created, and He gently blew upon it, as you would blow upon an ember to encourage its growth into a flame. He breathed His life and light into the point and it emerged a star.

At its birth the star emanated a faint hum that opened my ears to the hundreds and thousands of other sounds that surrounded us. I heard them only faintly at first, some higher, some lower, some rhythmic, others steady. Like music faintly playing a celestial song I could almost hear; the stars sang around us, joined by every heavenly body. And just like in the sanctuary the song of the King reached my lips, as I whispered at first, I matched words to the celestial sounds with perfection!

Wide eyed I looked to the King to confirm I was not imagining what I saw, heard, and felt. Taking my hands, He smiled encouragingly, as the universe joined me, in manifold witness. We sang boldly to the King, praising Him. Who is this King I serve that even the stars and heavens were taught to sing His praises!?

When *my* song was over, the planets and stars continued on, in their endless way, worshiping the King. My Lord smiled down at me, "This way, Anya." He reached forward and parted the inky blackness, like a curtain in front of us, as easily as we would draw aside the drapes of a window. We walked through it into a small room. Before us was a throne made of pure sapphire. It was at the top of several wide steps that led down and away from us into an expanse of what looked like sparkling ice.

"I brought you here so you can see what I see." He explained as He moved toward the throne, "Come sit at my feet and I will show you."

After the King had lowered Himself into the seat, I sat on the steps at His feet, my eyes wide, staring in amazement at the mechanism before me.

On the bottom most step before the white crystal expanse were four creatures standing as still as stone beside four large spherical objects that seemed to hover in midair. Each sphere had elaborate gold rings, of seemingly infinite descending size. Like wheels set within another wheel, set within another. All the rings appeared to be able to rotate and twirl freely within the outer rings. Presently, the wheels stood as perfectly still as the creatures, but at the King's command, the creatures began to push and pull the outer rings, setting the inner rings oscillating within. The sound of rushing water carried through the expanse. It was as delicate as the sound of wings pressing through the air but with the intensity of an army advancing violently.

The scene before me changed, the white crystal sea rushed past like clouds parting for the sun to shine through. Images were shown to me, images of every step of my journey. I realized that never once had I been out of the King's sight.

Then the images changed again, from what was past to what was becoming. Luke, Molly, the girls and Nana Betty found all the things I'd left behind in the trash bin and used them to retrace my steps. Putting the pieces of the puzzle together, they visited each of the friends I'd met on my journey, and all the people I'd encountered. The King showed me their lives, changed somehow, intertwined with one another, filled with hope, and inspired to share that hope with others.

"Was this because of the gift?" I asked breathlessly, filled with joy.

The King replied, "Yes, but more importantly from each connection you made. Every word spoken, each glance, each touch; each was a gift on its own, a message from you of My love that sent a ripple through the lives of everyone you met on your journey."

I could hardly believe it, but in my journey to deliver the King's gift, for almost every person I met *I* made a difference, left a positive impression for the Kingdom, and made their lives better or gave them hope.

I saw Luke and Molly and I saw the King's gift, a song of praise, right where it was intended to go, fully realized and inspiring hope in all that it touched. I *had* done it! The mission was complete, and I had succeeded! Overcome with joy and relief, happy tears streamed down my cheeks as the four creatures returned the wheels to their original positions and the crystalline expanse swallowed up the visions.

From behind me a glow remained and as I turned, my eyes were filled with a warm radiance, like the appearance of rainbows just fading from the face of my King.

Smiling, He held His hand up for a 'high-five'!

Filled with wonder and joy I slapped His giant hand with mine and the sound of our laughter filled the chamber. I was finally back home where I belonged and honored to be a servant of the Kingdom.

Epilogue

"OKAY! I THINK WE are live!"

Luke's face covered most of the screen before he backed away and sat down in a chair. In the chair next to him sat a clean-cut man wearing a sports jacket and sweater over his broad shoulders. The warm glow of the morning sun shone through the stained glass into the peaceful sanctuary where they were seated before the camera.

"Welcome fellow Pilgrims! I am so blessed to be here with you today. This morning we have a special guest at Simple Faith Church. Most of you have tuned in today because of a Simple Faith live stream that happened a handful of months ago that has gone absolutely viral." Luke chuckled.

"Thank you to everyone who has responded to the song. Truly, it was a gift from the Lord, it's His song and for His praise. That is why it has resonated with so many of us and I am honored that you have embraced the message. Some others of you, maybe even more of you, are here because of a friend that we met while doing street ministry. She was only here for a short amount of time, but she made an impact on my family and, as it turns out, many people she encountered." Luke nodded at the man next to him, the man shook his head in agreement.

"I can't explain everything that happened, but over a million and a half of you have watched the video. One minute she was here singing in this sanctuary and the next moment she was gone. The only thing I can do is quote Hebrews 13:2 'Be not forgetful to entertain strangers: for thereby some have entertained angels unawares.' I have no doubts that Anya was a messenger for the Lord and everything she did was to bring Him glory and point to His Kingdom. Honestly, it is what each one of us is called to do, to be an ambassador for the Kingdom of God and to tell others His story and the good news of salvation. Just like Anya's life intersected with the life of our guest today and influenced a radical shift, your life can do the same for someone. I hope by sharing these stories of a life changed for our King, Jesus, that you are encouraged to share the good news that you have been given. So, hold on tight, my friends, we are just getting started!"

Turning his focus to the man seated next to him, Luke suggested, "Why don't you go ahead and introduce yourself."

Taking a deep breath, the man bravely looked into the camera and declared, "I am Joe Shepherd."

Luke intervened "Okay, I heard that collective gasp on the other side of the screen. That's right. Joe Shepherd, of Joe and Joanna Shepherd. Beloved hosts of 'Let's Get Cookin', authors of over half a dozen cookbooks and owners of Jojo's Downtown restaurant."

Transitioning, Luke shifted in his chair to address Joe. "Most of the world has heard the tragic story of your wife's death and what happened. But you went dark, brother. No one has really seen you or heard from you for years. Just some crazy rumors floating around about 'The Shepherd' wandering the streets at night fighting crime. So, what happened, what changed and what's next?"

Again, Joe took a deep breath. "After my wife died, I lost it. I was so angry at God, at myself. How could I have let that happen to her? I had defended thousands of people all over the world but couldn't protect the person I loved the most. I pushed everyone else who cared about me away. I was not willing to deal with my grief and all the trauma from my past came crashing in on me again. I was hurting so bad I gave into addictions, anything that could numb the pain!"

Joe leaned forward with his elbows on his knees, "I was drinking every day and looking for a fight. Most of the time, I just wandered the streets in a drunken stupor bent on revenge. In my mind, if I could find the enemy and take him out it would make me feel better or I would die trying. Either way was fine with me. In all that time, God never stopped pursuing me. I had shut my ears and hardened my heart to his voice, but He was persistent. Until the day I finally listened, and things began to change."

Glancing over at Luke, Joe explained, "I was passed out on the floor of the restaurant, for probably the thousandth time and when I woke up, clear as day I heard a voice. 'Go to Lower Wacker. She needs you.' Out of spite I went, just to prove that it was all in my imagination. It was probably not a coincidence that I happened to be at the right place at the right time to do the right thing and rescue a girl from some punk thugs."

A soft smile played across his lips, "Little did I know that the girl I rescued had come to rescue me. She called herself a servant of the King, but I believe she was an ambassador of God himself. I had to admit to myself right then that it was the Lord speaking to me. The same Lord that I was so mad at, that I had turned my back on; He hadn't left me or forgotten about me. It freaked me out and so I ran away like I had run away from everything else! But I prayed that day. That was something that I hadn't done since I lost Joanna. I prayed that if this was real, that God will take away the hunger for revenge, help me to forgive and give me freedom."

Joe turned to Luke, "A few days later, you and your wife, Molly, found me again back in the same alley behind the restaurant where we had first met. I'd been sober for four days, waiting on the Lord. I hadn't let myself get sober for years. When you told me the story of Anya, I already knew God was real and that He had spoken to me. I became convinced that He wasn't done with me yet; I had something bigger to do."

Joe leaned back and nodded toward someone who was off camera, "That same day, I ended up coming to the aid of the same young man who had threatened Anya. He was just as confused as I had been. Danny was looking for a place to belong and had gotten messed up in the wrong crowd. He was beaten up pretty bad and he became my first mission. It was because of Anya that I first met Danny, but it's because of the Lord that he has become like a son to me." Joe voice choked up with emotion.

"God has given both of our lives purpose again. In all those years, I was not letting myself mourn the death of my wife; but I also was not honoring Joanna's life. She loved the Lord, no mistake about that! She ministered the love of God in everything that she did. The least I could do was to honor her by doing the same. If I could feed others that were hurting like I was, like Danny was and show them they had a place in the Kingdom of God, then Joanna's memory would live on."

Joe looked directly into the camera, "And that's why with Luke and Molly's help, Danny and I are pleased to announce the relaunch of Jojo's Downtown. This time, it's not going to be a fancy restaurant, but a place for anyone who needs it to come and get a warm meal, access to resources and most importantly to hear about the healing and freedom that can only come from a relationship with Jesus. Now I may never be a rich and famous chef like I once thought I would be, but God brought me the long way around so that I could do something bigger for Him and His glory. Though I may miss the years I wasted wallowing in my own pain I will never regret what King has been able to do with me since. I will forever be grateful that I crossed paths with Anya, a faithful servant of the Kingdom."

Introduction to Book Two

The Warrior of the Kingdom

1

The Invitation

"FOR ME?" I STOOD baffled in front of the herald at the doorway of the palace kitchen holding the sky-blue envelope with the King's Seal pressed upon it in golden wax. The elegant writing on the front clearly said 'Anya', but my mind could not comprehend why I would be receiving such a formal letter, and from the King himself.

The young messenger smiled and raised his eyebrows with a nod as he held the envelope further toward me. Relieved, when I finally took it from his hands, he gave a wink and with a skip in his step, he turned to continue down the passageway outside of the kitchen. Perhaps, to deliver other envelopes just like the one that I held?

Morning was well underway in the kitchen. Amid the hustle and bustle of preparing for a banquet the King was holding in a few days, the other staff present did not notice me standing in the doorway, still facing a closed door, looking down at this mysterious envelope.

Two years had passed since my journey to Luke and Molly's land. Once I had returned, I soon resumed my duties in the kitchens and of cleaning the palace. Settling back into my home here in the palace kitchens with Marita, I had many more responsibilities now and occasionally, Marita would even allow me to accompany her to the market to order the supplies from the merchants there. Sadly, these were my only ventures outside of the palace walls. Sometimes Marita would find me out on the kitchen patio which looked out over the glistening harbor, dreamily recollecting my journey as I could barely make out the white of a billowing sail in the distance. I could not help but wonder where those ships were headed now or where the roads that lead away from the palace and village ended.

Don't get me wrong, I loved my place here. It felt so secure and safe. Things were routine and predictable, but somewhere within me was a longing for something more. I could not really describe what drew me, or put my finger on the feeling, but as good as I had it as a servant in the King's palace, there was a longing in my heart that was not satisfied. I felt like I was meant for a greater purpose. "Do not despise these small beginnings, Anya" Marita would reassure me when she found me there with a faraway look in my eyes. "Perhaps you are being prepared for something more."

Little did I know that this letter I now held in my hand was the invitation to discover that something more, another layer of who I am, and who I was to become.

The chatter in the kitchen had stopped and I could now feel the eyes of the other servants looking at me, wondering why I still stood at the door. When I turned toward them, a gasp escaped from Tori's mouth when she saw what was in my hands. "The Kings seal!? Anya, what is it?"

"I'm not sure." I said, still staring down at the envelope.

"Is it for you?" Tori's eyes widened, scanning the envelope and I nodded slowly, "Well open it, silly!" Tori squealed. Though much older than me, Tori brought fun and joy into the kitchen and still had the spark of youth within her. The kitchen staff had gathered around me by now. I slowly broke the seal and opened the flap reveling a gilded edge of the card inside. With shaking fingers, I pulled out a card with the same elegant writing scrolling down the front. I held the card out and they all leaned in to read what it said, Tori read out loud:

> You are hereby, cordially summoned
> as a royal guest of the Most High King
> at an honorary banquet two evenings hence
> in the Royal Ballroom.
> Formal attire requested.

I checked the envelope again, just to be sure it still said my name! Me? A Royal banquet? But why? "Marita!" I cried out, dashing for the door to our quarters.

"Good heavens, girl! Such a ruckus!" Marita reprimanded as I burst into our small living space. Marita had been mending some aprons that had started to show wear and I thrust the invitation between her and her sewing. Quickly she dropped the sewing into her lap and snapped the card from my hand. She studied it silently for several minutes then said, "Alright then, we best find you something to wear."

I could not believe that this didn't surprise her. It certainly surprised me! It seemed that she should be asking the same questions as I was, but instead she jumped to her feet, pushed her mending off into the basket next to her old chair and turned to our small closet and started pushing aside clothing. Pulling out a few faded dresses that I'd worn many times for banquets where I was not the guest, but the one who prepared the plates back in the service hall.

She let out a dissatisfied grumble, "Hmh", Marita shook her head. "None of these will do.", she announced decidedly.

"Marita, the invitation says that the banquet is two days from now. How will I find anything formal to wear?"

"Leave that to me, child." She smiled with a determined twinkle in her wise eyes.